ISIS
ORB

ISIS ORB

A XANTH NOVEL

PIERS ANTHONY

OPEN ROAD

INTEGRATED MEDIA

NEW YORK

Copyright © 2016 by Piers Anthony

Cover design by Sarah Kaplan

978-1-5040-3737-2

Published in 2016 by Open Road Integrated Media, Inc.
180 Maiden Lane
New York, NY 10038
www.openroadmedia.com

ISIS
ORB

Chapter 1

HAPLESS

Hapless paced restlessly across his dingy excuse for a home. He wanted something, but he couldn't figure out what it was. Until he did figure it out, his life was in limbo; he couldn't go anywhere or make any key decision. He had never been any great shakes as a person, but now that he was living on his own he realized just how empty his existence was. Yet he couldn't think of what to do about it. So he remained a faded gray–eyed, dirt brown–haired, dull average excuse for nothing much.

He had considered doing what others did, and going to see the Good Magician Humfrey with a Question. But when he reconsidered it, he realized that it was probably not a good idea; he was no hero to participate in some grand design. If he even made it into the GM's castle, Humfrey would probably laugh him right back out of it. So squelch that.

There was a knock on the battered door. That made him jump; nobody ever came to call on him. It must be a lost traveler seeking directions from whoever happened to be close enough to ask. Him.

He pulled the door open with an unpleasant squeak. There stood a gnome in a crumpled suit. "Hapless," he said. "Invite me in."

How did this stranger know his name? "Uh, sure, I guess. Come in."

The gnome entered, then sat on the least rickety chair. "Hapless, I don't have time to waste, so listen carefully. I am the Good Magician Humfrey, and I have come to persuade you to come to my castle for an Answer."

Hapless answered with the grace for which he was known. "Huh?"

"Don't make me repeat myself; that wastes time. All you need to do is agree."

Hapless finally got a bit of ground under his emotional feet. "I don't want to do that! The Good Magician requires a year's service for a perplexing Answer."

"Or an equivalent Service of another nature," Humfrey agreed. "My Answer is always cryptic but worthwhile."

"This is ridiculous!" Hapless sputtered. "It's a trite formula! Some oaf comes with a stupid Question, gets a stupider Answer, then has to serve some complicated quest that completely messes up his life. Why should I get into anything like that? My life is already frustrating enough."

"Because formulas exist for an excellent reason: they work. You have no life to speak of; only by following this formula will you achieve your three life ambitions."

"*What* ambitions? I have no idea what I want."

"That is part of your problem. You want to play a musical instrument well, to have a good girlfriend, and to make a difference in Xanth. You will achieve all three only by taking a Quest."

Hapless opened his mouth to protest, then stalled. Because the moment the Good Magician spelled out what he wanted, he saw that it was true. It wasn't magic to make him desire things he hadn't before; it was a clarification of desires he had always had but had never been able to recognize. Humfrey had his number.

Still, he protested. "My talent is to conjure any musical instrument. But it's no good, because I can't *play* any instrument. No girl is interested in me because I don't have a useful talent. And as for making a difference, I have no idea how."

"Precisely. Your Quest will gradually clarify those aspects, so that by the time it concludes you will have succeeded in accomplishing all three." Humfrey stood. "I must be on my way. Your appointment at my castle is three days hence. Be there."

"I'll do no such thing!" Hapless said, working up a somewhat ineffective annoyance. "Why should I take your word about any of this nonsense?"

Humfrey rolled his eyes expressively, as if dealing with an idiot. "Because I anticipated your visit, and set up for it, making you the focus. When you foolishly changed your mind, all that work was in danger of being wasted. Five innocent folk will have their lives ruined, or at least never properly developed, a mean goddess will prevail, and two nice girls and a nasty one will remain unattached. Several of them are bound to come to me with Questions, which will then make their problems become my problems to solve. That will be a pain in the butt. I need to circumvent it. You yourself are largely worthless, but the others have marvelous lives to fulfill, and it's unfair to them to be so whimsically balked. So I am taking a hand for the greater good, not to mention my personal convenience, which means enlisting you, undeserving as you are."

Now this was interesting, not least because of the three girls. Two nice ones and a nasty one? That last had a certain guilty appeal. Nice girls weren't interested in him, but maybe a nasty one would be. He should be so lucky! "You—you think I could do all that? Just by taking the Quest?"

Humfrey hardly paused to consider. "I don't think, I know. However there is a qualification: you *could* do it, but whether you *will* remains in question. The future is never guaranteed. You will simply have to take your chances."

"I—I don't know. I don't much like taking chances."

Again the eye roll. "That's been your problem throughout. You don't want to take a chance on completely fulfilling your life and enabling several others to fulfill theirs? Knowing that the alternative is to settle into a lifelong slump of nonentity? You're boxing yourself in. You have to learn to think outside the box."

"Box? What box? I don't see any box."

"That's figurative, not literal, you numbskull."

"I have to figure outside a box? I still don't know what box."

The Good Magician looked at him as if about ready to tear out a handful of hair, and he didn't have much to spare. Then he changed his mind. "This box," Humfrey said impatiently, producing a small, closed, dull-gray box. "Think outside it, because what's in it isn't what you want."

"It isn't? Why?"

"Because that's its magic: to contain always the wrong thing." He thrust the box at Hapless.

Hapless took it. What could he do? If he turned this down he might never meet the nasty girl.

Humfrey walked to the door. "Be there," he repeated, and exited.

Hapless stood there, staring at the box. It stared back at him, in its fashion. It contained the wrong thing? Hapless didn't even know what the right thing was.

He got a dull idea. He could check inside the box, and whatever was in it would be wrong, and that might give him a clue what would be right.

He unfastened the closure and lifted the lid. Inside was a small picture of a rather pretty girl. She had flaring reddish hair, a cute nose, and a kissable mouth. "Who are you?" Hapless asked rhetorically.

"I'm Cylla Cybin, dummy," the picture answered.

Hapless was so surprised he almost dropped the box.

"Hey! Don't drop me, butterfingers!" the picture snapped.

"Uh, sorry. It's just that I expected something repulsive, like a dirty sock, not a pretty girl picture that talks."

"Pretty girl," Cylla repeated, mellowing. "Do you really think so?"

"Well, sure, but that doesn't matter."

"Oh? Why not?"

"Because what's in this box is wrong for me, so even if you were real, it wouldn't be good. The picture must be warning me to stay clear of you."

"Oh really," she said, as if considering potential ramifications.

"It's nothing personal. I'd love to have a girlfriend like you. But you're wrong, so that's that."

"And you're going to be governed by a stupid box?"

"Well, the Good Magician gave it to me, and told me—"

"The Good Magician! You saw him?"

"I guess, in a manner. He told me to go to his castle and take a Quest. And to think outside the box."

"I'm going with you."

"What?"

"You're hard of hearing?"

"But—but you're just a picture!"

Cylla frowned. "I am not just a picture. I'm a real girl whose picture somehow got inside your stupid box. That's not at all the same. I want to go see the Good Magician, but I don't want to travel alone, so I'll go with you."

"You want me to take your picture to the Good Magician?"

The picture's expression seemed to echo that of Humfrey, when he had to explain something obvious, to a dullard. "I don't care about the picture," she said carefully. "I'm talking about the real me. Take. Me. To. The Good Magician's Castle."

"But I don't even know where you are."

"You're in the village? Start walking north to the enchanted path. I'll meet you there."

What could he do? She was far more certain about things than he was. "Okay. Uh, when?"

"Now," she said firmly. "Get moving. We don't want to be caught out in the open when night falls."

How had he gotten into this? Hiking to the Good Magician with the wrong girl? But it seemed he had his marching orders. He grabbed his knapsack and popped the box into it, then stepped out of the house. He turned north and started walking.

As he came to the edge of the village, where the enchanted path began, there was a woman waiting. He knew it was Cylla, because the figure was just as shapely as the face was pretty. "About time," she said as he caught up to her. She fell in beside him, walking. "What's your name?"

"Hapless."

"It fits you."

For some reason this assessment did not thrill him. "I really don't think—I mean the box was telling me no."

"Let me see that box."

He fished in his pack and brought it out. Cylla took it, opened it, and peered inside. "Oh, that's wrong, all right."

"The picture?"

"The lipstick." She brought it out. It seemed the picture had been replaced to fit a new situation. "Totally wrong."

"What's lipstick?"

"Oh, you have lived a sheltered life, haven't you! It's color a girl puts on her mouth to make it more attractive."

"Oh. What's wrong with this?"

She grimaced. "I'll show you." She returned the box to him, then paused to rub the end of the stick across her mouth. When she dropped her hand away her lips looked like literal sticks. "How'd you like to kiss that?"

The notion was repelling. "You're right," Hapless agreed. "It's wrong. I'd hate to kiss that."

Cylla brought out a hankie and vigorously rubbed her mouth off. Her normal lips returned. She put her face close to his. "How about these?"

"Much better."

"Let me make sure." Suddenly she was kissing him.

Caught again by surprise, all he could do was float on the moment. No girl had ever kissed him like that before. In fact, no girl had kissed him at all. She certainly knew how to do it.

She ended the kiss. "Was that all right?"

His head was still spinning. "Uh—"

"I mean, there was no wood remaining? No taste of bark?"

Oh. "None at all," he agreed. "You're perfect."

"Good." She turned him loose and they resumed walking.

He remained unsettled. The kiss had been really nice, and she seemed good enough. So why had her picture warned him away? "Uh, the box, your picture—if it's right about what's wrong—"

"I'm wondering about that too. Obviously it feels we're not right for each other. It must know something we don't."

"Yeah, I guess so."

"But that's a romantic thing. It doesn't mean we can't travel together."

"I guess," he agreed with a tinge of regret.

"I heard that tinge. That's sweet."

"Uh, thanks, I guess."

"So let's figure this out. Maybe our talents don't mesh. What's yours?"

"I can conjure any musical instrument. But I can't play any of them. It's frustrating."

"Conjure one."

"What would you like?"

"A flute."

Hapless focused and conjured a flute. It appeared in his hand. He gave it to her. She played it, and a beautiful melody sounded.

She paused. "That's the best I ever played! It's a fine instrument."

"Not for me."

"You play it." She handed it back to him.

Hapless put it to his mouth and blew. A sour squawk emerged, reminiscent of a noise that made stained glass break into colored fragments and tumble into a garbage pit.

"Stop! You made your point. May I keep the flute?"

"Sure. But it will fade out after a day or so. They don't last."

"Still, it's a good talent. You could conjure another when the first faded."

"Yes. But it doesn't do *me* any good. I guess that's why I'm going to see the Good Magician. Maybe he has an Answer."

"If you could play as well as you conjure, you'd be a worthwhile man."

"But as it is, I'm not."

"Very well," she said briskly. "My turn. My talent is to make others hallucinate. That's probably why your box warned you against me."

"Hallucinate? I don't think I've been doing that. Except maybe when you kissed me."

"No, that was normal euphoria. Boys do that when girls smooch them, just as they freak out when they see girls' panties. It's general minor magic. Here's what it's like when I try." She took his hand.

He found himself standing in a forest of tree trunks with big wooden faces. "Get out of here, intruder!" one cried windily.

He tried to oblige, turning about. But behind him was a hungry-looking red dragon. He barely jumped back in time to avoid its snapping jaws. But then a tree branch caught him and hauled him in. It was a tangle tree!

"Ghaaa!" he cried as the vision ended.

"That's why my dates don't usually work out well," Cylla said. They were back in the real world. "It is obvious that I control the relationship, and they don't like that. So with you I was careful not to show it, until now, as a demonstration."

"I appreciate that," he said somewhat breathlessly. "But as long as you keep it under control, what's the problem?"

"You don't feel the need to dominate a woman?"

"I don't. It should be an equal partnership."

"I certainly agree, even if my other boyfriends didn't. Then there must be some other reason for the warning."

"There must be," he agreed, almost disappointed.

"I heard that tinge again. You're nice."

"Maybe the warning was wrong?" he suggested, this time with a tinge of hope that he knew she picked up on.

"I doubt it. But maybe we can find out tonight, when we camp."

He wasn't sure what she was hinting, but it strongly appealed. Still, he was uncertain, because of the box's warning against her. "Um, do you want to try the box again?"

She considered briefly. "Why not? So far it seems to have one wrong thing and one right thing."

He handed it to her, and she opened it and peered inside. "Well, now!"

"What is it?"

"A panty." She lifted it out: a limp pink cloth.

"But I'm not freaking out."

"Silly, you don't freak from an empty panty. It has to be fully displayed to be effective."

Oh. "That's wrong for you?"

"Of course not. Panties are a girl's best friend."

"Then why is it in there?"

"I'm sure I don't know. Maybe the box is addled. Here, I'll try it on. Mine are getting worn anyway, while this one is fresh. Close your eyes."

Hapless obligingly closed his eyes.

After a generous moment she spoke again. "Now look."

He opened his eyes—and promptly lost consciousness.

Her snapping fingers woke him from his trance. "Sorry about that. I simply had to test them. They work."

Oh. She had flashed him with the displayed panty, and he had freaked out. "So it's not wrong for you."

"Obviously. Just as I'm not wrong for you. That box has missed twice now."

That was curious, as the Good Magician had a reputation for being always right, if frustratingly obscure. Why would he have an erratic box?

Cylla returned the box to him, and he returned it to his pack. They walked on.

They encountered a man going the other way. "Hi!" he said.

"Lo," Cylla replied. "What's your talent?"

"To carve air into a solid mass. Like this." He moved his hands as if slicing something invisible, then held them forth as if presenting something.

Curious, Hapless put his hands out. There was a block of solid air, invisible but definitely there. "Nice," he said, impressed.

"We're moving on," Cylla said abruptly.

Hapless returned the block of air and ran to catch up with her. "Why did you go? It's a perfectly respectable talent."

"He's an airhead."

Was that a pun? It certainly did not seem fair. Hapless decided not to challenge it.

They crossed a meadow filled with flowers. Bees were servicing them. But one bee flew directly toward the two of them.

"Get away!" Cylla cried, batting at it. Discouraged, the bee departed.

"Why did you do that?" Hapless asked. "It wasn't threatening us."

"It was a Wanna Bee. Anyone stung by one of those wants to be something else."

Oh. She evidently knew her local wildlife.

As night approached, they came to a campsite. The enchanted paths were good that way, providing rest areas where needed. The idea was that travelers were safe on such paths, from danger, hunger, or serious inconvenience. They could sleep in comfort, wash in fresh water, and meet other friendly folk along the way. This greatly facilitated travel.

Sure enough, there was a good-sized pond, a number of pie plants with freshly ripening pies, milkweeds with pods of fresh milk, and pillow bushes near a covered shelter. Just about everything travelers needed.

They came to the shelter. "Um, about privacy," Hapless said. "We can take turns bathing in the pond."

"We can bathe together."

"But I might get a, um—"

"This is a problem?"

"Well, um—" He knew he was blushing.

"Hapless, we may be wrong for each other as life-mates, but we can enjoy ourselves as we travel. We can do or not do whatever we want. We are free."

Did she mean what he hardly dared think she meant?

"Hello, travelers!"

They looked at each other. They were not alone. That complicated things.

The fellow traveler turned out to be an ordinary looking young man. "Why don't you two get acquainted while I wash up," Cylla suggested somewhat sourly.

"Okay." He would take the stranger's attention while she had some privacy after all. It was amazing what a change a third person made.

Hapless addressed the traveler. "Hello. I am Hapless, on the way to see the Good Magician, as is my companion Cylla. My talent is conjuring musical instruments, though I can't play them."

"I am Eli, and my talent is also my curse."

"Curse?"

"My powers change every day of the week. On Sun-Day I feel burnt out but can produce light and even start a fire. Monday, which happens to be today, I have no talent but also no curse. Two's Day I see two of everything, but whatever I do is twice as effective. Wetness Day I am constantly rained on, but can control local wet weather. Thirst Day I'm thirsty but can quench anyone else's thirst, literally or figuratively. Fry Day I can cook anything into something edible, but it's so greasy it can be sickening. Saturn Day I am surrounded by rings of dust that separate me from others but I can also make them spin at high velocity to use as a weapon or defensive shield. Normally folk don't like to travel with me. But I happen to be going to the same place you are, in the hope that the Good Magician can provide me with a good woman who can handle my changes."

Hapless digested that. This man had a daunting array of magic that might indeed make it awkward to associate with him for any length of time. But if he was going their way, it would not be easy to separate from him.

"Yes, that's the way with most folk," Eli said, as if reading his thoughts.

"Oh, I didn't mean—"

"What's this?" Cylla asked from the entrance. She was clean with her hair loose so it could dry.

"My, what a vision!" Eli said, jumping up to embrace her.

"Um, I wouldn't," Hapless warned, too late.

Eli rocked back, staring wildly around. "Monsters! Earthquakes! Volcanoes!" he exclaimed, as if beset by all three at once. That actually might have been the case, in his hallucinations.

"They're not real!" Hapless shouted. "Just ignore them!"

Then Eli came out of it. "What was that?" he gasped, disheveled.

"Cylla has the power of hallucination," Hapless explained. "You surprised her and made her react. I'm sure she didn't mean to upset you."

"The bleep I didn't," Cylla snapped. "You had no business pawing me."

Things were off to a bad start.

"I apologize for being too familiar," Eli said. "You were just so lovely I couldn't help myself."

"Well, keep your hands to yourself," Cylla said, determinedly unmollified.

Hapless tried to change the subject. "Eli has a most interesting talent that is also his curse. It manifests in a different manner each day of the week, except today. Yesterday he was so bright he could start a fire. Tomorrow—" He paused, having lost track.

"Tomorrow I'll see two of everything," Eli said. "But I'll be twice as effective. The day after I'll get rained on, but will be able to help others quench their thirst."

"And of course you're going to see the Good Magician so you can get rid of your curse," Cylla said.

"Why yes; how did you know?"

"I just knew you were bad luck."

It occurred to Hapless that Cylla was as annoyed as he was about the addition of a third person to their company. But it really wasn't Eli's fault. So he tried to change the subject again. "Let me show you my box. It is supposed to contain a thing that is wrong for the one who opens it. We're not sure it's always accurate, though."

"That sounds interesting. Let's see it."

Hapless brought out the box and passed it across. "Just open it. It seems harmless."

Eli opened the box. "Spectacles?" he asked, lifting them out.

Hapless spread his hands. "Do you have a problem with your vision?"

"No."

"So you don't need them. Maybe that's why they're wrong."

"Maybe," Eli agreed dubiously. "Unless there's something else about them." He returned the box and tucked the spectacles into his pocket.

There was a silence that threatened to become awkward. "Let's see about something to eat," Hapless suggested. He didn't mention sleeping arrangements, which were now also a problem.

"Why don't I just move on," Eli suggested. "I can see that the two of you don't want company."

"But you were here first," Hapless protested. He really wanted to spend the night alone with Cylla, but fair was fair.

They looked at Cylla. "Oh, stay," she said with grumpy grace. "We'll manage."

The two men went out to forage for pies and milk, while Cylla set things up inside. When they returned, Cylla was just changing dresses, and her panties were showing.

"Snap out of it," Eli said, snapping his fingers. "We must have returned too soon."

"I freaked out," Hapless said ruefully. "But you didn't?"

"My father was Mundane," Eli said. "He faded out before he developed magic. He was immune to panties, and I guess I inherited that, though I do have magic. Panties are just clothing, to me."

If Cylla was aware she had been seen, she gave no sign of it. She had a table in place for the food, and they ate the pies.

As dusk closed in, Cylla and Hapless walked around the campsite, admiring its features. "I thought I'd freak him out for an hour so we could tryst," she murmured. "But he's immune. Now I *really* don't like him."

So the flash hadn't been accidental. Too bad.

They slept in the shelter, each rolled separately in a blanket harvested fresh from a blanket bush. Hapless was sorry they weren't alone, and that Cylla had been unable to flash Eli into unconsciousness. But that was the way of it.

In the morning they took turns washing up in the pond. Then Hapless remembered something. "Are you seeing double today?"

"I am," Eli agreed. "It's awkward, but I'm used to it."

"You see two of me?"

"Yes. You're like twins."

Then Hapless got an idea. "Try the glasses!"

Surprised, Eli fished them out of his pocket. He put them on. "Well, I'll be darned and hemmed! They work!"

"They do?"

"Now I'm seeing single. These are just what I need for Two's Day."

"Make that three misses," Cylla said. "That is, three times they weren't the wrong thing. The only time the thing was wrong was the lipstick." She paused, considering. "And if a man tried to get fresh with me, that lipstick might be just what I needed to turn him off. So I'm not sure the things have ever been wrong."

"Maybe I misunderstood," Hapless said. "I assumed that thinking outside the box meant that what was in it was wrong. Maybe what's in it is right, but it's still better to think for myself."

Cylla nodded. "That could be. The Good Magician is usually cryptic."

"These glasses certainly work for me," Eli said. "I wonder if on other days the box will have other things to counter my curses?" But he reconsidered immediately. "But then it might cancel the glasses. I'd better wait until tomorrow to try it again."

They had a breakfast of apple pie with cream from a rare creamweed. Then they set off together.

Soon Cylla slowed. "I'm not used to so much walking," she confessed. "Maybe you two should go on ahead without me."

"Now that would not be nice," Eli said. He looked around. "Is that a wagon?"

Hapless saw it: an old blue wagon, the kind that children used.

"What use is a wagon?" Cylla demanded. "Someone would have to pull it."

"Precisely," Eli said. "Get in, the two of you."

Perplexed, they did so. Cylla sat in front, her knees raised, and Hapless sat behind, his legs on either side of her. It was a tight fit, but actually rather pleasant for him, having her so close and snug.

"Ready?" Eli asked, taking the long handle. Hapless realized that the man could see under Cylla's skirt from that angle. Then he remembered that he was immune to panties.

"Ready," Cylla said a bit grimly. Was she annoyed that her panties might be visible, or that they had no effect?

Eli turned and pulled, and suddenly they were fairly zooming along the path. Then Hapless remembered: Eli was twice as efficient today. They were moving at twice the rate they would have on their own, and Cylla wasn't getting tired.

"He's a real help," Hapless murmured.

"I still don't like him," Cylla murmured back. "There's something about him that turns me off."

"Maybe that you can't freak him out by flashing."

"Maybe."

They made good progress, thanks to the doubled speed, and by noon came to a camping site they would normally have reached by dusk. So they paused only briefly, and went on to the next, accomplishing two days' travel in one.

"You really helped," Hapless told Eli.

"Glad to. But tomorrow will be different."

"Tomorrow we'll reach the Good Magician's Castle, so it won't matter."

They made a little campfire so they could have a hot meal.

They took turns again washing up, first Cylla, then the two men. There was a problem when she returned to the shelter: she had forgotten to put her clothing back on. "Uh, Cylla—" Hapless said, half stunned.

She glanced down at herself as if just now realizing. "Oh. I washed my clothing. It's not dry yet. I'll hang it up by the fire."

"Put something else on meanwhile," Hapless said.

She walked to a bush and harvested a small sheet. She wrapped it around her torso. "How's that?"

"That's fine. It's a good thing you didn't have your panties on, because . . ." He shrugged. Even without the panties, she had had considerable effect. She was an attractive woman.

"Where's Eli?" she asked as she went to the fire.

Hapless looked around. In half a moment he spied the man, frozen just inside the shelter. "He freaked out!" he said, surprised.

"But he's immune to panties," she said. Then she paused, catching on. "Which I wasn't wearing."

"He's not immune to bare flesh," Hapless said.

"That's interesting," she said thoughtfully. "I wonder if he knows?"

"I doubt he does, or he wouldn't have looked."

She nodded. "Let's not tell him."

Hapless shrugged again. "I guess it doesn't matter." He walked to Eli and snapped his fingers. The man recovered, and resumed walking, unaware that he had been in stasis.

The patter of rain on his face woke Hapless next morning. They were sleeping separately inside the shelter, yet the water was falling. Then he remembered Eli's curse. The man was sleeping, and it was raining solidly on him. The two of them were close enough to catch the edge of it.

"For pity's sake!" Cylla said, flinging off her wet blanket and scrambling out of the way. Hapless closed his eyes just in time. "The guy's a menace!"

"He can't help it. It's his curse."

"I suppose. Let's get out of here." She took his hand and led him outside, his eyes still closed so that he wouldn't freak out.

In due course they got dry and dressed, and harvested two umbrel-las from the convenient umbrella tree. Eli stayed with his sodden cloth-ing; he was used to this. "Sorry," he said. "I know I'm not very good company."

"But you helped yesterday," Cylla said.

Hapless was surprised; she seemed to have mellowed toward the man. After a moment he thought he figured out why: she preferred men she could control, and Eli had seemed uncontrollable by conventional means such as panties. But the discovery of his weakness for the absence of panties meant that she could after all control him when she wanted to, without resorting to her talent for hallucination. That made him eli-gible. In fact the box had called it: panties were the wrong thing for her, because they stopped her power over him.

And where did that leave Hapless? Well, the box had indicated at the outset that Cylla was not for him. He liked her, and maybe she liked him, but in the larger picture—outside the box—they were not for each other. He just had to accept that.

"Sorry about that," she murmured as if reading his thoughts. "I guess it was not to be."

"I guess the box warned me because otherwise I would have gotten the wrong idea."

"Probably it wouldn't have worked out, so we're saving ourselves heart-ache by realizing that at the outset."

"Yes," he agreed despondently. "And I guess it warned you that panties were not what you needed. Because they freak out the wrong man."

"Yes. I am coming to appreciate that. To think outside the box."

They trudged on through the rain. At least Hapless and Cylla had their umbrellas, and there wasn't far to go, thanks to the good traveling the day before. Before noon they came in sight of the Good Magician's Castle.

"I guess this is where we part company," Eli said. "We'll have to make our own ways through the Challenges."

"Do we?" Cylla asked.

"Don't we? Much as I'd like to have your company, I know you don't like mine."

"I am reconsidering. I think I can handle your curse if you can han-dle mine."

"Your hallucinations? Actually I find them intriguing, now that I know they *are* hallucinations."

"You do? Eli, maybe we don't need to go to all the complicated trouble of asking the Good Magician a Question and having to pay through the nose for his stupid Answer. What we each really want is a good partner who can handle us as we are. Maybe we can solve each other's problems instead, if that notion's not all wet."

"Oh, I'd like that!"

"So why don't we give it a try? I think the box gave us the clue, if only by indicating what was wrong for us."

"But the box gave me glasses that corrected my double vision. How does that relate?"

"I think I understand that. The glasses nullified part of your curse, but that's not your answer. You don't want to depend on things to cancel your problems, you want to handle them as they are. To embrace your talent, not reject it. Rather than wear glasses to do it, why not be with someone who maybe looks better doubled?"

He looked at her. "You would look twice as good," he agreed. He brought out the glasses and threw them away.

She folded her umbrella, letting the rain soak her, and stepped into him for a kiss. Little hearts radiated out.

Hapless walked away, knowing that he was no longer relevant to their scene. It was time for him to tackle the Challenges, alone.

What interested him was the way the box had broadened his thinking. He did need to think outside the box, not settling for the too-easy answers it seemed to offer. That would benefit him throughout his life. That was the real lesson of the box.

He oriented on the castle ahead. He had Challenges to tackle.

Chapter 2

MISSION

The castle looked distressingly ordinary, with a solid outer wall, high turrets, bright pennants, a moat with a visible moat monster, and trees and bushes surrounding the whole. Was it really the notorious Good Magician's Castle? It looked as if he could just walk up to it, cross the drawbridge, and go on in. It could belong to anyone with the status to rate such an edifice. But this was where the enchanted path had led.

Well, he would find out. He walked down toward the drawbridge, following the path between the trees.

And found himself in a bowling alley. He knew that was what it was, because cats were bowling. That made punnish sense; they were obviously alley cats.

He tried to pass it by, but it was closed, with no apparent exit. This must be the first Challenge. All he had to do was figure out the nature of its challenge, solve it, and move on.

He paused to consider the scene more closely, and noticed something odd. They were not using regular pins, they were using bowls. Bowls of berries. Green berries, yellow berries, brown berries, white berries, black berries, blue berries—ten different types. When a cat rolled the ball— which was a solid glass globe—it knocked the berry bowls over and the berries flew out. Then kittens came out from a service nook to clean up the mess, and new bowls were set in place. Well, they were entitled to play the game any way they wanted to.

So how was he to get past this? Was he supposed to get into the game himself, and if he won it he would move on? There was a huge problem there: Hapless was awful at bowling. When he rolled the ball, it was a challenge even to score on the gutter. Trying to roll a glass ball to knock down berry bowls was in invitation to disaster. There had to be some other way.

Tweaked by a notion, he brought out the little box and opened it. It was empty; no help there, even in a negative way. He was truly on his own.

Or was he? The empty box suggested that there was no way, but he was supposed to think outside the box. What was outside?

He shook his head ruefully. The whole world was outside! That was no help.

Maybe he simply had to try what he never would ordinarily, and bowl. That was certainly outside his box.

"Mind if I cut in?" he inquired, picking up the bowling ball before a regular cat could. The cat shrugged, not protesting.

Hapless heaved the ball down the alley. Sure enough, it veered off into the gutter with a splash. He had verified it: this was not the way.

Then he reconsidered. His concern was this particular scene. Suppose there were no legitimate way to escape it? Did that mean he needed to find an illegitimate way? To break the rules? He didn't like cheating, but wasn't sure that there was such a thing in a situation like this. Merely something that wasn't any normal part of this scene.

He studied the cats, who ignored him. They were rough-hewn specimens with scratches and missing patches of fur from fights. He didn't want to mess with them.

He considered the berry bowls. As he watched, a cat made a strike and berries flew all around, several of them striking Hapless before they rolled into the alley and on out of sight. One struck his belly, poking him; that would be a poke berry. Another bopped him on the head. He caught it and looked at it: a shad berry, smelling faintly of fish.

Fish. Didn't cats like fish? Wouldn't they prefer to eat those berries, rather than let them escape? But the cats were at the far end of the alley, so it seemed they didn't know what they were missing. Maybe the cleanup kittens didn't tell them, preferring to eat the berries out of sight.

A berry-shaped bulb flashed over his head. Maybe that was the way out!

He stood near a setting of ten bowls. When the bowling ball rolled down to bash the collection, Hapless snatched up the one with shad berries and carried it to the other end of the alley. "Get a whiff of this!" he said, and set the odoriferous bowl down before the cat.

The cat tried to ignore him, but the smell got to it, and in a moment it was delving into the berries. The other cats came, demanding their share. In half another moment all of them were fighting for the bowl, completely distracted.

Hapless walked down to the service nook where the kittens lurked. Sure enough, there was a small service door leading out. Hapless dived through it.

And he was in the next Challenge. Before him was a drab donkey. "Er, hello," he said uncertainly.

"Hello yourself, idiot," the donkey replied.

This set Hapless back a bit. He wasn't used to hearing animals talk in human dialect, though he knew it happened on occasion. "Um, I'm Hapless. Who are you?"

"I am Alec, simpleton. I see that you are well named. You're pathetic."

The creature was obviously trying to get his goat, or something similar. Was this part of the Challenge? It seemed safest to refuse to be baited. "You are evidently very intelligent."

"I'm way smarter than you, dumbbell," Alec agreed.

Ah. Now he caught the pun: Smart Alec, a wise-ass burrow. There would be no help here. He would have to figure out how to move on by himself. Which surely was the point of the Challenge.

Still, there might be a hint. Maybe he could draw the donkey out. "Who knows," Hapless said.

"Whose nose? Your nose is the scenter of your face."

Or maybe not. Hapless looked around. They were in a glade surrounded by saplings. There was of course no path out. He was stuck here with the irritating creature.

"Are you setting out roots, or merely trying to think?" Alec asked.

Hapless ignored him. Then he noticed something odd. The young trees were healthy and uniform, except in one section, where there was only rubble. That ruined the continuity. Why should an otherwise ordinary glade have such a discontinuity?

He walked to that spot. Now he saw that in amidst the piled brick fragments was a small eggplant.

"You need to be egged on?" Alec asked derisively. "Going to eggsplore? Getting eggscited?"

He had walked into that one, literally. It seemed there was nothing here for him either.

A large colorful bird flew down to perch on a brick. It was a crow, but a remarkably fancy one. "Who are you?" Hapless asked, surprised.

"Izadora Dahlia Crow," the bird replied, and flew away.

"Well, don't crow about it," Alec said.

Hapless shook his head, bemused. A colorful crow was a hint? Or merely another distraction? What was he missing?

He brought out the box and looked in it again, feeling foolish for doing so. It remained empty.

"Is that where you keep your brains?" Alec asked. "Only it's empty, unsurprisingly?"

Think outside the box. This whole glade was the box. He needed to disengage from the spot distractions here and see the larger picture, whatever it was.

Yet this different section had to contain a hint of some kind. What was the point of it, otherwise? He peered more closely at it.

There was a patch of white pebbles with dark dots, looking like some kind of candy. He picked one up and looked closely at it.

It looked back at him. It was an eyeball! Yet it smelled of candy.

"You going to eat the eye candy?" Alec inquired in the tone of a sneer.

Hapless hastily put it back in the pile.

Several bees flew over to inspect the candy. Some eyes seemed to be honey flavored. The bees picked up the honey, then buzzed crazily, rubbing themselves off. It wasn't enough; they fell to the ground, looking like little bee houses.

"Stupid bees," Alec said. "They're allergic to honey. It makes them break out in hives."

This was getting him nowhere. But he looked once more—and spied a small tree growing in the center of the crazy area. It was as if anything close to the tree was changed. Why? What would cause a change from order to disorder?

Then he got it. Reverse wood! It was reversing whatever came near. Maybe the roots of other plants were touching its roots, underground. So a plant became a brick. And—

Hapless found a handkerchief and wrapped it around his hand. Then he reached down to pick a leaf from the tree. The white handkerchief became a black sock, reversed, but still protected his hand.

Hapless brought it to the donkey. "What do you think of this, Alec?"

"It's nothing but a leaf," the animal complained. He nipped it from Hapless's hand and swallowed it. "Edible foliage, what else?"

"What is my best way through this Challenge?" Hapless asked him.

"Get on my back and ride on out." Then Alec looked surprised. "Did I just say that?"

"You did," Hapless agreed, getting on his back.

"Why?"

"Because you just ate a leaf of reverse wood. It changed you from obnoxious to helpful. Obviously you know the way out, because there's not enough grazing here in the glade for you to remain here full time."

"Oh, bleep." But the donkey walked to the other side of the glade, nosed aside a curtain of hanging vines, and marched on out through the aisle revealed. Hapless had thought outside the box again and found the unexpected key to the Challenge.

Then he was in a hall with two doors. Beside each door stood a young man. The doors looked much the same, and so did the boys; they might be twins. One door was labeled NULL, the other VOID. The boys had name tags saying the same.

Hapless approached them cautiously. "Do you folk answer questions?"

"Some," Null responded. "I can stop a Happening. My brother can reverse a prior Happening. We will gladly do so if asked."

"What's a Happening?"

Null shrugged. "Anything that happens. It's different every time."

"What's behind the doors?"

"A Happening."

"So I can go in there, and if I don't like it I can ask you to stop it, and you will?"

"Exactly."

"What's the catch?"

"I will do it only once."

"So I'd better not make the same mistake twice."

"Well, my brother might help you the second time."

"And if I don't go through one of those doors, I won't make it past this Challenge?"

The boy smiled. "That's it. So consider carefully."

"What's there to consider? I need to make it through."

Null shrugged. "Your choice."

Hapless shrugged back. He saw no real choice. "I'll try your door." He opened it and stepped through.

He was in darkness, and the footing was slippery. He fell on his rump and slid helplessly down somewhere. Then he came up against something and felt something else wrap around him. What was happening?

A glow developed, expanding into a light. Now he could see. He didn't like it.

He was on a kind of pedestal in a deep pit, securely bound by a rope that wrapped several times around him. He felt like a living sacrifice on an altar. Above was something moving. It flashed in the light as it swung back and forth. It was a pendulum! With what looked like a razor-sharp bottom edge. It was swinging lengthwise right above him. Worse, it was slowly descending.

He looked around, as at least his head was free. He saw the outlines of two doors back up above the slide. Both doors had led to the same place! His choice hadn't made a difference. What did that mean? That the doors were a fake choice, and his real choices were of another nature? He wished he had realized that before he stepped through one.

He struggled to escape, but the rope held him tight. The deadly pendulum swung a bit lower each time. A few minutes more and it would slice into him lengthwise, slowly cutting him in half. What could he do?

What else could he do? "Null!" he called. "Stop this Happening!"

Null appeared in his door frame. "Are you sure?"

"Of course I'm sure! I don't want to get sliced in half! Stop it!"

"As you wish." Null gestured, and the pendulum halted in place. It no longer swung and no longer descended. He had been saved.

"Thank you. Now get me out of here."

"I'm sorry, but I can't do that. You have used me up."

"But I can't untie these ropes myself! My arms are locked into my body."

"I'm sorry. I am limited to my job."

"You can't just leave me here!"

"I can't free you," Null said, and turned away.

Hapless was fuming, but also afraid. This was real mischief! He realized too late that merely stopping the Happening was not enough. He needed to get out of it entirely, but that was not what he had requested. That was the catch, that he realized too late.

Well, at least he had time to ponder. He would have to appeal to the brother, Void, this time with a more carefully considered request.

"Void, please Unhappen my entry to this chamber," he said.

"Are you sure?" Void asked, exactly as his brother had.

That made Hapless pause again. What was the catch to avoiding the whole trap? That question gave him the answer: this was the Third Challenge, and if he avoided it, he wouldn't get in to see the Good Magician. He would just have to give up and go home, a failure. As usual. After Humfrey had personally come to get him to come here, to undertake the Quest and save five people including two good girls and a bad girl. He didn't want to do that. But if to get the Quest he had to make it through this Challenge, and he couldn't do that, what then?

He could stay here, tied up, until he starved to death. That did not seem like much of an option. Was there other magic he could invoke? "Rope, untie me," he said.

The rope did not respond. So much for that.

Now that he thought about it, he remembered a story from somewhere, about a pit and a pendulum, from which this Challenge was obviously borrowed. What had the person in the story done? Ah, now he remembered: he had somehow gotten rats to gnaw through the rope, freeing him just in time.

Were there any rats here? "Rats, come gnaw on the rope."

If there were any rats, they did not respond. The borrowing did not go that far.

There had to be a way. But if there was, why was Void standing ready? Void was a prescription for failure. Was it supposed to be easy for him to fail rather than prevail? This did not make much sense to him.

Think outside the box. Well, this whole pit was a box, and he was hopelessly stuck in it. Unless he quit and went home. That was not a preferred solution.

Slowly the hint of a vague idea began to glimmer. No bulb flashed over him, but a bit of a tuber glowed. He was thinking either/or: either stay here and rot, or give up and go home. Those were box answers. He needed something else. Something outside. Something he had not considered before. What was that?

The glow increased. The tuber was trying to grow into a bulb.

Humfrey had come to ask him to come here, then made it impossible for him to get through. The Good Magician was not known as a person who liked to waste his own time. He had told Hapless to think outside the box, and even given him the box, not that it was doing him any good here. But the box wasn't supposed to help him; he was supposed to think outside it. Did that mean he should reject this entire situation?

The glow finally brightened into a flash. He had it. He hoped.

"Yes, Void, I am sure," he called.

Void gestured. Then Hapless was standing back in the hall, facing the brothers and their doors. Now he knew that it didn't matter which door he chose; it was all part of the same box.

"Thank you, both," he said shortly. Then he turned and walked back the way he had come.

There was Smart Alec, the wise-ass donkey. "What, you're giving up?" the animal asked cynically. "I knew you didn't have the gumption."

"Not exactly."

"Oh? Then what, exactly?"

"I am departing the box."

"Isn't that the same thing?"

"No."

"I don't understand."

"Of course you don't. You're part of the box." Hapless walked back to the service nook, and reentered the alley cats' bowling alley.

The cats were surprised. They paused in their game. "What are you doing here?" one asked.

"Stepping out of the box."

"The box?"

"Give me that ball." Hapless took it from him, turned, and rolled it down the alley. It was another perfect gutter ball. "This is not my game." He walked on, leaving the cats perplexed.

Now he was back in the forest surrounding the castle. He paused to take out the box. He opened it. It remained empty. He held it up like a magic mike and spoke into it. "Good Magician: are you there in the box?"

"Never," Humfrey's grumpy voice replied. "But I can hear you through it."

"Well, neither am I in it. I'm done with this foolishness. This entire setup is a box, and I'm through with it. I am no longer playing by other folks' rules. I am following my own rules. If you want me for your Quest, come and get me. I'll tackle that Quest my way, or not at all. Otherwise I'm going home."

There was a pause. Was the Good Magician going to let him go?

"Then come on in," Humfrey's voice came. The illusion lifted like dissipating mist, and the path to the drawbridge lay before him.

"Thank you." So he had won. He had bluffed out the Magician. He was relieved, because he had really gotten curious about the Quest.

Hapless marched along the path, to the drawbridge, and across it. The castle portcullis was lifted, and he walked on in.

A woman was there. "Welcome, Hapless," she said. "I am Wira, the Good Magician's daughter-in-law, and this is my daughter Liz." She indicated a three-year-old child.

"Hello," Hapless said. He wasn't good with children.

"Do you like lizards?" Liz asked brightly.

"I can take them or leave them," Hapless said.

"My talent is to summon and tame them." Indeed, she had a lizard on her shoulder.

"It's a good talent. I can summon musical instruments, but I can't play them."

"That must be very sad."

"It is. It's part of why I'm here."

"This way, please," Wira said, and led them on into the castle.

They came to an inner chamber where a severe-looking older woman stood. "Uh, hello," Hapless said awkwardly.

"Mother Sofia, this is Hapless," Wira said. "Hapless, this is Sofia Socksortor, Designated Wife of the Month. She's Mundane."

"I keep himself's socks in order," Sofia said. "That's why he married me."

"That is surely a worthy chore," Hapless agreed. He had heard of the Good Magician's notorious socks.

"Let me say, we admire your decision," Sofia said.

"To take a Quest?"

"To think outside the box. Hardly anyone does that today."

"They sure don't," Liz said brightly. "I'm going to grow up outside the box."

Oh. "Thank you." Hapless still felt awkward.

"Last week there was someone here whose talent was deciphering gibberish," Liz said. "He wanted to exchange it for another talent. His name was Xcjrqsntx, or Johnny for short."

"We talked him out of it," Sofia said. "It's a perfectly good talent. Who knows what else he might have wound up with?"

And surely less frustrating than his own talent, Hapless thought.

"Have a cookie," Liz said, proffering one.

"Stop that, you naughty child," Sofia snapped.

"But she was just being sociable," Hapless said.

"Sociable, my hind foot! That's fast food."

"Fast food?"

"Makes you go very fast. You don't need that at the moment."

"Aww," Liz said, her joke spoiled.

"He will see you now," Sofia said.

"I'll take him!" Liz said. "This way."

"Thank you," Hapless repeated, still feeling awkward.

Liz led him up a narrow, winding stairway to a dingy office where the Good Magician pored over a huge tome. "Hi Grandpa Humfrey!" Liz said even more brightly. In fact it raised the illumination of the chamber.

"Hello, Liz," the Good Magician responded, smiling.

"This is Hapless," Liz said. Then, to Hapless: "Don't aggravate him. He doesn't like anyone except Mom, and now me. Everyone else makes him grumpy."

"Thank you." How awkward could it get?

The child departed, and Hapless was left with Humfrey. "No need to inquire," the Magician said. "She's right. Everyone else is a pain in the sphincter."

This was too much. "You asked me to come!" Hapless said. "Then you tried to balk me."

"Until you got out of the box," Humfrey agreed. "You'd be useless for this mission inside the box."

"You mean the whole point of my Challenges was to make me rebel against their idiocy?"

"Yes."

Awkwardness was being displaced by annoyance. "This Quest had better come through."

"There is no guarantee. It depends on you, with a healthy dose of favorable luck."

"Are you sure you don't want someone else? My luck is seldom healthy."

"My auspices indicate that you have the best chance, indifferent as it may be."

"And if I succeed, I'll get a musical instrument I can play, a girl I can like, and I'll do Xanth some good?"

"Exactly. Now return the box."

Hapless passed over the box. Humfrey shook it once and gave it back. "Now its nature has shifted slightly. It will have what you need, though you won't necessarily recognize it at first. I borrowed it from Prize, Surprise's daughter, who conjures such boxes. It has been around; it even visited Mundania once. However the first five entries will be exactly what you need: the identities of the Companions you will enlist."

"Companions?"

"For your Quest," Humfrey explained patiently. "You will collect them singly, explain the mission, and when you have all five, you will proceed with that mission."

"And exactly what is this mission?"

"To fetch and use the Isis Orb."

"The what?"

"Must I get down to basics?"

"Yes."

Humfrey looked annoyed, but bore with it. "Then listen carefully." He took a deep breath. "You will seek, find, and collect together five divergent folk, each of whom has a very special wish, and enable them to achieve their desires. In order to accomplish this you as a group must locate and acquire the Isis Orb. This is a kind of talisman of great power; it will be a problem to learn its mechanism and control it. In fact you will need the five Totems for this purpose."

"Wait! You're losing me. I need to know more about this Orb. That's like an eyeball?"

"You don't need to know its history," Humfrey said shortly. "Just how to use it."

"Whose Quest is this: mine or yours?"

"Yours, of course."

"Then allow me to do it my way. Outside your box. I want that history."

Humfrey looked fit to explode, but there was also a certain grudging respect. Hapless had escaped the box, and was determined to stay out of it. Exactly as the Good Magician had advised at the outset. "You are familiar with the Demons?"

"With the capital D? I have heard of them, but never had personal experience with one. Aren't they supremely powerful?"

"Indeed. The Demon Xanth sleeps beneath this peninsula we call Xanth, and the trace leakage of radiation from his body accounts for all the magic of the Land of Xanth. Demons normally pay attention to mortal folk only when using them as a randomizing factor for some Demon Wager, such as whether a given person will turn left or right at a particular corner. Inestimable forces can be invoked in the accomplishment of these Wagers, and Demons gain or lose Status as a result. Mortals may not even know that they are the objects of Wagers; it doesn't matter to the Demons, any more than the personality of an ant would matter to you if you bet a friend which way it might turn. So it's best simply to ignore any concern about Demons."

"Then why bring it up?" Hapless demanded.

"Because it accounts for the talisman you seek. It happens that eons ago the Demon Xanth made a Wager with the Demon Earth, whose magic is Gravity, and lost. Thus Earth took a chunk of Xanth's magic in the form of the Orb and hid it in the deepest core of Xanth, where it would be safe from incidental discovery. It is that Orb you must recover."

"You called it the Isis Orb. Why?"

"That is another story. Isis, the Mundane Goddess of Fertility, learned about the Orb and went to claim it for herself. Now she has it, in a manner, to the annoyance of both Demons, but since it is their policy not to interfere in mortal matters without specific reason, they have had to let it be. So now she considers it hers, by right of Finders Keepers, though that will endure only as long as the Demons elect to remain clear. They may even have a Wager on whether anyone will succeed in wresting it from her, as you will try to do. To do that, you will require the five Totems of Air, Earth, Fire, Water, and the Void, each of which is dangerously powerful in its own right, and use them to control the Orb."

"Assuming Isis doesn't interfere," Hapless said.

"Exactly. Only then will you be able to use the Orb for your own benefits. Now are you clear?"

Hapless opened his mouth to protest, but Humfrey shoved the box in his hands. "Good. Then be on your way. Have a wonderful Quest!" His gaze returned to his huge tome. Hapless had been dismissed.

"This way," Liz said from the doorway. "We will get you outfitted for your journey."

Hapless followed her out, feeling as if he was back in the box. But if the Quest really won him the things he wanted, it would be worth it. He hoped.

Back downstairs, Sofia took charge. "You will start tomorrow. Your room for the night is ready. A bell will sound for dinner and in the morning for breakfast; follow it to its source and you will be fed."

"Uh, thank you." Hapless hesitated. "I'm not ready to retire yet. May I talk with you a while?"

"With me?" Sofia asked, surprised and seemingly flattered.

"And Wira, and Liz. There are things about Quests I still don't know, and maybe you could help set me straight."

"We will be glad to do that."

They settled down to talk. "For example, I am supposed to recover a magic Orb that will be guarded by a goddess, Isis. Who is Isis? He said she's the goddess of Fertility. Does that mean she makes plants grow?"

"Ah, Isis," Sofia said. "She's Mundane, Egyptian to be exact. Fertility is a euphemism; she's the goddess of sex. If you're up against her, she'd as soon seduce you as look at you, and make you her love slave."

"Love slave! I wonder—he said I would encounter a bad girl. Could that be Isis?"

"It certainly could," Sofia said. "She has a formidable reputation. It's not all bad; she's identified with the moon, with the solar disk between her horns. She is also considered Mother Nature. Sometimes she wears a highly symbolic veil; there's a statue with the words 'I am that which is, has been, and shall be. My veil no one has lifted. The fruit I bore was the Sun.' Some consider her image suckling her son to be the prototype of the Christian Madonna and Child. Not that this is widely known in Xanth."

"That's amazing! I think I would avoid her if I could."

"I hear that bad girls can be more interesting than good girls," Liz said.

"But you're going to be a good girl," Wira said quickly.

"Oh, of course, Mom." But she looked dangerously intrigued.

"I also don't know about this box," Hapless said. "Humfrey said something about the first five entries being the identities of the people I need. That just leaves me confused. How do I find them?"

"He can be obscure," Sofia said. "I've seen that box before. Don't do it now, but when you're ready to travel, tomorrow, open it and there will be a picture of your first Companion."

"Okay," Hapless agreed. "So I'll recognize that person. But how do I actually find him?"

"That is easy," Sofia said. "A path will open up before you. Merely follow it and it will lead you to that person."

"A path? Just like that?"

"An enchanted path that you can follow without danger. That part is easy."

"Just don't step off the path," Liz warned. "Then it's not easy. I tried it once, and nickelpedes came after me. I had to summon a big lizard to eat them."

"But suppose I need to—" He broke off, remembering that he was talking to a child. "Or are there rest stops?"

He didn't fool her or shock her. "Poop in a bag, then throw it across the line."

"Oh. Thank you."

"Liz is very practical," Wira said fondly.

"Himself is pleased with you," Sofia said.

"The Good Magician? He seemed impatient with my questions."

"That's his way. He was glad you asked them. It means you have some wit. Not every Quest taker does."

"Well, he came to see me, to get me to take this Quest. He told me to think outside the box. I hadn't done much of that before, but I'm learning."

"He did need someone," Wira said. "He searched for a long time, but none of the regular querents were suitable."

"Querent?"

"A person who comes with a Question. A query."

"Oh."

"Then he saw you in a magic mirror," Liz said. "You matched the specs."

"I had no idea!" He decided not to ask what specifications qualified him, lest it be ignorance and stupidity.

But Sofia answered anyway. "He said you have gumption, if only you could find it. That's what distinguished you from all the others."

So when he had in effect told off the Good Magician, finding his gumption, he had won some respect. That was good to know.

In due course they had dinner, and he went up to his room. It was a nice one, complete with a shower: a little chamber where warm rain was always falling. There was a bowl with a small dipper on the table, maybe for his refreshment. He dipped out some of the sparkling drink, then paused. Should he be thinking outside the box?

He compromised. He very cautiously touched his tongue to it.

He was rocked back by a punch in the mouth. Sure enough: this was a punch bowl. A fitting reminder.

In the morning he joined them for breakfast. Humfrey himself was not there; apparently he did not mix socially even with members of his family.

He thought of one more question. "You are the Designated Wife," he said to Sofia. "That implies there are others."

"There are," she agreed. "Over the course of a century or more he married and lost five and a half wives; then the Demon Xanth played a trick on him and gave them all back to him together. But in Xanth there's a rule: only one wife at a time. So now each of us takes a turn for a month, and that works well. When one of us gets completely fed up with him, the next takes her place, fresh and cheerful. This is my month."

"I'm glad it was. You have been very helpful."

"Thank you. Actually it's been nice talking with you. Few querents seem to have any interest in the rest of us here at the GM Castle. Himself has been even grumpier than usual recently."

Hapless had to smile. "As long as I'm not the cause."

"You are not. He's glad you are agreeing to take the Quest. No, what has disturbed him is covert interference by the Demon Destroy-Her, who may be using the Gourd Realm to contaminate other Demons with trace souls, getting them interested in mortal affairs, without Trojan's notice."

"Uh, Trojan?"

"The Night Stallion, horse of a different color, who governs the dream realm. He asked the Good Magician to investigate, but it's an extremely touchy business. We don't want more interference by Demons."

"I should think so," Hapless agreed. It had not occurred to him that the Good Magician could have problems of his own.

It was time to go. He walked out of the castle, crossed the drawbridge, and paused. Then he took out the box.

Did he really want to do this? He knew that once he started, there would be no stopping; he would be fully committed. Because of his gumption. But if he turned away now, he would maybe ruin the lives of five innocent people, and never get to find the one musical instrument he could really play.

Still, he was in doubt. He knew that his life would be at risk. If he went home now, he could settle in as a local farmer or worker and have a safe existence. But a dull one. If he accepted the Quest it surely would not be dull. For one thing, he would find his girlfriend. Or maybe two or three girlfriends, if he included the bad girl.

For some reason he found himself focusing on the bad girl. Who could she be? The Goddess Isis? Why would a goddess be interested in him? That didn't make sense; he was nothing. But if not her, then who? What could a bad girl possibly have for him that a good girl would not? Apart from naughty allure? Why was he so intrigued with her, when he didn't even know her?

It seemed he had good reasons to take the Quest, and good reasons to avoid it. Why was he thinking about what would surely be bad for him regardless? He could avoid that whole issue by skipping the Quest.

"Oh, fudge," he swore, and opened the box.

Chapter 3

FELINE

Inside the box was a picture of a cat with the word FELINE. That was all.

A cat? His first Companion was to be a cat? Hapless gazed at the picture with dismay. He really was not partial to cats. He didn't hate them, but he could certainly live without them. It would be a nuisance to associate with one on a presumably difficult Quest.

Then he realized that this was a kind of proof of the new status of the box. It was showing him what he hadn't known he needed. He never would have chosen a cat on his own, but it seemed he did need it. Even as odd a cat as this, with blue and white stripes.

He looked around. There was a path ahead of him that he hadn't seen before. The one that would lead him to the cat.

Hapless sighed and closed the box, returning it to his backpack. He set off down the path. After a few steps he paused and turned to look back at the castle. It was there, but then he noticed something else: the path wasn't. There were trees and brush between him and the castle, no path and no sign that one had ever been there. How could that be?

Oh—it was a one-way path. He had heard of them. Just to be sure, he faced backwards and stepped along it. Sure enough, it faded out the moment his feet left it.

He paused again, considering. Did this mean that if he accidentally stepped off the path, it would vanish and he would be hopelessly lost? He hoped not. Then he thought of a way to test it, maybe. He took off his pack, with the box inside, and set it on the ground. Then he walked away from it. The path remained, with the pack at the near end of it. It was the box that shut it down, not Hapless himself. That was oddly reassuring.

It meant he could anchor the path in place, if for some reason he had to leave it for a while. But he didn't plan to risk it. He might not be eager to have a cat as a Companion, but he didn't want to get lost looking for it.

He put the pack back on and resumed his walk. He didn't know how long a hike he had, so it seemed best not to waste time.

He admired the scenery as he traversed it: forests, fields, hills, dales, thickets, thinnits. It curved serenely around steep slopes, and found fords across streams. It was an easy path to travel.

Then it passed through a patch of dog fennel. Immediately the guardian dogs appeared, barking. One was a cute little hush puppy, wagging its tail. But they did not get on the path. It passed though a section of cattails, and the tails switched back and forth angrily, but again did not overlap the path. So it really was enchanted to protect him.

A butterfly came to land on his upraised hand. It consisted of a quarter pound of butter, with yellow wings. But there was something special about it. "Who are you?" he asked it.

"Don't you recognize me?" it asked in return. "I am not just any butterfly. I am the Chaos Butterfly."

"Chaos?" he asked blankly.

"When I flap my wings, a storm can form far away. It's an awesome power."

"That is impressive," he agreed, not quite believing it.

"Well, it's true." The butterfly took off and flew away.

Then he spied a bird coming in to perch on a rock on the path. It had to be harmless, like the butterfly, or it would not have been able to do so. "Who are you?" Hapless asked. "Do you have some awesome power?"

"I do indeed," the bird replied proudly. "I am the Tern of Events. Things can change significantly around me. Several villages are named after me."

"Oh, I see," he said, not really seeing. "Can you demonstrate?"

"Not to you. You are locked onto your path."

Ouch! Was he back inside the box, this time in the form of a path? "Well, I have a Quest to handle, and the path will lead me to it."

"So you say," the tern said, and took off.

Disgruntled, Hapless walked on. Before long he came to a glade where a shapely young woman stood. Her hair was striped appealingly blue and white. The path led to her and stopped.

How could that be? He had not yet found the feline. "Excuse me, miss," he said. "Have you seen a cat around here?"

She turned a sultry gaze on him. "No."

"Then something is wrong. This path was supposed to lead me to a cat."

"What do you want with a cat?"

"It's not what I want. It's what I'm supposed to find. I really don't care for cats."

"You're not making much sense. Why look for a cat if you don't like cats?"

"It's complicated," he said, nettled. He didn't like a disparaging glance from a pretty girl any more than he liked it from a butterfly or bird. Where could that cat be?

"Explain it, please."

"Why should you be interested?"

"Trust me: I'm interested. Answer the question."

Well, she had asked for it. "I am on a Quest for the Good Magician. He gave me a box containing what I need, even if I don't much want it. The box contained a picture of a cat with the word FELINE. It opened up a path to lead me to that cat. Instead it seems to have led me to you. Is the cat your pet?"

"No."

"Do you have it hidden away somewhere, like maybe in a bag? If so, would you please let it out."

She contemplated him disquietingly. It was as if she knew something he did not, such as the whereabouts of the cat. "Tell me more about this Quest. Why did you seek it?"

"Well, my talent is to conjure musical instruments, but I can't play any of them. It's frustrating. So if I succeed in the Quest, I'll find my instrument."

"And what is this Quest?"

"I have to find the Isis Orb and use it to grant my wish. To do that I need to find five Companions, and five Totems needed to control the Orb. It's complicated, as I said."

"And what do these Companions get out of it?"

"They'll get their own wishes granted by the Orb. So it's a group effort."

"And I'm standing in your way."

"As long as you don't tell me where that cat is, yes. I just want to find the cat and get on with the Quest."

She turned slowly, and her curves turned with her. "What do you think of me?"

"You're beautiful, including your pretty striped hair. I'd love to have a girlfriend like you. But I'm pretty sure you're not interested. So will you quit teasing me and tell me: where is the cat?"

"All you care about is my curves?"

"That's all I know of you!"

"And suppose I want someone to care about something other than my curves?"

He was getting fed up. "Then maybe you should find your own Quest, instead of interfering with mine."

"I am not interfering."

"That's what you say. Why don't you just go away?"

"I can't do that."

He was exasperated. "Where is that cat?"

"Watch me."

"I'm watching." Indeed, she was not at all hard to watch. She could probably freak out a man without ever flashing panties, if she tried.

She started changing. She seemed to melt down into a four-footed animal with a tail. It had blue and white stripes.

"Oh, my," he breathed. It was the cat. *She* was the cat. "Why didn't you tell me?"

The cat silently stalked off.

Bleep! He hurried after it. After *her*. "I'm sorry. I didn't mean to offend you. I simply had no idea."

The cat reached a nearby tree trunk and quickly climbed it. She lay on a branch just out of his reach and gazed down at him.

He had had enough of this. "Listen to me, Feline, if that's your name. I gave you a reason for my tackling this Quest, but that's not the whole story. The Good Magician *asked* me to take it, and finding a musical instrument is only part of it. Another part is that it seems I am the key to helping five other people accomplish their own wishes. Without the Quest they won't get what they want either. One of them is you. So whatever it is you want, you won't get it unless you cooperate and help me get the Orb. But if you don't care about that, okay, I'll go look for the next Companion and leave you out of it. I'm not going to mess with you. So get with it or get out; it's your choice."

The cat continued to stare at him.

"As you wish." He turned and stalked away from the tree.

"You win."

He turned back. There was the woman. He realized that she was fully clothed; the transformation seemed to cover that. "So what is it that you want that the Orb might grant?"

She smiled, looking dangerously pretty in the process. "This is ironic. I want to be loved for something other than my curves."

Hapless was amazed. "For something else? But you've got them. Why not use them? I'm sure you can catch the eye of any man you want to."

"I can. That's the point. There's a lot more to me than my curves. I want some of the rest to be recognized. A man who sees only curves is too shallow to bother with."

"That's all *I'm* seeing of you."

She merely looked at him. Bleep! He had just defined himself as hopelessly shallow. He laughed ruefully. "Got me there. I apologize."

"Let's get on with the Quest," she said. "The day is late. We'd better make camp, and look for the next Companion in the morning."

He looked around. The protected path had vanished, and he wasn't ready to start the next one. "There doesn't seem to be much here, and it's an exposed glade; we'll be in danger if we sleep here."

"*You'll* be in danger. I'll sleep high in a tree."

"Oh. Of course."

"You don't know what to do, do you?"

"I guess not. I hadn't planned this far ahead. I've lived in a village all my life. Never spent a night in the wilderness."

"You're not much of a man."

Was she trying to nettle him? "Not much," he agreed.

"And you're supposed to lead a Quest?"

"It wasn't my idea."

"The Good Magician enlisted you, you said. You must have some quality he respects. What is it?"

"I understand he said I have gumption."

She considered. "Maybe you do. You walked away from me."

He was surprised. "You respect that?"

"Yes. No man who has seen my curves ever just walked away. I had to change forms to get rid of them."

"Gumption," he repeated. "Well, that and a tame ogre will keep me safe at night, and I don't have an ogre." He thought of something else. "And you did change forms, so maybe it doesn't count."

She pondered briefly. "If you're supposed to lead this Quest, and I need the Quest to achieve my wish, and I'm supposed to be your Companion, then I guess it's up to me to keep you safe. If you get eaten by something during the night, the Quest will fade away."

"You don't have to do anything for me," he snapped. "I'll figure something out."

"There's that gumption again. You're going to go your own way, and damn the torpedoes." She smiled briefly. "Not that I have any idea what a torpedo is. But at the moment it's foolish. You need to do something to ensure your comfort and safety, and you're not getting it done."

"If you're quite through embarrassing me, what do you have in mind?"

She smiled again; it seemed to be becoming a habit. "I doubt I'm through doing that. There must be something you can do, if only we can think of it. Otherwise the Good Magician would not have entrusted you with the Quest."

"I suppose."

"Maybe your talent relates. You conjure musical instruments?"

"Yes. But I can't play them, so it's not worth much."

"I wonder. I've always wanted to play the kit, because it sounds like my nature, but never had one to practice with. Can you conjure me one?"

"What's a kit?"

"It's a very small violin, easy to carry around."

"Oh." Hapless focused. The kit appeared in his hand, together with its bow. "Here."

"Lovely." She took it, put the base of it to her chin, and stroked the bow across the strings. A perfect note sounded.

She paused, surprised. Then she launched into a tune. It was perfectly rendered and quite evocative. She really could play!

When the song ended, she shook her head. "This must be a magic instrument. I've had no practice; I know I can't play this well on my own."

"My instruments do play well," he agreed. "Except when I try them. Then they reek. It's maddening."

"Can you conjure another kit?"

He shrugged and conjured another. Now there were two.

"Try playing it."

He grimaced, then put bow to string. A gut-wrenchingly sour note sounded.

Feline winced. "I see what you mean. That is world-class discordance. You have no musical talent."

"Yes. Only musical ambition. If I can only find the right instrument for me, then as you say, they are magic, and it would play well for me. I've tried everything I can think of, but the result is always awful."

"Maybe that one is cursed. Let's exchange instruments."

They exchanged, but it didn't change the music: she played beautifully, and he played abysmally.

"Well, now we know," she said. "It seems the same instruments that are enchanted to play well for others, are enchanted to play ill for you. I appreciate your frustration."

"Yes," he agreed shortly. "So what does this have to do with my being safe for the night?"

"I had thought maybe music soothes the savage beast."

"That's breast, not beast. Everybody gets it wrong."

"I apologize. It's clear that you won't be soothing any breasts or beasts with your music." Then a bulb flashed over her head. "But maybe that's your answer: when a beast comes, play for it."

"Play for it? Why? So it will feel better about destroying me?"

"To drive it away. No creature could stand to listen to you long. Maybe that's your real talent: to drive away beasts."

He stared at her. "I never thought of that!"

"So maybe that's my contribution: to think of something. Now let's find something to eat and drink, before it gets too dark. And maybe something to make a tent."

"But you're going to sleep in a tree, as a cat?"

"Maybe." She gestured to one side of the glade. "On my way here I crossed a streamlet. A pie plant grew beside it, and a blanket bush. Those should do nicely."

"You knew this, but you didn't tell me?"

"You didn't ask." She walked in that direction.

He followed her, unable to avoid admiring her curves in motion despite his annoyance with her attitude.

"You're looking," she said without turning her head.

How did women always know? "Yes."

"Men do. I'd have to wear a poncho to stop them. It's annoying."

"So the Orb will point you to a man who doesn't look."

"Oh, I don't want that."

"You don't? I thought—"

"I want a man who appreciates me for something other than my curves. He can appreciate my curves too, as long as that's not the only thing."

"That does make sense."

They came to the streamlet, which was exactly as she had described. They drank the water, harvested pies, and pitched a small tent made from blankets. Feline nibbled a chunk of cheese she had harvested. "Hoo!" she exclaimed. "That's really sharp."

"Sharp?"

"Try it." She broke off a section and handed it to him.

He tried it. It was so sharp he almost cut his tongue. "Hoo!" he agreed. "What kind is it?"

"Swiss Army Cheese, I believe. Sharp like a knife with multiple blades."

"Sharp," he agreed.

As darkness closed they sat together in the tent. They still had the two kits, ready to use them at need.

"So who sleeps here?" he asked, just in case she meant to use it herself.

"We both do."

"But—"

"Don't be concerned. I will assume my cat form to sleep."

Oh. Of course. "Uh, should we take turns keeping watch? In case there are beasts?"

"No need. I sleep lightly. I will know if anything approaches, and will alert you. Then you can play to drive it away."

"But wouldn't you be safer, even so, up in a tree?"

"Not necessarily. There are predators in trees, too. A dragon could come and toast me, for example."

That was another thing he hadn't thought of. "I suppose so."

"Or an autocrat."

"A what?"

"AutocRat," she repeated, pronouncing it carefully. "A tyrannical rat that has it in for cats."

"Oh." As usual, he had no clever comment.

"Are you sleepy yet?"

"No. It will take me time to unwind." He refrained from saying that sitting so close to her curves was part of what was winding him up.

"Me too. So now must be the time for our histories."

"Our whats?"

"We didn't just come into existence when we met. Tell me your personal life history and I'll tell you mine. That way there should be fewer nasty surprises as we tackle the Quest. If those narrations don't bore us to sleep, maybe we can play games of tic-tac-toe."

He laughed. "I like the way your mind works."

"What, something other than my curves?"

Why did she have to spoil it? "Yes," he agreed shortly.

"You first."

"I'm pretty simple, as you already know," he said with attempted irony he knew wasn't working well. "I was delivered twenty-one years ago to a beefsteak tomato farmer who made a good living providing steaks to others. I was, I suppose—" He hesitated.

"Was what?" she prompted.

He plowed on. "A disappointment. I wasn't especially smart or handsome, and my talent was a waste. Also, I was sort of stubborn."

"Another name for gumption, maybe."

"Maybe. So when I grew old enough to live on my own, I moved out and spent my time conjuring every different kind of musical instrument I could think of, in the hope that, well, you know. They fade out after a day or so, so they didn't clutter the house. Then the Good Magician visited me and urged me to undertake a Quest."

"He didn't just promise that you'd find your playable instrument," she said wisely. "What else was there?"

He had to answer, now that she had put it directly. "He said that I'd have two or maybe even three girlfriends, one of whom would be a bad girl."

"Two or three?" she asked in a chilly tone.

"Well, I never had a girlfriend," he said defensively. "Maybe they're backlogged."

"And you think about the bad girl. Who is she?"

"Maybe the Goddess Isis. Though I can't think why she'd have any interest in me."

"That is a curiosity," she agreed.

"And he said I might make a difference in Xanth, apart from helping five other folk to realize their wishes. So I'm here."

She nodded. "You couldn't say no. Because underneath all your ineptitude and stubbornness you're a decent guy."

"I hope so."

"My turn. Twenty years ago my mother was lost in the forest; she had taken a wrong turn and couldn't find the right one. She was frightened and thirsty, so when she came across a small clear pond she squatted down to dip out some water with her hand and sip it. It gave her a really odd feeling. Then a tomcat came, chasing a rabbit. The rabbit leaped right over the pond, and the cat fell in, just as the cunning bunny had intended. Mother went to help him get out, because cats don't usually swim well. Too late they both realized that it was a love spring."

"Ooh, my," Hapless breathed.

"Right. By the time they scrambled out of the water, they had signaled the stork several times. They couldn't help it; love springs don't take no for an answer. Tom ran off into the brush, and Mom waded out the other side. She found a path and made her way home, but in due course the stork found her—they can be uncanny about such things—and delivered me. This was awkward because Mom wasn't married and she had told no one about her incident in the spring. That made her a bit of a pariah, because the other villagers suspected. She had to raise me alone. It didn't help that I had this weird hair."

"I think it's pretty."

"What, as pretty as my—"

"Stop it! I'm not trying to insult you. You won't let me be positive."

She considered that. "I guess maybe I am a bit oversensitive. All the boys teased me cruelly about my hair. It didn't help that when I discovered my talent, which is to assume either human or feline form, my cat fur was the same color as my hair. Sure, it made sense, but I wish both had been ordinary dull brown. I alternated weeks with my father, who worked in the Catnip and Catapult Works, but he didn't take me to work with him because the cats razzed him about my colors; he was ashamed of me, and blamed it on my mother. My mother blamed it on my father. I don't know where my colors came from. Whoever heard of a blue cat, let alone a blue striped one? So it wasn't much of a childhood or kitten-hood. At times I wished they'd never run afoul of that love spring."

"You had it worse than I did," Hapless said. "I'd have felt the same way."

She flashed him a smile of appreciation in the darkness; he felt its brief warmth. "Then when I came of age I got my curves, in both my forms. Then the boys' attitudes changed, but not for the better. Now all they wanted was to get their hands or whatever on my curves. But I knew them, and remembered their endless taunts. They were not worth my while. If there had been one halfway decent male among them in child-hood, I might have been satisfied to let him touch my curves, but there had been none. It wasn't any better with the local tomcats; all they wanted was one thing, and they meant to have it regardless of my own wishes. They were not at all subtle; they just wanted to jump on and in. I got into some really awful fights defending my so-called honor. I'd almost have been better off moving to the isle of Exsangui Nation, where vampires lurk; most residents die of blood loss. So now when some man even looks at my curves, I remember all that nasty teasing, and I—I react."

"I'm sorry," Hapless said. "I can't even claim that I would have been different; I teased girls too, and now they don't want to have anything to do with me. So my understanding is too late, for me or for you."

"The irony is that I'd really like to have a loving relationship with a good man. But I just can't trust any man, so it turns me off anything like that."

"I understand, I think." If only he had known *not* to look at her that way!

"So then I read a tea leaf, and it said I should go into the forest here and wait, and my problem would be solved. So I did, not knowing exactly what to expect. But I certainly didn't expect you."

"I'm not much of an expectation," Hapless agreed.

"I didn't mean it that way. At least now you know why I was cautious about you and why I still don't want you to touch me."

"I understand," he agreed sadly.

"I can't turn off my prior life. It governs me."

"So does mine, pretty much. But I think—now please don't take this the wrong way—that maybe we can understand each other, and maybe in time come to trust each other."

"I am struggling not to take that the wrong way," she said. "I can see that you're pretty innocent, and probably don't mean any harm. But you do look."

"I do look," he admitted. "I'm trying not to, but whenever I'm not concentrating, my eyes do their own thing."

"Well, maybe that's progress. Are we sleepy yet?"

"Maybe if we lie down and close our eyes?"

"Let's try it." She shifted into cat form and closed her eyes.

Hapless lay down beside her in the tent and did the same.

To his surprise, he dropped right off to sleep. The events of the day must have tired him more than he realized.

He woke to a nudge. Feline was beside him, in all her human curves; he could feel them against his side. "Nickelpedes!" she whispered. "Play your kit!"

Nickelpedes! Those little bugs were a terror by day or night, because they gouged out nickel-sized chucks of flesh from tender anatomy. He scrambled to a sitting position in the darkness, then fumbled for his little violin in his pack. He found the bow. He put it to the instrument and played. Wouldn't this be an awful time for his musical talent to improve!

He need not have worried about that. Foul notes screeched out, sounding like fingernails practically ripping apart a blackboard. He felt Feline clapping her hands to her ears. He kept playing, hoping it was even worse for the nickelpedes.

There was an angry clicking of little claws as the nickelpedes milled about, balked. Then they retreated, unable to handle the dreadful sounds. It was working.

"You did it!" Feline exclaimed, and kissed him on the ear. That was an unexpected thrill.

"I guess I did," he agreed, putting away the violin. "I never thought to use my lack of musical talent that way, until you suggested it. Thank you."

"You like my suggestion," she said, sounding pleased.

"Yes. Actually I like you too." He felt her stiffen beside him, and hurried on. "When you kissed me just now, I liked it, and I can't even see your curves."

"But you know they're there."

Why had he even mentioned them? "Yes. So I guess that spoils it. But it was a good suggestion."

She was silent a moment, pondering. "So you liked my kiss because of my curves. But you liked my suggestion because it helped save us from the little monsters."

"Yes, to both."

"I guess that's half a loaf. If you discover anything else you like about me, let me know."

"Gladly. I don't suppose you'd let me kiss *you* on the ear?"

"No," she said coldly.

Bleep. He had lost it again.

"Wait! Don't be mad. You—you said your eyes do what they want; you can't help it. Well, my reactions are like that. I know you were just trying to be friendly, and I froze you out. I'm sorry. Go ahead; kiss me on the ear."

He wasn't sure how to handle this. Would she be mad if he did, or if he didn't? So he compromised by being honest. "Feline, I don't know which way you want it, and I don't want to upset you either way. I don't have much experience with girls, and you're complicated regardless. Tell me what to do so it's all right."

"You really don't know?"

"I really don't. I'm a klutz, I know that much, but I'm trying to learn."

"Kiss me."

He was surprised; he had expected to be bawled out for his incomprehension. He didn't argue; he turned his face toward where he felt her in the dark and kissed where her ear should be, sort of hunt and peck.

Only it wasn't her ear he met. It was her mouth. She had turned her head.

He thought he would float out of the tent. It was amazing. Cylla had kissed him, but this was better.

Then it ended, and he sank back down to the ground. "Oh, my," he breathed.

"Someone kissed you before," she said. "Who?"

He remained dazed. "Her name was Cylla Cybin. Her talent was hallucination. But I think I hallucinated again, just now."

"So I'm your second kiss."

"Yes."

"Yes what?"

"Yes, yours was better."

"Thank you. Don't get ideas."

"I got ideas. I can't help it," he admitted, ashamed.

"Well, keep them to yourself." But she did not actually seem annoyed.

"I will."

"I am thawing a bit."

"I'm glad."

"Something else is coming. Something big."

Hapless grabbed for his kit.

"Two things," she said. "Big snakes. I'm not sure whether they like music or dissonance."

"We need to know," he said. "If we play the wrong kind, we'll get eaten."

"I know. But we don't have to guess. We'll both play."

"Good idea!"

They sat side by side, each with a violin. Two gross serpentine shapes loomed before them, visible mainly by their glowing eyes. The eyes were set distressingly far apart; these were huge creatures.

Hapless and Feline played their kits, the sweet and sour notes together. The four eyes ahead blinked in unison, confused. Then they retreated and were gone.

"It worked!" Feline said.

"Your idea worked again."

"Are you angling for another kiss?"

"No. But I would have if I'd thought of it in time."

"Well, you get one. Do it."

He kissed where her head was. This time he landed on her ear. She was teasing him. The odd thing was that he liked it just about as well. But his experience with Cylla had taught him that seeing a girl or kissing her did not necessarily make for a permanent relationship, however nice she might be.

Then she reverted to feline form and purred herself to sleep. He lay down beside her and slept also.

He woke before her in the morning, surprised to see her in her human form. How long had she been that way?

"You're a fun girl," he murmured, and drew himself out of the tent. He went to the stream, stripped, and washed himself off.

When he emerged from the water, there was Feline watching him. It was too late to be embarrassed, so he simply climbed back into his clothes without comment.

She stripped her clothes and waded into the water while he averted his gaze. So her clothing was separate, despite becoming her fur when she was a cat. Her blouse was blue, her skirt white, her slippers one of each color. He hadn't noticed before, being too obsessed with her curves. Now he saw also that her bra was white, her panties blue. It was nice clothing.

"Oh, take a peek," she said.

He turned and looked. She was absolutely lovely in her nudity. Then he dutifully looked away again, and went about foraging for breakfast. Nudity did not guarantee a full relationship either.

Soon she rejoined him. "You played that correctly."

"Thank you. I'm still learning."

"And I'm still thawing."

They smiled briefly at each other. Nothing was guaranteed, but the signs were promising.

"I think it's time for the next Companion," he said as they stood up to collect their things. "I have no idea who that might be."

"When you open the box, you see a picture, and a path appears?" she asked.

"Yes."

"And the path is enchanted to be safe? No monsters, no getting lost?"

"Yes. But there's no guarantee if you step off it. Uh, I was told that if you have a, er, natural function, to do it into a bag and then toss the bag across the line. That way you take no risk."

"Yes. What I'm thinking is that next time we face a night camping out, that we stay on the path. If it's between Companions, then invoke the next

Companion, then camp on the path that forms. We don't have to follow the path to the end immediately."

He gazed at her, impressed. "That's a clever idea, Feline! Guaranteed safety. No more nervous nights."

"No more kisses in the scary dark."

He hesitated, uncertain whether she was teasing him. "I'll miss that."

"You won't be missing much."

"I'll miss it a lot! I'm sorry if that turns you off, but when you kissed me I nearly floated into the sky. I'm not going to pretend it's nothing."

"Let me clarify," she said, with an obscure smile. "If I want to kiss you, I'll kiss you. We don't have to be in danger or in the dark. Just don't push it."

"Oh. I won't." But he remained somewhat disappointed, for no good reason.

"Like this." She stepped into him and kissed him firmly on the mouth. Again, he felt like floating. He had the wit not to put his arms around her.

"Oh. Thank you for that clarification," he said when she let him go. Indeed, he appreciated it enormously. She could be very friendly, if he just didn't presume. It was her way. She didn't mind being appreciated; she just didn't want to be sought only for her curves. His appreciation of her ideas had been unfeigned; that was what turned her on.

"Open the box."

Indeed, it was time.

Chapter 4

ZED

Hapless opened the box. There was a picture of a male centaur with the printed name ZED. But there was something odd about him.

"He's got stripes!" Feline exclaimed.

So he did. "Black and white, all over his body. Like a mundane zebra," Hapless agreed.

"And he must want to get rid of them, because other centaurs don't have them."

"He must. Centaurs are notoriously conservative. They don't even like magic."

"He surely needs us. Well, let's be on our way."

"Yes." This seemed straightforward. Where was the catch?

They started down the enchanted path that had appeared when the box opened. It crossed the stream using a mini bridge that Hapless was sure hadn't been there before and meandered on into the forest. There was a pretty water lily, but when he tried to touch it, it dissolved into water, which was of course what it was made of.

Above there were pretty clouds, supported by winged foundations. There was something suggestive about them. "What are those?" Hapless asked.

Feline looked. "Flying buttresses. You know, female flying butts."

"Oh." He was embarrassed.

"I like this path," Feline said. "Not only is it safe, it's fun. Was it like this when you found me?"

"Pretty much."

A small cloud floated across the path. "What's happening hear?" it inquired.

They paused, surprised. "Hear?" Hapless asked.

"Present location, not there, at this place—"

"Here?" he asked.

"Whatever," the cloud agreed irritably. "Are you up to something interesting?"

He was slightly annoyed. "What does a cloud care?"

The cloud expanded, forming a head, arms, legs, and finally a lovely female torso clad in extremely abbreviated apparel. "I'm not a cloud. I'm Demoness Metria. I'm attracted to interesting things."

"Oh. I'm Hapless. I'm not very interesting."

"I can see that. But this is an unusual path, and your companion is a cat woman. That could be interesting."

"You can tell my nature just by looking at me?" Feline asked.

"Crossbreeds are routine, and generally dull," Metria said. "But ad hoc enchanted paths aren't common."

"Add what?" Hapless asked.

"Temporary, special purpose, formed for one reason, with respect to this particular thing, pertaining to—"

"Convenient?"

"Whatever. Wait, that's not quite right. In fact, I had it right in the first place. Are you trying to mess me up?"

"I just didn't know the term."

She glared at him. "Next time, keep your ignorance to yourself."

His irritation increased. "Or what?"

"Or I'll flash you with my pan—"

He came to as Feline snapped her fingers near his ear. ". . . ties," he heard the demoness conclude. Her short skirt had already dropped back into place. It seemed she had suited action to word.

"We're just going to help a zebra-striped centaur," Feline told the demoness. "So leave us alone. It's not nice to flash innocent strangers."

"A zebra-striped centaur! Now *that's* interesting. I'd better stick around."

"Fudge a la mode!" Feline swore. For some reason it seemed she wasn't keen on having a shapely panty-flashing demoness join their party.

Metria looked at her cannily. "Or are you just pretending about the stripes, so you can enlist my assistance? I don't trust this." She faded out.

"Is she really gone?" Hapless asked.

"Of course she is," Feline said firmly while shaking her head no. It seemed that she had had some experience with small d demons.

"That's a relief," he said. "I don't want to get flashed again." Actually he would have liked to have a piece of glass or something to filter the effect, so as to see her panties without freaking out.

Feline fished in her purse. He hadn't realized that she carried one; maybe it appeared only at need. She brought out a bandana. She stretched it taut across her face, and he realized that she could see him through it, filtered. Then, wordlessly, she handed it to him. She was helping him get his peek, if the opportunity came.

He realized that he was getting to like her pretty well, and not just because of her curves. She understood him, without judging him.

"It's a good thing she didn't realize that we're on a Quest for the Good Magician," she remarked. "She'd really be curious then."

Metria reappeared. "I heard that. You're on a Quest!"

"Oh, fudge," Feline said. "We thought you were gone."

"Now get out of here," Hapless said. "We don't want your kind along."

The demoness puffed up, literally. "Tell me all about it, or I'll—"

"You'll what?" he demanded.

He managed to get the bandana in place just in time to intercept her flash. And he saw the panties: pink polka dots with nothing inside the dots. He was amazed. He had had no idea that demonesses wore anything like that. Even through the filter, he barely retained awareness. What a peek!

Feline snapped her fingers. "Wake," she said as Metria dropped her skirt again.

Hapless blinked as if just coming out of a trance. "What happened?"

"She flashed you again. You have to stop aggravating her."

"Well, our Quest is none of her business."

"Tell me anyway," Metria said. "Then maybe I'll go away, my curiosity satisfied."

Hapless sighed. "It's for the Isis Orb, that should grant our wishes. We're gathering Companions."

"Isis! She's worse mischief than I am. That's saying a lot."

Could they learn something worthwhile? "What, she's a demoness?"

"No, she's a goddess. They rank somewhere between small d demonesses and big D Demonesses. You don't want to mess with her. Your stupid bandana won't protect you from *her* panties."

She had known. She must have wanted him to see without quite freaking.

"You *wanted* him to see!" Feline said accusingly.

"Well, I didn't come down on the last sunbeam, pussy. Nobody has panties like mine. What use are they if no one remembers them?"

"Point made," Feline said thoughtfully.

"Just what kind of mischief is Isis?" Hapless asked. He already knew something about the goddess, but if he was destined to tangle with her, he wanted to know as much as he could.

"She likes to make men her love slaves," Metria answered. "Then she can make them do whatever she wants. Oh, to have power like that! I'd conquer Xanth."

"You want to conquer Xanth?"

The demoness considered briefly. "Maybe not actually conquer it; ruling it would be too much responsibility. But to have my panties recognized as supreme—that would be fun. All the men would have eyes like pink polka dots."

"Isis could do that?"

"Yes, if she wanted to. I'm not sure what motivates her. If she wanted to be queen, she could have used the Orb to grant her wish. Instead she just keeps it without actually using it. That's odd."

"It is," Hapless agreed. "What does she look like?"

"Anything she wants to. But always beautiful and sexy. They say there's no man she can't seduce in minutes without even showing her panties. I'd like to see her in action; I might learn what little I don't already know about that." The hem of her skirt lifted on its own until it almost, but not quite, showed her panties. She evidently had excellent control.

"Well, we're bound to see her, in due course."

Metria shrugged. "She wouldn't need anything special to deal with you. I wouldn't learn anything. Well, toodle-oo." She faded out.

"Why am I annoyed?" Hapless inquired rhetorically.

"Because she obviously dismisses you as too easy for a hint," Feline said. "But she raised a good question: why does Isis keep the Orb if she's not using it?"

"Maybe she wants folk like us to come for it, like a special flower to attract bees."

She nodded. "The next question is, then what does she want with us?"

"I have another: why would the Good Magician send us to her?"

"That's another good one," she agreed. "Are we mere pawns in some larger game? I don't like the smell of that."

"I thought it was Demons who made pawns of people."

"Well, then, could this be a Demon bet?" she asked. "I heard it was one of those that got Princess Harmony her suitors."

"If I really thought it was a bet, I'd do my best to mess it up."

"You can't mess up a Demon bet. They take all that into consideration. You really can't do anything about it; one Demon wins and one loses, whichever way it turns out."

"So I guess we'd better ignore that chance."

"That's easiest," she agreed.

The path soon debouched into a larger track. There in the center of it was a kind of wheeled wagon labeled CENTAUR STAGE COACH.

They paused. "Is that a pun on center stage, or on stage coach?" Hapless asked.

"Both," a centaur answered, appearing from behind the coach. "Get in."

"But we're on a Quest," Feline protested. "We can't just ride randomly."

"This isn't random," the centaur said. "It's available for those on centaur business. Since you're on a temporary centaur trail, you must qualify."

Hapless looked at Feline. "Does this make sense?"

"It must. He's a centaur. They always make sense."

"It couldn't be a fake centaur, designed to get us off the enchanted path and into mischief?"

She paused, considering. Then she addressed the centaur. "If I asked you whether you are a fake, what would you say?"

"Of course not. Centaurs don't do fake."

"Then thank you for the ride." She went to the coach and stepped up into it.

"Uh—" Hapless said uncertainly, too late. Then he shrugged and joined her.

The centaur took hold of a strap at the front of the coach and set off down the trail at a trot. Soon they were moving along at a good clip-clop.

"The way I phrased it, he had to give me a true answer, either way," Feline explained. "So it was a good verification."

"That is not the case," the centaur called back. "You confused it with the truth-teller/liar syndrome, where each always honors his code, and the liar lies about what he would have said and so tells the truth. In the real world, the liar knows that sometimes he can be a more effective liar by telling the truth."

"Uh-oh," Hapless said, chagrined.

"Fortunately I am legitimate," the centaur continued. "Enjoy your ride, but be more careful in the future."

Feline blushed. "I'm sorry. I thought I had it figured."

Hapless took her hand. "You tried. And it got us a good ride."

"Brace yourself. I'm going to kiss you."

"I don't need to brace myself for—"

She intercepted him with a kiss so forceful that he fell over on the seat. He had needed bracing after all. He had learned not to take too much for granted with women, but he was really getting to like Feline. Would that be mischief?

They rode on, looking out the small windows. The scenery was fairly racing past. In fact the wind of their passage leaked in and chilled them. There was a blanket, which they pulled over them, but their ears still were cold.

"Use the ear wigs," the centaur called back.

These turned out to be hairy caps—wigs—with padded muffs that did indeed keep their ears warm. "Thank you!" Feline called.

"I think we got the wrong ones," Feline said.

He looked at her. The wig made her look like an old-time barrister. "You look elegant."

"Thank you. You're beautiful yourself."

"I am?"

Then she fetched out her little makeup mirror and handed it to him. He held it up so he could see his own face.

His wig made him into a long-haired blonde.

"Um, maybe we can exchange?"

She pulled off her wig and gave it to him. He gave her his. Now she looked like the blonde, and actually she was quite appealing that way.

She made a wry face. "You like her better than you like me."

"I, uh—"

Then her frown-face cracked and she burst out laughing. She had been teasing him.

"Brace yourself," he said. Then he kissed her. She could have dodged it, but didn't. So far each kiss had been better than the last, and this was no exception.

"Oh, my," she said when it ended. "A little heart."

Now he saw it, floating away like a soap bubble. "Does this mean we're getting serious?"

"You just love my curves."

"I, uh—"

"Got you again," she said, smiling.

He spread his hands. "I do like your curves. But I like your personality too."

"I am slowly coming to believe that," she said seriously. "But let's give it time. Other girls have curves too."

He was glad to leave it at that.

The coach slowed, then stopped. "We have a problem," the centaur said.

They got out and looked, leaving the ear wigs in the coach. The trail ahead went to a bridge over a deep ravine. It looked all right, with a tall center pole from which cables curved gracefully down to help support the planking. "What is the problem?" Hapless asked.

"The inspector says this bridge might not be safe."

"Inspector?" Feline asked.

"Me."

They turned. There was a man who looked to be about 61, give or take a few months. "And you are?" Hapless asked.

"Peter Reddick, from Mundania. I helped build bridges there. Now I inspect them. It's a living." He smiled. "Though it seems I died."

Hapless exchanged most of a baffled look with Feline. What did this mean?

"Some Mundanes come to Xanth when they're through with Mundania," the centaur mentioned. "He evidently caught on."

Oh. "This bridge looks all right," Hapless said.

"It's not," Peter said. "I need to inspect it."

"How do you know, if you haven't inspected it yet?" Feline asked.

"It's a sense I have. It may be magic, this being a magic land."

"A talent," Hapless agreed. "To sniff out unsafe bridges."

"Exactly. I don't know how it's unsafe, but you shouldn't risk it."

"But we're going somewhere," Feline said.

"You won't get there if the bridge collapses when you're crossing."

That was a sound point. "So are you going to inspect it?" Hapless asked.

"Yes. I just got here. My sense indicates that it was in good order, but something about this situation makes it unsafe."

"This is an enchanted path," the centaur said. "It should be safe."

"Unless the enchantment summoned me to make sure," Peter said.

"Does this make sense?" Feline asked the centaur.

"Yes. Enchanted paths may take new untried routes, as they can't choose their destinations. The bridge could have been safe with regular use, but not for the coach; it may be conditional safety. So help was summoned."

"Then let's get it inspected," Hapless said impatiently.

Peter put a foot on the bridge. He tapped the sides. "This seems solid, but it may take awhile to verify its structural integrity. I don't have the tools I had in Mundania."

"Can we help?" Feline asked.

"I'm not sure. I'd like to check out the cables, but they would not be safe for you to try to climb, and—"

He broke off, because Feline had become the cat. She leaped on a thick cable and scampered up it. It vibrated from her slight weight, and there was a faint rattle.

"It shouldn't do that," Peter said. "It's supposed to be secure." He went to the cable anchorage. "Uh-oh."

"Loose?" Hapless asked.

"Yes, and it shouldn't be. This has corroded over time, and though normal weight would not have dislodged it, the weight of that coach probably would have. You could have been dumped into the ravine."

"Uh," Hapless said, taken aback. So the threat had been real.

Feline scampered back down, rejoined them, and returned to human form.

"Fortunately I can fix it." Peter worked on it, and soon pronounced it secure.

"Thank you," Feline said, and kissed him on the cheek.

"Glad to have been of service," Peter said, dazed. Hapless knew how that was. Those kisses were potent.

They returned to the carriage and the centaur hauled them across. The cable remained securely connected. "I am relieved," Feline murmured. "I did feel that rattle when I was on it."

"Yes. That's what gave him the clue."

They waved to Peter from the other side, and he waved back.

"I think I have learned something about enchanted paths," Hapless said.

"What is that?"

"It's not just where they go, but how they get there."

She nodded. "I think someone is angling for another kiss."

"I wasn't!" he protested. "I just am coming to appreciate things I never thought of before."

"I didn't say you were."

He looked at her. "It certainly seemed as if—"

"I meant me." She leaned toward him and kissed him.

Oh. She had gotten him again. He didn't mind at all.

Soon the coach slowed again. "I hope it's not another obstruction," Hapless said.

"What. You don't like being stuck alone with me?"

This time he was ready. "I like it well. But an obstruction will interrupt our alone togetherness."

Feline laughed, "Well put. But there should be other occasions."

The coach halted. "I think we have a problem," the centaur said.

They got out and looked. The trail ahead was moving, shifting positions from side to side. One moment it led through a forest; the next, through an adjacent field. Then across a swampy area. When it moved, the scenery reappeared where it had been, uninterrupted. It was weird.

"It's as if it can't make up its mind," Feline said.

"I know how that is," Hapless said. "I am often that way myself."

"It is supposed to be locked onto its destination," the centaur said, perplexed. "That should not be moving."

Hapless got an idea, not enough for a bulb flash, but still interesting. "It's locked onto Zed. A zebra-striped centaur. Maybe he's moving."

"A striped centaur?" the centaur said, frowning. "That's irregular."

"You don't approve?" Hapless asked, knowing the answer.

"Naturally I don't. Zebras have striped hides; centaurs don't."

"Unless maybe his folks met at a love spring," Feline said. "A zebra and a centaur."

"That would be miscegenation. We definitely don't approve of that."

"My parents met at a love spring."

"Well, you're a cat. You have lesser standards."

"Lesser standards! What are you, a bigot?"

"Everyone knows that cats have no morals. Centaurs, in contrast, do."

Feline opened her mouth, showing catlike teeth. Hapless rushed to get between them. "We thank you for the ride, centaur. We'll take it from here."

"He's snatching for a scratching!" Feline spat.

"We can stay on the path," Hapless said. "Maybe it will move us with it."

"You're taking the part of that catty creature?" the centaur demanded.

"Catty creature!" Feline exclaimed. "You horse-faced hoofer, what makes you think—"

Hapless wrapped his arms about her, picked her up, and hurried down the switching path. "Thank you!" he called back to the centaur.

The centaur shook his head, then turned and hauled his coach back away from them. Immediately it dissipated, and he was left in the brush. "Serves him right," he muttered as he set Feline down.

"You did take my part," Feline said.

"Well, sure. We have to get where we're going, and—"

"Weren't you afraid I'd scratch you?"

"I guess I'd rather get scratched than see you insulted."

"Are you trying for another kiss?"

He paused, taking stock. "If it's a choice between scratching and kissing, I'll take the kiss."

She swiped at his face with claws extended. He scrunched his eyes shut, unable to get his face out of the way in time. Then her kiss landed. She had been teasing him again, at least in part. It was another wonderful experience.

"You do like me for more than my curves," she said.

"For your curves and your kisses," he agreed.

"Are we still on the path?"

"I think so. But it's weird the way it's switching."

"It is."

They stood and watched the scenery change around them. The path was keeping them on it as it jumped from place to place.

Then they saw what was at its end. A zebra-striped centaur was dodging back and forth, and the path was switching to keep up with him.

"He's trying to avoid it!" Feline said, amazed.

"Why would he do that?"

"We'll just have to catch up and ask him."

They ran along the switching path, getting closer to the centaur despite the changing background.

"Hey, Zed!" Hapless called. "What are you doing?"

The centaur paused at the sound of his name. That was all the path needed. It latched onto his hind hooves, securely anchored.

"Oh, bleep!" Zed swore.

They reached him and stepped off the path. "We're coming to help you," Hapless said. "Why were you trying to avoid our path?"

"Because I changed my mind," Zed said. "I thought I'd undertake a Quest to find my true wish. Then things got weird and I realized it was a mistake, so I tried to cancel it. But that creepy path kept coming after me. Now I'm stuck."

"What is your true wish?" Feline asked.

"To find true love."

"You no longer want true love?"

"Oh, I still want it. But I don't think I'll find it by traveling along weird paths."

"Well, this path is gone," Hapless said. "You don't have to take any path you don't want to."

Zed looked around. There was now no path, just scenery. "I don't?"

"It was just to lead us to you," Feline said. "You can quit now if you want to. Otherwise we should get acquainted, because we'll be keeping company for a while."

"Who would want to keep company with a striped centaur?"

"Have you looked at me recently?" Feline stroked her own striped hair.

"Um." The centaur was plainly taken aback.

"Try thinking outside the box," Hapless said. "Consider doing something you haven't tried before, like joining a Quest."

"That's a novel notion."

Hapless plowed ahead. "I'm Hapless. My talent is to conjure musical instruments, but I can't play any. My wish in part is to find an instrument I can play."

"I see," Zed said cautiously.

"I'm Feline. I'm a human/cat crossbreed." She changed to cat form, and back. "My wish is to find someone who will love me for something other than my curves."

"You're a striped cat!" Zed said.

"Like a blue and white zebra," she agreed. "You get mocked for your stripes? Tell me about it."

"I apologize," Zed said. "You folk are like me. Misfits. No affront intended."

"None taken," Feline said. "That's what we are."

"Now we understand each other," Hapless said. "Are you with us? You can go your own way and we'll go on without you, but we figure there is a reason we are being put together and we'd rather have you along."

"Go my own way?"

"In due course we'll activate the path to the next Quest Companion," Hapless said. "If you don't get on that path with us, we'll separate and probably never meet again. So it's your choice."

Zed considered, then took hold in the centaur manner. "You mentioned thinking outside the box. I am interested. But I prefer to know more. How did you get started on this Quest? There has to be more to it than just enjoying each other's company."

"The Good Magician came to see me, and talked me into it," Hapless said. "He said I was needed for the Quest, and others would suffer if I didn't take it. So I did."

"Just to find an instrument you can play?"

"Well, he said I would also accomplish something meaningful, and have two or three girlfriends."

"Feline looks like one," Zed said. "You need more?"

Hapless felt a bit out of sorts. "I don't know whether Feline is one. The Good Magician mentioned two good girls and one bad girl."

"Well, villains are the reason that heroes exist. Maybe you need a villainess in order to become a hero."

"I don't know. But I think I'd settle for Feline."

"Except that you like her human curves too well?"

Centaurs were sharp! "Yes."

"So the two of you could quit the Quest now and be satisfied, if she were amenable."

Hapless felt himself blushing. "Yes. Except I wouldn't have accomplished anything meaningful or have found my musical instrument."

"How do you feel about that?" Zed asked Feline.

"I wouldn't want to deny him his instrument."

"That's evasive."

"That's curvaceous."

Zed laughed. "I'll join the Quest."

"What, because I threw you a curve?"

"I like your curves."

"I'm not sure I understand," Hapless said.

"Your motives are not straightforward. This intrigues me. I think I will like your company, even if I don't get my wish, so it won't be a waste of effort."

"Then let's camp the night and set off again in the morning," Hapless said.

"No," Feline said. "Let's set off now, and camp the night on the path."

Oh. "Yes, of course."

"Did I miss something?" Zed asked.

"An obscurity," Feline said.

"The paths are enchanted," Hapless explained. "So we can camp on them safely. That makes it easier."

"Ah. This is sensible. Here there be dragons."

"Literally," Feline agreed.

"Well, figuratively at the moment. This has been my stamping ground for a few days, and it is clear of dragons and other threats. We'll be safe until nightfall."

"Then let's relax and get to know each other until then," Hapless said, relieved.

"There's a little spring nearby, and a small plantation of pie plants. But there are brambles intervening. I can carry one of you there, as I know a safe route."

"Make that two of us," Feline said, and changed to cat form.

"Two," Zed agreed, smiling.

She jumped into Hapless's arms. Then he mounted the centaur, carefully. "I have no experience riding anything," he warned. "I may fall off."

"That would be awkward," Zed said. "Fortunately I have a riding blanket."

"Blanket?"

"You're sitting on it. It will keep you in place."

Hapless looked. There was the blanket, striped to match the centaur's stripes so that it wasn't obvious. This was supposed to keep him on?

"Meow," Feline said from his shoulder.

"Exactly," Zed agreed. He stepped forward—and Hapless remained securely in place. The blanket was working!

Soon the centaur was trotting through the brush, and Hapless was gaining confidence. This was a nice way to travel.

They reached the spring, and Hapless dismounted. Feline jumped down and became human, her skirt flaring to show her legs almost to her panties. He suspected she had done it on purpose, and didn't mind. He did like her curves, however that complicated their relationship.

"You're sure this is not a love spring?" Feline asked. "It's pretty."

"Nor a healing spring," Zed said. "Or Lethe. It's just water. I checked it carefully. I've had enough mischief from love springs."

"Your parents met at one?" Feline asked as she harvested a hot pizza pie.

"My father was a Mundane zebra who strayed into Xanth and was lost. My mother was unfamiliar with the area. Both were thirsty. You may interpolate the rest."

"We may what?" Feline asked.

"Fill it in for ourselves," Hapless said.

"Oh, yes. The way it was with my parents."

"We do seem to have that in common," Zed agreed.

"New subject," Feline said. "Do you play a musical instrument, Zed?"

"No."

"There's something I want to find out about Hapless's talent. When he conjured me a kit—that's a small violin—I played it better than I had any right to. I'm wondering whether it would be similar for you."

"I'm sure I would make a mockery of any instrument I attempted. I have no experience."

"But have you ever dreamed of one, foolishly? In your most secret imagination?"

"Are you trying to embarrass me?"

"Not at all, Zed. This could be the opposite. I think Hapless's talent has ramifications we hardly comprehend, and if we only understood it better, we might succeed in finding the instrument he can play. No one else needs to know about this experiment. Please?" She smiled winningly.

Hapless was impressed. She was charming the centaur, who did have a human component and surely appreciated her curves.

"When I attended centaur school," Zed said, "There was a class on music and its instruments. There was a passing reference to the saxophone, a mundane instrument invented in their year 1840 by one Adolphe Sax, a single-reed hybrid of the clarinet and oboe with a mellow tone. There was something about that description 'hybrid' that appealed to me. The lowest commonly made is the subcontrabass, rarely seen today. I thought it might be fun to play such a rare and special instrument, but of course I never mentioned it, let alone thought to attempt it, already being laughing stock enough."

Feline turned to Hapless, lifting a curvy eyebrow.

Hapless had never heard of the instrument described, but the centaur's description was more than sufficient for his talent. He focused, and one appeared in his hands. It was large and looked phenomenally complicated, with keys and levers galore and a huge curved bell. Overall it resembled an extremely fancy letter S.

"Try playing it, Hapless," Feline said.

He put the mouthpiece to his mouth and his hands on the keys. He blew.

An awful noise sounded. Both Feline and Zed winced. This was definitely not his instrument.

"Now you, Zed," Feline said. "Surely you can't do worse than that."

"I am not at all sure of that," the centaur said. But he took the saxophone and lifted it to his face, his hands on its convoluted body. He blew.

A lovely full-bodied note emerged.

All three of them paused, surprised.

"I think you can play it," Feline said.

"I think it was a fluke." But he tried again.

This time a marvelously evocative melody came. It was absolutely beautiful.

"Oh, let me join you!" Feline said.

Hapless conjured a kit for her, and she joined in, making it a duet. Now the beauty was compounded. It was perfect harmony.

They came to the end of the refrain and paused, awed. "I never dreamed of that!" Zed said. "This has to be a magic instrument, because I'm sure I have no such talent."

"Mine too," Feline agreed. "Now it is confirmed: Hapless summons magically playable instruments. For anyone but himself. They fade away after a day, but he can re-conjure them."

"I hardly believe this, but I like it," the centaur said. "Let's play some more."

"Gladly." They resumed their serenade of the glade.

Hapless didn't want to spoil their enjoyment, but he was sick at heart. If only he could find an instrument for himself! His talent was teasing him horrendously, showing him what others could do while denying it for him.

He walked away, depressed. All he could hope was that somehow in the course of this Quest he would at last find his instrument. The Good Magician had promised as much, but he still did not really believe it. Bleep!

Then the music went sour and stopped. He turned to look back. The two were staring at their instruments. What had happened?

Hapless hurried back. "What—"

"It stopped," Feline said. "Suddenly neither of us could play."

"Why should that be? You both were doing so well. Try it again."

They tried it again, tentatively. The music was lovely.

"It must have been a fluke," Hapless said, relieved for them.

"I am not sure of that," Zed said. "Our ability faded when you departed. We should verify that."

They verified it. When Hapless got beyond a certain distance, the ability ceased. They could play well only in his presence.

"Now we have gained further comprehension of your talent," Zed said. "Not only can you conjure instruments, you make them play well."

"But then I should be able to play one myself!" Hapless protested.

"Surely so. We merely have to find which one is right for you."

They left it at that. There was at least hope amidst the frustration.

Chapter 5

NYA

When evening came, Hapless brought out the box and opened it. Inside was a picture of, well, he wasn't sure, with the word NYA.

The others looked. "Crossbreed," Feline said. "Like a winged serpent."

"Female," Zed said. "With lovely face, arms, breasts."

"But a dragon's tail," Hapless said. "A dragon/woman crossbreed?"

"Dragon/naga, maybe," Zed said. "Nagas are already human/serpent crossbreeds. The dragon could provide the wings and tail."

"Nya Naga," Feline suggested. "No panties."

But plenty else to attract the wandering male eye. "This should be interesting," Hapless said.

"So unglue your eyeballs and shut the box."

Hapless smiled. "Are you jealous of her attributes?"

"Of course I am. But with luck she'll be able to change to full serpent mode so it won't be a problem."

Problem? Hapless exchanged a look with Zed as he shut the box. She thought the view of a bare human female torso was a problem? Best not to argue the case.

The path had appeared when the box opened. "We'll follow it tomorrow," Hapless said.

"It is interesting to see it from the other end," Zed said.

They made a blanket tent, and Feline curled up in cat form. Zed simply stood, not needing to get off his feet to rest.

"Why hello, handsome stallion."

Hapless woke with a start. So did Feline. She assumed girl-form beside him in the darkness. "Beware," she whispered.

Then they looked out and saw in the near darkness that it was a lovely lady centaur with zebra stripes, that even crossed her provocative bare bosom. She was beckoning Zed.

"Who are you?" the centaur asked. "A demoness?"

"No, I'm C Duce the cemoness. Come to me and I'll give you such a thrill. I collect—"

"Don't do it!" Hapless called. "It's a trap!" Because obviously this was a demoness, whatever she called herself.

"Surely so," Zed agreed. "The stripes give her away."

"Oh, fizz," the mare swore. Then she changed to full woman form, gloriously nude. "Is this better, handsome man?"

"Don't answer her," Feline hissed. "She wants to engage you in dialogue so you'll forget she's off the path."

And it would be folly to step off. Hapless didn't answer.

"What, cat got your tongue?" C Duce asked snidely.

"Hey!" Feline said. Evidently the demon had seen her change.

"Have you considered this?" the creature asked. Smoky panties appeared.

Hapless managed to cover his eyes with a hand just in time, but Zed didn't. The centaur stood frozen in place. "That won't work," Hapless said. "A freaked-out person can't step off the path."

"Fizz and clods!" the cemoness swore. Hapless mentally translated that to liquid and solid natural functions, and smiled. Those weren't quite what she collected.

Feline snapped her fingers near Zed. "Wake. You have no business freaking out over a fake human form."

"I apologize," Zed said, recovering.

"Stay out of this, cattail," C Duce snapped.

"Or you'll what?" Feline demanded.

"I'll tear your fur out." The centaur became a cat.

"Oh, yeah?" Feline asked, stalking toward her as she changed form.

"No!" Hapless cried, diving for her. "She's trying to trick you into stepping off the path!" He picked her up, preventing her from crossing the line. "You can't fight a demon."

She changed back, and he was embracing a disheveled woman. "You're right. Thanks." She kissed him.

"Nauseating," the cemoness groaned, changing to woman in underwear form.

"Did I hear my name?" This time it was a ball of smoke on the path.

"Oh, no, it's Metria," Hapless muttered.

"Because she appears on the enchanted path," Feline agreed. "Meaning she doesn't wish us harm, annoying as she may be."

"Exactly. It's a complication we hardly need."

"Not necessarily."

"What are you two gesticulating about?" Metria demanded as her form formed.

"Doing what about?" Feline asked as she disengaged from Hapless.

"Intercommunicating, conferencing, discoursing, lecturing, confabulating—"

"Talking?"

"Whatever," the demoness agreed irritably.

"There's a foreign demoness just off the path trying to mess us up," Feline said. "She freaked out both males with her soiled panties."

"Soiled panties!" the off-path temptress shrieked. "I'll have you know they're genuine hot stuff!"

"So it's true," Metria shrieked back. "You're poaching on my territory!"

"I begin to see where this is leading," Hapless whispered appreciatively.

"*Your* territory? *My* territory!" C Duce said indignantly. "This stupid path leads right through it."

"But the path itself is my territory," Metria said. "So get your stinking tail out of here."

"Stinking tail?! I dare you to cross the line and say that."

"Oh, I will, you half-donkeyed freak!" Metria strode to the edge of the path and across it, sprouting claws. She had no concern about needing the path; it was just a convenience to her.

Immediately the two were engaged in a hissing, scratching, hair-pulling, bra-snapping, panty-shredding fracas. The three on the path watched, amazed.

"I don't believe I have encountered that speech-impaired demoness before," Zed murmured. "But she is intriguing."

"That's Metria," Hapless said. "She likes to mess in with interesting things. But she's another panty-flasher."

"Oh?"

"Polka dots with no cloth in the dots."

"That's really intriguing."

"Note that she considers the enchanted path to be her territory," Feline said, annoyed.

"Because she has access to it," Zed agreed.

Meanwhile the fight continued. Now the demonesses had graduated to dragon forms and were breathing smoke and fire at each other. It seemed to be an even match.

"Maybe we should move quietly on," Hapless suggested.

The others nodded. They left the little tent and walked on along the path, which ended behind them. The tent remained, and the battle, but all else was untrespassed wilderness. There was a faint glow marking the path, so they had no problem staying on it.

"Please?"

They paused. It was two children, about age 11, boy and girl, standing just off the path. She had bouncy curly hair, while his was straight.

"What is it?" Feline asked.

"Our name is Ari," the girl said, flouncing her curls cutely. "My brother lost his voice, so he can't talk; only I can understand him. We're on a quest to find it."

"To find his voice? I'm not sure that's something you can find by wandering through the forest. You should be home."

"Ari can't go home without his voice. Mom would know we'd been playing where we shouldn't. Then we'd both be in trouble, maybe even grounded. It's right here somewhere. Please, will you help us look? It's not safe to stay out here too long at night, and we're frightened."

Feline looked at the others. "They're children," she said, and stepped across the line.

"No, wait!" Hapless said, as usual too late. He looked at Zed. "I've got to help Feline." Then he dropped his pack and stepped across too.

The two children morphed into goblins. "Gotcha, fools," they said together.

"Oh, bleep!" Feline swore. "We fell for it."

"He wasn't silent at all," Hapless agreed, chagrined.

"We're taking you to the mound for the cook-pot," the goblins said together. He had a club, while she had a coil of rope. They were closing in on either side.

"That's what you think," Feline said. She became the cat, her claws extended.

Hapless feared that wouldn't be enough. He conjured a musical instrument: a trombone. Then he took it apart, taking a bone in each hand. It was a shame to ruin such a fine piece, but this was an emergency.

Feline pounced on the girl goblin with a screech, tearing at her hair. Hapless swung at the boy goblin, left and right, conking him on the head, bonk bonk! Goblins' heads were the hardest part of their bodies, so this didn't really hurt him, but was effective as a demonstration. In only a moment and a half the two were fleeing, defeated. The surprise had been reversed.

"We make a good team," Feline said as she resumed girl-form, satisfied. "I'd kiss you, but you might bonk my head."

"I bonk only goblins. If he had continued to fight, I would have bonked his feet. That would have hurt him more."

"I don't want my feet bonked either." She lifted a foot, not quite high enough to show a panty, teasingly.

They laughed together, then turned back to the path.

It was gone. There was only untrammeled wilderness. "Uh-oh," Hapless said.

"It was more of a trap than we realized. Those goblins may have been simply decoys, setting us up for the real threat."

Indeed, now they heard a heavy tromping, as of an ogre approaching.

"Here." It was Zed's voice, close by.

They both jumped, startled. "I hear you, but I don't see you," Hapless said.

"I'm standing beside your pack, at the end of the trail."

Hapless looked, but still saw nothing. Meanwhile the tromping was making the ground shake. "You must be invisible."

"I'm not," the centaur reassured him. "I can see myself and you plainly. But perhaps I am shrouded by illusion. That should dissipate once you return to the path."

"How can we return to the path if we can't see it?" Hapless demanded. The ogre came into sight. Twice the height of a man and broad in proportion, wielding a monstrous club. Mere trombones would not balk this beast!

"Fi fo fum fee," the ogre chanted. "He she feed me." He smiled, showing tusk-like yellow teeth.

"Close in on my voice," Zed said. "I will reach across and take your hands when you are close enough."

They went to the patch of brambles that masked the voice. Sure enough, they were an illusion. They reached out. Then Hapless felt his hand taken, and saw that Feline was similarly caught. They were drawn forward another step, and the path formed around them. Zed was holding their hands.

The ogre stood amidst the brambles, scratching his hairy head. Where had they gone?

"Thank you," Feline said, relieved. "That was nervous business."

"I begin to see a reason for my presence on this Quest," Zed said. "Not merely to find my own true love."

"Well, when you find her, give her this," Feline said, and kissed his ear. Hapless saw the ear brighten as the kiss landed. She did have the touch.

"It does seem that we are meant to be a team," Hapless said as he put his pack back on.

"Yet I wonder," Zed said. "If the path and I were covered by illusion, how is it that the cemoness and the goblins were able to see us?"

"They must be specially attuned," Hapless said thoughtfully.

"Maybe we should learn that tuning," Feline said. "So we don't get caught out again."

It was late, and they were tired, but they did it right then, taking turns stepping off the path and being guided back. Gradually they became aware of it, seeing its faint light as a phantom guide through the wilderness. Zed did it too, appreciating the need. Only when they were satisfied did they settle down again for the night, pitching another blanket tent.

Feline hesitated as the two of them lay down together in the tent. "Can I trust you?"

"I certainly hope so," Hapless said, perplexed.

"Good." She went to sleep in human form, lovely in her repose.

Oh. When he thought about it, he was inordinately pleased. She did trust him.

In the morning they resumed their hike, appreciating the surrounding scenery in a way they had not before. There were indeed demons, goblins, and ogres in these parts, not seen because of the protection of the path.

The path approached a mountain, but instead of going around it, it ascended, winding around it like a serpent, climbing high along a road inset into its steep slope—an inset that surely didn't exist outside the enchantment. The ground spread out below like a variegated tapestry, with forests, fields, rivers, ponds, and in the distance, the sea. As they looked at each feature, that feature enhanced itself, the forest becoming greener, the river smoother, the pond larger, and the sea more formidable. Hapless knew that was a standard aspect of Xanth, where not only animals but plants and geography had their awareness and liked to be admired.

"I do appreciate you, all of you," he murmured, feeling a bit foolish. "You are a wonder to behold." Then the whole scene brightened appreciatively, and he no longer felt foolish.

At last they came to a lofty dragon's nest atop the highest crag. It looked exposed, but Hapless could see that it was soundly bound to the rock and was secure. The precipitous path went up to it and stopped, as if hesitating to leap on into space.

"Welcome, Quest," a dulcet voice called. It came from the figure within the nest, not a dragon but a naga, with a serpentine tail and torso, topped by a human head, hands, and yes, breasts. Not all naga sported more than their heads on serpentine bodies, but each crossbreed was a rule unto itself.

"Uh, hello, Nya," Hapless answered, his eyes striving valiantly and not completely successfully to remain cool while confronted by that bare bosom. "We—we have come to enlist you as a Companion. If you're—you're interested."

"Of course I'm interested," Nya Naga said. "All my life I have struggled to discover my purpose in life, and now at last I have the chance to accomplish it. I was thrilled to see the enchanted path come my way."

"Uh, yes." Feline nudged him, and he realized that he was drifting, mentally or emotionally. "So we should—should get to know each other, because there will be challenges and we can't be sure we'll survive."

"That's why you need a dragon in your company." She shifted, becoming a winged dragon. It breathed out just enough fire to incinerate a buzzing fly that had come in too close, then shifted back to naga form.

"Uh, yes, I guess. This is my friend Feline, a human/cat crossbreed."

Nya eyed Feline. "Friend or girlfriend?"

"Girlfriend," Feline said before Hapless could deny it.

"That explains the cuttingly sharp glances," Nya said. "What is your concern, Feline?"

"Your bare boobs. You could use a halter."

"I can't use a halter, or a bra, because when I change forms, they could remain around my body, entangling it. Anyway there is no social need." Nya glanced at Zed. "Is there, centaur?"

"None," Zed agreed. Obviously the naga knew that centaur fillies regarded clothing as superfluous, and wore it only when tutoring human children, if then. She had trumped Feline at the outset.

"I'm glad that's decided," Nya said graciously.

Hapless didn't dare look at Feline, who was surely steaming. "And this is Zed Centaur."

"I'm sure we'll get along," Nya said. "You are concerned about your coloration?"

"Yes. My father was a zebra. But what I really want is to find true love regardless of my colors."

"And I want to find someone who will love me for something other than my curves," Feline said.

"And I want to find a musical instrument I can play," Hapless said.

"But you look half smitten with Feline."

It was that obvious? "It's complicated. It seems that I am fated to have two or three girlfriends, one of whom will be bad. While the prospect is intriguing, it does make things awkward with Feline."

"Well, I will put your concern about me at rest, Feline," Nya said. "I would love to have a suitable boyfriend, but I think he needs to be dragon or naga, not human. Human men are too partial to panties, which I will never have. At any rate, my primary concern is to find my purpose, as I mentioned. So an eyeful is all either male of your party will ever have of me. I don't begrudge them that, but that's the limit."

"Fair enough," Feline said, though Hapless wasn't sure that was her complete sentiment.

"This nest," Zed said, looking over the edge. "Is there a reason for it to be so isolated?"

"Yes. It is safe from everything except flying predators, and as a dragon I have little reason to fear those. Closer to the ground it could be overrun by assorted ground predators, which could get messy. I prefer to sleep in peace."

"Are you able to converse in your dragon form?"

"Only with other dragons," Nya said. "I can understand human dialogue, but lack the mouth to speak it. So if you want conversation, it will have to be in this form." She glanced at Feline as if mildly amused.

"This form is fine," Zed agreed.

Feline kept silent, and Hapless saw fit not to comment on forms. "We would like to get to know you better, as Feline said. In an emergency, we need to know each other's capacities well enough to make quick decisions. We will happily fill you in on our personal histories."

"Mine is simply told," Nya said. "I am a dragon/naga crossbreed, the result of an encounter at a love spring, as it seems is the case with two of you. The dragons tolerate me but do not welcome me, because I am a crossbreed. The naga don't even welcome me; dragons make them nervous. So I was sent away to get a centaur education, and I have respect for centaurs." She glanced at Zed. "Not romantic, I assure you. But their minds are excellent. So I live mostly alone, and I can handle that. But this is a life largely without purpose, and I am so situated, emotionally, that I crave purpose. There must be some reason for my existence; I do not believe in sheer coincidence. That's why I am eager to join your Quest, and I will support it in any manner I can."

Hapless nodded. "More could hardly be asked. There is one other thing, perhaps not important. Do you play a musical instrument?"

"I've always been partial to the harmonica, but I do not play it well, to my regret."

"We may be able to remedy that," Hapless said. He focused, and a fine harmonica appeared in his hand. "Try this."

She took it and put it to her mouth. She blew into it. A lovely melody came forth. She paused, surprised. "This must be magic."

"Not exactly," Zed said. "His talent is to summon such instruments, and to facilitate their playing, but he himself can't play any. We appreciate his frustration."

"I see," Nya said thoughtfully. She played a medley, clearly enjoying it. "May I keep this harmonica?"

"They last for only a day or so, then fade," Hapless said. "But I can summon another. Do keep it, and you can always have another one if you wish."

"Already I like this Quest."

"Let's play a theme together," Zed said. "It's a fine way to bond."

Hapless conjured the kit violin for Feline, and a saxophone for Zed. "Do you know 'The Crossbreed's Lament'?" Feline asked.

"Oh, yes!" Nya and Zed said almost together. Hapless wasn't familiar with it, but it didn't matter because he didn't need to play it.

The three played it together, in three-part harmony, and it was wonderful. Hapless, as an audience of one, was entranced despite his sadness at not being able to join them. At least his talent was worth something to others, if not to himself. Then it occurred to him that maybe that was a reason for his presence on the Quest: he could help others bond, when otherwise they might not.

"You play divinely on that little violin," Nya told Feline.

"Thank you," Feline said, thawing. "Your harmonica is great too."

"And that sax," Nya said. "I never heard one played before, but it's hard to see how any other could be more mellow. That's a remarkable instrument."

"They all are," Zed said. "We are magically competent, thanks to Hapless's talent. We couldn't do it without him."

And there it was: they could not be competitive when they made such lovely music together. Neither could he resent it when they credited him for their abilities. Yet still he wished that he could play an instrument himself.

Then they settled down for dinner. Nya had a fair supply of foods, and was glad to share it, as in the morning she knew they would leave the nest, maybe never to return. Then they took turns relieving themselves over the edge of the nest; sanitary facilities were simple. It was not at all private, but that was part of the bonding: they were becoming a kind of family.

But at dusk there was mischief. It started innocently enough. "The enchanted path that brought you here was impressive," Nya said. "There is no path up the mountain; I knew it was magic the moment it formed. Now it's gone."

Indeed it was. The mountain had reverted to sheer impassibility. "The

Good Magician gave me a box," Hapless explained. "At first it contained only what was irrelevant to my need. I had to learn to think outside the box. Then it contained the paths. When I opened it, there was the picture of Feline in cat form, and the path went to her. Then it showed Zed, and the path chased him down. Then it showed you."

"We have to stay on it," Feline said, smiling. "Or else."

"Or else what?"

"Or else we are suddenly lost in the wilderness," Zed said. "The path can get covered by illusion so we can't find it. We have practiced finding it regardless, just in case. But it's better just to stay on it."

"May I see this magic box and path?"

"Sure," Hapless said. He dug into his pack, found the box, and drew it out. He held it toward Nya.

Just then an erratic gust of wind passed by and flipped it from his hand. "Bleep!" he swore as it dropped into the deepening shadows below.

"I'll fetch it," Nya said. She changed to dragon form, spread her wings, and paused. Two bits of fire jetted from her nostrils, making whistlings that sounded like "Uh-oh." Then she changed back to naga form.

"What is it?" Feline asked, alarmed.

"Rocky Roc is coming. I don't fear most winged monsters, but I can't fight the roc. Maybe he's just passing by. Hitherto they've ignored me."

"And if he isn't?"

"Then we're in trouble."

"Which we could have avoided if I set up the next path," Hapless said ruefully. "I messed up again."

"Not your fault," Feline said. "Bleep happens."

He really appreciated her support. But the roc did not veer off. It was coming straight for the nest. It was so big it looked like a flying mountain. It could just about clutch the entire nest in one clawed foot.

"I'll try to talk to him," Nya said.

"You speak roc talk?"

"In dragon form I speak the pidgin tongue of the winged monsters. There's normally a kind of pact. It's crude but gets the job done." She changed.

"Pigeon?" Hapless asked. "Bird talk for the big bird?"

"Pidgin," Zed said with authority. "That is a brutally simplified language that occurs when folk of different languages need to communicate. Drastically reduced vocabulary and syntax. Sometimes a pidgin will evolve into its own language, called a creole, which is more sophisticated."

"Oh." Hapless felt ignorant, again.

The dragon issued a smoky hiss. The approaching roc responded with a raucous cry. The naga reappeared. "Rocky says I have one minute to vacate before he drops the nest into the sea."

"But why?" Zed asked. "If you haven't done anything?"

"He didn't say. He's just mad. He called me 'burn breath.' You can't argue with an angry roc. Especially not in pidgin. We have to vacate."

"Can you carry us?" Hapless asked.

"I'm not that big a dragon. I could carry a cat, and maybe a human for a short distance slanting down, but not a centaur."

"Could we stay in the nest, then swim to shore after it lands in the sea?"

"No. It is securely anchored to the crag, and hauling it off that will destroy it. Only fragments will reach the sea."

"So we're doomed if we don't repel the roc," Hapless concluded.

"I'm sorry. I'll take man and cat to the forest floor, but I can't help the centaur."

Feline caught Hapless's eye. "Play your music. Loud."

He nodded. "There may be a way. Clear the center."

"I don't follow," Nya said, perplexed.

"Just do it," Hapless said. "Trust me."

They squeezed to the edge of the nest as the roc looked close, the draft of his wings blasting them. As a huge taloned foot reached out to clutch the entire nest, Hapless conjured an organ. It filled the center with its standing keyboard and surrounding pipes, leaving little room for them. He sat at its keyboard and jammed both hands on the keys. "Cover your ears!"

The talons closed on them as the others put hands on their ears. Then a horrendous sound blasted out from the vibrating pipes, like a sick whale with a very bad hiccup. BLUURBST!!

The roc rocked back as if struck, which actually was the case. The sound was utterly awful, blown on the winds from the pipes. He tumbled down out of control before spreading his wings and catching the air again. He spiraled back up toward the nest.

Hapless played another chord. HOOHARGH!! It sounded like nausea deluxe being scratched on a severely broken blackboard.

The roc shuddered, but this time did not go out of control.

"Tell Rocky we'll play a whole symphony if he comes close," Feline said with a certain satisfaction.

Nya went dragon again and hissed. The roc cocked his head but did not retreat.

"Let's try the positive next," Zed suggested. "Tell Rocky we'll eschew the bad sound if he behaves."

The dragon hissed again. The roc hesitated.

"Let's give Rocky a sample," Zed said. "Tell him we'll play him some nice music, so he knows the alternative."

The dragon hissed once more. This time the roc responded with a caw.

The naga reappeared. "He says he'll listen briefly, before he braves the awfulness again." She reverted to dragon form.

"Let's do it," Zed said. "This is our chance to be positive."

The roc squawked once more. This hardly required translation: "This better be good."

The naga form reappeared, complete with harmonica. Feline and Zed found their instruments. "What music?" Nya asked.

"Rock music, of course," Zed said.

They played a rock symphony. To Hapless it sounded rather violent, but it was way better than his organ rendition.

And the roc was charmed. He squawked approvingly. Music had again soothed the savage breast or beast.

They had negotiated the crisis. Hapless abolished the organ. The others continued their serenade. When it concluded, the roc did not attack.

"Best to find out why Rocky was angry," Zed said. "So we can be sure not to set him off again."

Nya went back to dragon form and hissed. The roc responded.

She became the naga. "He says the dragons are calling him loathsome. He doesn't like that."

"Well, sure," Zed agreed. "No one likes to be ridiculed. How well we here know that! So it seems he doesn't want any dragons in his territory."

"Yes."

"I wonder. Language can be devious. What is one person's idiom may be another person's insult. Pidgin lacks nuances. I suspect a misunder-standing."

"Dragons do talk," Nya said.

"I have a notion," Zed said. "What is pidgin for 'loathsome'?"

Nya turned dragon and made a hissing sound.

"And what is pidgin for 'handsome'?"

She made a similar sound.

"Can you tell the difference?" Zed asked Feline and Hapless.

"No," they said almost together.

"So the dragons could have remarked on the handsome roc, but the translation sounded like the loathsome roc."

Nya, still in dragon form, nodded. She hissed again to the roc. They heard the two similar words again as she made the point.

The roc looked taken aback. Then he spun about in air and departed.

The naga returned. "That was it! He concedes it was probably a confu-sion. We're safe." Then she looked at Zed. "You're smart."

"I am a normal centaur, apart from my coloration. We practice sen-sible thinking."

"I know. As I said, I respect centaurs." She paused. "I think I need to go fetch your box now. It should be lodged in a crevice not far down."

"That would be nice," Hapless agreed. He had really come to depend on the box, which he realized might not be best. But he wanted to get along with the box remaining as an option, so he could think outside or inside it.

Nya turned dragon and launched into the air. In two thirds of a moment she was flying below the nest.

"We functioned as a team," Feline said. "But I hope we don't have to do anything like that again soon."

"I'll try to take better care of the box," Hapless promised. "I don't know what shape the path is in."

"It should still be there," Zed said. "If the path ends at the box, which our experience indicates, we remain on it, and it terminates below us."

They peered down into the gloom. Now Hapless saw the faint outline of the path dropping down. The centaur was correct.

"But if the path hasn't terminated, why were we vulnerable to the roc?" Hapless asked, confused.

"You did not actually touch Nya," Zed said. "So a bit of the path remained. But we stepped off it, going to the sides of the nest. So we weren't safe."

"That makes sense," Feline agreed.

In another moment and a third Nya was back with the box held delicately in her mouth. She dropped it into the nest then changed. "I think I can wait until morning to see into that box," she said. "I have had enough adventure for today."

Hapless picked up the box, immensely relieved. "Yes."

The others were glad to agree. The nest seemed safe enough, now that the roc was gone. Nya dug out a blanket from an alcove, and Hapless shared it with Feline in human form. Zed remained standing, as usual, while Nya curled up in dragon form to sleep.

Hapless remained disturbed by his slip with the box. "I got us all in trouble," he murmured.

"And helped get us out of it," she replied. "That was lovely dissonance with the organ. Rather, a loathsome sound. I almost puked."

"Still, I should have—"

She shut him up with a kiss. "Now go to sleep."

What choice did he have? If he argued further she might assume cat form and ignore him. He much preferred her human form, especially when it was right up against him. He slept.

He woke in the night. "You're dreaming of me," Feline said accusingly. "I can tell."

He didn't dare ask how she could tell. "Uh, yes. Sorry."

She laughed. "That's okay. It's natural, since you're wedged against me. See that you don't dream of any other woman."

Was she teasing him? "I'll try."

They returned to sleep. He absolutely loved the way she nestled against him. If only they didn't both know that he was destined to have one or two more girlfriends. Until that situation was resolved, he couldn't commit to her.

Hapless woke as the first beam of dawn splashed across the nest. Feline remained asleep, lovely in her dishevelment, including her striped hair. "I wish you were my girlfriend for real, you lovely creature," he whispered.

Her eyes popped open. "I heard that."

Bleep. "I should have kept my mouth shut," he said, embarrassed.

"You're still enamored of my curves."

He could not deny it. Her curves fascinated him. "Yes."

"You're not even bothering to lie about it," she said accusingly.

That was somehow worse. "Sorry about that."

"Not even to get what you want of me, in your dreams."

"Yes," he repeated, ashamed.

"I'm not sure you *can* lie, about anything."

She was nailing him. "That's true."

"So when, if ever, you tell me you love me for something else, I'll know it's the truth."

"Yes." He already liked her a lot, but he couldn't swear it was exclusive of her curves.

She gazed at him a moment longer. "You're hopeless."

Now at last he could disagree, albeit with a smile. "No, I'm Hapless."

"You are. You think I'm mad at you."

"Yes."

"Well, I'm not." She kissed him. "Now let's get on with the day."

Not? How he wished he could be sure of that!

"That was an interesting sequence," Nya remarked.

"Extremely," Zed agreed.

Hapless blushed, remembering that there really was no privacy in the togetherness of the nest. Then he saw that Feline was blushing too. That made up for a lot.

Chapter 6

QUIN

They washed, breakfasted, and made ready to go. "I think I'm through with this nest," Nya said. "I doubt we'll be returning this way."

"Not if we achieve our wishes," Zed said.

"So I'll shut it down and donate it to Rocky Roc. He can use it to safely store incidentals."

"But you just had a fight with him," Hapless protested.

"He yielded graciously. He's not a bad bird." She shifted to dragon form and emitted a loud hiss.

There was an answering squawk from far away.

The naga returned. "He appreciates the gesture," she said.

Hapless made a mental note: Nya did not hold grudges. He liked that.

She turned to him. "You were about to show me the box last night when we were rudely interrupted. Shall we try again?"

She wasn't blaming him for the mishap, either. He liked that too.

"Let's," Feline said a bit tightly. She evidently misconstrued the nature of his gaze. He hastily removed it from Nya's front.

Now Hapless carefully brought out the box and opened it. As he did so, the faint outline that connected the box to Nya disappeared; that path was gone. There was a picture of a dragon with a human head and bird's wings on the forepart. The word was QUIN. "What's that?" he asked.

"Another crossbreed," Nya said. "It looks like Dragon/harpy."

"You should find him interesting," Feline said.

"I do. We evidently share dragon ancestry. But what counts more is his personality."

"Always," Feline agreed.

"Look at that path!" Zed exclaimed.

Now the others looked. The path led from the nest straight out into air, faintly glowing. It resembled a long narrow bridge, but it had no supports below or cables above. It just proceeded, going into the distance in a straight line, far above the ground.

"Can it support our weight?" Zed asked. He meant *his* weight; he was the heaviest of the Companions.

"We'll just have to see," Hapless said. Assuming an air (awkward word in this context) of greater confidence than he felt, he stepped out on the aerial way.

"Wait!" Feline said. "You can't go first."

He paused. "I can't?"

"You carry the box, and the path ends at the box, remember? You have to go last, or you'll strand the rest of us here."

She was right. "Sorry." He stepped back.

Feline tried it, looking as if she were ready to switch to cat form the moment the path let her down. But it remained firm; it supported her. The footing was invisible yet solid.

Nya was next, in her naga form. She slithered gracefully along it, and it supported her too.

Then Zed set hoof on it. It held. He tried another, and it remained firm. Then the rear hooves. It held his full weight. "I can't say I'm completely easy with this," he said. "But neither can I fault it. It does the job."

Finally Hapless got on it. He glanced back, and regretted it, because the path no longer existed behind him. There was just a gap of air separating him from the nest. Could he fall into it? He decided to face resolutely forward, avoiding the issue.

They walked on in single file, though the path was broad enough for two. Where was it going? Regardless, they were committed.

Rocky Roc returned. He did a double-take.

Nya shifted to dragon form and hissed. The roc nodded. Then, evidently curious, he flew to the path ahead of them—and sheared off, unable to cross it. The enchantment prevented any overlap.

Nya hissed again. Rocky nodded again, and flew on to inspect the nest he had inherited. It was too small for him to perch on, but certainly could be useful to cache items. He was clearly pleased.

They picked up speed, preferring to get through this stage of the journey efficiently. The scenery spread out beneath them. At one point they passed over a moderate mountain with a goblin mound at its top, only a short distance below them. The goblins spied them and looked up in wonder as they passed. The males froze in place until the females bopped them on their heads, making them stir. One female shook her fist at them.

"Well, they shouldn't look," Feline snapped.

Oh. The males had peeked up under her skirt and gotten smitten by the sight of her panties. It did serve them right. Feline could have avoided the issue by assuming cat form, but evidently preferred to assert her power to walk where and how she chose.

The path moved on, crossing a lake. Water birds looked up, surprised. Probably they could not see the path, only the file of creatures on it, seemingly crossing in mid air.

In due course they came to another high nest. There was the harpy dragon watching them approach. He had evidently figured out their purpose.

Feline stopped just short of completion. "Let me introduce us," she said. "You are Quin, clearly expecting us. We are members of a Quest, hoping to win the fulfillment of our wishes. I am Feline, a human/cat crossbreed." She switched briefly to her cat form. "This is Nya, a naga/dragon crossbreed." Nya switched briefly to dragon form, and back. "Next is Zed, a centaur/zebra crossbreed." Zed nodded. "Last and least is Hapless, who runs the Quest. He can conjure musical instruments, but can't play any himself. Do you play any?"

"Actually I do," Quin said. "My original harpy form has wings and legs, but when I change I can reshape myself somewhat and form those legs into human arms. I can be dragon, harpy, or in between. It's awkward, but it works. I favor the accordion, but I don't have an accordion to play, so it's academic."

"Not any more." She looked back. "Hapless?"

Hapless conjured a fine accordion and presented it to Quin as he stepped into the nest. Now all of them were there, and it was crowded, but they fit.

"Oh, my," Quin breathed. "This is absolutely beautiful." He fitted his hands into the straps and played a scale. "Oh, yes!"

"We will play music together," Feline said.

Hapless obligingly conjured instruments for the others. They played an impromptu melody, harmonizing perfectly. Every sound complemented the others.

"Wait," Quin said, stopping. "Where is your instrument, Hapless? Why are you not playing? You are surely the best of all, considering your talent. Why are you not allowed to participate?"

Hapless spread his hands. "I'm not forbidden. I am unable. No instrument works for me. It's frustrating."

"What, even a magic one like this? I can tell it is enhancing my own ability, because I never played this well before. Why can't it do the same for you?"

"That is my curse," Hapless said. "The magic seems to be reversed for me."

"I am reluctant to believe that," Quin said. "Show me." He passed the accordion back to Hapless.

Hapless took it and played an awful riff.

Quin winced. "Point made," he said, taking back the accordion. "You are cursed."

"We're all here because we have wishes to fulfill," Feline said. "What is yours?"

"I want to find out how to become human, instead of a part human mishmash. I have been trying to shape my dragon heritage into a human body to go with the human portion of my harpy body, but it doesn't work; I have too much tail and no human legs."

"Why not just settle for one or the other, then?" Nya asked.

"I would if I could, but I can't."

"Can't decide which one?"

"Can't settle for either, or for a grotesque combination."

"You definitely belong on this Quest," Feline said. "None of us want to settle for what we've got."

"I would love to join your Quest," Quin said. "But I fear I can't."

"But the path brought us right to you," Hapless protested.

"Maybe it made a mistake. I am not free to go."

"What's going to hold you back?" Nya demanded. "Your other half is a dragon!"

"My conscience."

"That's mischief," Zed said knowingly.

"So you want to join, and have a wish to fulfill, and the path thinks you're the one," Nya said tightly. "But you think you shouldn't do it?"

"Exactly."

"Maybe we should hear your reason," Zed said. "Perhaps we will have some input to help you decide."

"If you wish."

"Oh, we wish," Nya said. "Talk."

"As you request. I wouldn't want to bore you with my personal problem."

Hapless made a mental note: Quin was remarkably polite for a harpy or a dragon. That probably got in him in trouble with both factions.

"Bore us." Feline said. "Your problem is our problem." The others nodded agreement.

They settled down to listen.

"I am the unfortunate result of a love spring tryst. My father was a small flying dragon who happened to catch a harpy alone, so naturally he launched to catch her in his jaws. She dodged, evading him, but in the process they collided and both fell into the pool below. Then things changed, and instead of making war they made love, and I hatched from the first egg she laid thereafter."

"We know how that is," Nya said. "Most of us have similar origins."

"Yes. My mother took care of me, reluctantly, but the other harpies barely tolerated me because I was a crossbreed. The same was true with the dragons; my father did not want to be seen with me, though I am a legitimate steamer."

Hapless found that interesting. Nya was a fire breather. Dragons came in different types.

"We understand that too," Feline said. "But that isn't reason not to join the Quest. Rather the opposite."

"He is getting there," Zed said.

"Now a bit of background on the harpy culture," Quin continued. "The great majority of them are female. Maybe only one in a hundred is male, and in some generations the ratio is leaner than that. That means that most harpies who want to breed must do so with members of their ancestral stock, vulture or human, alternating generations. That is a challenge, because the average harpy is a wretched creature, not at all attractive to others. They have to settle for corrupt male vultures or humans who will go for anything remotely female and who will not stick around long after trysting. They far prefer to have a male harpy, even if he has to be widely shared.

"Which is the other reason I was tolerated: they knew they might eventually need me. They were not eager to make it with a crossbreed, and neither was I to make it with a harpy, but we were up against difficult alternatives. I would far prefer to have a dragon girlfriend, but the dragon ladies spurn me. So I wish to find a way to morph into full human, as my mind is human.

"Fortunately, a male harpy came to their local flock, and of course they welcomed him and left me to my own devices. Hence this isolated nest. But then the goblins raided and captured him. Now he is prisoner in the bowels of the mountain. They are holding him for an impossible ransom, something like a mountain of gold. Probably the goblins just want to get permanently rid of the harpies. If the harpies attack the goblins in an effort to rescue him, the goblins will kill him. So it is an impasse. Meanwhile it seems that I am all that the harpies can be sure of, and I will have to serve if Hardly Harpy remains captive much longer. I owe it to them for their prior sufferance. So I can't depart until that case is settled; it wouldn't be ethical."

"Hardly Harpy?" Feline asked.

"He doesn't act like a harpy, hence his name. He's actually a nice guy with an open mind. He can tolerate the wretched behavior of the females, but he doesn't treat others that way. He's smart and independent, making up his own mind about things. I like him."

"We can't fault you for your ethics," Zed said.

"I would love to go with you, even if there is little hope of success. You understand about crossbreeds. But I can't, as long as Hardly remains captive, and that could be a long time. You will do better going on without me."

"What do you think, Hapless?" Feline asked him.

Hapless would have preferred not to be put on the spot. But he was the nominal leader of the Quest, and had to answer. To his surprise, he had an answer. "We need to rescue Hardly Harpy. Then Quin will be free. The box must have counted on that."

"And how will we do that?" Feline asked.

Now it was time to think outside the box. "First we need information. Quin, is there any route to where Hardly is being held that we can use without getting ourselves caught and eaten by the goblins?"

Quin considered. "There may be, but there's a caution. The mountain is honeycombed with cave passages throughout. The goblins occupy some, the harpies occupy some, and assorted other monsters use the rest. Those passages are not safe."

"What about music? Would it soothe those savage beasts?"

"Some, perhaps, but not all."

"Suppose Hapless plays?" Feline asked.

Quin considered, surprised. "They would not like that. It might drive them away."

"So we could proceed with impunity?"

"I doubt it. The goblins have many devious traps like concealed pits and deadfalls that will operate regardless of the music. We would have to use safe routes, which would be guarded by goblins."

"I know something of goblins," Nya said. "The naga have dealings with them, generally hostile. There are places they don't go."

"They are wary of nickelpede-infested sections," Quin agreed. "And the haunts of large serpents. Also sizable subterranean rivers and flooded caverns, where sea monsters lurk. So there are fair regions free of goblins. But the same menaces would keep us clear of them too."

"Except for our music," Nya said. "We might either charm them or repel them so that we could traverse their territories."

"Perhaps. But the chamber where Hardly is kept would be sealed off from any such regions. They don't want him dead until they decide to kill him. We would not have access from there to him."

"Have those caves ever been invaded by a centaur?" Zed asked.

"Not that I know of. A centaur would be limited to the larger passages, and still vulnerable to the slings and arrows of the goblins."

"Unless protected by special music," Zed said. "Then he could use his hind hooves to break through a suitably thin partition, perhaps surprising the goblins."

This seemed to be coming together. But Hapless realized that they needed one more thing. "Is there a map of the caves?"

"I believe I have one," Quin said. "I never thought to use it." He brought it out.

They pored over it. The interior of the mountain was a three dimensional labyrinth of passages both natural and artificial. "We'd get lost in that, even with the map," Feline said. "If the goblins didn't find us first."

"The box," Quin said. "I believe you said you are supposed to think outside it?"

"Yes," Hapless agreed uncomfortably. "Except when it makes a path we have to follow."

"And you followed a path to me."

"Yes. You saw us arrive."

"I wonder whether it is possible to think outside the path, as it were."

"If we leave the path, we're lost," Feline said. "We've done it. Now we know better."

"Though we did learn to see that path from outside," Zed reminded her. "We don't have to stay on it all the time. But we do need to stay close."

"I am thinking that you have not seen the complete path," Quin said.

They looked at him. "What is your point?" Nya asked. "You saw us arrive here. That concluded this particular path; you can see that it no longer exists across the air."

"My backpack ends the path," Hapless said. "Or rather, the box in it does. When we reached the nest, that path was over."

"Are you sure?"

Was this person stupid? "Of course we're sure," Hapless said. "We've done this several times."

"Or are you thinking within the box?"

Hapless looked at him with frustration. Was the crossbreed being deliberately obscure? "When it comes to following the path, we either follow it or we don't," he said. "We're here. That's it."

"Here is my reasoning," Quin said. "The path leads you to your destination, in this case me. You have to stay on it or you get lost. But I am not presently available. So either that path is in error, or you have missed a loop."

"A loop?" Feline asked.

"The loop through the mountain labyrinth."

"Where?"

"There." Quin pointed to the air between them. There was the faint glow of the path, and it wasn't leading toward him but toward the mountain.

The path did not go directly to Quin. Instead it turned aside, avoiding him, and entered a tunnel into the mountain—one that probably had not been there before.

"Oh, my!" Zed said. "The loop that enables us to rescue the prisoner so that you can be free to join us! We just assumed the path had terminated. We were not thinking outside the box."

"This is my thought," Quin agreed.

Hapless whistled. "You're outside the path, and outside the box, so you saw what we didn't."

"This is phenomenal," Zed said. "But it remains problematic. If the path has not yet reached you, how can you join us in raiding the goblin hive?"

"Do I have to be on the path to accompany you?" Quin asked. "Or if I am, does it count? A loop is a loop."

They considered that. "I think I could not loop around to follow myself on the path," Hapless said. "Because the box erases it as it catches up. But you're not yet there, so maybe you can, confusing as it seems."

"Certainly we can try it," Nya said.

"And the path should be enchanted to protect us," Hapless said. "As long as we stay on it. We can do this."

"But quietly," Zed said. "Because Hardly isn't protected, and if they see us coming, they'll kill him. Keeping ourselves safe is no good if we carelessly mess up our chance to complete our Quest."

"Quietly," Hapless agreed. "We can still use the map, to spy where goblins and other creatures are likely to be, so we can avoid alerting them. When's the best time?"

"Evening is approaching," Nya said. "We could rest."

"Or we could do the less likely thing, and go immediately," Zed said. "It will be night, but inside the mountain that won't matter. The faster we act, the less likely we are to give the goblins time to catch on that something is afoot."

The others looked at Hapless. It was his decision. "Act now. Rest later," he decided.

"I'll lead," Feline said. "You trail, Hapless, to keep the path firm. Quin, you follow me with the map, so you can warn us what's around us. Zed and Nya in the middle. We'll talk in whispers, if at all. If there's likely mischief, make a hand signal."

"Good enough," Hapless agreed, endorsing her organization. "Have your musical instruments ready."

"No," Zed said. "They aren't silent."

He was right. Hapless hadn't been thinking. Again.

They started off in single file. Hapless saw the others enter the mountain before him. When he got there he found that there was a faint glow of the path so that they could follow it without banging into a wall.

He had expected the caves to be dark and gloomy, but glowing moss illuminated their walls in assorted colors and they were somberly lovely in their fashion. There were chambers linked to chambers, each with its own descending stalactites and rising stalagmites. Portions were wide avenues, but the path chose to twist deviously through obscure connections. They followed it, trusting the enchantment to know what it was doing. Tight as it squeezed in places, there was always room for them to pass, including Zed, their largest member.

The map indicated that they were approaching a goblin trail. Their path paralleled it. They increased their caution.

Quin raised his hand in warning. They halted in place, silently.

There were sounds. A gob of goblins tramped through the main section of the cavern, carrying bags of air potatoes evidently harvested from the surface. They were on the other side of a line of stalagmites, and did not see the Companions. In three and a half moments they were gone.

Hapless breathed. The enchantment had protected them from discovery. If the goblins had seen them, what then? Would the gobs have been balked, as monsters had been on prior paths? Maybe, but that would have alerted the goblins to their presence, and they might have moved or killed their captive. The parameters were uncertain.

Parameters: there was a sophisticated word, he thought as they resumed motion. It meant variable boundaries that shifted depending on circumstances. If the party was unobserved, they could probably reach the prisoner without difficulty. But if they were discovered, they might have to follow a different, more complicated course. There was no single perfect route; it all depended on multiple factors.

Their passage spiraled generally downward, wending through large and small caves. One contained a collection of bats hanging from the ceiling. Spooked, the bats dropped into the air and flew rapidly through a hole in the wall, surely heading for the outside night.

They came to an underground pool. Something lurked in it. "Kraken weed," Zed whispered. "We don't want to mess with that."

"But the path leads across that water," Feline whispered.

The others looked at Hapless. "Trust the path," he whispered back.

Feline set foot on the water. The kraken was immediately alert, focusing on the spot. But its tentacles did not penetrate the space reserved by the path.

The water dented, but held. Feline walked across it, and the others followed, as they had walked across the air before. The kraken reached for them with a hundred tentacles, entirely surrounding the space that was the path, but could not get inside it. They walked through the tunnel of tentacles unharmed.

"I am impressed," Quin murmured. This was evidently his first venture on an enchanted path.

"If we are pursued, on our return, the kraken will be a good barrier," Zed whispered.

Farther along, there was a nest of giant spiders. They looked, approached, but could not touch the path or the folk on it. Still, it was nervous business, passing their gnashing mandibles.

Another cave was evidently the haunt of a troll. He was sleeping, and did not wake as they passed through. If he had awoken, and spied them, would he have made a commotion? Would that have changed their chances? Parameters, again.

Then they came to a den of tigers. They must have strayed from Mundania and found refuge in the mountain. They saw the intruders and approached, looking annoyed.

Feline changed to cat form. She stood there for a long moment, almost a moment and a half, one striped cat silently facing down others. Then she reverted to human form. The big cats turned away, acknowledging her right to pass with her party. It seemed that cats did not interfere with cats, even crossbreeds.

Finally they reached what seemed to be the lowest level. The path tunneled through a wall, and there were two individuals, a female goblin and a male harpy. The harpy was bound to the floor by a shackle on one leg and a chain.

The goblin opened her mouth to scream. Zed reached down to pick her up, clapping a hand over her mouth so that she could not warn the other goblins. She was helpless and silent.

"Hardly Harpy, I presume?" Feline said to the male. "We have come to take you away from all this."

"Who are you?" Hardly demanded suspiciously. "What trick is this?"

Hapless stepped forward. "I am Hapless Human, and these are my Companions of a Quest."

"I don't believe you. It's just another tease the goblins arranged."

Quin was in dragon form. He changed to harpy form. "I am Quin, harpy/dragon crossbreed. You may know of me."

"I do. There can't be two of you. But what's your interest in rescuing me? Or are you here to kill me, so you can have all the hens to yourself?"

"I want to join the Quest so I won't have to mess with the hens," Quin said. "But I can't ethically depart until I get them a better replacement. So we really are here to rescue you."

"Come with us," Feline said. "We have an enchanted path."

"Put Glenna down."

"The gobliness? She'll scream to alert the goblins."

"No she won't. Let her go or I won't go anywhere with you."

Hapless glanced at Zed and nodded. The centaur set the lady goblin down and let her go. She didn't scream.

"Glenna, I have to go," Hardly said.

"I know," she said. "I'll miss you." A tear crossed her cheek.

Hapless realized that the goblin was not so much a guard as a friend. Maybe both.

"Come with me."

"I would only be in the way. The harpies would never let me stay."

"True," Hardly said. He stepped onto the path and walked through the wall.

The others followed. The wall became solid as Hapless brought up the rear. They were safely on their way.

"I love you, Hardly," Glenna called.

Hardly froze. "She never said that before."

There was a harsh cry by a male goblin. "He's escaping! This is your fault, Glenna!"

Now Glenna screamed. They were going to take their rage out on her.

"Rescue her too!" Hardly said.

Hapless tried to reason with him. "She's a goblin. We really can't—"

"I'm not going without her. I won't let her be tortured to death."

"But—"

"Now!" Hardly stepped off the path toward the wall.

Hapless looked at Zed. "Can you—"

The centaur went to the wall where the hole had been, turned around, and delivered a two-hind-foot kick. The stone was blasted apart. He spun about and plunged through, Hapless following.

Two goblin males were holding Glenna and a third was facing her, obviously about to rape her before they killed her. Goblins did not pussy-foot when it came to brutality.

Hapless conjured a tuba and blew into its mouthpiece with all his might. BBLUURRPP! It was the most horrible sound, stinking of flatulence and vomit.

The goblins fell back, stunned, Glenna among them. Zed reached down, picked her up again, and plunged back through the gap in the wall. Already the goblins were regrouping. Hapless blasted them with another foul-smelling note, then threw the tuba at them and leaped after the centaur.

Hardly and Glenna were hugging, his wings around her body. "I love you too," Hardly told her. Then they kissed. Little hearts floated around them.

"We have to get out of here," Hapless said. "I don't know if the path remains intact."

"We'll soon find out," Feline said grimly as goblins poured through the gap.

Hapless conjured another tuba, but before he could play it, the goblins were piling into them and bouncing off the invisible wall surrounding the path. They had made it.

"I couldn't tell you before," Glenna told Hardly. "I knew you wouldn't want to be with a goblin."

"I always liked you, but I thought you were just taking care of the prisoner."

"That, too," she agreed. They kissed again, generating more hearts.

"Get on the centaur," Hapless told them both. "We'll sort this out later."

They got on Zed's back, and the group moved out while the goblins grabbed at them without connecting. Hapless played another stench on the tuba and the goblins fell back, unable to handle its awfulness.

They came to the tiger den. The big cats formed an impromptu phalanx and marched on the goblins, who grimly stood their ground. "MAAKE MMYY DAAY!" the lead tiger growled. The goblins retreated.

"Thank you," Feline said to the tigers. "That was a truly catly deed." Then, to Hapless: "Cats like music. I wonder if we could thank them better with a nice tune?"

Hapless, seeing that the cave was now free of goblins, agreed. He conjured instruments, and the others played an impromptu predatory cat medley for the tigers. They loved it.

The troll was still sleeping. They passed through his cave without waking him, again.

Then the spiders. They played a buzzing melody that sounded like a swarm of giant flies. The spiders appreciated it.

And the kraken. They scored with a sound like the rushing sea. Music did not have to be melodic in the human manner to be effective.

Finally they emerged to the nest. They had rescued Hardly, but there was a complication: he had a girlfriend.

"Oh, Hardly, they'll never accept me," Glenna wailed.

"We'll see about that," he said resolutely. "I will settle this in the morning." He stroked Glenna's shoulder with a wing. "I regret I will have to be untrue to you, dear, but I think you understand the situation."

"I do," she agreed bravely.

They settled down for the rest of the night in the crowded nest. Feline was jammed up against Hapless. "Sorry I can't give you more room," she said.

"I'll survive." They both knew she could have made room by assuming cat form.

In the morning Hardly, smudged by repeated kisses, assumed control. "Let me settle my business with the harpies, so you know you are free to go, Quin. Then we'll part company, amicably. I do appreciate being rescued."

Hapless was not at all sure how this would play out, but was satisfied to let the harpy handle it.

Hardly pursed his lips and made a shrieking whistle. Immediately there was an answer. In three and a third moments a flock of harpies flew in toward the nest and hovered. They were every bit as dirty as reputed, with stringy soiled hair, battered wings, ugly faces, and smudged bare jugs that would have challenged any halter to beautify. It was clear why they were not popular birds.

"What's this?" one screeched, spitting as she spoke. It seemed that the screech was the normal harpy mode of speech.

"These members of a Quest rescued me from the goblins," Hardly announced evenly. "Mark them carefully. You will treat them with courtesy and respect, now and in the future."

They looked, and did not argue, foreign as these concepts might be to them. It was plain that he *had* been rescued, saving them a mountain of gold or worse. It was also plain, as Quin had said, that he was his own man, taking no guff from the dirty birds.

"And this is Glenna Goblin," he continued, gesturing to her. "She succored me when the goblins threatened to abuse me, at serious risk to her own welfare. She stayed with me throughout, taking care of my needs without asking anything in return. She has now been banned from her kind, because she helped me escape. I am grateful, and I love her. We will stay together, and you will treat her with respect."

Hapless looked from the wretched filthy harpies to the lovely little goblin girl. It was plain why even a harpy male preferred her.

There was outrage. "No way!" a harpy screeched.

"She will be my girlfriend," he continued inexorably. "You will be my harem. It's a package. You can't have one without the other. Take or leave it."

The harpies were silent. They knew it was this deal or nothing.

"I'm sure other harpy flocks will be happy to accept these terms, if you don't. Shall we depart?"

They hesitated. Hardly spread his wings as if to fly away. That much was a bluff, because Glenna couldn't fly, but it accented the point.

The harpies hastily caved. They knew it was the best offer they were ever likely to get. At least Hardly understood them.

Hardly faced the members of the Quest. "I thank you for your service.

If you should return this way, the harpies will welcome you." He glanced at a harpy who was opening her mouth, and she quickly closed it. "And I thank you specifically, Quin, for enabling this outcome. You have been a true friend."

"You are welcome," Quin said. Hapless knew it was heartfelt, because Quin would have been stuck for it otherwise.

"Now we shall proceed to our apartment in the mountain," Hardly said. "This way, my dear." They left the nest and went to a hole in the mountain. In two thirds of a moment they were gone.

"I am relieved," Quin said.

"So are we," Hapless agreed. It was an understatement.

Chapter 7

FARO

They had not gotten a full night's rest, but they were eager to move on before any further complication could find them. Hapless opened the box.

There was a picture of a female winged centaur, with the name FARO.

"Well, now," Zed said.

Hapless agreed. Lady centaurs were well endowed, and normally did not wear clothing. If Nya was interesting in this respect, Faro was more so.

"Ahem," Feline murmured.

"She has nice hair," Zed said. "We appreciate it."

She did have nice long brown tresses that curled from her head through her mane and down around her front. Hapless was happy to leave it at that.

"Isn't that a boy's name?" Feline asked.

"Yes, normally," Zed said. "But names are fickle; they don't always remain with their original genders. This one means 'I do well,' and there's also a card game."

"Well, let's go recruit her," Feline said with resignation. "She'll be able to fly with you dragons."

The new path proceeded to the mountain, then straight down it at an impossible angle. "We can't follow that," Feline said. "We'll fall off."

"Not necessarily," Zed said. "I have heard of some very special paths."

"We'll try it," Hapless said. He nerved himself and marched along the path.

"Wait!" Zed called. "You have to be last."

Oh. Yes. He kept forgetting. "Sorry."

Zed went first. When he reached the mountain, he turned and walked down the slant without difficulty.

The others stared. Why wasn't he falling?

"I'm on the level," Zed called, seeing their astonishment. "It's part of the enchantment."

"All right," Feline said bravely. "I'm next." She went to the mountain, turned so that she was facing down, and walked without difficulty. "I'm on the level!" she agreed, thrilled.

Nya followed, then Quin, both in their dragon forms so that they could fly if they had to. They didn't. Finally Hapless. Sure enough, it was as if he remained level and the mountain turned sidewise, so that it was beneath his feet. He was becoming more impressed with the paths; their enchantments could be imaginative.

They trekked down the mountain to the trees below, then through the forest to the sea. Then over the sea, walking on the water. Sea serpents eyed them, but did not attack, evidently having seen such paths before.

When they were well out to sea, a storm struck. They saw it coursing across the sky heading toward them. "It doesn't know we're protected," Feline said, chuckling. She made an impolite gesture toward it.

"Caution," Zed said. "That could be Fracto."

"Who?"

"Cumulo Fracto Nimbus, the worst of clouds, self-styled king of all clouds. He likes to rain on parades and picnics."

"I don't care who he thinks he is," Feline said. "He can't touch us as long as we're on the enchanted path."

"Still, it's probably better to ignore him."

"Oh, poo!" She made another gesture, larger and more insulting.

The cloud reared up, becoming black with rain. It splatted against the path. When the drops went around, outlining the protective tunnel without reaching them, its fury redoubled. Winds howled, battering the path.

Then the cloud got smart. Instead of attacking the path directly, it whipped up the surface of the sea. Giant waves formed and crashed against the tunnel, heaving it upward, then dropping it low. The path rested on the ocean's surface, and when that surface moved, so did the path. Up and down, up and down and around. It was as if they were inside a thrashing serpent.

Hapless felt himself getting motion sick. Feline joined him, looking no better. Before long they both spewed out the contents of their stomachs. That set off the others, and soon Zed, Nya and Quin were spewing too.

"Make it stop!" Zed begged.

"I guess I'd better," Feline agreed. She faced the wall. "Fracto Cloud! I apolo (heave!) gize!"

The storm continued unabated.

"Try a feminine wile," Nya murmured.

"Oh, bleep!" But Feline opened her shirt, presenting a fine peek to the cloud. "I'm sorry I (cough!) insulted you!" The cough really shook her assets.

The wind died out. The battering stopped. The path settled back to the surface of the sea. The cloud, having made his point, moved on and the sun came out.

"You were right, Zed," Feline said as she closed up her shirt. "Caution is best."

"It usually is," the centaur replied.

The path was quiet, but they did not feel like resuming their trek immediately. They moved on beyond the puke, seeing it dissolve into the sea as Hapless's pack left it behind; then they rested in place. After a while as digestion improved they ate token amounts from Hapless's pack. Then they got moving again, slowly. It was a lesson of sorts.

Well before dusk they made camp for the night, still on the water. Hapless set his pack down so he could join the others. They set up with their musical instruments and played diverting, relaxing music. That helped despite his own musical frustration. Then they ate a bit more and settled down to sleep. Hapless noticed that Nya and Quin were both in dragon form and conversing in hisses; evidently they were getting along. Zed stood alone, thinking his own thoughts. They surely concerned the pretty centaur filly they were about to recruit. True, she was winged, and there was not a lot of interaction between flying and land centaurs, but this was a special situation. It had to be intriguing.

"I was foolish," Feline said as she came to be with him for the night. "I brought this motion sickness upon us. I'm still recovering."

"You didn't know."

"Zed tried to warn me. I didn't listen."

"Next time you'll listen."

"Oh, yes." She pondered briefly. "I think I should make it up to you. I've been teasing you; it's time I stopped. So if you want . . ." She trailed off suggestively.

He was tempted, but knew better. Anyway, they were too public here. "Not that way. I haven't yet learned to ignore your curves."

"I knew you'd say that."

"I'm pretty predictable."

"Yes. I like that about you."

"You don't like an adventurous spirit?"

"Oh, I do. But that's not you, and I wouldn't try to change you."

"Thank you," he said uncertainly.

"I wonder who they are?"

"Who?"

"Your other girlfriends. The good girl and the bad girl. Do you think they're as pretty as me?"

"Are you teasing me again?"

"Teasing myself, maybe. I'm jealous of them."

"When they don't even exist, yet?"

"That's the key: yet. I want to put them into the past instead of the future. What's the use tantalizing you if you have someone else to go to? Maybe even two someone elses?"

There wasn't much he could say about that, so he didn't try. Feline nestled against him and they slept.

In the morning they handled functions by tossing bags off the path, ate some more, and got moving again. They were all pretty much recovered from the sickness. The path continued across the water. The trek was actually becoming dull.

"Land ho!" Feline called out.

The others looked. There was an island ahead. That made sense, as what was the point in crossing water otherwise?

And there on the small beach was the flying centaur watching them approach. She had brown hair on her equine body and human head, with a marvelous shock of auburn hair trailing back into a mane, and large folded wings, exactly like her picture. Overall she was a glorious creature, and not merely for her bare front.

The centaur waved. Zed waved back.

They reached the beach. Zed did the honors. "Faro Centaur, I presume?"

"The same," she agreed. "I dreamed that there would be a Quest I could join, so I could get my wish. You must be that Quest. It seems unlikely that anything else would arrive on an enchanted path that leads across the sea to my front hooves."

"We are that Quest," Zed agreed. "What is your wish?"

"That is simply told. I am a flying centaur, but I don't fly because I have acrophobia. I am afraid of heights. I want to get over it."

"So you are in effect a land centaur," Zed said.

"In effect," Faro agreed. "Not by choice."

"Did this phobia come upon you recently?"

"Not at all. I have had it all my life. I can fly, but not high enough to make it worthwhile. The other centaur children nicknamed me Fear O' Heights. That is easy to derive from my name."

"That is cruel."

"But also true. My fear limits me and I wish to abolish it." She grimaced. "My classmates sought to encourage me by stranding me on this island. They figure that when I get frustrated enough, I will fly away from it. That isn't working; the mere thought of flying high paralyzes me."

"Couldn't you fly low over the water?" Zed asked. "Virtually skimming it?"

"I could, but I won't. The sea predators are lurking, waiting to snap at my legs and pull me down. To avoid them I would have to rise at least a body length, and I can't."

She glanced at Zed. "If I may inquire, why are you on this Quest? You appear to be normal, apart from your interesting coloration."

"I want to find true love. I am actually a crossbreed. My sire was a zebra. This tended to isolate me as a foal and as an adult."

"I understand how that is." Obviously she did.

"Allow me to introduce the other members of the Quest," Zed said. "Hapless Human, who wants to be able to play a musical instrument. Feline, a human/cat crossbreed who wishes to be loved for something other than her curves. Nya, a naga/dragon crossbreed who wants to find her purpose in life. And Quin, a harpy/dragon crossbreed who wants to become human."

"So you are mostly crossbreeds and misfits," Faro said.

"So it seems," Zed agreed. "It may be a requirement for the risky challenge of a Quest. Sensible folk don't do such things."

"They don't," she agreed. "I think I need to know more about the Quest."

They explained about the Totems and the Isis Orb, with its power to grant their wishes.

Faro nodded. "It is said that the devil is in the details. What are your details?"

"Well, for one thing we play music," Zed said.

Hapless conjured instruments, and the others played a nice harmonic melody.

"What instrument do you play?" Hapless asked.

"I have always been partial to the drums, but I am only a mediocre player."

He conjured a fine three-drum set and presented it to her. She tried it, and was instantly proficient. Even without other music, the beats were compelling. "It's magic! I know I am not that good. It makes the player a virtuoso."

"Only in my presence," Hapless said ruefully. "And only if played by someone else."

"You summoned it. You can't play it?"

Hapless took the drums and tapped on them with the drumsticks. The result was a horrible thumping like a herd of lost wounded elephants. He had made the point.

"I'm so sorry," she said. "That's like having wings but not being able to fly."

He found that a nice analogy. He liked her, and not just because of her front.

"I suppose we should be on our way," Feline said.

"I suppose we should," Hapless agreed. "Obviously the Orb is not on this isle." He brought out the box, explaining how it worked.

"Oh, are there more Companions?" Faro asked. "I understand that five is the normal number. That is, a leader and five supporters."

"I believe it varies," Zed said. "We'll soon know."

Hapless opened the box. They gathered around to peer into it.

The picture was of a fiery faun, with the words FIRE TOTEM.

"A Totem!" Zed said. "Not another Companion."

"That means the roster of Companions is complete at five," Feline said. "That's a relief."

"A relief?" Quin asked. "Why?"

"No more bare breasts," Nya said, laughing as she shook hers. "Two sets are enough."

"Three," Feline said, flashing hers. But she seemed irritated rather than amused. "Regardless, more than five Companions would become cumbersome. We need a manageable group."

Quin eyed the picture. "I'm not sure how manageable that is. That's a fire spirit."

"We can worry about that when we get there," Zed said. "Is there a path?"

They looked, and made out the path. It rose into the air and arced across the water.

"Uh-oh," Faro said.

"Maybe we can walk it," Zed said. He put a fore-hoof on it and pressed down.

His foot landed back on the ground with a thud.

"Or maybe not," Feline said, testing it herself with no better success.

"It seems that is not so much a path, but a guide," Zed said. "A line to follow so we won't get lost. Unfortunately not all of us can follow it."

"Four of us can't," Faro said.

"It may not protect us either," Zed said. "We shall have to think outside the box."

"Let's split into two or three groups and storm-brain for ideas," Feline suggested. "Then get together and compare them."

"That seems good to me," Zed said. "Maybe three pairs?"

"Choose your partner," Feline said.

"You. You understand stripes."

She laughed. "That makes sense to me. "Give me a ride." She vaulted smoothly onto his back. He walked beside the shore as they talked.

"Dragon form?" Quin asked Nya.

She changed as he did. The two launched into the air.

"I think we're the leftovers," Hapless said to Faro. "Sorry about that." Facing her, he saw that her human portion stood significantly taller than he was. In fact her breasts were at his face level. That mixed his feelings.

"I'm not sorry," she said graciously. "You understand frustration."

"I do." He put the box in his pack and set the pack on the ground to anchor the new path. It would not go anywhere without him.

"You don't need to walk," Faro told him. "I can carry you."

"You're not a beast of burden."

"There's no burden."

"I weigh what I weigh. You have no call to handle my weight as well as yours."

"You evidently lack experience with flying centaurs."

"You're the first I've met," he agreed. "And I must say, you're very pretty, either as human or equine."

"Thank you. I'm probably the prettiest flightless flying centaur extant, and the only one. But that's not my point. You don't know how we fly."

"Don't you flap your wings, like birds?"

"We do. But that's not enough. Our wingspan is not sufficient to lift us into the air. We are too massive for our wings." She unfolded her wings and spread them wide. It was impressive; they reached out a centaur body length to either side, and from above her head down to touch the ground. She was framed in white.

"They look big enough to me. They're huge!"

"I won't bore you with the square-cube rule," she said seriously as she folded her wings. "Simplified, the larger the body, the bigger the wings need to be, in proportion. A hummingbird can have stubby little wings; a roc would need wings filling the sky."

"But rocs' wings are in proportion," he protested.

"Yes. They use a device similar to ours. Let me show you."

"Show me?"

"Get on my back. We're going to fly. Not high, I assure you, but at least clear of the ground."

"I don't understand."

"Allow me." She reached down, caught him under his shoulders, and heaved him up, clasping him to her generous bosom. Then she turned around and swung him onto her back, behind the wings. He was amazed in several respects: by her evident arm power, by the way she pressed him against her, and by the way her torso twisted around until her head was facing back toward her body. He was astride her as her head returned to the forward position.

"I'm on your back," he said. "But I'm not sure—"

Her tail flicked against his back, then against her own side. Was she swishing flies away?

Then he felt strange. It was as if he were about to float away. "I, uh—"

"I lightened you," she explained. "Then myself."

"Oh, you didn't frighten me. Surprised me, though."

"Not frighten. Lighten. I made you light. Now hang on to my mane." She started to trot forward.

He grabbed a handful of her lovely mane as she spread her wings again. She jumped, and suddenly they were flying. He saw the ground beneath her hooves. This added to the weirdness. "Uh—" he said.

"We are airborne. We both weigh only a fraction of what we did a moment ago. This is part of the magic of flying centaurs: we can flick ourselves light. That is our secret of flying. When I said you would be no burden, this is what I meant. The effect doesn't last long, but if you get heavy I can flick you again to keep you light."

"I'm impressed."

"I'm impressed with your magic. You conjured a fine workable drum set and several other instruments, and they all play beautifully. I can't do anything like that."

They were moving swiftly along the beach. They passed Zed and Feline, and Feline waved. Hapless waved back, feeling giddy. "Really impressed!"

"You like her, don't you."

She had noticed. "Feline? Oh, yes. She may be my girlfriend."

"May be? She is jealous of your attention to other females."

How observant was this filly? "I suppose. When a woman has assets, I look. It's a male thing."

"If you like her, and she likes you, what is the problem?"

"It's complicated."

"I don't mean to pry, but if I am to associate with the Quest I prefer to understand the other participants as well as is feasible."

"Okay. It's that Feline is curvy, very attractively so. Men notice. But she wants to be loved for something other than her curves. So I'm trying to do that. But, well, curves like yours don't help."

She laughed. He could only imagine what that did for her front. "This is universal female magic, but human males are particularly vulnerable to it. Centaurs don't take it nearly as seriously, nor do they employ storks to deliver their offspring."

"They don't? How do they get babies?"

She told him, drawing a parallel to the way it was in Mundania. He was amazed and somewhat sickened.

"However, we have more serious matters to consider. The route to your Totem is one that challenges our resources. If I could fly high I could transport your non-fliers there, but that is my problem. It seems I need the Orb to abate my fear of heights, but that I need to abate my fear in order to reach the Orb. This is a catch-23 situation, or thereabouts."

"A what?"

"In Mundania they seem to number their tosses and catches. It means a paradoxical problem. A person needs A to get B, but needs B to get A. My mind is centaurishly logical, and I do not see a solution."

"Well, you have to think outside the box."

"This means a non-logical solution?"

"Not necessarily. It means to come up with something nobody thought of before. And—" He froze, as an idea bulb banged into his forehead. It must have been fooled by his forward motion, and collided instead of floating.

Her head turned around to face him in that weird way she had. "Yes?"

"This is so crazy, maybe it's not worth mentioning."

She glided down until her hooves hit the ground, and she trotted on it before coming to a halt. "Those can be the best ideas."

"It's that maybe you should be blindfolded for flying."

"But then I would not see where I was going."

"Yes. Exactly."

"There may be something I am missing."

Hapless tried to clarify it. "If you were blindfolded, maybe you would not see the heights, so would not fear them."

"And I'd crash! Flying blind is folly."

"Not if someone else guided you. If I rode you and called out where to go."

She considered that. "This is so far out that it just might work. I never would have thought of it."

"Of course you'd have to trust me, and you've known me only an hour or so. So it's not something immediate."

"Let's try it now."

"Well, if you really want to."

"I don't really want to, but I will surely lose my nerve if we delay." She produced a bandanna from somewhere. "Blindfold me."

He took the bandanna and tied it around her head, covering her eyes. "Of course you could just close your eyes."

"I would open them involuntarily. This is better. I am now unable to see."

"Okay. Try walking."

She walked a few steps.

"Turn to the left. There's water close by."

"I feel it," she said as her left side hooves splashed.

"But one pace to your right it's dry."

She moved rightward. "Dry," she agreed.

"Now fly. The coast is clear."

Faro spread her wings and flew.

"Veer slightly left." She did. "Now we're over the water." He saw a ripple heading their way. "Climb! There's something coming."

She made powerful strokes and ascended. A green serpent's head popped out of the water, snapping at where her feet had been a moment before. "Sea monster," Hapless reported. "Now we're out of its range."

"This is working," she said in developing wonder. "I can see the monster in my mind, but I'm not afraid of the height. I could fly across the water to land."

"Maybe so," he said cautiously. "For now, we'll stay low." But they were at about treetop height, which he suspected would freak her out if she realized.

"This is exhilarating," she said, climbing higher. "But I could never do it without you. I need to be sure that someone is guiding me."

"I am doing that. Curve to the right, so we don't leave the land."

She curved right. They flew on around the island. There were Zed and Feline. He waved to them again.

They paused to stare. Faro was flying well above them.

"Spiral down and land," he told her. "I think we have done enough for now."

She did so. He called out the proximity of the ground as they approached it, and she trotted her legs so as to strike the ground running. They landed a short distance in front of Zed and Feline.

Hapless reached forward and pulled off the blindfold.

"You flew blindfolded?" Zed asked, amazed. "I would have thought you would start out more cautiously."

"I flew *because* I was blindfolded," Faro said, exhilarated. "Hapless thought of it."

"This doesn't cure her fear of heights," Hapless said modestly as he dismounted. "Just masks it, as it were. She still needs the Orb for her cure."

"It will do," Feline said. "Now you can leave the island."

"Now I can," Faro agreed. "Provided I have Hapless with me."

Both Zed and Feline nodded. Neither seemed completely comfortable. Hapless wondered whether this was because Feline had her eye on him, Hapless, and Zed had his eye on Faro. They might not like Hapless and Faro associating too closely. But there did not seem to be much alternative.

"That brings us up to three fliers," Nya said. "Faro can carry Hapless, and Feline too, in cat form. But Zed will be more of a challenge."

"This is navigable," Faro said. "We can make a harness to support him, then I can flick him light, and a dragon can haul him on a line. It may not be the most comfortable mode of travel, but it can be done."

They looked at Zed. He shrugged. "If you can fly blindfolded, I can swing on a line. But I would hope to return to the ground soon."

"Yes," Faro said. "The ground is more secure."

"That harness may be a challenge," Zed said. "I may be made light, but I would prefer to have one that could support my full weight, just in case."

"I have friends in the village who may be able to help with that," Faro said.

"Village?" Hapless asked, surprised. "We flew around the island, and I didn't see any village."

"It is Eleven Elves, settled by ground-dwelling elves. As you know, there are many species of elves, the best known of which are the Elm elves whose strength is inversely proportional to their distance from their tree. These are separate, but they have their skills. They prefer to remain inconspicuous, to avoid mischief from passing dragons and monsters with too much time on their claws. But the elves are friendly, once assured there is no danger." She glanced at Nya and Quin. "I trust I can reassure them?"

"Yes," the two said almost together.

"We want no trouble," Nya said.

"We're on a Quest," Quin said.

"Then let's proceed to my stall," Faro said. "We can make the harness this afternoon, and test it, and plan to depart tomorrow morning after a good night's rest."

That prospect appealed to all of them.

They followed Faro to the village. As they approached it, the little houses came into view: eleven of them, one for each elf family. The centaur's stall was at the edge, much larger.

An elf came out to meet them. He was barely knee high to Hapless, but as he approached he shimmered and became man sized.

"This is Elmer Elf, who speaks for the village," Faro said. "Whose talent is illusion. Elmer, these are my new friends. They are on a Quest, and seek no quarrel. They want only to get a good night's rest so they can be on their way tomorrow. I will go with them, though it will be sad to leave you."

Elmer eyed them. "Do I have their word to join us in peace? One looks human, another has cat ancestry, and two have dragon ancestry, by the look of them."

Faro turned to them. "If you will introduce yourselves, and give your words, you will be welcome here, as I am."

Hapless stepped forward. "I am Hapless Human. I give my word. My talent is to conjure musical instruments, though I can't play one myself. The others are musically competent. We can serenade your village with a concert, if you wish."

"That will be nice," Elmer agreed.

Feline stepped forward. "I am Feline, half cat." She changed briefly to her cat form. "I give my word. In fact, if there is any service I can do for the folk here, in return for your hospitality, let me know."

"There is a rat who is raiding our granary. He's too cunning for us to catch, and too vicious for us to kill."

"I will spend the night in that granary. I think that by morning that rat will be permanently gone."

"Thank you."

Zed stepped forward. "I am Zed. I give my word. If that rat is not gone by morning, I will hunt it." His bow appeared in his hands, an arrow nocked. Centaurs always hit what they aimed at.

"It is too cunning to show itself by day," Elmer said. "Otherwise Faro would have gotten it."

Faro smiled as her own bow appeared in her hands. "True."

Nya and Quin slid forward together. "We are Nya and Quin," she said. "We are half dragons. We give our word, and will entertain your children in our dragon forms if you wish, or simply remain clear if you prefer. We understand your caution."

Elmer eyed them. "Just how tame are you in dragon form?"

"Completely. Our minds are unchanged, only our bodies. We will harm no one here." Then both changed to dragons and bowed their heads.

"This will do." Elmer raised his hand in a signal, and the other elves appeared. They had been there all along, invisible.

"Do you give rides?" Elmer asked.

Both dragons nodded. The tiny elf children approached them, at first cautiously, then more confidently. Soon they were climbing over the dragons. Then they were treated to a brief slow ride, on the ground. Flying would be too risky. It was clearly a rare experience for them. The dragons were more than earning their keep.

"But do not do that with any other dragon," Faro warned.

The elf parents nodded appreciatively. They knew.

In due course they went to Faro's stall, where Hapless and Feline set about making the harness for Zed. The elves had fine leather thongs that they skillfully wove into the harness, building it around Zed as he stood there. In a surprisingly brief time it was done.

"There will be a banquet," Elmer announced. "In the interim you may play your concert, if you are amenable."

They assembled in the central village square and Hapless conjured instruments. They played several lovely Elven melodies and harmonies, complete with Faro's resonant drumbeats, and the elves were clearly charmed.

"How is it that your group plays so well?" Elmer asked Hapless. "Surely the members of your Quest were not selected for musical ability."

"It seems to be part of my talent," Hapless said. "I can conjure the instruments, and in my presence they play well. But I myself am abysmal. That's my reason for the Quest: to find an instrument that I, too, can play well."

"When you find it, you will surely play extraordinarily well. Your magic should guarantee it."

"I hope so," Hapless said with feeling.

The concert concluded to resounding applause. Then came the banquet, and it was like a concert of its own; the elves knew what they were doing, and there was plenty of food and drink.

"Do you know, I could see living in a village like this," Feline said as she ate beside Hapless. "The elves are really nice when you get to know them. Faro is well off here. Oh, I know she has to get over her fear of heights; she's incomplete without flying high. But apart from that she's not suffering."

Hapless could only agree.

Daylight remained after the banquet. The dragons gave the children more rides, and this time a few of the bolder ones accepted flying. They made short hops up over and around the village and back. It was an experience they would never get elsewhere.

"We really appreciate your hospitality," Hapless told Elmer.

"I think we are the ones who owe you. We will never forget this visit, and we will be sorry to see Faro go. She's a fine filly. But we knew she must seek her destiny."

"I can't speak for the future," Hapless said. "We are not assured even of surviving the Quest. But if we do, and achieve our wishes, perhaps we can visit again."

"You will be welcome."

The dragons, tired, settled down to sleep in the stall. So did Zed. Faro gave Hapless and Feline a small tour of the area. Behind the stall was a fine acorn tree, and in it lived a tree fairy, Faro's friend. This was Spelfie, who was visible only when someone was thinking about her. She was a pretty little thing, like a winged human child, but plainly adult. Her costume was scant, and Hapless suspected that Feline was not eager to have him look at it too closely. She wore a petite wood crown.

"Actually I'm only visiting," the little fairy explained. "I used to associate with my own tree, but a jeweler cut it down to make a house. When he discovered that it was my tree, he was chagrined. So he made this crown out of its remaining wood, and that enables me to roam freely, no longer bound to a particular tree. But without that limitation, I ate too much junk food elsewhere, and got fat."

"You don't look fat," Hapless said.

"This is how I look without the illusion," Spelfie said, and became quite fat. After barely half a moment she returned to her slim appearance, but Hapless knew that Feline no longer resented her. That was a relief.

"Oh, look—there's the opti-mist," Faro said. "It sometimes appears in the evening."

Hapless looked and saw a small cloud floating close above the ground. It brushed by them, and suddenly he felt much more positive. They had found their fifth Companion, enabled her to fly, and surely their Quest would succeed.

"It puts a positive slant on things," Faro said. "That has helped me endure my confinement to the island. Oh, the elves are nice and the island is fine; it's just that I so very much want to fly on my own without being crippled by fear."

"Surely you will when the Quest is done," Hapless said.

"And a rainbow!" Feline said.

There it was, arcing beyond the mist, raining little bows. Feline picked up a pretty red one and put it on her hair. It remained though the rainbow faded.

"There's Julius," Faro said, waving to a man beyond the littered bows.

"Hello, Faro," the man said. He was clearly old, but spry. "I was just collecting some of these bows; there's no telling when they might be useful."

"These are my new friends Hapless and Feline," Faro said. Then, to them: "This is Julius Saucier, from Mundania, so he doesn't have a magic talent yet, but he can almost work magic with wood. He's a creative carpenter. You should see the grandfather clock he made, with all wooden gears. He even made a wood crossbow; I don't need it, of course, but it's a nice instrument."

"It's been a real pleasure getting to know Faro and the elves," Julius said. "I couldn't have asked for a better place to retire."

Retire? Unless he had found a special route to Xanth, Julius was dead. Hapless kept his mouth shut.

"I'm sorry, but I will be leaving tomorrow," Faro said. "I'm joining a Quest."

"We will miss you," Julius said. "You prettify the local scenery."

Faro smiled. "Thank you."

They moved on. "I want you to meet my friend Corny."

"Is that a nickname?" Hapless asked.

"Not exactly." She showed them to a field where a unicorn grazed. "Don't try to get too close; she's shy. It took me a while to get to know her."

When they got close, Hapless saw that the unicorn's horn consisted of a corncob. "Corny Unicorn," Feline murmured.

They returned to the stall. "My feelings are mixed," Faro said. "I am eager to join the Quest, but I'll miss these sweet folk of the island."

"You'll be able to visit them anytime," Feline reminded her.

"Yes. I depend on that."

Faro went to stand beside Zed to sleep on her feet.

Feline joined Hapless for the night, sharing a blanket. "She's such a nice filly, I really can't resent her no matter how much you associate with her."

Because he would be riding and guiding Faro. "I'm pretty sure she's not my other girlfriend."

"What, despite those matchless frontal curves?"

"I appreciate her for other reasons."

That shut her up.

Chapter 8

FIRE FAUN

In the morning they returned to Hapless's pack with the box still anchoring the new path, such as it was. He picked up the pack and put it on, and the faint outline of the path remained. They all could see it, except Faro; they had had practice with paths, and she didn't need to.

Several of the elves came to watch. This was a novel experience for them, too.

Zed got into the harness, and Faro flicked him light. The two half dragons changed to dragon form, with Quin donning the other end of the rope so that he could haul the main harness up. Zed was now feather light, so it wasn't at all difficult.

Quin and Nya took off together, spiraling upward near the path. Zed lifted as the line went taut. He did not look comfortable despite being safely light. Hapless couldn't blame him; his position seemed precarious.

"Close your eyes!" Faro called.

Zed did, and looked more relaxed.

The elves waved, and the dragons waggled their spread wings in response.

Feline assumed cat form and joined Hapless on Faro's back, taking hold just in front of the great folded white wings while Hapless rode behind them. Then he tied the blindfold around the centaur's head, as she twisted her front section to face him, securely covering her eyes. He knew Feline was glad Faro couldn't fly facing back; she knew where he would be looking.

"Take off," he told the centaur.

She trotted forward, then spread her wings. She pumped the air and lifted.

"Spiral left, ascending," Hapless said.

She did. When they were high enough, Hapless oriented on the path. He guided the centaur to it. "That's good; fly level."

The elves waved again, and Hapless waved back. "Can you waggle your wings?" he asked Faro. "They are waving to you."

Faro did. The elves applauded. Then they were left behind as the path went out over the water.

They were on their way.

The path achieved cruising level then curved to follow the shoreline. Where was it going?

There were birds in the air. They glanced curiously at the odd group but stayed clear, as well they might; who would want to tangle with two dragons and a flying centaur?

Then a pair of young griffins oriented on them. They were the color of shoe polish, two shades. They squawked as if looking for trouble, and headed toward the group. Nya detached from the formation to intercept them, but this did not faze them; they merely separated so that she could not toast them both. She flew toward one, but the other slipped by and came toward the swinging centaur.

"Can you hit a target blindfolded?" Hapless asked Faro. He was conscious that they did not have the protective shield of the other paths.

"Yes, if you spell out its location precisely."

He wasn't sure how to do that, since both parties would be moving. Then he got a notion. "When a griffin squawks, could you hit that sound?"

"Yes."

"Draw your bow."

The bow appeared in her hands, arrow nocked.

"The griffin is at three o'clock," he said, using the standard directional system. "Same elevation as we are."

Faro twisted her torso to aim at three o'clock.

The griffin considered, then flew away, knowing better than to dare a centaur. The other did the same, no more eager to dare a fire-breathing dragon.

"They're gone," Hapless said. "We bluffed them off."

"Bluffed?"

"I really didn't want to have to shoot it," he said. "You would have lost the arrow, unless we landed to recover it from the body."

"Meow!" Feline meowed, her tone saying "Nice catch."

They continued flying. No other creatures challenged them. Maybe word had gotten around.

Then the path abruptly curved, proceeding inland. "We must be orienting on our target," Faro said.

"I guess so. So far it's just forest land."

Soon there was a glowing wall ahead. "The region of Fire!" Hapless exclaimed. "Naturally that's where the Fire Totem would be!"

"Now it makes sense," she agreed. "I trust there's a route past the firewall? Flames are not good for wings."

"Uh, yes, I think. The path is angling up."

They angled up. The firewall was like a thin mountain, with peaks and valleys, all well above the ground. Only high fliers could cross over it. The outline wasn't fixed; where there was a gap one moment, there would be a new flame the next moment. There did not seem to be any safe crossing at this level.

Then the path angled in toward one of the higher flames. What was it doing?

But as they approached it, the flame dissipated, leaving a gap. The path had found a temporary pass, and zoomed through it. The flames closed in behind, too late.

Now that path led down to the ground. They landed in a charred lot surrounded by adjacent fields that had not yet been burned out; their flames were hot. But here it was merely warm.

Hapless removed the veil. "We're here," he said. "Great flight."

Faro looked around. "I merely trusted you to guide me."

"And I trusted the path. It knew what it was doing."

Feline changed to human form. "But where is the Fire Totem?"

They all looked around. There was no sign of a fiery faun.

"It must be a rest stop," Zed said, stepping out of his harness. "But we are surely close."

"Surely," Faro agreed. "There's a mound of rocks here. Maybe it covers an underground den."

Then Nya spied something. "Look. In the next field."

There was the fiery faun. He was manlike, naked, with small horns on his head and goat hooves in lieu of human feet. Fauns were human/goat crosses, and it showed. He was busy with a flaming torch, setting fire to any bushes that were not already burning.

Hapless slowly figured it out. "This must be where the faun lives when not actively setting fires. He should return here when he's done with the next field. We will have to be ready for him."

Then Zed figured it out further. "We need the Fire Totem, but the picture was of a fire faun. Could they be the same? Or could one be the guardian of the other?"

"That could be it," Quin said. "We need to catch the fire faun to make him lead us to the Fire Totem."

"And how do we do that?" Feline asked.

"There's something else, now that I ponder it," Zed said. "On Quests of this type, where amulets or tokens or Totems need to be gathered, it is generally one Companion to one artifact. I suspect that the Companion who is destined to carry the Totem is the one to obtain it from its guardian."

"Who is supposed to get the Fire Totem?" Hapless asked.

"That is the question," Zed said. "Perhaps we should decide that now, lest the wrong one come to grief."

Feline gazed across at the fire faun. "Someone who can handle fire, I should think. Like maybe a dragon."

"That lets me out," Quin said. "I'm a steamer."

They looked at Nya. She nodded. "I am a fire breather, yes. I must be the one. Does anyone have any idea how?"

"Excellent question," Hapless said. "While we ponder that, I have another notion to pursue. If the Totems represent the five Elements of Fire, Water, Air, Earth, and the dread Void, how do the rest of us align? If we don't match up, maybe this is a bad idea."

"Water," Zed said. "That is typically fluid, yielding, changeable—"

"Curvaceous," Nya said.

Feline straightened up. "I must be Water," she agreed, surprised.

"Then Air," Zed said. "Who is like air?"

"Someone who flies?" Hapless asked.

"That narrows it down to three," Zed said. "Nya, Quin, Faro."

"I'm taken," Nya said.

"And I can't fly alone," Faro said. "I doubt I qualify."

"Which leaves me," Quin said. "Steam is like air. I must be Air."

"Earth," Zed said. "I am land bound and solid. I must be Earth."

"That leaves the worst one," Hapless said. "The Void, from which nothing escapes."

"And by elimination, that must be me," Faro said. "Though the prospect terrifies me."

"Your acrophobia relates?" Zed asked.

"Oh, yes. I'm afraid of heights. The Void might seem to be the opposite, but it is similar: a fall into it has no returning. I'm afraid of that fall."

"Could your fear qualify you?" Zed asked.

Faro winced. "Oddly, it might."

"But that could be positive," Zed said. "You have found a way to fly. Could you similarly find a way to conquer the Void?"

"There is logic there," she agreed with a shudder. "But not one that appeals to me."

"Another thing," Hapless said. "She conquers heights by being blindfolded. I don't see how that would work with the Void."

"Unless she could also navigate the Void blindfolded," Zed said.

"Something else," Feline said. "Faro got the Void by elimination. Elimination means taking away things. It's consistent."

"Again, it is a consistency I don't much like," Faro said. "But if it must be, it must be. I am the Void."

"Which leaves us with the first question," Nya said. "How do I handle the fire faun?"

There was silence. None of them knew.

"Well, I have another question," Hapless said, his nose uncomfortable as it tried to pop out of joint. "Why don't I have a Totem? You figured it would be Faro by elimination, but you forgot me."

The Companions exchanged an awkward glance. "Well, you're not a Companion," Zed said. "You're the Quest leader."

"That doesn't mean I can't participate," Hapless said hotly.

Nya looked at Feline. "Maybe you can explain it to him."

"Explain what?" Hapless demanded. "That you don't think I'm competent?"

"I'll try," Feline said. Then she took his arm to lead him aside, as if he were a difficult child.

He refused to go. "I get to conjure musical instruments, but I can't play any. Now I get to lead the Quest, but I can't participate! What's wrong with me?"

"Nothing's wrong with you, Hapless," she said soothingly. "You're a fine person and we need you. It's just not your role to get a Totem."

"Because you think I can't handle it?" He was getting angrier by the moment.

Feline drew him close and kissed his ear. That put him into a third of a trance. "It's not a matter of competence. It's just that each of us needs to perform the role we are assigned, and yours is to organize the Quest. You don't need a Totem for that."

"I don't see why not!"

She drew her skirt tight against her body so that the line of her panties showed beneath it. That intensified his trance to two thirds. "Hapless, please be reasonable. Let's—let's go behind those rocks for a bit of privacy, and consider."

He still had some resistance, being inherently stubborn. "Consider what?"

She kissed him again. "Our relationship." She took his hand and stroked it across one of her curves. The effect was phenomenal. He wanted to hold her and kiss her and proceed to summoning one or more storks, though he had little idea of the technique.

"You're trying to seduce me!" he said, catching on. "To change the subject. I won't have it! I don't want you that way."

"I knew you wouldn't," she said.

This annoyed him anew. She was using seductive tactics to manage him. "Then why are you leading me on? When you don't plan to follow through?"

She met his gaze seriously. "Hapless, there's one difference between us. You wouldn't lie to get what you want. I would."

He opened his mouth, but nothing came out.

"I will be seductive when I don't actually intend to seduce," she said. "So it's a lie, of a sort. It's part of the art of being female."

Finally he squeezed out a word. "Why?"

"Because you are being unreasonable, and I need to get you to accept your role without resenting it."

"My role?"

"Your role as the leader of the Quest. Just as you can't play an instrument, but you enable us to play, you can't have a Totem, but you can enable us to get our Totems so we can complete the Quest. We all must play our parts."

He remained resentful. He opened his mouth to protest further.

She stroked her hand across her skirt as if to make her panty line show again.

He gave it up. "Okay."

She kissed his other ear. "Now you're being reasonable"

"I'm not being reasonable! I just don't want to get freaked out."

She smiled. "That will do."

They turned back to face the others, who had frozen like a tableau. Now that Hapless had been rendered reasonable, they resumed animation. "How do I handle the fire faun?" Nya repeated.

"I think this is your challenge to handle alone," Faro said. "But we can give you advice."

"Maybe you can fight fire with fire," Zed said.

"I'll try." She walked to the edge of the burned-out section and called to the faun. "Hey, faun, I need your Totem."

"Go bleep your bleep, snakeskin!" the faun called back, using language that would have singed the foliage if it had not already been burned.

"Don't speak to me that way!" Nya snapped. "I'm a lady."

"Yeah, bleep?" he asked, employing a term that would have made a female dog snarl. "You're missing the part of a lady I can use." He touched his exposed front.

"Stop being obscene."

"Make me." He made an obscene gesture.

Hapless realized that this was a battle of attitudes as much as of words or bodies. The creature was trying to freak her out. Fauns were like satyrs, but less obsessed with sex. The kinship was evident, however.

"Stop. Or I'll—"

"Or you'll what, you bunless freak?"

"I'll turn dragon and toast you soundly."

"I'd like to see you try, naga trash."

Nya turned dragon and sent a blowtorch blast of fire that completely enveloped the faun. Hapless was impressed; she truly had dragon fire when she needed it.

But it had no effect on the fire spirit. "Is that the best you can do, worm tail?"

Nya flew forward and coiled her sinuous body around the faun. She put her snoot to his face as if kissing him and blasted out another volley of fire. It surged right down his throat and blew him up like a balloon. But then he exhaled, blowing it out again and returning to his original shape, undamaged.

"That was some kiss, snake lips," he said. "Do it again."

Seeing that, Hapless knew that she would never overcome the faun with fire.

Disgusted, Nya uncoiled and retreated to the lot where the others stood. "Fire is not doing it," she said, frustrated.

"So we see," Feline said. "But you know, he is getting less insulting. Maybe he likes you."

"He's a foul-mouthed hothead!"

"A typical male," Feline agreed. "Deal with it. Try seducing him."

"Seducing him! I want to blow his head off!"

There was a trace of obscurity in Feline's smile. "Well, that's one way to do it. I was thinking of a less extreme technique. Try being sinuous atop the rock pile."

The naga considered. Then she slithered to the rocks. She got behind them with only her forepart above. It looked as if she were a human woman standing behind the pile with only her top half showing.

"Hey, faun!" she called. "Want another kiss?"

The faun looked, and Hapless saw what the fire spirit saw: a lovely human girl's top half, bare.

"Forget it, naga crossbreed; I know your nature." But he was clearly interested.

Nya smiled blindingly as she did an upper body dance that Hapless found remarkably compelling. "Are you sure?"

The faun hesitated. It seemed he wasn't sure. She had impressed him with her fire kiss, and now was adding to it via her human charms.

"All I want is the Fire Totem," Nya called.

Wrong move. "No way," the faun said, and turned away. The spell was broken.

"Bleep," Feline muttered. "She impressed you more than him."

Hapless should have known she'd be watching him.

Balked a second time, Nya appealed to the Companions. "What else is there?"

"Play music," Faro suggested.

Hapless conjured a harmonica and brought it to her. She put it to her mouth and started playing. It was absolutely lovely from the outset.

The fire faun had been walking away. Now he paused, turning toward the sound. He was listening!

Nya shifted her melody, going to fire music. Her body seemed to glow with the heat of it, and it was a hot melody.

The faun slowly walked toward her as if in a trance, his hooves clicking on the hard ground. She faced him, still playing. He came right up to her, reached a fiery hand to touch her—

And dropped to the ground as the little Totem. Nya stopped playing, reached down, and picked up the object. "I believe I have my Totem," she said, satisfied.

The others went to join her. She passed the artifact around so they could all appreciate it. When Hapless held it he saw that it was a miniature replica of the fire faun. Or rather, it was the fire faun himself, compacted to this inert form. No wonder he had not been eager to be converted!

"Now if only I knew how to use it," Nya said.

"Does it have a separate use, or is it merely necessary to complete a spell to control the Orb?" Zed asked.

"I feel its power," Nya said as she took it back. "It is tuned to me; only I can use it. I know it can do things for me; I just don't know what. Or how."

"Then we had better figure it out," Hapless said. "Because the other Totems may have similar powers, and we may need to use them before we're done."

"It's fire," Feline said. "I wonder whether it can help us with fire."

"There's more than enough fire here in the Region of Fire," Faro said. "I fear for my wings."

"Let me see," Nya said. She slithered toward the nearest firewall, holding the Totem before her as if to ward off the flames.

When she reached the wall, it abruptly flared brighter. It intensified, radiating additional heat so that she had to slide back. It raged.

Then it puffed out, leaving a gap in the wall.

"I don't understand," Nya said, retreating.

"I think I do," Zed said. "The proximity of the Fire Totem causes the fire to flare up. But then it uses up its fuel and flares out."

"It's filling in again," Quin said. "Slowly."

So it was. The fuel fumes were building up, sustaining the normal blaze. They had discovered one property of the Totem.

"But I feel there is more," Nya said. "Its power infuses me, makes me feel stronger."

"Don't flare up and expire!" Quin said.

She smiled. "It's not that kind of power. It seems to be enhancing mine, somehow."

"You have two forms," Quin said. "Maybe it facilitates the change."

"Maybe," she agreed uncertainly. "But I don't think that's quite it."

"You have some human ancestry, via your naga side," Feline said. "Could it help you change to complete human form?"

"Maybe," Nya said. She focused—and became a complete human woman.

"Oh, my," Faro breathed. "Power indeed."

"What I want," Quin said. "When I get my Totem, will it grant my wish? To become human?"

Nya looked at him. "If it's like mine, it should," she said. "But I can also feel that the power is from the Totem, not myself. When I no longer have it, I won't be able to assume this form. So it's not a permanent solution, any more than Faro's blindfolding is the complete answer for her."

"Surely true," Faro agreed. "Still, it's impressive."

"I wonder," Zed said. "Would your Totem enable you to fly without the blindfold?"

"Oh, I wonder too!" Faro said. "And then the Orb could make it permanent."

"But what really counts for the moment," Hapless said, "is that now we know how to tame a Totem, assuming music works on the others. That's a major step."

"It is," Nya said. She reverted to her naga form. "I think I need to rest a while to assimilate this development."

"We'll camp here now," Hapless decided. "So we can all ponder."

But it was not a great campsite. There was nothing to eat, and no trees with pillows or bedding. New grass was growing rapidly, but it was dry, and probably would be burned off again in an hour or so. It seemed likely to be a nervous and hungry night.

Nya perked up. "The Totem can help," she said.

"How?" Hapless asked sourly.

"There's a den below the rocks where Fiery Faun lives when he's off-duty. As possessor of the Fire Totem I have the right to use it." She smiled. "Fiery is hardly pleased, but is obliged to help me."

"Can we trust this?" Feline asked suspiciously.

"Yes. It seems that Fiery won a good burn site with a nice den by signing up for the draft registry. That means he could be drafted at any time for Totem duty. He figured it would never happen, because there hasn't been a draft for a century. But now it did, and he's stuck for it. If he doesn't cooperate fully he could be fired, that is, dishonorably discharged, and that would be a blot on his record he would never live down. So he has not only to do it, but to do it in a way that satisfies me, because my report will make all the difference. A good report will give him an honorable discharge and he'll be able to retire in comfort early. So this Totem service can help him or hurt him and he knows it. He will do his absolute best to please me. He can see into my mind now, and knows that I am completely committed to the Quest, so now he is too."

"Well, now," Feline said, satisfied.

But Zed wasn't. "What about the other members of the Quest? Will he try to mess us up?"

"No. He doesn't have to serve you, only me, but if he does anything to mess up the Quest, he's in violation. So he will leave you alone, unless I give him a specific order. And of course your own Totems will be similarly committed to you, when you have them."

"Let's see this den," Faro said.

Nya slithered around the rock pile. "There," she said, indicating a particular rock.

Hapless went to heave it out of the way. Behind it was a hole to a tunnel below the pile. It was big enough for a man to crawl through, but not a centaur.

"We'll stay above," Faro said. "We don't need a den."

"We don't," Zed agreed. He seemed pleased to have this chance to be with Faro, alone.

"Let me check it," Nya said. "I'm experienced with subterranean passages, and I have the Totem." She slid into the tunnel.

"I'll follow," Quin said, assuming dragon form and slithering after her. Feline shifted to cat form and followed.

Finally Hapless went. He had to proceed bent over, but soon the tunnel widened and deepened and he was able to walk upright. He came into what appeared to be a living room chamber. He caught up to the others, who had halted.

There, facing them, was another fire faun. This one was female and quite nicely shaped beneath her flames. Her long red hair curled down around her bare body. She had cute little horns and dainty hooves. "Darn!" she swore.

"We—" Nya started.

"You drafted Fiery," the faun femme said bitterly. "Now he'll have to serve as a Totem maybe for weeks until you finish your stupid Quest."

"Yes," Nya said. "Then we'll let him go."

"That doesn't solve my problem."

Nya took passing stock. "What is your problem?"

"The big Fire Fandango is tonight. We were all set to dance up a firestorm. Now that's ruined. Why couldn't you have had your Quest some other time?"

Nya was taken aback. "We didn't realize—"

"Now how am I going to dance for the prize? I can't do it without a partner."

Feline changed to human form. "I may have heard of this," she said.

The faun looked at her. "What's it to you, cat woman?"

"The dance can be any two people, right? It doesn't have to be just man and woman."

"Well, yes, but I practiced with Fiery. I can't get another partner, male or female, on such short notice."

"Hapless will take you to the dance," Feline said.

Hapless was startled "What?"

"We messed up her dance performance," Feline said. "We should make it up to her before we move on."

"But—but I don't know the first thing about the fandango. Or the second or third thing."

"You'll take the Totem. Then you'll know. It will also protect you from the fire."

"Now that might work," the faun said. "Hello, Hapless. I'm Fiera."

"But—"

"Then it's decided," Feline said. "I'll come too."

"Wait!" Hapless said. "Don't fandango dancers have to play the castanets?"

"How did you know that?" Feline asked.

"That's the fourth thing," Hapless said. "They're little finger clickers, but considered musical instruments. I can conjure them, but can't use them."

"Exactly," Feline said. "That's why I have to come too."

"I'm not making any sense of this," he said.

"Here is the sense of it," Feline said patiently. "You take her to the dance. You conjure the castanets. You dance, I'll play them."

"I'm not making much sense of this either," Fiera said. "Why would he dance without the castanets?"

"Because he can't play any musical instrument. He conjures them, but that's all. But anyone else who plays one of his instruments can do it well. It's his talent and his curse."

"Ah. But there's a problem: if he borrows the Totem, it will protect him from the fire and make him competent in the dance. But then you will have no protection."

"I think I can finesse that. But we'll need your help, I think."

"If this can get me to the dance with a competent partner, I'll do what I can."

"Good." Feline turned to Nya. "Can you lend the Totem to Hapless for the dance?"

"I could, but it won't do magic for him, only for me," Nya said.

"I think it will work for him if you ask it to. Your word is its law, no?"

"I can try," Nya said dubiously. She lifted the Totem. "Totem, I want you to go with Hapless for this purpose, to protect him from the fire and make sure he knows his way around. That's so he can take Fiera, since you can't. Will you do that?" Then, answering a silent query. "Yes, I believe this will facilitate the Quest, because we're trying to get along with the folk we encounter along the way." Then she nodded and handed the Totem to Hapless. "He will do it."

Hapless accepted the Totem. Immediately he felt its power. *My mistress wants this, so I am obliged to do it, snothead. Don't foul it up.*

Just so.

"Now the other detail," Feline said. She came to stand before Hapless. "Fire Totem, I know you can hear me. Hapless will take your girlfriend to the dance, and you will protect and guide him for that. But I need to come too, for a key aspect, so I need to be protected from the fire too. Can you make me immune to the flames for a few hours?"

Why the blazes should I, catbox?

"The Totem wants to know why," Hapless translated.

"Because I think I can help Fiera win her prize, as she wants to. You'll have to trust me on this."

"Oh, I want to win it!" Fiera said.

I don't have an order from my mistress. I don't have to do it, whiskerface.

"The Totem prefers a more specific reason," Hapless said.

"Then let's put it this way: do you want your girlfriend attending the dance with a stranger who can't keep his eyes and maybe his hands off her curves? But suppose they are accompanied by his jealous girlfriend who will be watching them all the time?"

The conspiring pussy has a point. I'll have to do it.

"The Totem agrees with your reasoning." Hapless was just translating, though he was not entirely pleased with her description of his tendencies.

Feline smiled. "I thought it might." She held up her hand, and Hapless touched it with the Totem. There was a crackle of power.

Now the schemer is immune to fire.

Then it was time to get ready. They garbed Hapless in the dance outfit Fiery would have used, and Feline in a spare dress Fiera had. Both outfits were burning hot, but now they could handle them without suffering. They both looked surprisingly sharp, Hopeless thought. Then, prepared, they left Nya and Quin to relax in the den while they headed out to the dance.

The two centaurs were startled to see the three exiting the den. "We're going to the Fire Fandango," Feline explained brightly. "Carry on."

Fiera led them through several burning fields to a larger rock pile. Beneath it was a much larger den where dozens of fire fauns had gathered. "Fiery couldn't make it," Fiera explained. "But these folk are filling in. Treat them like respected visitors." That sufficed.

Hapless and Fiera stepped onto the dance floor. "Conjure me casta-nets," Feline whispered.

He did, and she donned them while Fiera donned hers. They were little shells that attached to the fingers so that they could be knocked together, producing evocative clicking sounds. In amateur hands they could be awful, but in expert hands they could be fantastic.

"But I don't know how to do this dance," Hapless protested.

Follow my lead. Better, let me have your feet.

Hapless turned over his feet. The music started. Then suddenly he was dancing, tapping the floor with precision while snapping his fingers. Meanwhile Feline on the sideline played her castanets with marvelous dexterity in time with his steps.

He danced with Fiera and it was wonderful. She really knew how to use her fingers, hooves, and torso, and was about as sexy as she could be without freaking him out. But he was matching her in everything but the castanets, and those were so well played and timed by Feline that he almost felt as if he were playing them himself.

Then they changed partners, and he got to dance with other lovely fire girls. He had never been so well treated by so many beauties. It was like a slice of heaven.

Then he saw Feline watching him, and stifled his rapture. Still, he was having a fine time. No girl had ever been jealous of his attentions before.

Midway through the dance, they paused to have the contest. "Give me the Totem," Feline whispered urgently.

"But—"

"Totem, I need you so I can help Fiera win a prize," Feline said. "With your help I believe we can do it. Do you want her to win?"

Bleep. Turn me over to the she-devil.

Hapless did. When the Totem left him he reverted to his normal incompetent self. It was not a nice feeling. But he was doing the right thing. He hoped. He sat down and watched the contestants.

One couple after another performed, doing intricate dances as they clicked their castanets most intricately. They were good, very good; it was a stiff competition. The panel of judges watched, listened, and made notes.

Then Fiera's turn came. Feline went with her. The music started, and the two women addressed each other, doing a fine coordinated dance as they clicked their castanets. Hapless realized that Fiera had phenomenal natural skill; she did indeed have the talent to win a prize, with an equivalent partner. The hidden key was Feline: she had the body, the coordination, the curves, while the Totem she carried lent her the skill in this particular dance and Hapless's talent lent her the phenomenal ability with the castanets. It was Fiery Faun's skill being drawn on here, and he certainly had it. Thus the two shapely women became a marvel of lovely symmetry, doing a dance that fascinated him. Feline lacked the petite hooves of a true faun, but her human feet were appealing in their own right. In that moment he loved them both.

Then he looked quietly around. All the men, and many of the women, were similarly rapt. They all loved the dancers. The performance was that good.

It didn't hurt that it was clear that Hapless was far from the only one who admired well-displayed curves.

They won. Fiera hugged the trophy, transported by her joy. She kissed Feline, then kissed Hapless. "Thank you!" she breathed.

Feline returned the Totem to Hapless. "That was glorious," she murmured.

Gotta admit, the cattail pulled it off. The credit was grudging, but genuine.

After the dance they returned to the home den. The others welcomed them back and admired the trophy. Hapless returned the Totem to Nya. Then they all collapsed into sleep. It had been a considerable day.

Better, Hapless felt reasonably satisfied that they had done the right thing. They had gotten the first Totem without doing serious harm to anyone else. He hoped that kind of success would continue.

Chapter 9

EARTH DRAGON

In the morning the plot of land had been burned over again; pockets still guttered. The centaurs must have had to step lively to avoid the flames.

Hapless opened the box. There was a picture of a huge six-winged steamer dragon, with the words EARTH TOTEM.

"This can't be right," Zed protested. "That's not a land-bound creature, it's a winged monster."

"You know better than that," Faro said. "The totems don't have to be restricted in nature. All the elements are in all the Regions except maybe the Void: air is everywhere, ground is everywhere, and nothing could live anywhere without water. I suspect there's some fire spread about too. The Regions are merely where particular elements are dominant. So a flying creature can represent Earth, if that's the way it is. Maybe it needs to fly in order to get around the Region efficiently."

"Excellent point," Zed agreed, looking at her fondly. It occurred to Hapless that they could have gotten to know each other well during the night. "I stand corrected."

"You were always correct; it was just a slip of attention."

"I was distracted by your nice—wings." He had evidently changed the word as he detoured around it.

She inhaled. "Thank you." She probably had picked up on the original word.

"Time to follow the path," Hapless said, as he felt a glare from Feline lurking in case he got too interested in that word.

This time the path stayed on the ground. It led from the box to a distant firewall. They followed it, avoiding sections that were still actively burning. The Region of Fire wasn't so bad when they were used to it.

They halted before the firewall. Nya slid forward and touched it with a finger. That section blazed up and flickered out. They quickly stepped through.

They were in the Region of Earth. It was mountainous, with an active volcano directly ahead. "See—fire," Faro said, pointing to the smoking cone.

"You're right," Zed said. "Volcanoes are creatures of earth, but do have fire."

The path did not go to the volcano. Instead it meandered to the right as if in no hurry to get anywhere.

"There's something odd about this," Feline said. "Where's the dragon? Why isn't the path going straight to it?"

"Maybe we should pause to consider," Zed said. "I have no idea how to catch a dragon, let alone pacify it. Quin or Nya could have flown after it, and maybe fought its steam with steam, but I can't."

"It does seem odd that a centaur should have been selected to capture a flying dragon of any kind," Feline said.

"Well, maybe we got it wrong," Zed said. "We decided who would be what, but we didn't know the actual alignment."

"Yet it worked out with the fire faun," Nya said.

"You had fire to oppose it," Quin reminded her. "Maybe I'm supposed to oppose this dragon with my steam."

"We had better decide soon," Faro said. "Because there's the dragon."

They looked. The monstrous six-winged dragon was flying toward them, puffing steam. It was male, and so big it seemed it could carry any of them away, even maybe a centaur.

"Well, I'll try," Zed said bravely. His bow appeared in his hands, arrow nocked.

The dragon saw that, and sheared away. He knew about a centaur's infallible aim.

"But he's too big to be killed by an arrow," Quin said. "*I* could be killed, but I'm only a quarter the size of that one."

"He probably would feel the sting, though," Faro said, her own bow appearing. "And if you aimed for an eye, you could blind it. If I loosed another arrow at the same time, we could take out both eyes. It might not like that."

"It might not," Zed agreed with a smile.

"But we thought it should be just one Companion to a Totem," Zed said.

"Maybe it doesn't know that," Faro said.

"It must know. The path has to go to it. The fire faun saw that, and knew."

"But it doesn't," Faro said. "The path bears off to the side."

"Maybe it's the wrong dragon," Feline said.

"I doubt it," Zed said. "That dragon gave me too knowing a look."

"But if the path doesn't track him—" Faro said.

"I don't understand that," Zed said. "The path should go to him, and if he's moving, it should move after him, as it did with me. Why isn't it?"

"There are too many mysteries here," Hapless said. "We'd better stop right here and figure some of them out, because any mistake could be lethal."

They formed a circle facing each other. "We'll storm-brain again," Feline said. "Only all together this time, because that dragon could pick us off individually if we separate."

"Two questions to answer," Hapless said. "Why doesn't our Companion match the challenge, such as our steamer dragon going after the steamer dragon? And why is the path ignoring the target? Could they be related?"

"Maybe we do have the wrong Companion for this Totem," Quin said. "So the path refuses to focus. That's its way of telling us we're going wrong."

"That makes so much sense it's bound to be wrong," Feline said.

"That is cat logic?" Nya asked.

"Yes. Sometimes the way to catch something is not by bounding straight at it, but by circling it and sneaking up from behind."

"How do you sneak up behind a flying dragon who can see you coming?" Quin asked. "You'd never catch me that way."

Then Hapless got a notion. "Maybe not sneaking. Herding."

The others looked at him, perplexed. "You can't herd cats," Feline said.

"Or dragons," Quin said.

"Ah, but we can," Hapless said. "By getting all around the Region of Earth, and closing in on the dragon from all sides. I think he's confined to the Region, so we can surround him."

"He would just fly over us," Nya said.

"Not if we balked him with music. That can reach up and fill the area."

"Music! That's how I enchanted Fiery Faun."

"Yes. It should work on the dragon too. Music can reach into the sky so he can't avoid it."

"And if he knows about it, he will want to avoid it," Zed said thoughtfully. "So he could be herded in toward the center."

"Or to one corner, where you will ambush him with your saxophone," Faro said. "No fire or steam needed, or even arrows. Just a clever idea." She glanced at Hapless. "I confess, at first I didn't see why you should be the Quest leader. But I am coming to appreciate it now."

"It's just an idea," Hapless said, embarrassed. "Maybe wrong."

"And maybe right. Let's put this together: with music, we don't need to worry about physical weapons, so they're irrelevant. With herding we don't need to have the path go direct. The path goes around because that's the way to catch our dragon: surrounding him. So you were right: the two matters are related, and are the key to success. You're a genius."

"Oh, I don't think so," Hapless protested. "Even if it's right, it's just a lucky guess."

"Which seems to be part of your nature," Feline said. "Lucky guesses."

"Let's do it," Faro said. "We can circle the Region and drop off Companions every so often. Then we'll start playing our music. With luck the dragon won't know which of us is the one, or maybe it could be any of us, but the path knows where it will finish, and that's with Zed."

"Maybe," Hapless agreed. It seemed far-fetched, but what else was there?

"The dragon might not," Zed agreed with a smile.

"Question," Faro said. "How are we to know when everyone is in place, since we won't be able to see each other and we won't want to shout and alert the dragon to our plot?"

"Excellent question," Zed said, gazing at her appreciatively. "But I believe I have an answer. My double bass saxophone has an extremely low range. I can play the very lowest note, which may be slightly below the range of human or dragon hearing, so it won't alert the dragon."

"Excellent answer," Faro said, returning the appreciative gaze. "But how can we hear it, if it is beneath our hearing?"

"By the vibration in the ground. It's one way Mundane elephants communicate. They feel it in their feet."

"And we of the serpentine persuasion should be able to feel it in our bodies," Nya said. "While the flying dragon won't, as he has no contact with the ground."

"That was my thought, yes."

"I will need to keep my paws on the ground," Feline said.

"And I can take off my shoes," Hapless said. "But first, let's test it." He conjured the sax, and Zed took it and played a silent note.

"Hooo!" Quin said.

"Oh, yes," Faro agreed.

Feline changed form, then back. "Yes, definitely."

Hapless removed his shoes. There was the vibration. "Got it. So we have our signal. We start herding with our notes when we feel this."

A nod circled the group.

They resumed motion, following the path. The scenery was beautiful, with lush fields and forests. Indeed, all the elements were represented here, but the dominant theme was Earth: the landscape itself. The volcano might have fire, but it was constrained by the massive cone of rock. There were rivers and lakes, but they flowed and formed exactly where the lay of the land directed. There was air, but it was passive, filling in where the contours of the ground allowed. Earth governed here, without question. Only the Void was absent, and that was of course a rule unto itself.

The path led them to the slope of a mountain so high it had snow on its summit like a white cap. This, too, showed the power of Earth: it controlled the temperature, and could freeze the top of a mountain if it wanted to, so that the water there could do nothing.

"You know, I always took the ground for granted," Feline said. "Not any more. I am admiring its majesty."

"Much of our existence is shaped by geography," Nya said. The two females seemed to be becoming friends, having more than gender in common. Sometimes they shifted into their cat and dragon forms to inspect spot features of the terrain.

The path meandered to a high ledge overlooking a fetching valley. Then it did something odd: it looped before moving on.

"Hold up," Hapless said. "I don't much trust anything I don't understand, and I don't understand why the path should loop. None of the paths have done that before."

"This is a good point," Zed said. "The path may not be smart in itself, but it does know where it's going, or rather, where *we* are going. If we ignore its hints, we could be in trouble."

"What trouble threatens here?" Hapless asked.

There was a rumble. Then a patch of snow broke off from the snowcap and slid down the mountainside. It descended to a lower slope, where it buried several trees.

"Avalanche," Zed said succinctly. "And by the look of it, this is a prime location. The slope above this ledge is steep, and snow is piled up. It could crash down at any time."

"So we don't want to linger here long," Feline said. "Because if an avalanche came, we non-fliers could not escape it."

But Hapless wasn't satisfied. "I don't see why a loop would be a warning. A loop doesn't go anywhere; it just circles around itself. That's more like telling us to stay here."

"We are missing something," Zed agreed.

"It's too bad we have to leave it," Feline said. "It's a nice lookout to spy on the dragon. We can see all across the Region of Earth from here."

"Ah," Zed said, a bulb flashing over his head. "A lookout should stay here. Or rather, a herder. To stop the dragon from coming this way."

"But the avalanche!" Feline protested.

"A flier could avoid it."

"Who?"

"That would be me," Faro said. "I could fly just high enough to avoid the avalanche, if I had to."

"That makes sense," Hapless agreed. "This will be your post."

"Give me my instrument."

Hapless conjured the three-drum set and gave it to her. She put it on and played a brief drum solo. "I will hold the fort."

The others moved on. The path led down the far slope to a broad level area where no plants grew; it was solid sand. It was hot. In the center of the parched section there was another loop.

"Station Two," Hapless said. "The desert post. Who can handle this?"

"I can," Nya said. "I am now impervious to heat."

Hapless conjured her harmonica. She took it and played a few lovely notes. "I am ready."

"Then so are we," Hapless said. Then he thought of something. "Oops."

"I don't like the sound of that," Feline said.

"I just realized that you won't be able to play beautiful music in my absence," Hapless said ruefully. "So our herding won't work."

She stared at him. "Oh, litterbox! I forgot."

"We all did," Quin said.

"Can you think outside the box?" Zed asked.

Hapless strained, knowing that it was up to him to salvage the situation. Finally a dim bulb flashed. "Maybe we can bluff him."

"I'm afraid I don't see how," Zed said. "Dragons may not be the smartest creatures, but they make up for that in ferocity. Only superior combat power or evocative music will daunt him."

"Unless we do something he will never think of."

"And what would that be?"

"A single note. Even without talent, we can do that. Well, maybe I can't, but the rest of you can."

"A note is not a symphony," Nya said. "It will not enchant the dragon."

Hapless glanced at her. "You know this from your Totem?"

"Yes. It takes special evocative music."

"And the dragon knows this?"

"All the creatures on the Totem draft know it."

"Good. I need your help, Nya."

The naga smiled. "If it's okay with Feline."

He ignored that dig. "I need you to fly back to Faro and explain to her that she will have to use a sustained note when she plays her drums. That is, nothing fancy, as she won't have the skill in my absence. Just a regular beat, like a prelude to a full rendition."

"But that won't enchant the dragon," Nya repeated.

"That's right. It won't. But it will warn him that the music is about to begin. He will turn away, lest he be caught by it."

She considered. "He won't know it's a bluff."

"That's right. As long as she doesn't actually try to do more. She doesn't need to enchant him, just warn him away."

She nodded. "You're right. That is outside the box." She changed to dragon form and took off, flying back the way they had come, though it was no longer marked by the path.

"You've got nerve," Feline said.

"One of my few qualities," he agreed.

Soon Nya returned. She landed, then assumed naga form. "Faro understands. She'll do it."

"Good enough. You'll do it too, on your harmonica. Just a single warning note." He conjured her harmonica.

"Got it," she agreed, accepting it. She played a single note.

The remaining four of them moved on, following the path around the Region of Earth in a slow left turn. The desert ended and a rocky terrain appeared. "Only small plants grow here," Feline remarked. "No trees."

"Surely more mischief," Quinn said.

The ground shook. Cracks appeared and rocks rolled about.

"It's an earthquake!" Zed said.

"Fortunately, a small one," Quin said. "That explains why there are no trees: they don't have time to grow here. Only weeds."

In the middle of the quake zone was another loop.

"But it's not safe here," Feline said. "There could be a big quake."

"Unless a person can fly above it," Quin said. "So this must be my station."

"It must be," Hapless agreed. He conjured Quin's accordion. "Can you salvage it when a quake comes?"

"I think so." Quin donned the accordion, then shifted to dragon mode. The straps remained around his serpentine body. He flew in a loop and returned. Then he shifted back to harpy form. The accordion was undamaged. He played a single note.

"That's it," Hapless agreed.

"Look," Feline said. "The dragon is returning."

"Good," Hapless said. "Play your note, then when the dragon comes closer, serenade it. It won't be smart enough to know that my presence makes a difference."

"Got it." Quin faced the creature and played the note, followed by a lively melody.

The dragon retreated. He had gotten the message.

"Ideal," Hapless said.

Three of them moved on. They now were about halfway around the Region. They could still see the big volcano in its center. It was as if the volcano was watching them, daring them to approach to within its range. Was that also a bluff? Hapless doubted it.

They entered a forest covering a hill. The crest of the hill was bare and full of holes like a giant ant mound. "Goblins," Feline said. "I hope we skirt that."

Unfortunately they didn't. The path led right by it, then made a loop.

"This one must be mine," Feline said. "Goblins are afraid of cats, as you saw."

"But you're a small cat."

"Still big enough to dispatch a goblin. Give me my kit."

Hapless conjured the small violin. She took it and played a riff.

Goblins swarmed out of the mound and charged in to surround them. "Fresh meat!" the goblin leader said.

Feline faced them. "Now we can do this two ways," she said evenly. "You can attack us and we'll make you hurt by stomping you." She glanced at Zed, who obligingly stomped his feet menacingly. The goblins backed off slightly, knowing they would take losses. "Clawing you." She changed to cat form and arched her back while spitting. The goblins retreated another step. "And revolting you." She glanced at Hapless. "The tuba," she murmured, before changing back to human form.

Hapless conjured the tuba and played a brief but sickening siege of retch music. The goblins turned greenish and retreated further.

"Or we can declare a truce and I can play you a selection from 'Goblin's Goblet,' and then remain a while to back off the dragon so he won't steam you today." She played a few notes, and the goblins softened visibly. She evidently did know the song. "So which is it to be?"

The goblin leader hesitated.

Zed stomped one forefoot. Hapless took a breath to blow another ill note. Feline switched to cat form for a quarter of a moment.

"Truce," the leader said quickly.

Feline smiled. "That's so nice of you." She played the kit again, and it was truly evocative, smelling of overflowing goblets of wine. It was intoxicating. The goblins loved it.

When she finished the piece, the goblins staggered back to their mound, too soused for combat. "Go get the dragon," Feline said, playing the single note.

Hapless paused a good three fifths of a moment. Feline had handled the crisis with elegant finesse, and he liked that almost as well as he liked her curves.

"Move it," she said sharply as if reading his thought. Almost wasn't good enough.

Hapless and Zed moved on. "She is a worthwhile person," Zed said as they followed the path on around the Region.

"She is," Hapless agreed. "But apart from her hang-up about curves, I am fated to have one or two more girlfriends. That complicates things."

"That would," the centaur agreed.

The scenery continued to be beautiful, with a pleasant river coursing beside the path. They crossed it on a pleasant covered bridge. At the far side there was another loop.

A troll rose up. "Stop. Pay Troll," he said.

They paused. "This is a trollway?" Zed asked.

"Of course it is, stripe face! Trolls live under bridges, and this is mine. Now pay up or I'll eat you."

"What is the toll?" Zed asked.

"What do you have?"

"If we are to negotiate payment," Hapless said, "let's introduce each other. I am Hapless Human and this is Zed Centaur. Who are you?"

"I am Trover Troll."

"That's an odd name."

"Not at all. A trover is a legal action for the recovery of personal property wrongfully converted by someone else for his own use. Such as your using my bridge to cross the river without paying for it."

"I disagree." Hapless said. "We are following a magic path that indicates where one of us should stay. I think this is my station. I know nothing about payment."

"Ignorance of the law does not exempt you from its strictures."

"But we may have a problem," Zed said.

"Maybe not," Hapless said. "Feline showed the way." He conjured another tuba and played a sour note.

The troll rocked back as if struck. "What was that?"

"That was the first note of a sickly serenade I will play if you require it."

"I don't want anything like that! I want my toll paid."

"Here is the deal," Hapless said carefully. "The toll I am paying you is *not* to churn your guts with the serenade. You won't be eating anything with your stomach roiling to this music."

"That's no payment!"

Hapless played another note. Even the nearby foliage wilted, and the flowing river water turned greenish.

"Ugh! Okay, okay, just stop the nausea!"

Hapless smiled. "I knew you'd be reasonable."

"You have more guts than I thought," Trover said. "I mean that in the worst possible way."

"I think you have this station in hand," Zed said. "I will move on to my own. But the troll was not my problem."

"Not?"

"It's that I won't be able to play my sax in your absence."

Oops again. "I keep forgetting that. I just can't be everywhere at once."

"And if you desert this post, the dragon will fly through it to escape our net."

"This is interesting," Trover said. "You are trying to catch the Earth Dragon?"

"It's not your business," Hapless said, sorry he had forgotten about the troll.

"Ah, but it *is* my business. The Earth Dragon is the key to the Region of Earth; all Earth power is ultimately invested in him. If you capture him, you will gain control of the Region, with phenomenal powers, and will have dominion over us all, me included. You might banish me from my beloved bridge."

Both of them looked at the troll. "You're not as stupid as you look," Zed said.

"Well duh, centaur! I couldn't possibly be as stupid as I look, now could I?"

Hapless was impressed. Trover had personality.

"Then what are you doing lurking under a bridge and demanding tolls from passers by?" Zed demanded. "This is hardly a way to exert your supposed intellect."

"It's what trolls do, centaur. The same way that centaurs use their intellects to teach classes and educate ignorant humans. Trolls who do not haunt bridges maintain the Trollway that efficiently takes folk anywhere in Xanth, for a fee. It's our nature."

"What of the trolls who eat children and terrorize villages?"

"Well, we do have some riffraff. There are not bridges enough for every troll, and the leftovers tend to degenerate. They are our lower class, fit mainly to be looked down on, just as are poor humans."

"Now wait a moment!" Hapless protested. "No one deserves to be looked down on."

"I will happily leave you to your ensuing discussion," Zed said. "After we solve my problem with the instrument."

"This discussion with Hapless promises to be interesting," Trover said. "So maybe I can get rid of you by solving your problem."

Zed looked at him with suppressed contempt. "You can solve it?"

"I will make you this deal, stripe hide: if I solve it for you, you will then depart and leave us alone."

"Done, bridge trash."

The troll turned to Hapless. "Acquaint me with the essential: why can't the centaur play his saxophone when apart from you? Are you his mentor?"

"Hardly," Hapless said. "It is my talent to conjure any musical instrument, but I can't play any, and others can play them well only in my presence."

"I believe that you can't play, but not that you enhance the playing of others."

"I can demonstrate. What instrument do you play?"

"A tro instrument, of course, like the trombone. Remember, I'm a troll. But I'm not good at it."

Hapless conjured a trombone, finely crafted of bones. "Try this one."

Trover took it and blew a note. It was beautiful. He blew another, his surprise showing around the mouthpiece. Then he played an entire melody.

He set it aside. "Point made. Evidently your talent exports your musical ability to others. If I can play that well, obviously the centaur can. But since it's a side effect of your talent, others have to be near you for it to operate. So why don't you simply accompany your friend to his station, so he can play his sax unimpeded?"

"Because we have to herd the dragon," Hapless said, and explained.

"Ah. Then the solution is obvious. When your five members play, herding the dragon to Zed for the coup de grace, you will all be converging on the centaur. Thus when he plays, you, Hapless, will be in range, and his instrument will be effective."

Hapless exchanged an amazed look with Zed.

"You win, troll," Zed said, the contempt mysteriously absent. "I'm on my way."

Hapless conjured the double saxophone, and Zed carried it with him as he followed the path on around the Region of Earth.

"Excellent." Trover refocused on Hapless. "Why do you feel that no one deserves to be looked down on? Is it not natural for superior creatures to scorn inferior creatures?"

Hapless realized that he was in over his intellectual depth. But he tried. "It may seem natural, but it's not nice. Each creature is unique in its own way, and does not deserve to be scorned for that. I'm an indifferent human with no special qualities other than maybe stubbornness, but even I deserve some respect for being what I am. We recently encountered a fire faun, and he turned out to have an interesting culture that I came to respect. So contempt may be largely a product of ignorance."

"So then contempt should be for the contemptuous?"

"Yes, actually. They deserve their own medicine."

"I agree."

"So therefore you should not—" Hapless paused. "You what?"

Trover laughed. "I agree. That dismays you?"

"Um—"

"I think you and I are going to be friends."

"But you were saying—"

"I argued a case with which I disagreed, for the sake of argument. You refuted it. You are my kind of person. I admit that surprises me, but I have learned not to judge on too slender a basis."

"I—I guess I was prejudiced against trolls."

"And I against humans. But it seems there are exceptions."

"Exceptions," Hapless agreed weakly.

Then he heard the rush of air as the dragon approached. He quickly took the trombone and blew a foul note. The dragon swerved away.

"This is an interesting technique," Trover remarked. "I would swerve away too."

"Something I don't get," Hapless said. "You don't seem disturbed that I'm helping to herd the dragon to his likely captivity, even though you understand that this could change the power structure of the Region of Earth. What's with you?"

"I try to maintain perspective. To view the larger picture. I am satisfied with the existing order, but it is possible that change will be for the better."

"Change could be risky for you."

"Perhaps. But when I saw the magic path form, and noted the loop indicating that this is a station, I realized that this must be a Quest and that the Good Magician may be involved. As a general rule it is best not to interfere with the Good Magician. Things tend to turn out as he anticipates, however deviously."

"So far they have," Hapless agreed.

"I reasoned that if there was a station beside my bridge, there must be a reason. It would have been easy for the magic path to avoid my area. So it seems that my peripheral participation was wanted, and that aroused my curiosity. I was not aware that the Good Magician even knew of me."

"The Good Magician wanted us to meet and talk?"

"That would seem to be the case," Trover said. "The question is why."

"It must facilitate the Quest in some way."

"Indeed. Can we fathom what way?"

"I have had trouble making much sense of any of it. I just follow the paths and try to do my best."

"Commendable. I wonder why you were selected for this mission."

"I wonder too. I am not especially smart, handsome, or lucky, and my talent is more frustrating than useful to me."

"I appreciate that; you are realistic. Yet there must be a reason. Perhaps a quality of character?"

"My character is not special either. I think I just happened to be the nearest available person who wasn't otherwise occupied. The same may be true for the others. None of us is anything special."

"Yet you seek the Goddess Isis."

"We seek the Isis Orb, which I guess we'll have to get from Isis somehow."

"Isis is mischief. She has designs on Xanth. Had she been the one to travel this path, I would have done my best to torpedo her, dangerous as that would have been. One does not lightly cross a goddess. I was relieved to see you instead."

"Well, we have met and talked, but I'm not sure how it benefits either of us."

"Sometimes benefits are not immediately apparent."

"But what about the trolls who raid villages and eat babies? If you don't think they are your lower class, what are they?"

"They are trolls of a differing persuasion. Who is to say which persuasion is best? Again, it is much as it is with humans or other creatures: each is a rule unto himself. We judge others at our peril."

Hapless found that hard to answer. So he said so.

"You are honest."

"Too honest, my girlfriend says."

"Compulsive honesty can be a social liability, true, but it surely has its place." Trover shrugged. "This trombone you conjured for me: may I keep it?"

"As long as it lasts, which will be a day or so. My conjurations are temporary."

"Thank you." Trover lifted it and played a lovely melody. "It's such a delight to play it competently, even though I know this is your talent rather than mine." He resumed playing. The bones were really performing in his hands.

Hapless took off his shoes, so as to be able to feel the low sax note when it came. Meanwhile he listened with pleasure to the music, yet again with that tinge of jealousy. If only he could do the same!

They chatted about this and that. Then Hapless felt the vibration. It was time. "I must move on, Trover," he said. "It has been surprisingly nice getting to know you."

"Likewise. Perhaps we shall in some unlikely circumstance meet again."

Hapless put his shoes back on and followed the path toward Zed, keeping an eye out for the dragon. Soon the dragon did show. Hapless lifted his tuba and played a warning note. The dragon retreated.

Now he began to hear another note. This was Feline's kit, beautifully ominous. It was a bluff, as she could not play a competent melody, but it seemed to be working.

The dragon flew back toward Hapless. He inhaled. The dragon quickly left.

Another note sounded: Quin's accordion. And Faro's drumbeat. And
Nya's harmonica. All were advancing south. The one note that didn't
sound was Zed's saxophone. Would the herding work?

It did. The dragon flew toward Zed, evidently thinking that he lacked
the skill or courage to play compelling music. Now the central volcano
shuddered, evidently aware that something was happening. They needed
to get this done quickly.

Hapless hurried to get closer. The dragon angled down for a strafing
run, evidently planning to take out the centaur as a warning to the others.
He was getting dangerously close. *Play, Zed!* Hapless thought. *Before you
get fried! I'm close enough now.*

Suddenly Zed lifted his sax and played the most potently evocative
music imaginable. Caught too close, the dragon tried to reverse course,
but only succeeded in spinning out of control. He crashed to the ground,
righted himself, and tried to crawl away. Hapless almost felt sorry for the
creature.

Zed marched on in, playing. The dragon was stunned. Zed came and
touched his tail. The dragon disappeared.

Zed stopped playing. He bent down to pick up the new Totem. "Gotcha," he said.

The volcano blew out a boulder as if clearing its throat, then settled
back down to mere smoke. It knew it was pointless to protest their victory.
The dragon would return in due course.

The others closed in to admire the Totem. It was in the form of the
dragon, six wings and all, and most resembled a work of art. "Congratula-
tions," Faro said, kissing him on the cheek. "Will it enable you to fly?"

"I never thought of that!" Zed held up the figure, concentrating. Nothing happened. "No," he said, disappointed. "Flying is not an Earth basic
characteristic. But it can do plenty else."

"Do demonstrate," Feline said. "We all need to know what we as a
group have."

"It can start an avalanche." He glanced at a nearby hill, and there was
a dirt slide. "And an earthquake." The ground around them shook warn-
ingly. "And a volcano." A tiny volcano popped up near them like a blister
in the ground, spouting a jet of smoke. "I can make them all bigger, if
you want."

"No need," Hapless said quickly. "Those effects are dangerous, and we don't want to invoke them unless there is reason."

"Agreed," Zed said, satisfied. "Thank all of you for your cooperation. I couldn't have done it without you."

"We're a team," Faro reminded him.

So they were.

Chapter 10

AIR GRIFFIN

They relaxed, glad to be reunited and with the second Totem conquered. But three Totems remained, for Air, Water, and the Void, and they were surely formidable.

"Which do we tackle next?" Hapless asked.

"Isn't that for you to decide?" Feline asked.

"Actually it's for the box to decide," Nya reminded them. "It did for Fire and Earth."

"Oh. Yes, of course," he agreed, disgruntled. It was a familiar state; he simply wasn't sharp at obvious details.

"But let's not open it until morning," Quin said.

They were glad to agree. They played themselves a concert, then foraged for their evening meal. There was a pleasant pool nearby where they could safely wash. The Region of Earth had become docile, once its Totem was won.

They settled for the evening, the two centaurs standing together, the two dragons resting side by side, and Feline with Hapless. A quest with six participants, maybe forming into three couples. But there was a lot yet to be accomplished, and—

"And there's that other girlfriend you're trying for," Feline said.

He was put slightly askew. "Are you sure you're not telepathic?"

"Fairly sure. I can tell when your focus is not entirely on me, and there's not much else it can be on except the other woman. Men have small minds; when they aren't on one girl, they're on another."

He was not completely satisfied with that assessment, but wasn't sure he could refute it. "And I'm not trying for anyone else. It's what the Good Magician said. It's fate, maybe; I didn't ask for it."

"Two good girlfriends and maybe one bad one," she agreed. "And the bad one fascinates you the most. Maybe I should just preempt the others, since I'm here first."

What did she have in mind? He was intrigued. "Maybe you should."

"I could seduce you, and you'd be mine. The others would be too late."

She knew her power. "Yes."

"But there's a caution."

"That fate will have its way regardless?"

"Make that two cautions. The second is that it could mess up the Quest. You might not continue if you already had your girl."

"I suppose. But I still want to find my musical instrument."

"Yes. So it's not sure."

"What's the first caution?"

"That I'm not quite sure I want you. You're sort of lunky for a human, and you like me mainly for my curves."

She had him dead to rights. It was those curves that gave her the power to seduce him, if she chose to invoke them. He didn't even try to argue. "Yes."

"And you're honest to a fault. I'm not used to that, in a man."

"I'm sorry."

"Oh shut up and sleep or I'll kiss you."

"But—"

She shut him up with a kiss. By the time he recovered from it, he was asleep.

"But I do like you more than is convenient," she murmured, snuggling against him. Maybe he only dreamed that, since he was asleep. Regardless, she was worth dreaming about.

After their morning ablutions, they gathered around Hapless for the opening of the Box. He lifted the lid and they all peered in.

There was a picture of a horrendous six-headed griffin, with the words AIR TOTEM.

"That's what I have to pacify?" Quin asked, dismayed.

"It's a flying creature," Nya said. "Makes sense for Air."

"I may have to chase it down in air. That means I'll have to play my accordion while flying, and that Hapless will have to be within range. Those are fair challenges."

"Maybe I can run along behind you as you fly," Hapless said. "If the terrain permits."

"If," Quin agreed grimly. "The powers that be are not making this easy."

"If Quests were easy, everyone would take them," Faro said.

The path led from the box to the south. That made sense, because the Region of Air was south of the Region of Earth. They followed it, and the ground was reasonably even and uncluttered.

They came to the boundary wall, which scintillated, looking like a curtain of solidified air. They stepped through it and found themselves in another fairly pleasant landscape, with fields and forests, mountains and valleys, and rivers and lakes. The path led straight toward its center.

"Why do I suspect it will not be this simple?" Quin asked rhetorically. Why, indeed.

They followed the path toward a jagged mountain in the Region's center. At the very top of the highest jag was what looked like a huge nest. In the nest was a large bird. Or maybe a griffin.

"A griffin is a cross between an eagle and a lion," Zed said helpfully. "It has the head and wings of the eagle, and the body of the lion. Details can vary, however."

"Such as having six heads," Quin said.

"That is unusual, but it seems not outside the range."

"It must get hungry, supporting all those heads," Feline said. "It may be hard to stop all the heads at once; one will get through your defenses to peck you."

"Thank you for that clarification," Quin said dryly.

"We may need to think about this, lest we get in trouble," Hapless said.

"Uh-oh," Nya said. "The beast stirs."

Indeed, it seemed that the griffin had spied them. He spread his wings and launched into the air. In no more than three scant moments, or two and a half generous ones, he was swooping down on them. The creature was huge, the size of a centaur, with each of the six heads looking more vicious than the others.

They scattered, taking cover wherever it was offered. Hapless got under a rather prickly bush.

The griffin flew on by, leaving only a six-throated screech behind. Evidently he was merely assessing the situation. But there was no doubt he was the one they were after, because the faint sparkle of the path tracked his motions.

"So now he knows we're after him," Feline said, reappearing from behind a small tree. "And he doesn't like it."

"No element of surprise," Zed agreed.

"Uh-oh," Nya repeated. "Now the Region is reacting."

"Reacting?" Hapless asked.

A stiff gust of wind caught him in a buffet, almost knocking him off his feet. More winds followed. A storm was brewing.

"The Region of Air features wind," Faro said. "We're in for a blow."

"Does the Region care about what we're after?" Hapless asked.

"In a way. You never can be sure, with the inanimate."

"We'd better get under cover before it blows us away." That was not much of an exaggeration.

They hurried on toward the craggy mountain. The wind picked up until Hapless could hardly keep his feet, and he saw that even the centaurs were having some difficulty. Only the serpentine dragons were handling it, being too low to the ground to give the wind much purchase.

"Found something," Nya called. "Cave entrance."

"But is it safe?" Feline asked.

"Surely for dragons. We'll explore it first."

The two dragons disappeared into the ground, while Hapless, Feline, and the two centaurs huddled at the entrance.

Soon they returned. "The cave is clear, but it may not be safe," Nya reported. "It's a wind tunnel."

"A what?" Hapless asked.

"A tunnel for wind. It is actually a straight hole in the hill, no dips or curves, no obstructions. Flying creatures can test their abilities there, as the wind increases. When the wind velocity exceeds their ability, they get blown out. They can practice, learning to fly more strongly. But it's not good for us, as the wind velocity will increase to tornado force and blow us out too. We would become projectiles, smacking into something and getting battered or killed."

"But we have to get out of this storm!" Indeed, the wind was still increasing.

"There may be a way," Zed said. "We two centaurs are massive enough to block the ends of the tunnel, so the rest of you could get shelter within it until the storm blows over."

"Let's do it!"

Zed placed himself at the tunnel entrance, and Faro went to the exit. Zed lay down across the entrance, cutting off the wind there. They made their way to the other end, where Faro made way for them to pass her, then lay across it as Zed had. She folded her wings tightly to prevent wind eddy currents from tugging at their feathers. The wind tunnel was quiet, perhaps for the first time in eons.

It was a relief to be out of the howl. Nya and Quin assumed their naga and harpy forms so they could talk. "We are operating as a team, again," Feline said. "Helping each other to get along."

"Each episode brings us closer together," Nya said. "But it's no guarantee that we will complete the Quest successfully."

Time passed, but the storm did not abate. "This is not getting us closer to winning the Totem," Quin said.

"We are pinned here waiting for a storm to pass," Nya said. "But suppose it doesn't pass? This is after all the Region of Air."

There it was. "This tunnel may be a trap," Hapless said. "Not in the sense of getting ambushed by a monster, but because we can't stay here forever. I fear we'll have to get out and brave the storm after all."

"I fear you're right," Quin said. "But we'll need a plan."

"A plan?"

"You have to get close enough to the griffin to enchant him with your music. I have to be close enough to you so that you can play well enough. That storm seems to be making both impossible. You can't fly nearly as well as the griffin in this wind, and if you're high in the air, I can't be near you. Just blundering along won't do."

"Good thinking," Feline said. "So let's work out the plan."

There was a silence. No one had a plan.

Hapless realized that it was up to him, again. He did not regard himself as a strategist, but he had to come up with something. Only his creative mind was blank.

"Think outside the box," Feline reminded him.

If thinking inside the box meant having Quin pursue the griffin and not catching him, and not being able to play music competently if he did catch him, that was certainly a losing strategy. But what else was there? If they didn't pursue the griffin they would never catch him, and if Quin couldn't catch him, how could Hapless help? Herding was out of the question in this environment. The whole thing seemed to be a loss. Were they going to have to give up?

Give up? That was no good. Yet the thought gave him a faint glimmer of a notion that hovered just outside his range. What was it?

"Too bad we can't make the griffin come to us," Nya said. "Then we could nab him."

The bulb lit. "Come to us!" Hapless said. "If we can't chase the griffin, we can make the griffin chase us."

"And do what—eat us?" Feline asked.

"He'd have trouble eating two dragons, even with those six heads," Nya said. "He's not going to come to us. He'll just stay away from us until we give up and go away."

"That's what he hopes," Hapless said. "But he's thinking inside the box."

The three others looked at him. "Maybe you're a bit too far outside the box for us to follow," Quin said.

"Here it is," Hapless said. "Even the griffin must get tired fighting the wind in this stormy Region. That's why he has his nest in the crags: where he can safely rest between storms. He's probably up there now, since we're no threat to him, trapped down here under the storm."

"I follow you so far," Feline said. "So why should he come down to us?"

"Because Quin will fly up to the nest, playing his accordion. The griffin knows he can't stay there for that. So he'll fly away, leaving Quin with nothing."

"Exactly," Quin agreed. "And even if he stayed, I would not be able to charm him, since you would still be down here underground."

"That does seem to make sense," Nya said.

"So where's the catch?" Feline asked Hapless.

"Well, Quin will doggedly pursue him around and around the Region of Air, through the storm. He won't be as fast as the griffin, especially carrying the accordion, so there's really nothing to worry about. Finally the griffin will tire of the chase and return to the nest to rest. Quin will follow him there. At which point the griffin, fed up with this stupid game, will launch into the air, ready to bite Quin half a dozen times in a single lunge."

"While I'm trying to play a useless accordion," Quin agreed. "This is suicide. He'll eat me for dinner."

"No," Hapless said. "He will be mesmerized, and when you touch him he'll compact into the Totem, and it will be done."

They looked at him again. "Is there perhaps a detail you omitted?" Nya asked.

Hapless considered. "Oh. Maybe there is. It is that I will be up near the nest, having climbed the crag while you distracted the griffin with your clumsy chase. So when he attacks you, your music will get him."

They considered that. "You have a way to reach the nest on your own?" Feline inquired.

"I hope to have Nya's help. Naga can climb well, can't they?"

"We can," Nya agreed. "But you're human, not another naga."

"But you should be able to ferret out a feasible route, and help me navigate it."

"Maybe. But this is highly chancy. You could fall and kill yourself."

"It's well outside the box," Hapless agreed.

They considered again. "Maybe we could rope the two of you together," Feline said. "So that when you fall, she can catch you, as it were."

"But it just maybe possibly might work," Quin said dubiously.

"Which is a better chance than the box offers," Hapless said.

"I wonder," Quin said. "Would the height make you nervous?"

"Oh, yes," Hapless agreed. "I dread it with something between fear and terror. Riding Faro was easy, but climbing a windswept snowy ledge is something else."

"But?"

"But it's something I think I had better try."

"This would require considerable nerve," Nya said.

"I think the word is gumption," Feline said. "Hapless may not be the smartest, strongest, boldest, or luckiest man extant, but he's surely the gumptionest."

"Thank you for that vote of confidence," Hapless said.

"You're welcome, you idiot." She kissed him on the ear.

"Then let's move out," Hapless said, emboldened by the gesture. "We have to get to the base of the mountain."

"While I distract the griffin," Quin said. "Conjure me my accordion, please."

Hapless did. Quin put it on, then changed to dragon form, which was better for flying. He growled, and it sounded like "I'm ready. I hope."

They moved to the end of the tunnel. "We're coming out," Feline called. "We have a Plan."

"The storm is unabated," Faro said. "I can't fly in this; it's dangerous." Indeed, her hair and mane were flying across her face, obscuring her vision, and the wind was so strong it wouldn't be safe for her to open her wings. They were tightly clamped to her body, acting like a partial cloak.

"Stay on the ground," Quin said, resuming harpy form for a moment. "I'm the only one flying at the moment. I'm more sinuous." He reverted to dragon, except for his arms, which remained to clasp the accordion. It looked awkward, but he seemed to know what he was doing.

"And me," Nya said. "I will try to bolster you." She shifted to her dragon form.

"I fear this is mischief," Faro said.

"You and I both," Feline said. "But our air-headed leader is determined. We need to get to that mountain."

Zed joined them, having seen them emerge. "Nya and I will try to shield you," he said. "Stay between us, and hang on, those of you with hands."

Hapless and Feline wedged between the two centaurs and grabbed hold of manes. That did seem to lend some stability. Then the centaurs stepped forward together. It was working. For one step.

Meanwhile the two dragons faced into the wind and spread their wings. They were immediately pushed backwards, not forwards. Then they rose into the air, actually flying backwards. Both Hapless and Feline stared.

"It's not as backwards as it looks," Faro explained. "The wind is in effect providing their forward speed. They are flying in its current to gain elevation. Then they'll turn and ride it. It's not something I would care to try, but they'll be all right as long as they maintain their balance and orientation. Their serpentine torsos can't be broadsided as readily as my equine body can be."

Sure enough, in another windblown moment the two dragons tilted and veered rapidly to the side, suddenly gaining speed. In another quarter of a moment they were out of sight.

Now the storm, as if sensing that something was up, intensified another notch. Rain spattered, then thickened. But the centaurs moved on. Fortunately the wind was now coming from the direction of the mountain, as if determined to blow them away from it. They all ducked their heads and plowed on.

The rain became a drench-pour. Visibility was cut to two body lengths, then one. The ground became muddy. They kept moving.

The rain became hail, which peppered their hides. It stung, but Hapless squinched his mouth and eyes closed and kept moving.

"Too bad Nya isn't here," Feline gasped. "She could use her Totem to melt the ice."

The storm, as if seeing that this wasn't working, shifted to sand. It became a sandstorm, blasting abrasively at their skin. They shoved on.

The sand mounded before them, becoming a dune that threatened to bury them.

"But I am here," Zed said. He focused on the mound, and it shook, forming cracks, and the sand drained into the fissures opening in the ground.

There was an angry howl as the wind was balked. But sand and ground were in the province of Earth, and Air could not override that.

They trudged on, trusting that their direction was correct, or that the centaurs could orient on the mountain despite the poor visibility. Their trust was vindicated; they came to the base of the mountain, and soon found a measure of shelter in a wind-carved grotto. The scream of the wind as it cut around the sharp edges was almost painful; it knew it was being balked.

Hapless spit out sand. "Next step: scale the mountain."

"Oh," Feline said. "You were going to have Nya help you climb, but she forgot; she's helping Quin fly."

"That's right," Hapless said. "I always mess up the details."

"Maybe I can help you. Cats are good climbers."

"Feline, I'd love to have your company. But I don't think you can do this, and you might get hurt. I'd hate that."

Then a shape loomed out of the swirl. It was Nya. She plowed into the sand beyond the grotto, then slithered into it. "Almost forgot!" she exclaimed.

"But what about Quin?" Feline asked.

"He's handling the wind and heading for the griffin's nest. The griffin will have to move. We know how that should play out. Now what is more important is to get you up near the nest without being observed."

"What if the griffin sees him?"

"That's mischief. I'll try to protect him, but that griffin is probably more than my match."

"So Hapless better not get seen."

"Yes. With luck Quin will be able to distract the griffin long enough."

"Are you sure you want to try this, Hapless?" Faro asked. "We can ponder alternatives."

"Not at all sure," Hapless admitted. "But I think I'd better try it, all the same. The path leads up the mountain. You can still ponder alternatives, in case I don't make it."

"Ah yes, the path. It shows the way and you follow it. Is that courage?"

"I don't think so. I just have a job to do, so I'm doing it."

"Gumption," Feline repeated.

"Then let's get to it. I'll try to find you good footing if I can."

"Thank you."

Nya slid out of the grotto and up the steep slope of the rock outside. Her naga form was good for this; her snaky belly had traction.

Hapless tried to follow, bracing against the wind, but immediately discovered problems. His hands and feet found no purchase on the rock, and the wind quickly blew him aside when he tried to climb. This was no good at all. If he had this much trouble at the base, how would it be at the top?

He conjured a guitar with picks for his fingers. He put on the picks and let the guitar blow away in the wind, jangling as it went. He set his hands against the rock, and the picks dug in just enough to make it possible for him to climb. He might not be able to make music with them, but scraping rock worked. His shoes did cling reasonably well.

"It's better up here," Nya called back from beyond the outcrop.

Hapless made it to a kind of ledge that formed a narrow ridge. The path followed that. It was indeed better. But when he looked back, the path was gone; he would not be able to return the way he came, because he would not be able to remember all the details. Well, that was something to worry about later.

They continued on in a rough spiral around the mountain. It was not a big mountain, and before long they were on the second loop, well above the first. Hapless was getting used to clinging to the rock; the wind could not really get at him as long as he remained in the crevice.

"Uh-oh," Nya muttered.

He did not like the sound of that. "What is it?"

"Traffic."

"Uh—"

"Caterpillar. A large one. Harmless to us. Evidently up here to graze on the high mountain lichen."

"So what's the problem?"

"We're in its track."

Now he saw the caterpillar heading toward them on its myriad little legs. It was about the size of a Mundane bus, its surface green, its antennae reaching forward. The track was the only place it could walk. If they didn't get clear of its route, they would likely be bulldozed off the track and the mountain. "We'd better get out of its way."

"Yes. But this is not a convenient spot to leave the path."

Hapless looked to his right, where the rock fed into a drop-off of lethal height. Then to his left, where the wall rose almost straight up. Inconvenient was a fair understatement. "Can I climb over it?"

"No. Its skin is poisonous, as a discouragement to predators."

"Then I guess we'll have to back off to a widening where we can let it pass."

"That will cost time. You need to get close to the nest before nightfall. Quin is not a good night flier."

"You have a better idea?"

"Yes. I will hook onto the ledge above this one, and stretch down to help you get off the path for long enough. When it passes, you can drop back onto the path."

"This looks precarious."

"It is. You will have to trust me."

"I trust you. I'm just not sure how this will work. I don't see how you can scale that cliff."

Nya smiled, and shifted to dragon form. She flew up off the path, climbed to the upper ridge, landed on it, and changed back. Then she hooked her tail over the ridge and let her body slide down across the cliff toward him. She reached her arms down. "Catch my hands."

"But they're out of reach."

"Not if you jump."

"But I'm too heavy for you! My weight would pull you off the ledge."

"I don't think so."

He wanted to argue further, but the caterpillar was marching toward him at a fair rate. Its bug eyes stared at him like fixed headlights. It obviously was not about to brake to a halt. He had either to take Nya's hands, or retreat back down the path.

He gambled that he was not putting both their lives in peril and leaped up to barely catch her hands in his. Their fingers linked. Then with surprising strength she pulled her body back upwards, hauling him along. "Lift your legs to clear it," she said.

He managed to draw his legs up under him, against the cliff, so that he was hunched just clear of the caterpillar. Slowly it passed beneath him, segment after segment.

He looked up. Nya's eyes were closed as she concentrated on holding him. Her breasts were pressed flat against the rock. She was doing her utmost. If her tail got tired and let go . . .

He let that thought trail into an ellipsis, not caring to complete it.

"I can't hold on much longer," she said.

That was the dreaded completion. "If you can't, then let me go," he said. "At least you can save yourself."

She didn't answer. But he could feel her body and his nudging lower as her overworked tail stretched. She wasn't fooling about her limit.

Finally the last segment of the caterpillar passed. "It's gone!" he gasped, "I'll drop down now."

"I'm slipping! Catch me!" Indeed, she was sliding down the cliff.

So he did not let go; he was already dropping. His feet touched the ledge and he sank down on it, drawing her into him upside down. They landed in a tangle, her breasts mashing his face. She was panting with her effort. He wasn't sure where the rest of her was, so he just lay there holding her tight.

"We're safe now," she said. "Thank you." Then after a pause. "You can let go now."

Oh. He released her and she drew her torso off his face. "I was afraid you'd fall," he said somewhat lamely.

"You were right. Half of me was over the edge. But you held me in place until I could wriggle back onto the path. I really appreciate that."

What could he say? So he said nothing. He knew that later, when he wasn't afraid of them falling, he would remember that moment. He only hoped she had not been aware of it.

"Of course if I had gone on over, I could have changed form and flown to safety."

Oh, again. "I forgot." So his extra effort had been unnecessary.

"There's no need to blush."

Was she teasing him? "It was awkward."

"I won't say a word to Feline."

"Thank you."

They resumed travel up the mountain.

The mountain narrowed, until the ledge was barely a nick in the slope. He could see it spiraling on up above him and on down below him. There was no longer room to walk; he had to spread himself flat, like Nya, and crawl. At least that gave the wind less body area to tug at.

It was cold; the wind carried fog, and the fog wet down the rock, and the water froze into ice. It was awful, but he kept crawling onward, though his fingers got numb. What else was there to do?

Then the worst happened: his numb fingers slipped, and his body slid over the brink and down the steep slope. "Hapless!" Nya cried. But she acted: when he came to the marginally larger ridge on the loop of the spiral just below him, the dragon thumped up against him, pushing him against the mountain, and he was able to get hold again. Then the naga formed just ahead of him. "I guess this is too tough a climb for you," she said with regret. "We'd better go back down."

"No." He resumed crawling upward.

When he got to the same place as before, he saw that the ridge had filled with ice, so that it was no longer a ridge. That explained his slip. He conjured a metal flute and used it to pound the ice, cracking it and prying it out so that the crevice was there again. Then he crawled on.

Only to slip again as his numb fingers no longer responded to his mental urging. He was back down at the next loop, getting braced again by the dragon.

The naga reappeared. "Hapless—"

"No!" He jammed on.

And fell a third time. And a fourth. He simply could no longer hold on. The day was getting late, and half the peak was in frigid shadow, but still he crawled, or tried to. It might be a useless effort, but he couldn't quit.

"Hapless—"

"No!"

"Hapless, listen to me!"

"No!"

She faced him, her forepart downward on the ledge. Then she kissed him.

There were no hearts or special effects, but the shock of it jolted him out of his fog. What could possibly be on her serpentine mind? "What?"

"I had to get your attention, so I copied Feline. Hapless, I figured out another way to help you."

"Not if it means giving up the Quest."

"You are positively oink-headed! But here it is: I'll turn dragon, and blast out the ice and warm the stone. In fact I can use the Fire Totem to heat the rock itself. I should have thought of it before. That should enable you to crawl on without falling. Just so you know what I'm doing."

Oh.

"Okay," he agreed weakly. It wasn't just his hands that had gone numb; the rest of his body was following, and his mind too.

She turned dragon, then made a strafing run. She blasted out fire, and the ice fairly steamed into the air and was quickly blown away. Then she returned to Naga state and slid ahead of him.

He advanced to that spot—and it was warm! What a blessing! "Thanks!" he gasped, and moved on, invigorated. With warm rock, there was no freezing, and his numbness was fading.

They completed two more loops. But night was hurrying in, and they still weren't close enough to the griffin's nest. Worse, the griffin came in to the nest, and spied them. He gave a screech of outrage and dived at them.

"Oh, bleep!" Nya swore. She shifted to dragon mode and launched out to intercept the griffin.

"No!" Hapless cried. The griffin was substantially larger than the dragon, and though it did not have fire, it did have those six heads. It circled the dragon, seeking an opening. Nya was doomed.

The dragon blasted out a stream of fire, but the savvy griffin dodged it and dived in while Nya was taking a new breath. He caught the dragon's torso in his front talons and held it there as the heads oriented for a lethal sextet of bites.

Music sounded, coming rapidly closer. Accordion music. Quin was catching up to them, in an awkward intermediate stage, playing his instrument as he flew.

"Squawk!" the Griffin said, and it sounded like "Bleep!" He tried to dodge out of the way, but his talons were caught on Nya's body and he couldn't get clear in time.

Quin flew right up to the caught griffin, his music louder and clearer. The griffin froze in place, mesmerized.

Then Quin crashed right into them, and the griffin disappeared. He had become the Air Totem, and Quin had hold of it.

Quin and Nya fell apart, righting themselves in air. They had made it! They had won. No thanks to Hapless, who hadn't made it to the nest in time.

Nya landed on the ledge above him and became the naga, and Quin landed below him and became the harpy. "It worked!" she said. "You brought the griffin to you! And gave Quin the magic he needed to play the enchantment."

Hapless stayed in place, realizing that it was true. He had been so focused on reaching the nest that he had forgotten that it was Quin and the griffin he needed to be close to, and the two of them had come to him. It had worked after all.

"Now let's abate this wind," Quinn said. And the wind died. He controlled it, because he possessed the Totem of Air.

After that it was relatively easy. Nya and Quin helped him slide down the mountain, catching him when he lost control, and before long they were all at the foot.

The two centaurs hailed them, and Feline pounced on Hapless, hugging him pleasantly close and kissing him. With that support he finally let go and fell into the sleep of utter fatigue.

Chapter 11

MERGE

Hapless woke with his head on Feline's lap while she stroked his hair. He could hardly imagine a nicer way to be. "Oh, Feline," he said. "You didn't need to stay up just to cushion me."

"Oh, I did, Hapless," she said. "You had quite a time. Nya told me all about it. How you got frostbit but wouldn't give up, then got the Air Griffin to attack you so Quin could catch him and get the totem. You're such a hero!"

"I'm no such thing," he protested. "I'd have fallen off the mountain if Nya hadn't helped me."

"She said you kept her from falling off herself."

He hoped Nya had kept her promise not to tell one detail of that situation. "She exaggerates. She could have turned dragon and saved herself."

"Yes. But you were too frozen to think of that. So you had the right motive."

So it seemed the naga hadn't told. "At any rate, Quin and Nya did it. They're the heroes."

"You all are." She leaned down to kiss him.

He remained uneasy. Nya hadn't told, but did that make it right? "I—there's something I have to tell you, Feline."

"Don't worry; your fingers will recover. Nya used her Totem to heat them through to the core so they wouldn't be lost. She said you just kept plowing on regardless of the pain."

"Not that. It's that when we fell, after the caterpillar passed, she, well, she fell on top of me. Her—front landed on my face."

"Her bare bosom?"

"Yes." Would she explode? Would she dump him on the ground?

"Now that's interesting."

"That it happened?"

"That you told me."

"I wanted to keep it secret, but that would have been deceiving you by omission, so that would have been a lie."

"And you couldn't lie."

"I couldn't," he agreed.

"How do you expect me to react, Hapless?"

"I don't know whether you'll be angry, mad, or furious. Whatever it is, I guess I deserve it."

"Why?"

"You don't like me looking. This was touching. That must be worse."

"Because you appreciated her curves?"

"Yes."

"More than you appreciate mine?"

How bad was this going to get? It was treacherous territory. "No. But she was bare."

"That makes a difference?"

"Yes," he said, fearing her explosion.

"Close your eyes."

Was she going to hit him? He closed his eyes, trying not to flinch.

She shifted around some, then took his head in her hands and lifted it to a new location. She pressed him firmly down. Her lap had been soft; this was softer.

Then he heard her heartbeat. She had set his head against her bared breasts! She was matching what Nya had inadvertently done, and raised the ante.

"I—" he said, overwhelmed.

"Whose curves are better?"

"Yours! And I love you for them. I wish I didn't, but I do."

"I suppose it can't be helped. Now go back to sleep; you are not yet fully recovered."

He didn't try to argue. Instead he relaxed and went back to sleep.

He woke again hours later, much improved. Feline was no longer with him; instead it was Nya keeping an eye on him. "You told her," she said when she saw that he was awake.

"I had to." Yet Feline had left him in Nya's care! That suggested that she trusted him—and Nya.

"I think she loves you."

"I think I love her too."

"You make a good couple."

"Maybe we could. But there's those other women I am fated to meet. That complicates things."

"It does," she agreed. "I have to say I hope those others don't work out."

"I hope so too."

"Are you ready to travel?"

"I think so."

"But first you need to eat." She brought him a pie. He had not realized that there were pie plants in this area.

"There aren't," she said. "Faro cased the area and brought some back."

So low-level flying was still a good deal swifter than walking. He ate the pie appreciatively; now that he was rested, he was famished.

Feline returned. "Ah, I see you're up. We should get moving. There are two more Totems to get, and they are not close by. We'll have to portage around the Regions to get to Water."

Evidently they had done some organizing while he was out of it. That was fine with him. He had not sought the burden of leadership, and exercised it only because he seemed to have no choice. "Water," he agreed.

"The day's half gone, but we can camp in Xanth proper, to the south. With luck we can avoid the region of flies."

They had been studying the map, too. "Avoid," he agreed. "Unless the path takes us that way."

"We don't plan to open the box until closer to our destination," she said seriously. "We feel more comfortable being out of the box for a while."

"So do I," he admitted. "The paths show the way, but it's not always easy."

"Not always easy at all," Feline agreed.

They set off, traveling south. Soon they came to the scintillating border and passed through it. Normal Xanth lay beyond. It was a relief to see it, after several days in the Regions.

"We'll go west around the border of Air, then north past Earth and Fire," Zed said. "That way we can be reasonably rested and fed before we tackle the Region of Water."

And the Region of the Void after that, Hapless thought. Water should not be too bad, but he dreaded the deadly mystery of the Void.

Feline cupped her ear. "What's that?"

"A child," Faro said. "Crying."

"We have to help it."

"We do."

The two of them set off at a tangent.

Hapless hesitated. "Go with them," Zed said. "We'll explore for the best route around the Regions. You can readily find us." He, Quin, and Nya moved on.

Hapless hurried after the woman and the centaur. In an instant under three moments they found the child. It was a cute five-year-old little girl with curly mouse-brown hair and hazel eyes, standing in a little-girl-sized glade and sobbing.

Feline dropped to her knees and hugged the child. "We'll help you," she said. "I'm Feline Catwoman, and this is Faro Centaur. The man in the background is Hapless. Who are you?"

"I'm Myst. I'm lost."

"Where is your mother?"

"I don't know!" Myst wailed.

There was half a pause. Then Faro filled it in before it went too far. "You don't know because you're lost, of course. We meant to ask *who* is your mother?"

"Merge." This was not completely helpful either.

"You wandered away while she was busy?" Feline asked.

"Yes."

"Tell us about it," Faro said.

"She was dousing pun virus, and I got bored, and I had this little picture in my mind of a really neat toy. So I looked for it. But I didn't find it. Instead I got lost."

Dousing pun virus? Hapless couldn't make sense of that, so he focused on the simpler part. "What neat toy?"

"A little bonger with five colored planks. And two sticks."

Hapless did some mental translation. It could be a musical instrument. "Like this?" He conjured a toy Xylophone with five colored panels.

"That's it!" Myst exclaimed happily. She picked up the two padded sticks and started bonging. She made a pretty tune. Then she paused, surprised. "It worked!"

"His instruments do," Feline said. "Hapless, you stay with Myst while we locate her mother. We'll follow her trail back." She changed to cat form, sniffed the ground, and bounded off in the direction the smell indicated the child had come from. Faro followed.

Hapless knew nothing about children. But Myst was happily playing the Xylophone again, reveling in her sudden proficiency. She didn't mind being baby-sat. Feline had left him there because if he left, the music wouldn't work any more and the child would be disappointed.

So he focused on the confusion as he sat on the ground opposite her. "What was your mother doing, Myst?"

"Dousing pun virus," the child repeated over the sound of her music.

"Maybe I'm too dull to understand that. What does dousing mean?"

"She splashes her water on."

Hapless decided to wait for an adult explanation on that. "What is your mother like?"

Myst kept on playing. "She's great! She lets me do anything I want."

Just so. "What about your father?"

"Don't have a father now."

"Uh—"

"I'm 'dopted."

Oh. "Your mother adopted you?"

"Yes. She wanted to marry, but there wasn't a man, so she 'dopted me by herself. That's fine. But I know she'd like a man, if she found the right one."

A single mother looking for a husband. That could be a dangerous combination.

Myst paused in her playing. "I like your bonger."

"It's called a xylophone."

"That's too big a name for me. Can I have it?"

"You can have it for a while. But it won't last."

"It won't?" She threatened to tear up again.

"My talent is to conjure musical instruments. But after a day they fade."

She looked really disappointed. "That's sad."

"But I can conjure another."

Sunlight reappeared. "Great!" Then she surprised him by jumping up and hugging him and kissing him on the cheek. All he could do was put his arm around her to steady her. He knew nothing about children, but he liked this one.

At that point Feline and Faro returned, with another woman. She had waist-length hair that seemed to be of several colors, and a perfect body. This must be Myst's mother—and here he was holding her daughter. It was embarrassing.

Then their glances met. The scene froze. There was a glowing line connecting them, then a flash as a coruscating red ribbon appeared to tie the two of them together. Hapless could not look away; he was locked into this link with the woman.

"It's a Love Knot!" Faro exclaimed. "They are destined for each other."

"Oh, no!" Feline moaned.

The ribbon and love knot faded. The scene resumed motion.

"Are you going to marry Mommy?" Myst asked.

He answered before his mind connected. "I don't know."

"Why not? You seem like a nice daddy to adopt."

"It's that I already have a girlfriend."

"Oh, phooey! Dump her. Mommy's better."

"I can't do that."

"Maybe it's time for introductions," Faro said. "Hapless, this is Merge. Merge, this is Hapless."

"Who is the other woman?" Merge asked grimly.

"Me," Feline said.

"Oh, bleep! We were becoming friends. You were so nice. You found my child and led me to her."

"Yes. I don't know you well, Merge, but it is already clear that you are no scheming hussy. If anyone deserves Hapless, you do."

"Don't I have a say in this?" Hapless asked.

"No," the two women said almost together.

"You got tied by the Love Knot," Faro explained. "And you already loved Feline. You have no choice. You were slated to have two good girlfriends anyway."

"And one bad one," Feline said grimly.

"And one bad one?" Merge asked.

"That's a more complicated story," Feline said. "Maybe we should make time to exchange detailed personal histories, since we're likely to be seeing more of each other, regardless of our preferences."

"Maybe we should," Merge agreed. "We hardly know each other. But please, may I ask one thing? This is new and unsettling to me and I fear for the future."

"Yes, kiss him," Feline agreed.

They already understood each other that well?

Merge walked toward Hapless, who stood up to meet her. Myst ran to hug her around the waist, then took her hand and walked back with her. "I already kissed him," the child said proudly.

Merge stepped into him, put her arms around him, drew him close, and kissed him firmly on the mouth. Little hearts radiated out. Myst caught one and hugged it to her. Hapless was overwhelmed with the wonder of it. Heaven was kissing him!

Merge stepped back, and Faro caught him before he fell. "Sit down until you acclimatize," she said.

He sat. That was indeed best.

"We are six folk on a Quest," Faro said as the others settled. "Each of us has a wish to fulfill, and we understand that if we find and control the Isis Orb, we will have our wishes granted. But it hasn't been easy. First we had to round up the Companions; I was the last. Hapless is the leader. He conjures musical instruments but can't play any; that's his wish: to find his own instrument. Now we have to catch and tame the guardians of the five Regions of Fire, Earth, Air, Water, and Void, then use them to control the Orb. But we expect the Goddess Isis, who it seems has the Orb, to make it difficult. We aren't sure that all of us will survive the Quest. We are now on our way to the Region of Water." She took a breath. "Hapless and Feline have a thing going. But we always knew that he was destined to have two good girlfriends and maybe one bad one. So it's not your fault, but it does complicate our Quest."

"Who is to be the bad girlfriend?"

"We're not sure, but we think it could be Isis herself. That would be really complicated."

"So Feline and I could both lose out to the goddess?"

"Yes."

Merge looked at Feline. "I think we had better be friends. I already know he'd be better off with you than with Isis. She has a reputation."

"I think so too," Feline said. "I'd much rather see you get him, than the goddess. But he is intrigued by the bad girl."

"Well, he's a man. Men are stupid about such things."

"Exactly."

The two smiled at each other. They were definitely on the same side.

"Now my history," Merge said. "I was originally five sisters." She shimmered and fractured into five nude young women with brown, black, red, yellow, and light blue hair. "We were all aspects of the original," Brown said. "But didn't know it," Black said. "Until folk on another Quest came," Red said. "Needing our help," Yellow said. "And enabled us to merge," Blue said. "Whereupon we became me," the reunited Merge concluded. "I possess the Urn of Pun Virus Antidote Elixir, which we use to douse the virus that is killing puns." She lifted the urn she carried, which Hapless somehow hadn't noticed until this moment. "That is what I was doing when Myst got lost. I wasn't paying proper attention to her."

"It was my fault!" Myst cried. "You told me not to wander off."

"That's why I hope to marry," Merge said. "It takes two to raise a child properly."

"How did you come to adopt Myst?" Faro asked.

"That is a story that would fill a book by itself. But greatly simplified, my friend Astrid rescued five children from the future, and then the members of our Quest adopted them. I took Myst, and I love her, but she can be a challenge."

"I sure can," Myst said proudly.

"Maybe you should demonstrate, dear," Merge said fondly.

"Sure. Say you want me to take a bath, and I don't want to. You can't even catch me."

"Oh, I think I could," Feline said, smiling.

"Try it, Aunt Feline."

Aunt Feline?

Feline walked toward the child. Myst backed off. Feline pounced, wrapping her arms about her. Myst slipped through her grasp and floated away. She had become a patch of mist!

"That's her talent," Merge said. "It's what made her hard to adopt. All the children were difficult."

Myst reformed. "See?"

"Now I see," Feline said ruefully. "But what's this about you being from the future?"

"Xanth was going to be destroyed in fifty years," Merge said. "So Astrid and Fornax brought the children back so they wouldn't perish."

"Fornax?" Faro asked. "Is that a coincidence of names?"

"No. She's the Demoness Fornax, from the antimatter galaxy. But she helped Astrid, maybe because in a way they are similar."

"Similar?"

"Well, Astrid isn't a Demoness, or even a demoness. She's a basilisk."

"A basilisk!" Faro exclaimed. "Their very look can kill!"

"Yes. So she wears dark glasses. She's really a very nice person, quite beautiful, and my friend. So is Fornax, actually." She turned to face Hapless. "I know it's too late and all, after the Love Knot, but before you marry me you have to know that in addition to the challenge of my daughter, I have some unusual friends you may not much like. You'd probably be better off with Feline."

"If I have a choice," Hapless said wryly.

"Yes. So maybe I'd better go away now and not complicate your Quest or your life."

"No!" The odd thing was that it wasn't Hapless who spoke—it was Myst. That was most interesting.

So it was Hapless's turn. "I can't let you go, Merge. I love you. But I love Feline too. I think I need time to consider."

"I don't think I could walk away anyway," Merge confessed. She turned to the child. "But dear, what is he to you? You hardly know him."

"He's got the Xylo, Xylo—bonger. I can't play it without him."

Was that really her reason? Or did she truly want a father?

"Then I think you should come with us," Feline said carefully. "So we can get to know each other better. At least until we enter the dangerous Region of Water. Would you want to do that?"

Merge closed her eyes. "I wish that when he lies down to sleep at night, you could hold his right hand and I could hold his left hand."

"You actually want to share him?"

"You had him first. I don't want to interfere with that. But I do want to be near him. So yes, sharing seems to be in order."

Feline glanced at Faro. "What do you think?"

"Given the situation, this seems fair. Merge didn't choose to love Hapless; fate decreed it."

"I'm the interloper," Feline said. "I wasn't fated. I was just there. And I'm still not sure he's right for me."

"I don't understand," Merge said.

"Feline wants to be loved for something other than her curves," Faro explained. "Hapless likes her curves."

"Well of course he does. He's a man. What else would he be interested in?"

"Her personality?"

"He's a *man*," Merge repeated. That seemed to settle it.

Actually, Hapless liked Feline's personality very well. But it was hard to separate it from her curves.

"We have to rejoin our group," Feline said. "Come walk with us, Merge."

"Can I ride the horsie?" Myst asked.

"That's a winged centaur, dear, not a horse."

"Come here, Myst," Faro said. She picked the girl up, swung her around, and set her down just forward of the wings. The child was thrilled.

"But your xylophone," Merge said, going to pick it up.

"Don't bother," Hapless said. "I'll conjure another when she wants it. They only last a day anyway."

"This interests me," Merge said. "You can conjure any musical instrument?"

"As far as I know. But I can't play any. Yet. I have to believe that there is one for me, if I can only find it."

"Have you considered singing? The voice is a musical instrument of a sort."

"Maybe that's it," Feline said. "Hapless, try conjuring a song."

This seemed crazy, but he tried.

A girl appeared. She opened her mouth and sang.

"You conjured a *person*?" Merge asked. "A singer?"

"I—I never tried that before. I didn't know it would happen."

"Who are you, child?" Feline asked the girl when she finished her song.

"I'm Monti. I'm not a child; I'm thirteen. How did I get here?"

"It seems that Hapless conjured you. He conjures musical instruments."

"Oh." The girl looked at Hapless, clearly unimpressed. "I'll be on my way." She turned to go.

"One detail, Monti," Feline said. "His conjurations last only a day. Then they go back where they came from."

"Oh, bleep!" the girl swore. "Then I'd better make the most of it." She walked away, singing.

"Life is full of surprises," Merge said.

"Do you fancy a musical instrument?" Feline inquired.

Merge laughed. "I've been too busy mopping up anti-pun virus patches to think about anything like that. Now we seem to be catching up and I can start relaxing." She pondered briefly. "Myst likes the Xylophone. Maybe that would do for me too. An adult one."

"Let's find out," Feline said. "Hapless?"

Hapless conjured a full-sized marimba on a stand. "Oh, my!" Merge said, amazed. "That's beyond all my expectations. I would be incompetent to play it."

"Try it anyway," Feline said wisely.

"If you wish." Merge picked up the sticks and tentatively touched them to the wood. A lovely pair of notes sounded. Surprised, she tried again, and soon was playing a pretty melody.

"That seems to be part of Hapless's talent," Feline said. "Anyone playing one of his instruments in his presence is gifted, but not when he's absent. He finds it most frustrating."

"I should think so. His talent seems to be designed to tease him," Merge agreed, sending him a sympathetic look. He was already in love with her, but that look would have moved him regardless.

"We'd better move on before the others double back to look for us," Faro said.

They walked on, generally westward, Feline and Merge chatting amiably. They were definitely getting along, though Hapless suspected that with women that could be deceptive.

Then there came a voice from the south. "Hallooo!"

"Oh, that's Astrid!" Merge said. "She must be worried because I didn't return to check in."

"The basilisk?" Faro asked sharply.

"Yes. But don't be concerned." Merge put her hands to her mouth and called back. "Hallooo!"

In barely over a moment and a half the other women appeared, trailed by an eleven-year-old boy. The woman did wear dark glasses. The two hugged.

Then Merge turned to introduce them to each other. "This is my dear friend Astrid, and her son Firenze. And these are Feline, Faro, and Hapless, my beloved."

"Your what?" Astrid asked. She was phenomenally shapely, an astonishing beauty.

"Oh, I should explain. These kind folk rescued Myst when she got lost. Then when I first saw Hapless, a Love Knot formed. It wasn't something we planned on; it just happened. Worse, he already has a girlfriend."

"Hello Hapless," the basilisk lady said, looking as if she wanted to remove her glasses.

"Uh, hello," he said incompetently.

"Hapless, Feline, and Faro are three members of a Quest to fulfill their wishes," Merge said. "He conjures musical instruments but can't play any himself. But he found a nice little Xylophone for Myst, and a nice big one for me. We can play them competently as long as he is near."

"He's nice, Aunt Astrid," Myst pronounced. "Maybe he'll be my new daddy."

"You like him that well?" Astrid asked.

"Sure. It's a real nice Xylo—bonger."

Astrid's mouth quirked. "That surely suffices, dear." She was a basilisk? She really seemed quite human.

Now three more figures joined the group: Zed, Nya, and Quin. This prompted another round of introductions.

"We're glad you're safe," Zed said. "We turned back because you didn't rejoin us, and we smelled a hostile dragon in the area."

As if summoned by the mention, the dragon appeared. It was monstrous, as big as their two dragon forms combined. Quin and Nya instantly transformed to intercept it.

"Wait!" Astrid said. "There is no need for violence. I will send it away."

"Dragons don't readily send," Zed said.

"Wait," Myst said, smiling. "Aunt Astrid has her way."

Astrid strode out toward the dragon. "Halt!" she cried.

The dragon, swooping down for a strafing run, was so amused by the challenge that it almost crashed. Then Astrid removed her glasses, catching it with a glancing glance. Then the dragon did crash.

Stunned by the glance, the dragon picked itself up and crawled away. It had learned about basilisks.

"It didn't die," Hapless said.

Astrid put her glasses back on and turned to him. "I looked at it with my peripheral vision, so it was jolted but not killed. I thought a warning would suffice."

"It did," Hapless said, impressed not only by her power but her discretion. She was, as Merge had said, a nice person.

"Aunt Astrid was honored by all the cele, celeb—important folk," Myst said. "They all came and ap, appl—clapped. Even princesses. Even Demons."

"No need to mention that, dear," Astrid said modestly. "It was nothing, really."

"Only saving five children, and Xanth," Myst said, hugging her.

"I heard of that," Zed said. "That was you?"

"That was her," Myst said before Astrid could demur. "We all love her."

Hapless looked at Merge, who nodded.

"Did you find the virus?" Astrid asked Myst, changing the subject.

"Oh, sure. I forgot. It's just up ahead."

"The virus?" Zed asked.

"Myst can sense the virus in the air, when she vaporizes," Merge explained. "It's very helpful. That's why we are in this area; some patches remain." They walked toward the area.

"I remember when the virus came," Zed said. "We centaurs aren't too partial to puns, but when they were suddenly gone, we missed them. Xanth is largely made of puns."

"We have been eradicating the virus," Merge said. "And restocking puns from the storage vault of Caprice Castle. It's a dirty job, but someone has to do it."

"There!" Myst cried, pointing. There was a line of something like fire, but instead of burning foliage it was turning puns into glop.

"Oh, it's spreading!" Merge said. "I will have to fragment." She split into her five component selves.

"I'll help," Feline said. "Just tell me how."

"Take my urn," the closest fragment said. This was Blue, with the long blue hair. "I'll get another." The urn, like the person, had become five. It seemed that it, unlike the clothing, was part of the magic.

Hapless had been too distracted by the lovely nude forms to think of helping. Now he did. "I—"

"Take mine," Red said, handing him her red urn with a smile. She was just as pretty as Merge, but he discovered that he was not smitten with her despite her tantalizing nudity. She was incomplete; it was the full person he loved.

"How—"

"Just pour it on any area where the virus is operating. The elixir will do the rest." Red moved on with a swirl of her flowing hair.

Hapless went to the line of change. A pretty round stone was just dissolving into slush. It was a pomegranite, a plant that fruited granite rock. He quickly poured elixir, too late to save the stone, but in time for the foot stool made of feet next to it. He felt a sense of accomplishment: he had saved a pun. Two puns: next to it was a pomegranate that was a small palm too, Palm of Granite, the sweet-tasting food for sculptors. He had also stopped the advance of the virus; the seeming fire no longer burned where the elixir had doused the ground.

Meanwhile the others were similarly busy. Feline managed to throw a wash of elixir in the air, saving several passing thoughts. They moved on, offering fleeting notions that could not quite be caught. One brushed by Hapless, and he did catch it: it consisted of numbered speech balloons. It was the Thought that Counts.

Zed, who admitted to not much liking puns, had just saved a mushroom: a room filled with mush. Had he not done so, there would have been no more room, just rotting mush. Faro saved a patch of Kumquats and Goquats that would force folk who ate them to compulsively come and go. Quin saved an outhouse, a cousin of the toilet tree, part of the family of waste treatment plants. That really stank! Nya just missed saving a Frayed Knot, unfortunately.

Then Hapless thought that Blue was before him, but instead it was a Blueberry Blonde, being pursued by the virus. He doused her with elixir, saving her from a fate worse than death: rotting glop.

Then suddenly it was done: they had wiped out the patch of virus, saving half a slew of puns. Now they all understood what Merge's business was. The five iterations approached each other, their hair twined together, and they merged headfirst into Merge. "Thank you!" she said. "That was a bad one. Had we not caught it in time it could have spread into the whole area and left it desolate."

"And thank you, Myst, for catching it," Astrid said to the child. "Are there any more patches in this region?"

"No. This is the last one."

"Then Firenze and I will rejoin the others." Astrid and the boy walked back the way they had come.

"I should go with them," Merge said wistfully.

"You can't," Feline said. "We're still getting to know each other."

Hapless remained privately surprised that they were getting along so well. It seemed that Merge was not the jealous type. Feline was that type, but apparently accepted Merge as part of fate. Maybe she was glad that the second girlfriend was not a cheap hussy. Far, far from it!

"That must be it," Feline agreed. It was unsettling the way she understood his unvoiced thoughts. Almost as unsettling as his knowledge that eventually he would have to choose between them. He truly dreaded that.

"You should," Feline said darkly.

"That was a workout," Zed said. "Let's rest."

They all settled on the ground. Hapless lay on his back. Two hands took his: Feline on one side, Merge on the other. That felt wonderful, but it also intensified his dilemma: how could he ever pick one over the other? He loved them both.

"Not until we deal with the bad girlfriend," Feline said.

"And suppose I can't resist the bad girlfriend?"

"We'll help you do that," Merge said.

And suppose the bad girl was a goddess?

"Maybe Aunt Fornax will help," Myst said, plumping down on his feet. Could she read his mind too?

"Demoness Fornax can't intervene in Xanthly affairs, dear," Merge said. "Remember all the trouble she had to let us get into, because the other Demons would have squelched her if she helped?"

"Um, yes," Myst agreed. Evidently it was a powerful memory, because she fuzzed into mist for a moment.

There was surely another interesting story there, but Hapless decided to let it be. At least it clarified that they remained largely on their own.

In due course, having discarded several undue courses, they resumed travel. They turned north and walked west of the Regions.

They reached the Region of Water by evening. They could tell because the boundary curtain looked like shimmering water. "I think this is it," Hapless said.

"But the day is late," Feline said. "We should wait until morning."

No one questioned this. If Feline wanted Merge and Myst to remain with the party a little longer, she surely had her reasons. Hapless would have thought that Feline would want to get rid of Merge as soon as possible, but he already knew he had little if any understanding of the motives of women. So they made camp, foraged for supper, then washed in the water curtain. Hapless tried not to stare as Feline, Merge, and Myst stripped naked and used it as a shower.

"Oh, go ahead and look," Feline called to him. "Chances are you'll wind up with one or more of us."

So he looked. Feline had luscious curves, yes, but Merge matched them; they were two outstandingly beautiful women. Whichever one he wound up with, it would not be just for her curves.

"I'm going to look like that when I grow up," Myst said, returning wrapped in her towel.

"Which one?" he asked, dazed.

"I haven't decided yet."

They finished. "Your turn," Feline said.

Strip naked in front of them? "Uh—"

"You looked at us. Now we look at you."

He was stuck for it. He took off his clothes and showered, and they did look. "Men aren't as interesting as women," Myst concluded diplomatically.

The two centaurs stood a bit apart, as usual. The two dragons lay another bit apart. That left Hapless with two women and a child. They settled down under a blanket, all still bare. Feline took his right hand, Merge took his left hand, and Myst held on to a foot. He couldn't do anything except lie there. Regardless, it was a suburb of Heaven.

In the morning they organized for the next stage of the Quest. Merge and Myst hugged Hapless and kissed him tearfully. Then they did the same with Feline, whom the child addressed as Aunt.

It was time. They gathered around, and Hapless opened the box.

Chapter 12

WATER GORGON

The picture was of a lovely mermaid with snaky locks of hair. The words were WATER TOTEM.

"Uh-oh," Feline said, looking over Hapless's shoulder.

"What?"

"That's a gorgon."

"Uh-oh," he echoed weakly as he saw that the locks were not snaky, but actual little snakes.

"I'm supposed to tame that?"

Feline was the one designated to go for the Water Totem. He shared her dismay. "There must be a way."

"We should pause to consider before we take that path," Zed said. For the path now ran from the box directly to the water curtain.

They paused to consider. "Do I understand this correctly?" Merge asked. "You have to try to conquer a gorgon?"

"I'm designated for Water, yes," Feline agreed grimly.

Myst burst into tears.

"You really care about me, Myst?" Feline asked, surprised and touched.

"Yes, Aunt Feline."

"Even though I might take Hapless away from your mother?"

"No, you will share him."

They would share him? As they had holding his hands at night? How far would that go? That seemed fraught with mischief, but also insidiously tempting. Hapless decided to stay out of this dialogue.

Feline looked at Merge. "How do you feel about this?"

"Hapless cares about you, so I do, too. I don't want anything bad to happen to you. You're a nice person I want to keep as a friend, regardless whom Hapless chooses."

"But if I—"

"He will still be in good hands."

Feline considered. "I still don't know how I feel about Hapless. But I know I do want you for a friend."

Then the two women were hugging and crying together.

Hapless looked at Myst. "It's a female thing," she explained. "We cry when we get emotional."

The other Companions were studiously neutral. This was his picklement.

"And you too, Myst," Feline said over Merge's shoulder.

The child joined them, hugging and crying.

After a suitable interval, Feline drew apart. "Let's go get that Totem," she said briskly.

They got on the path. Hapless was last, of course. He turned to face Merge and Myst once more, to make some evocative parting statement. "I, uh," he said with his accustomed flair.

"We'll check right here every day," Merge said tearfully. "At noon. Until you return."

"Uh, yes." He followed the others. He couldn't help wondering whatever the two women and the child saw in him. He suspected the other Companions were as mystified as he was.

The path led through the porous shower curtain. Suddenly they were in a completely different scene, on the edge of a broad placid lake.

"We'd better mark the spot," Feline said. "So we can find them." She changed to cat form and dug in the ground, throwing up a mound of dirt.

"Uh, yes," Hapless said again. He had not thought of that. In fact, taken as a whole, he was feeling wonderfully inept.

Feline returned to human form. "A boyfriend is just a boyfriend, but a woman friend is forever."

"But what if I marry Merge?"

"I may be mad at you, but still friends with her. But right now we need to focus on that gorgon, or it will all become academic."

"Maybe there are local residents who will know something about her," Zed said. "That could help."

Indeed, the path led to a small village. The houses were made of shimmering sheets of water. The path took them to one door. The sign said SEEP INN.

A shapely young woman with a kerchief and dark glasses stood outside the door. Her complexion was pleasantly green. "Are you folk looking for lodging?" she asked. "I have fine waterbeds, and I serve water rolls for breakfast and water chestnuts for dinner. We have fine water logs for the fire."

"There's fire in the Region of Water?" Hapless asked.

"Well of course. We are not savages. The fact that this is the Region of Water does not mean that other elements are excluded; they are merely muted."

"I think you lost a letter from your sign," Feline said. "Shouldn't it be Sleep Inn?"

"The sign is fine. When the lake rises and floods the village, the water seeps in. We like it that way."

"We are actually looking for information," Zed said. "We are on a Quest, and won't be staying long."

"A Quest? I took you for tourists." The woman smiled. Her teeth were greenish too. "I am Colorado."

"I thought that was a region in Mundania," Zed said.

"No. It's my nature. Color-ado."

"Uh—" Hapless said.

"I change color with the temperature. When it's cold I turn blue. When it's hot I'm red. When the sun's too bright I turn yellow. At the moment I am comfortable."

"That's fascinating," Zed said. "My colors are unfortunately fixed."

"I noticed," Colorado said, smiling again. Hapless noticed that she tended to smile more when addressing a male. She was an intensely attractive woman. He seemed to be encountering a number of those on this Quest.

"We need to find the gorgon," Feline said with a bit of an edge.

Colorado froze for a long instant, then recovered. "This is not wise. Carmen is not friendly to women."

The gorgon had a name? Well, why not.

"She is friendly to men?" Feline asked.

"In her fashion. She gets lonely at times because few folk seek her company. So on occasion she takes a boyfriend. That's not good."

"But doesn't her mere look turn folk to stone?" Hapless asked.

"Not exactly. First, a person has to meet her gaze directly. Just seeing her, or she seeing you, has no effect. But a shared glance is deadly. So many of us here wear protective glasses, just in case." She touched her own. "Second, it's not stone, it's water. She's a water gorgon, and her direct look turns a person to water, which collapses in a puddle and flows away. That's why she's not popular."

"I learned that once a gorgon married the Good Magician," Zed said. "They teach such things in centaur school. She donned a mask to stop from turning folk into statues."

"And we know of a basilisk in human form," Nya said. "She wears dark glasses to stop from killing people."

"Yes. There are three gorgons, with different modes of killing," Colorado agreed. "Carmen dons dark glasses when she goes after a man, otherwise she would merely liquidate him. But it's still not good. She plays with him for a month or three, then tires of him and washes him out. All our men know that if Carmen loves you, that's the end of you."

"Then why would any man, er, date her?" Zed asked. "Knowing that it's the end of him?"

"She has most effective curves, if you like that type," Colorado said. "Women don't see much magic in them, but men are instantly fascinated. Especially when she converts her tail and makes legs. When she dons panties, a man is helpless. It's too bad. We'd rather be rid of her; there are not many men left in our village of Waterloo, and fewer yet moving in. They've heard about the gorgon."

"A man would have to be a fool to go with her," Feline agreed. "Yet many men are fools."

"It does come with the territory," Colorado said. "They see those curves, and what little minds they have are gone."

Feline nodded thoughtfully. She of course had her own curve issues. "Nevertheless, we need to get to the gorgon," she said. "Dangerous as she may be."

"Well, she is the Guardian of the Region," Colorado said. "If you try to mess with the water, she'll seek you out quickly enough. I don't recommend it."

"Our Quest requires it, unfortunately."

"Then move your party far away from here, lest the gorgon makes waves."

"Waves?"

"Big ones can wash away whole villages. If she gets angry."

"We'll go far from here," Feline agreed.

"Please do." Colorado looked plainly worried.

The path led on along the shore, having gotten them the information they needed. The two dragons flew lazily overhead, the two centaurs walked, and Hapless and Feline trailed, so as to keep the path clear for the others.

A young man was walking the opposite way. "Hello," he said, plainly impressed by Faro. He was bright blue all over.

"Hello," she responded as if not noticing the direction of his gaze. "Are you all right? You seem blue."

"I was foraging for supplies for the Inn, but a rascally bird dropped an ice water bomb on me. Now I'm freezing cold." Indeed, his teeth were chattering.

"Blue with cold?" Feline asked as she and Hapless caught up. "Are you like Colorado?"

"I *am* Colorado," he said.

There was half a pause. "We just talked with a woman by that name at the Inn," Feline said. "Your sister?"

"I have no sister. I run the Inn. I have no idea whom you encountered."

"Let's warm you up," Feline said, signaling Nya to come down. The dragon did, converting to her naga form, which seemed to impress the young man just as much as Faro did, perhaps for the same reason. "Colorado needs warming," she said.

Nya held her Totem and focused on the man. He changed rapidly from blue to green. "Oh, that's better," he said.

"So someone is impersonating you at the Inn?" Faro asked.

"Must be," Colorado agreed. "I can't think who or why. Can you describe her?"

"She wore a kerchief, dark glasses, and was extremely shapely," Feline said. "Do you know anyone of that description?"

He laughed. "I wish I did!" Then he reconsidered, paling visibly. "Unless—"

"Unless?"

"No, that's impossible. It must be someone playing a prank. I'd better get home and put a stop to it." He hurried on.

"That was curious," Faro said. "He must have thought of someone."

"And didn't want to identify her," Feline said.

"We shouldn't let the concerns of other folk distract us from our Quest," Zed said.

"If the path leads us to the gorgon, can we safely follow it?" Feline asked Hapless. "I mean, if she sees us coming we'll be helpless, because we won't be able to look at her, and she'll be able to attack us with a wave or worse."

"Maybe we should pretend to have no idea how to find her," Hapless said. "So she doesn't see us coming. Does that make sense?"

"Not a lot. But it's better than nothing."

Nya reverted to dragon mode and rejoined Quin in the sky. The centaurs, Feline, and Hapless resumed their walk along the shoreline.

They came to an isolated shack by the shore with a rickety fishing boat tied up beside it. "Maybe there," he said.

The others passed on by the shack, but Hapless and Feline paused to knock on its warped door. In barely one moment it opened to reveal yet another surprisingly well-formed woman wearing a heavy kerchief, dark glasses, a short skirt, and a light halter. "Yes?"

"Uh, we are travelers looking for the gorgon," Hapless said, fighting off the distraction of the well-filled halter. The woman seemed somehow familiar. "Could you direct us?"

"You're looking for the gorgon?" the woman demanded, amazed. "She's dangerous. Everyone knows that."

How much should he say? Lying was not in his nature, but neither did it seem smart to advertise their mission.

Feline stepped in, knowing his limitation. She could lie when she needed to. "We want to interview her for a special project."

The woman turned to Feline. "And you are?"

"Feline. I'm a cat woman." She changed briefly. "And this is Hapless. He's on a Quest to discover a musical instrument he can play." She grimaced. "So far everything he has tried is awful."

Hapless found her technique interesting. She was lying by indirection. What she said was true, but it was a diversion from the reason they wanted to find the gorgon.

"Maybe he should try the foghorn," the woman said with a third of a smile.

Something about her dismissal of his ability annoyed Hapless. So he did what he knew better than to do: he conjured a foghorn and blew it. POOOO-POO! The noisome sound smelled like conjugated poop. Worse was the fog that poured out of it, filling the area with its putrid stench.

"As I said, awful," Feline said with the other two thirds of the smile after the three of them had finished coughing and the air cleared.

"So I see," the woman agreed. "I am impressed." Her gaze returned to Hapless with a certain guarded appreciation. "May I try it?"

He handed the foghorn to her. She put it to her mouth and blew. This time it made a loud, deep, melodious sound, as of a wind blowing across a scenic waterfall, and the fog didn't smell.

"Exactly," Feline said. "Everyone else can play them, but not him."

"Perhaps a water drum," the woman suggested. "Or the water bowls. Can you conjure those?"

"Sure." Hapless conjured the water drum, which was a large half gourd shell filled with water, with a small gourd floating in it, tapped with the fingers to make the sound. Then the bowls, which were several open glassy bowls filled with water to different levels. When the woman leaned forward to tap their rims with bamboo sticks, they made different notes.

"I never played these so well before," the woman said.

"That seems to be part of his talent," Feline said. "Other folk play the instruments he conjures very well. Isn't that true, Hapless?"

Hapless remained frozen.

Feline snapped her fingers at his ear, bringing him out of it. He had freaked out when he saw down inside the woman's marvelously shapely halter. "Uh, yes," he agreed belatedly.

"You intrigue me," the woman said. "You have nice magic. I may have a use for it, between bouts of ellipses."

"Uh—"

"Bouts of what?" Feline asked in a deceptively neutral tone.

"You heard me, catnip. The Adult Conspiracy censors out the details, leaving only suggestively trailing fragments."

"We're not interested in that."

Actually Hapless was interested. What did this shapely creature have in mind?

Instead of responding to Feline, the woman faced Hapless. "Let me show you the surf."

"Uh—"

"We're just looking for the gorgon," Feline said sharply. "We don't need to see the sights." Hapless wasn't sure which sights she meant. He had become to a degree acclimatized to the bare breasts of some of the Companions, but that halter was potent.

The woman pointedly ignored her. "Just let me put on my water moccasins," she said, lifting one foot high to set it on a bench so she could put on the slipper. Her short skirt slid back along her thigh, heading for neverland.

Hapless knew what was coming. She was going to freak him out with her panties. Feline wouldn't like that. He started to jerk his eyes away— and saw a faint glitter touching her heel.

He recognized that glitter. It was the path. It led to the woman's feet.

This was Carmen, the gorgon. The path had looped around, as it sometimes did, touching itself without being complete. Carmen must have seen them coming and set herself up to intercept them. She intended to make him her boy toy for a month or three before discarding him. Feline didn't know it, so he couldn't conjure her kit and have her fascinate the gorgon; by the time he explained, they would both be washed out. Or he would be in a freak-out trance and Feline would be water.

They needed to get out of here. Now.

"What did you say your interest in the gorgon was?" Carmen asked Hapless, as if to distract him from what she was doing.

Despite his realization of their imminent peril, the sight of that exposed thigh was messing with his mind. It made him speak more freely than was wise. "We need her for our Quest. We need her to be a Totem."

"A Totem! Never!"

Hapless made a supreme effort. He tore his gaze away from those luscious legs just before the panty showed, and lurched against Feline. "Go!"

"What?" she asked, annoyedly confused.

He grabbed her about the shoulders and shoved her away from the house. "Away!"

"Hapless, what are you doing?"

"It's Carmen!"

Now she recognized the name. "The gorgon? This is mischief."

"So you caught on," the gorgon said, removing her dark glasses. "That's too bad. Now I'll have to treat you unkindly." She pulled off her kerchief, and the uncovered snakes hissed in unison. "I will make a wave."

They ran from the house. Hapless saw Zed and Faro waiting for them a short distance ahead. "Get out of here!" Hapless yelled. "It's the gorgon!"

But the centaurs ran the wrong way, back toward Hapless and Feline. Before he could protest they caught up, and Zed swung Hapless onto Faro's back. Feline turned cat and jumped onto Zed's back. Then both centaurs galloped madly away from the house, not looking back. They knew what was what.

"No you don't!" the gorgon cried. Suddenly a wave was forming in the water, rising higher as it rushed for the shore. The gorgon was the guardian of water; she could make it respond to her command. It was clear that it would crash on the shore and wipe them out.

"You go ahead," Faro called to Zed. "She's after Hapless."

Zed nodded, then increased his speed. He was very fast when he put his mind to it, thanks to his zebra heritage. The wave might not catch him before he got out of its range. Faro didn't race; instead she spread her wings and leaped into the air. "Guide me!" she told Hapless, closing her eyes.

"Turn right," he said. "Climb."

She did so, and in about 2.1 moments was sailing over the incoming wave, barely skimming over its hump. The water beyond was calm; they had escaped the trap.

"What happened?" Faro asked as they glided on, more relaxed.

"We stopped to ask directions from a pretty woman," Hapless said. "Only she turned out to be the gorgon in disguise. She liked my talent, and was going to freak me out and make me her boy toy. But we ran."

"And there wasn't time for Feline to enchant her with violin music," Faro concluded.

"That's it. Had we but known, we could have been prepared, and Totemed her right then."

"Ever thus," Faro agreed. "It seems to me that gorgon is dangerously canny."

"Yes, this may be more of a challenge than we thought."

Hapless saw Zed and Feline on the sand safely beyond the wave. The dragons were gliding down to join them. He directed Faro, and they landed close by. "I knew you could get me there," Faro said. "I trust you."

"You fly beautifully when you are blind," he agreed.

They walked and slithered as a group, discussing what had happened. "I wonder what Colorado thought of?" Hapless asked.

"I believe I can answer that," Zed said. "He thought of the gorgon."

"The gorgon?"

"She was impersonating him, to talk with us anonymously, as it were," the centaur said. "She wanted to know what we were up to, and we told her."

"But she said she was Colorado!"

"She lied. Did you ever see her actually change color?"

Hapless realized that it was true. The woman had described the condition, but not actually performed it. He remembered the kerchief that would have covered her snakes. "We could have nabbed her!"

"The box led us right to her," Feline said. "And we let her get away."

"We did not think outside the box," Hapless agreed. "We just assumed the gorgon was far away."

"Then it led us to her again," Feline said. "And she fooled us again."

"And now she knows all she needs to about us," Hapless said. "And what we want to do to her."

"We'll never catch her after this," Feline said. "She'll wipe us all out if we ever get near her again."

"There is an aspect," Faro said thoughtfully. "Didn't you say she was playing up to Hapless?"

"She bent low to freak him with her halter," Feline said indignantly. "Then she was going to flash her panties. She was going to stun him long enough to wash me out, so she could have him all to herself."

"Could she be the bad girlfriend?"

That made them all pause a good three quarters of a moment. "Oh, no!" Feline breathed. "Carmen could love him for a while, and it would be the end of him."

"Literally," Faro agreed. "That seems to be a feasible definition of a bad girlfriend."

"So there's the answer," Faro said.

The others looked at her blankly. "Isn't that the problem, rather than the answer?" Zed asked.

"The problem is avoiding her gaze," Faro said. "The solution is making her jealous. She's getting a thing for Hapless. That makes her vulnerable. She won't want to wash him out yet. So she'll keep her specs on."

"But he can't just go to her," Feline protested. "Even if she wants to play with him a while before washing him out, it will ruin the Quest."

"He won't go to her. She will come to him."

"I'm still not seeing this," Feline said.

Faro spelled it out. "You will go with Hapless to a place near Carmen, to be sure she can overhear you and perhaps see you," Faro said carefully. "The path will show you where. You will play up to him in an obvious effort to seduce him. She will have to act to prevent that, because she doesn't want a used man, she wants a fresh one. She's an imperious creature; you know the type. She will be furious that you are interfering with her target. Common sense will dissipate, leaving blind outrage. When she charges foolishly in, concentrating her deadly gaze on you, you will greet her with your music. That will be the end of her."

Feline nodded, seeing it at last. "Something about your reasoning appeals to me."

"I thought it might."

"The rest of us will keep our distance," Zed said. "This is your challenge, Feline."

"It is indeed," Feline agreed.

They moved on until they found a suitable campsite. The others set about foraging for pies, blankets, and milk pods, while Nya in naga form quietly slithered along beside the path ahead, out of sight. Naga were very good at slithering unobserved, especially in the dark, and if she got caught she could use her Fire Totem to make a distraction and escape.

In due course Nya returned. "She has a secluded beach she uses to entertain men," she reported. "It is stocked with food and things men like, such as swords, cans of beer, and pictures of nude women. Between bouts of whatever, she retires to a deep neighboring pool where she can rest while keeping an eye or two on the men. They can't see her in the pool, but she sees them via her snakes peeking just over the surface. It seems the men are mostly so befuddled by the mere thought of being with her that they don't even try to escape. But when they do try, she quickly washes them out."

"She certainly knows how to handle men," Feline said almost approvingly.

"In the morning, follow the path to that beach," Nya said. "She will be in the pool beyond, resting. Pretend not to know she is there; you are merely looking for a private place to play with Hapless. Then strike when she emerges from the pool and comes at you."

"Strike?" Hapless asked, as slow on the uptake as usual.

"Conjure Feline's violin. Give it to her. Close your eyes, both of you; you must not look at the gorgon. Chances are she won't recognize the significance of the music until too late."

"But what if she does recognize it?" Hapless asked.

"Then you are lost. It's a calculated risk."

"I'm not sure I—"

"We'll take it," Feline said.

"I don't know," Hapless said as he lay with Feline under their blanket. "This seems awfully risky."

"Just play your part," she said. "You know you have to be in the scene so that my music will be competent."

"Still, if our timing is at all off—"

She kissed his ear, pleasantly delivering a quarter stun. "Then I might succeed in seducing you before she arrives. Would that be such a horror?"

"But—but—what about Merge?"

"She will surely have her turn."

"Are you teasing me?"

"Hapless, I have not yet begun to tease you," she said, taking his hand and putting it somewhere on her body that was remarkably soft yet firm. That freaked him out, and he disappeared into a pleasant slumber.

ooOOoo

He woke in darkness. Feline lay beside him, softly sleeping, his hand still on her bare bottom. He loved the way she trusted him. In fact, he loved *her*. If only he could be sure that it was something other than her curves that compelled him. And what about Merge, and little Myst? He loved them too. How could he be so emotionally jumbled?

But that wasn't what had awakened him. There was an eerie yet compelling sound.

ooOOoo

What was it? It was coming from the lake. He had to find out its source. He carefully crawled out from under the blanket, naked—had Feline removed his shorts? What a tease she was!—and made his way to the shore.

ooOOoo

It was clearer now, coming from the water. There was a figure there, a shape in the shallow surf, illuminated by the moonlight. A female face, magnificent breasts, a slender torso. She switched her flukes, moving toward him. It was a mermaid.

Then he saw the snakes on her head. It was the gorgon, in her natural state! Just like the picture in the box. "You!"

"We gorgons are distantly related to the sirens. We can issue the call when we choose to. Only our target can hear it."

"That ooOOoo?" Only when he tried to emulate it, it sounded more like OOooOO, horribly atonal.

"Come to me, Hapless," she said. "I promise I won't molest you or wash you out. I just want to talk."

He might be crazy, but he trusted her. "I am coming to you, Carmen." He waded into the water.

"Moonlight is too weak for my power to work," she said. "You can safely look me in the face."

He reached her, and looked into her eyes. They were like bottomless pools, drawing him in.

She kissed him. He clasped her in the water. She was all woman above, no woman below. "I promised not to molest you," she said. "As you can feel, it's impossible when I'm in this form."

"Impossible," he agreed faintly.

"It requires a liquid hour to convert my tail to legs, and another hour to change back, so I don't do it casually. But I will do it for you if you truly want it."

"Uh, I wouldn't put you to that trouble." Because he suspected that if she made legs and he got between them, he might never get free of her.

"This way." She swam out into deep water.

"Uh, I'm not sure how far I can swim. I'm not good at that either."

"I'll tow you. Relax." She swung an arm around his neck, drew his head close against her left breast facing up, and swam backstroke, hauling him along with ease. Her powerful flukes propelled them so rapidly they left a dark wake in the water. He might have been alarmed, but the support of her breast pacified him and he was at ease.

Soon they came to a moonlit islet in the lake. They sat in the shallow surf, facing each other. She was absolutely lovely; even her snakes formed esthetic curls around her face.

"Uh, what—" he asked, exerting his penchant for sparkling dialogue.

"There's something about you, Hapless. I want to be your girlfriend."

His girlfriend! "What, because of my nonexistent musical ability?"

"Actually it is a formidable talent, conjuring musical instruments and enabling others to play them. I felt its power when I played the water bowls. But it's more than that."

"It can't be my masculine appeal. I'm not good at anything."

"True. But you are a virgin. That's rare in a man, and has considerable appeal to an experienced female like me. I'd dearly like to be your first intimate experience. But it's more than that, too."

She could tell that he'd never made it with a woman? "Uh, more?"

"Yes. It relates to your personality."

"My gumption?"

"Yes. There is some way that you are almost unique among men. I would revel in your continued company, and treat you very well. I am centuries lonely for the association of a man I could respect. All the considerable resources of the water realm could be yours. For example, I could enable you to breathe water so that you could explore the deepest seas without drowning. If you will only be mine."

She was serious? The idea was wickedly tempting, and not just because of the evocative breast she had provided for a pillow. "I am fated to have two good girlfriends and one bad girlfriend. You must be the bad one." Maybe that would turn her off.

"I must be," she agreed. "Though I am not a bad person, Hapless. I don't wash out anyone without reason. I protect the Region of Water from pollution and exploitation. It's a worthy calling."

Indeed, it seemed so. But there was that in him that could not accept it. "We are here to capture you and render you into the Water Totem, that we need to complete our Quest."

"I thought it might be something like that. That's why I changed and intercepted you, the moment your party entered my realm. But I'm not interested in being your Totem; it would interrupt my lifestyle."

"Well, that's the way it is. I must complete my Quest."

"You will not be moved?"

"Yes, I won't." Would that cause her to wash him out immediately?

"Even if I put on my legs and wrap them around you?"

She would do that? He'd be doomed. But still he resisted. "Yes. You could seduce me, but you couldn't divert me from my quest."

"Oh, you are so infernally desirable when you are determined to do what you believe is the right thing. I do want to win you for my own."

"No." Though his passion was crying yes!

She sighed. "So it seems we must be opponents. Very well. I will return you safely to your camp, as I regard this session as a de facto truce. But thereafter it will be war."

Bleep. He hated the thought, quite apart from its deadly danger. "War," he agreed.

"I will give you a day or three to reconsider, and welcome you to my embrace if you do. But do not try to approach me if you mean to Totem me. I think this is fair warning."

"Fair warning," he echoed. Why couldn't he just accept her wonderful offer and embrace her in love? But he couldn't; it would be betraying his Quest. Not to mention Feline and Merge.

"Time to return," she said. She put him against her breast again and towed him back across the lake. If this was intended to remind him of what she offered, it was effective; he was completely reminded.

She kissed him again and turned him loose in the shallows. "Oh—here is a trinket to remember me by. It will tell me where you are. If you decide you want no part of me, above or below, ever, simply throw it away." She removed a clear gem-like stone from her ear and touched it to his ear. It took hold, and it was cold; he realized it was ice, but it was pleasant rather than painful. It did not melt.

She kissed him a third time. Then she was gone. She had made her case.

He returned to the blanket where Feline still slept; he hadn't actually been gone long. He set his hand back where she had left it, and sank back into sleep. He didn't wake until morning. He was back in his shorts; had they ever been off?

When Feline stirred, waking him, he knew he had to tell her. "Uh—"

"Uh?" she repeated as she sat up. "Are you trying to be communicative?"

"I saw the gorgon in the night. Her song summoned me. She said she wanted me for a boyfriend."

"Oh, you dreamed it! I suppose she does have some curves that might appeal to a sleeping man."

Had he dreamed it? "Uh—"

"What's that on your ear?"

He remembered. There was the confirmation. "She gave me an ice gem to remember her by. She said to throw it away if I completely rejected her."

"And will you throw it away?" Her voice was deadly neutral.

He considered, and realized that he couldn't. "No." And waited for the storm to break.

"So it's like that. The bad girlfriend. Indeed, it is past time for me to deal with her. I'd better stop pussyfooting."

He had escaped the storm. For now.

After the morning ablutions, and his explanation to the others about the ice gem, the two of them followed the path on around the lake. Then it deviated, picking its way through a thicket of water rushes to a narrow pass between misty mountains to a private valley with a smaller pond. There it was: the perfect spot for seduction.

What made him nervous was that he knew that Carmen the Gorgon was nearby, surely in the pool beyond, and watching. But they had to pretend they didn't know. That it was coincidence they had come here at this time.

"It's lovely," Hapless said, speaking a line they had rehearsed. "But what is here that you wanted to show me?"

"Put on your blindfold."

He put on the bandanna he had brought. Its thin material covered his eyes without blinding him; he could see fuzzily through. "Now what?"

"This," Feline said, removing her shirt.

He stared. It was the first time he had seen her bare top when she wasn't washing. Her curves were phenomenal. He would have freaked out without the protective bandanna. "Uh, that's really something. But you could have shown me back at the camp."

"Yes. But others would be watching. I couldn't do this." She took his right hand and made it stroke her front. That would have freaked him out, but for the translucent thin gloves he wore for this occasion.

"Oh, Feline!" he said. "What are you doing?"

"I am seducing you. Before anyone else gets you, like that lady dog gorgon. Now get your clothes off."

"But Feline!"

"Do I have to do it for you?" She started removing his shirt.

"That's more than enough!" It was the gorgon's voice. She was striding out of the water in wet natural splendor, having evidently rendered her tail into legs during the night. She was in fighting trim, with no bluffing concerning her ability to seduce him. Her hair snakes were rampant. She was not about to let another woman steal his precious virginity.

"It's the gorgon!" Feline cried. "O, woe is us!"

"No, woe is *you*, cattail," the gorgon said, coming up to them. "Him I'm saving for ultimate pleasure. You thought you could poach on my territory? Look at me, strumpet!"

"Now!" Feline hissed, averting her gaze.

Hapless belatedly remembered. He conjured her kit and handed it to her.

"Get away from her," Carmen snapped. "I've got better things for you than she does."

"No!" Hapless exclaimed, turning away as if to escape. "I'll—I'll toss the ice!" He reached for his ear.

Carmen tackled him. They fell to the sand together. "Feel this!" she said, grabbing his hand and hauling it to her body. He knew she was about to freak him out with a panty touch. If she had panties on. He could not resist her. She meant to get him out of the fray and captive so she could deal with Feline directly.

Then the music started. Feline was playing her little violin with all the skill his presence bequeathed.

He felt the gorgon freeze, transfixed by the music. He was able to crawl out from under her touch. He did not look at her. "Oh, bleep!" she swore helplessly. "In my rage I forgot about that detail."

The music continued, getting louder as Feline closed on the mesmerized gorgon. Then suddenly the gorgon was gone. In her place was the Water Totem, in the mermaid form.

"Gotcha." Feline said with immense satisfaction, picking up the Totem.

"I guess the seduction is over?" Hapless asked, trying to make a joke of it. That didn't work.

"Do you want it to be?" Feline asked.

"I, uh—"

"That's what I thought. Well played, Hapless; it almost seemed as if you wanted it."

It had been an act, yes, to lure the gorgon in, but he *had* wanted it. He had somehow fumbled it away, as usual. Now he had lost his chance with both Carmen and Feline. He felt a dark depression coming on.

She put a soft hand on his shoulder. "Yes, I am teasing you, Hapless. But there will come a time, I promise. Maybe not long, now; someone's going to take your virginity, and it might as well be me."

The depression sprouted wings and flew far, far away.

They returned to the camp. "We got the Water Totem," Feline announced, brandishing the miniature figure of the gorgon.

"Great!" Zed said. "That leaves only one to go."

"One to go," Faro echoed grimly. She would be the next to face the challenge, probably the worst one of them all.

"What powers does it give you?" Nya asked.

"I don't know. Let me see." She held the totem in her hand, concentrating. "The power to make waves. And—" She broke off, looking astonished.

"To turn folk to water with a look?"

"Yes," Feline agreed faintly. "Only I don't have to do it. Only when I focus on it. So the rest of you aren't in danger." Then she paused, surprised.

"And?" Nya asked.

"And I can bring Carmen back to full life, only under my control. She will help us any way she can."

"Can you trust her?" Zed asked.

"Yes. She is my slave for the duration, until I free her."

"I think it was too easy to capture her," Zed said. "Especially considering that opal she gave you, that informed her where you were at all times."

"Opal?" Hapless asked.

"The water gem on your ear. The clear opal. It's valuable apart from its magic. Such gifts are not carelessly given. She must really like you."

"Uh—"

"Maybe we should talk with her."

"If you wish." Feline touched the Totem, and it expanded to the gorgon. Who promptly fell down, because her tail could not support her on land.

"Oh. Sorry," Zed said, reaching down to lift her up. He set her on a stone, where her tail sufficed to brace her. She made a remarkably pretty figure. The several males were obviously impressed, the females less so.

"To answer your question," Carmen said, adjusting her dark glasses, the only apparel she wore. "Yes, there was some ambiguity. I realized that Hapless was not going to give up the Quest. So if I wanted to continue my association with him, I would have to join the Quest. Otherwise I would lose him entirely. I did not want to do that. There's something about him."

"There is," Feline agreed.

"I knew that I would not be allowed to join the Quest in my wild state. So I had to accept the tame state." She sighed impressively. "It's a nuisance, but what else is there?"

"That smells like love," Faro said.

Carmen shrugged, as impressively. "Or fascination. It can be compelling."

"It can," Feline agreed. Then the gorgon shrank back into the Totem, and the males' eyeballs reverted to normal. A cynic might almost have suspected that the cat woman was not completely at ease with the gorgon's tame state.

At any rate, they had the fourth Totem. But the worst was still to come.

Chapter 13

VOID HORN

It was Faro's turn. "Let's do it," she said.

Hapless opened the box. The picture was of a floating megaphone, with the words VOID TOTEM. The path led north.

"One thing we need to be aware of," Zed said, drawing on his centaury store of background information. "The perimeter of the Region of the Void is what is known as an event horizon. It is a one-way crossing. It is possible to enter the Region, but not to leave it. If we cross, we will be completely committed."

"But the Quest would be impossible if it ended in the Void," Nya said. "There must be a way through, and the path will show it to us."

"The path will show us the way to the Void Horn," Quin said. "That's not the same. Presumably if we capture the Horn, we will be able to move on out of the Void."

"And exactly what is the Void Horn?" Feline asked. "It doesn't look like a ravening or seductive monster, but it must be dangerous."

"Yet still possible to tame," Zed said. "If we can just figure out how."

There was half a silence.

"So should we cross?" Hapless asked.

"Is there any other way to complete our Quest?" Faro asked in return.

A furtive glance circulated. It died out before completing the circuit, as if swallowed by the Void.

"As the gorgon said," Zed said, "It's a nuisance, but what else is there?"

The others looked at Hapless, prompting him to confirm the decision. He realized that leadership consisted largely in following tacit directions. Then, having used up the other half of the silence, he spoke. "We'll cross."

They trekked north, past the village, around the lake, and to the shimmering boundary wall. This was the dread event horizon. The path led directly though it. Hapless nerved himself and stepped through.

There was no sinister chill, no jolt of pain. He simply crossed the line and stood in a pleasant landscape sloping gently down. Flowers grew amidst the greensward. The air was fresh. He turned to tell the others, but discovered he could not take even a single step back; he could go forward or sideways only. But at least he could reach back. He poked one hand through the curtain.

Someone took it. Feline, by the soft feel of it.

Then she stepped through and stood beside him, holding his hand. "I thought maybe you wanted company."

"Oh, yes," he said gratefully.

"This doesn't look so bad."

"You can't go back. It's one way."

She experimented as he had. "So I see. Well, the others will be along presently. We forgot that you should have crossed last, but I think they know where we are."

She was right; the path ended with him. It would have vanished behind him. In the tension of the moment it had slipped his mind. But it did extend before him, proceeding to the right side.

The two dragon crossbreeds were next, crossing together. "This is nice," Nya said appreciatively.

Finally the two centaurs, crossing in step. Their party was complete.

"What now?" Hapless asked.

"Now we trust the path," Feline said. "We go find the Horn."

"Somehow I dread that," Faro said.

"So do we all," Zed said.

The path meandered around the Region, drawing gradually closer to the downhill side, which might be the dread center. The trees and bushes that grew on the slope seemed to be leaning away from that lower part as if nervous about it. Small wonder; it reminded Hapless of a giant maw.

There was a commotion down the slope, at the edge where it became more like a gulf. They paused cautiously to inspect it from a distance. A jolly jumbuck was caught in a brier patch. No, it was using the patch to keep from sliding down into that maw.

Something was coming. It was the Horn, floating up from below, the letter A prominent on its side. It oriented on the jumbuck, nudged the animal's haunch, and made a weird keening sound. Air blew in from all directions to disappear into the horn. It was a giant suction. Instead of blowing, the horn was sucking.

And the jumbuck got sucked into the horn and disappeared.

"Now we know what it does," Feline whispered.

"But the letter in the picture was O," Zed said.

Hapless checked. The centaur was of course correct. This was not the same megaphone.

Then as they watched the letter A changed to the letter D.

"From Avoid to Devoid," Zed said. "It may change each time it feeds."

"So when it feeds on us it will be O?" Faro asked nervously.

"Ovoid. I am not making sense of that."

The Horn, its appetite satisfied for the moment, floated back down the hill toward the gulf.

They stopped where they were and considered. "We need to understand this thing better," Zed said. "Evidently the Void Horn has a purpose here, serving the interest of the Void. What would it be?"

"That jumbuck must have wandered in here to graze," Nya said. "Not realizing that it couldn't retreat. When it caught on, it clung to the brier patch, trying to escape its fate. Then the Horn came after it, seeming to know it was there."

"Let's try this for sense," Zed said. "Things normally head toward the center of the Void, not because they want to go there but because there's not much other direction they can go. Some may catch on before the final slide. They can't retreat, but they can stop sliding. That's a snag. It may interrupt the normal process of the Void. So it sends the Horn out to relieve the snag."

"The Horn is an aspect of the Void," Faro said. "That's why it can travel against the current. If we capture it, we'll be able to do the same."

"That is centaur thinking," Zed said. It was obviously a sincere compliment.

"But what about those letters?" Feline asked. "Why do they change?"

"They may be an indication of its current state," Zed said thoughtfully. "A could mean it is hungry. D could mean it is sated. O must mean something else."

Hapless realized that they were making progress, but he wasn't sure it was enough. It was obviously dangerous to approach the Horn at any time. He needed to think outside the box.

Then he got a notion. "Chicken music!"

The others looked at him.

"We use music to tame the Totems," he said. "What kind of music would tame the Horn? Ovoid means egg-shaped. That could mean it could be affected by chicken music. We have to play chicken music when it's at O."

"What is chicken music?" Feline asked.

"I don't know, but maybe Faro does." He turned to the winged centaur. "Play some chicken music." He conjured her set of drums.

"This is insane," she muttered.

"Way outside the box," Hapless agreed.

She donned the drums and began to beat on them with her hands. At first it was just an interesting syncopation, but then it started animating. It was as if a flock of chickens were pecking up bugs and grain. Pecca! Pecca! Peck peck peck PECK!

"That's chicken music," Zed agreed.

"It may ignore music at other times," Quin said. "But it has a thing for chickens. Maybe a number of them wander in here, so it gets to feed on them often."

"But the problem remains, how can we be on hand when it is at O?" Faro said, easing up on the drumbeat. "That thing must travel to wherever there is a snag, and we won't know when it's at O."

Feline looked at Hapless. "We need another outside-the-box idea."

Hapless concentrated. What would regular folk never think of? That might by some freak work? That seemed to make no sense at all, yet could circle around and work by surprise?

"A play!" he exclaimed almost before the idea bulb flashed.

"What do you mean?" Zed asked.

"A play about love, messed-up love. Like maybe a boy with two good girlfriends and a bad girlfriend, and he can't make up his mind between them, but he really needs to."

"This is not a play," Feline said. "It's personal history."

"Only this one's about Void Horns. Boy and girl horns. With letters that change."

"Hapless . . ." Feline said as if talking to an idiot with a bomb.

"But it might relate," Zed said. "We don't know what kind of social life the Void Horn has, but if the gorgon is any guide, it's lonely. Such a story might appeal to it."

"Is it male or female?" Nya asked. "That could make a difference."

That brought them up short. Hapless had assumed male, but realized that something that took things in could perhaps more readily be female. Unless there were other things to determine gender. "I don't know."

"Well, we had better make a determination, or we'll have no story," Zed said.

"Um," Feline said.

Hapless looked at her. "Isn't that my line?"

"My Totem—Carmen Gorgon—says she can help."

"Then why not let her?" Zed asked.

"I, um—" she said, evidently torn. "She wants to seduce Hapless."

"But you control her, don't you?" Zed asked. "You can forbid it."

"Not if she gets Hapless to choose her. I don't control *him*."

Hapless kept his mouth shut. Feline might not control him, technically, but she had an awful lot of influence on him. Yet he still wore Carmen's opal. She still wickedly tempted him.

Faro took hold. "Feline, you got your Totem. We all have, except me; I'm the last. We need my Totem to get out of the Void and complete our Quest. I realize that you're not eager to animate Carmen, whose interest is in fascinating Hapless, but if she can help, we need her. If we reject help that just might maybe could enable the Quest to succeed, then we are all lost."

"But what if she takes Hapless?" Feline wailed.

"It seems you have a theoretical choice: to risk losing Hapless while enabling completion of the Quest, or to claim Hapless at risk of losing the Quest. That's the hard equation. You need to make your choice."

Hapless or the Quest. That was stark.

The others gazed at her. They all knew that they were all lost if they didn't get out of the Void. Including Feline herself. Including Hapless. There was nothing to be won by giving up the Quest.

"Oh, hairballs!" Feline swore, in tears of frustration.

Then Carmen appeared, nude except for glasses, falling as her tail flailed. Hapless quickly caught her, and found himself clasping her face to face, her phenomenal upper section plastered to him. He was more aware of it with every breath she took. Her snakes curled around her head and his head, drawing his face in toward hers; they seemed friendly now, and not at all scary. "We've got to stop meeting this way," she said, quickly kissing him.

Feline's fear was justified. About the only thing that prevented Carmen from seducing him this instant was that she was in tails and had no place. Not without legs.

"She's going to have to make legs," Faro said. "Otherwise she can't function here."

"Do it," Feline said grimly.

"That will take time," Carmen said.

They set her up on another rock, and slowly her tail started changing. They harvested clothing from a clothes horse grazing beside the path; the thing was made entirely of clothing, but looked like a horse with clothing on. Carmen donned a blouse and kerchief, both of which filled out impressively. Her tail was now covered by a skirt, except for the tips of her flukes. This partial concealment had the effect of making her look even more fetchingly human, with perhaps a bouffant hairstyle and a super-uplift bra. The males of the party still found her quite interesting.

"How can you help?" Feline asked grimly.

"I am a creature of a Region," Carmen said. "I know about the Regions. The Void is special in significant ways."

"Tell us something we don't already know," Feline said, her grimness unabated.

"The Void is a kind of black hole, with its event horizon. The question is what happens to the things that are drawn into its singularity. The physical objects are in a kind of stasis, but what about information? As a practical matter, that may be lost."

"This makes sense," Zed agreed. "It is a fate we prefer to avoid. But what is the relevance?"

"The Void Horn must have had a past, before it was captured by the Void and put to work here. But we may never know what that past was. Even the Horn probably does not remember."

"Granted," Zed said. "But our interest is in capturing it, not in tracing its unfathomable history."

"That is where you are wrong. It needs a history. History lends identity. Without memory we all flounder."

"You said you could help us," Feline reminded her, her grimness starting to curdle. "Get on with it."

"We can make a history for the Horn that can become as valid as any other, since its prior history was destroyed. A history that facilitates our need."

"I am not clear how a manufactured history could enable us to capture the Horn," Zed said.

"You wondered whether the Horn was male or female." It was clear that Carmen had heard their dialogue. "Change the history to make it male, and it will become male, as there will be nothing to gainsay it."

"We can make it male," Zed agreed. "That won't capture it."

Carmen smiled. She was even prettier then. "But it may do just that, Zed. Consider the psychology of the guardians of the Regions. Mine, for example. I have immense power in my Region, am virtually immortal, and no denizen dares oppose me. But I am lonely. When a fresh male with some gumption comes into the scene, I am interested. Not to exert my power, as I already have plenty of that, but to abate my loneliness, at least for a while. S*x is fine (even here in the Void a bit of the Conspiracy remained operative), romance is better, but what truly counts in the long haul is companionship. Hapless could make an intriguing companion. I would not be lonely while with him. That provides him considerable appeal that is not based on his appearance or abilities. He would be compatible company. S*x and romance are merely tools to recruit him. His hidden quality of character is what makes him worthwhile."

"Get on with it," Feline gritted.

"We have no evidence that the Horn desires company," Zed said. "In fact it seems eager to swallow anything within range."

"That is the beauty of the special quality of the Void," Carmen said. "We can provide him with a history and personality that desires exactly that. Such desire is potent, as my own case illustrates. It can trump common sense. Therein is our potential power over it."

"Does the Horn have common sense, or any sense at all?" Faro asked. "Or is it just an appetite?"

"At present it's just an appetite," Carmen agreed. "But we can give it character, making it become a worthwhile collaborator. Because of the nature of the Void."

"I am not following this stage," Zed said. He spoke for all of them.

"We can craft a fictional character to be what we need for the Quest. That is also appealing to an entity that has no character, because of the erasure of the Void. We can make the Horn into that new person. He will accept it because he will crave its definition once he discovers the nature of definition. He will not be able to resist it, any more than a man can resist a seductive woman." She glanced at Hapless and spread her forming legs under the skirt. That electrified him, though no detail showed.

"Watch it!" Feline snapped.

"Merely flexing my forming legs," Carmen said. "To get the ligaments and muscles aligned. It's a cautious process."

Now Hapless had a question. "You were in legs when Feline converted you to the Totem. But then you were in tails. Why?"

"The Totem is my natural form. I reverted to it the moment I was converted. If I revert to it now, I will be in tails again and have to start the leg process all over. That would be awkward."

Feline did not comment. It was plainly a warning.

"How can we get the Horn to orient on such a character?" Zed asked. "We don't even know if it understands our language."

"It understands," Carmen assured him. "All Region creatures do. It helps us deal with visitors." The word almost sounded like "victims."

"So do we just tell it of a nice persona, and see if it reacts?"

"Better to show it in the play you were considering. Dramatize it." Carmen glanced again at Hapless. "How did that go, again?"

"Boy with two good girlfriends and one bad girlfriend," Hapless said. "It needs a plot, a story line, but that's the essence."

"I believe I can develop that story," Quin said. "I have had a certain interest in drama. Let's make the boy a prince—"

"Prince Voila," Carmen said. "A VOI name, so that the Void Horn will identify. Played by Hapless, of course."

"Point taken," Quin said. "Prince Voila must marry and rule his kingdom when his father the king dies. He has two girlfriends, but can't choose between them."

"Princess Feline," Feline said. "First good girlfriend. My part."

"I will play the bad girlfriend, of course," Carmen said. "Who tries to seduce the prince away from his kingdom and lock him up forever in her Castle of Er*tic Pleasure."

"Now wait!" Feline protested.

"Where else would she take him?" Carmen inquired. "If you want to corrupt a man, you use what you've got. Is there any other way to take a prince away from two good girlfriends?"

That stymied Feline. But she came up with another objection. "Still, we need the second good girl. Nya and Faro are female, but I see this as a human trio. Our cast of characters is incomplete."

"That is a problem," Zed agreed. "Maybe we need to storm-brain for an idea."

"Metria," Hapless said before he thought.

"That would be mischief," Feline said. "She always—"

A small cloud of smoke appeared. "Did I hear my denomination?"

"Your what?" Hapless asked.

"Class, family, category, designation, appellation—"

"Name?" Hapless asked.

"Whatever," the cloud agreed irritably. "What's happening here? Something interesting?"

"We're planning to put on a play," Hapless said.

"Not interesting," the demoness agreed. "So I'll toodle-oo."

"Wait for it," Zed murmured. "I have heard of this demoness."

The cloud nudged uphill, bounced, tried again, then exploded into Metria's dusky humanoid figure. "What the bleep! Why can't I pop off?"

"You're in the Void," Zed said.

"No one goes in the Void! Because it's a one-way trip."

"So it seems," the centaur agreed with a faint suggestion of half a smile.

"What are *you* doing here?"

"We're on a one-way trip," Zed said with a straight face.

"You uttered my name!" Metria said accusingly.

"I did," Hapless agreed.

"That brought me here. What's going on?"

"We're on a Quest, remember?" Hapless said. "This is another stage of it. The Void."

"So now I'm stuck here with you cards?"

"Us whats?"

"Kings, Queens, Jacks, Tens, Nines—"

"Jokers?"

"Whatever! I'm stuck?"

"Unless you care to help us escape it."

The demoness considered. "You have a way to escape the Void?"

"We hope so. But we'll need you to play a part."

"What part?"

"Prince Voila must choose between two good girlfriends and one bad girlfriend. We're missing a girlfriend."

Metria eyed him. "Do they get to smooch you?"

"Uh—"

"Yes," Feline said mischievously.

"I'll be glad to serve. I'll make the meanest of girlfriends."

"Uh—"

"We need another good girlfriend," Feline said.

The top of Metria's head blew off and smoke billowed out. "No way! I'm not good, I'm bad."

"But we already have the bad girlfriend."

"Who is this hussy? I'll show her who's bad!"

"Me," Carmen said calmly from her rock.

"And who the bleep are you?"

"My name is Carmen."

"I don't know any Carmen or even any trainmen. Have you ever acted in a play before? I'll bet you're a bleeping amateur who wouldn't know evil if it smacked you in the face!"

Carmen simply lifted her dark glasses and looked the demoness in the face.

Metria dissolved into a splash of water that splatted into the ground.

"Uh—" Hapless said belatedly.

The water gathered itself into a puddle that quickly boiled into smoky steam. The steam formed back into the demoness. Demons were not as vulnerable as living folk were. "You're a gorgon!" Metria spluttered.

"I'm a gorgon," Carmen agreed, replacing her glasses. "A really bad girl."

Metria regrouped. "Hold on there, water pill. I know something about gorgons. They're not mean spirited, any more than basilisks are. They just have trouble with their looks. One even married the Good Magician. She was a good wife. Not evil."

"We're not evil," Carmen agreed.

"So there! You're not entitled to the role of bad girlfriend. I am."

"You want to be the bad girlfriend?" Zed asked carefully.

"Of course I do! All I do is make trouble."

A look circled the group. It even included Carmen's dark glasses. It was followed by a nod.

"Then take the bad girlfriend role," Feline agreed reluctantly. "Carmen will be the second good girlfriend."

Carmen shrugged. "It is not a familiar role, but I will do my best."

"And I will do my worst," Metria said, satisfied.

They worked out the play in more detail, and rehearsed it, though their lines were somewhat impromptu. They practiced moving about the stage only left and right, never forward or back, so as not to lose their place in the Void. They were ready. They hoped.

Zed assumed the role of Narrator. "Void Horn!" he called. "We have something for you."

Somewhat to their surprise, the Horn came floating up out of the pit. And to their gratification it was now wearing the letter O. They had a lucky break, maybe.

The Horn started inhaling. "Wait!" Zed cried. "We have a story for you. It's about eggs. Listen and learn."

Would it listen? This was the crux. If Carmen was correct, it would give them at least a little time to make their case. Because at the moment it was Ovoid.

The centaur plowed right in. "Once upon a time, there was a kingdom of Chicken Little. It had hens galore, laying eggs by the gross for export to other kingdoms, in trade for other goods. That's how it made its living." He paused.

The Horn hung in the air, listening. So far so good.

"The King of Chicken was getting old," Zed continued. "His handsome son Prince Voila was slated to inherit the kingdom. But first he had to marry; it was the rule. But there was a problem. Prince Voila had two girlfriends, and he couldn't choose between them. The first was Princess Feline, of the neighboring kingdom Cat Call. It specialized in cats, and if he married her, the cats would quickly eat up the rats that were raiding the hen houses and stealing the eggs. That was a very good recommendation."

Feline stepped up, smiling, looking pretty.

"The second was Princess Carmen, of the kingdom of Water Fall, where they specialized in waterfalls and whirlpools. If he married her, they would never run out of water for their hens. That was important too."

Carmen stood, her legs now complete, and smiled. She was more than pretty.

"But then a bad girl came into the picture," Zed said. "She was Princess Metria, of the kingdom of Demon Straight. She didn't care about eggs; she just wanted to haul the prince into her secret castle and indulge him in perpetual passion."

Metria stepped up, her descending décolletage almost showing Too Much and her rising skirt hem showing More Than Enough.

"Naturally the prince was interested," the Narrator said. "And naturally the Prince's family was against this girl. So were the two Good Girlfriends. But there was just something about the Bad Girl. For one thing, she had magic. She could change her clothes without touching them." Metria demonstrated, her scant outfit becoming even scantier.

"Action," the Narrator said. "The Prince receives a message. The dialogue is extemporaneous." He faded back.

Suddenly Hapless was in the role. He was Prince Voila, torn by indecision. There was the message in his hand: IT IS TIME, COME TO ME AT MY SECRET CASTLE TONIGHT AND I WILL GIVE YOU SOMETHING THAT WILL REDUCE YOU TO A QUIVERING MOUND OF SATISFACTION. (signed) BAD GIRL.

Wow! He suspected she had something interesting in mind. He pocketed the message and went to lunch.

Princess Feline was there, as pretty as ever. "Oh, Prince, I was afraid you had forgotten our luncheon date," she said.

"I would never do that," he protested, though in truth it had slipped his mind. He had been distracted by the message. What was the Bad Girl planning to give him? A really fancy dessert?

"And of course you have a swimming date with Princess Carmen this afternoon. I'm sure she looks good in a swimsuit." She paused half a moment. "And she'd better be in a swimsuit."

"Uh—" He had been secretly hoping she'd be nude. She was reputed to have a fabulous figure.

"What's that in your pocket?" Feline asked, fishing it out before he could protest.

"Uh—"

"Why, this is a note from Bad Princess Metria," Feline said. "Naturally you're not planning to go there, are you?"

"Uh—"

"Because she couldn't possibly have anything good for you. You know that, don't you, Prince?"

"Uh—"

She gave him a slantwise look and dropped the matter. The luncheon proceeded normally. The meal consisted of Eggs Galore, a popular entree in the kingdom of Chicken Little. Prince Voila didn't care to admit that after a lifetime of eggs he was ready to try something else.

That afternoon he met Princess Carmen at the pool for their swim date. She was in a swimsuit and cap, and her figure was splendid. But her mood diminished it. "Feline tells me that you received a Note from Bad Girl Metria. You threw it away unread, of course."

"Uh, no." He almost could have wished that the two princesses did not get along so well together, sharing information.

"And she wants to give you something. You're not interested, of course."

"Uh—"

She gave him a look that slanted the opposite way from the one Feline had, and dropped the subject. Their swimming proceeded normally. It was certainly fun being with Carmen, as it was being with Feline. But what did Metria have in mind? The mystery fascinated him.

At nightfall he sneaked out the back way and went to the Evil Castle. He felt guilty, but he just had to know what goodies the Bad Girl had for him. "Ah, Prince Voila!" Princess Metria said. "I'm so glad you could make it."

"Well, you said you would give me something."

"So I did!" She put her hand to her blouse as if to remove it. "I'm sure you'll like it."

"Not so fast, trollop," a voice came. It was Princess Feline in a Royal Tither.

"Get out of here, catgut," Metria said. "You're not invited."

"And what about me, jade?" another voice came. It was Princess Carmen.

"You're not invited either, watercress. This party is just for Prince Voila."

"You're going to seduce him and make him forget his obligation to his kingdom!" Feline said.

"What if I am? It's his choice, not yours, cat's whiskers."

So that was what she had for him. Seduction. That was not something the Good Girls offered, because they had to be pristine until marriage. His interest intensified.

"Yes, it should be his choice," Carmen said. "Let's make this an even playing field. We'll all give him his choice, and may the most beguiling girl win."

Metria assessed the situation. "All right." She evidently felt that she had the advantage here.

"Then let it be the Seduction Game," Feline said. "Winner takes all."

"Agreed," Carmen said.

"Agreed," Metria said. She faced Hapless. "Just so you know the rules. Each of us takes turns with each round. The one who first seduces you wins you. She'll marry you."

"But Good Girls can't—" He protested.

"Can't advertise it," Feline said. "Because Princesses must Appear Pristine. But few really are."

"Royalty is all about Appearance," Carmen said. "Reality hardly counts."

"But—"

"Actually since this is a Family Show, a full freakout will do in lieu of a seduction," Metria said. "It's a standard substitute in show business."

"It is?"

"Round One," Feline said. "The Look." She took center stage as the others faded back.

"Uh—"

Feline peeled away her princessly gown and stood nude. Her curves were absolutely lovely. But he didn't freak out, maybe because she wore no bra or panties.

"My turn," Carmen said. She stepped out of her clothing, becoming nude. She was even more shapely than Feline, but he didn't freak out.

Then she did a slow dance, and that accented her curves and put him at the very verge of a freak. But he didn't.

"And mine," Metria said. Her clothing evaporated, literally. She was so shapely he knew it was artificial, since she could assume any form she chose. Then she danced, and that magnified the effect. His eyes started glazing, but he didn't freak. Quite. Then she turned slowly around, and the first hint of a panty line formed.

"Foul!" the other two princesses said almost together.

"Oh, posh," Metria swore as the line disappeared.

It seemed she had tried to sneak the hint of panties in, but been caught. Well, she was the Bad Girl; they were expected to try to cheat.

"Round Two," Feline said. "The Kiss."

The kiss? The Prince was unfamiliar with this game, but wasn't sure how a kiss could be competitive.

Feline remained nude. She stepped up to him, took him in her arms, drew him close, and kissed him. He floated.

She ended it and stepped back. He dropped back to the floor. It was only an inch, but quite enough to make the point.

Then Carmen stepped up. She kissed him. He floated two inches.

Finally Metria kissed him. Three inches. Four. Five.

"Foul!" the other two chorused.

"You're levitating him," Feline said.

"Using external magic," Carmen said.

"Oh, fudge," the demoness swore. She had been caught again.

He still had not been seduced, though that was more a matter of chance than any resistance on his part.

"Round Three," Feline said. "The Feel."

The Feel? He was feeling dizzy; did that relate?

She took his hand and brought it to her shoulder. It was a very nice curvy shoulder. Then she stroked it down across her front. Oh—that kind of feel. His hand went numb and he slid around the edge of freaking out. Only the fact that there were two others watching prevented it from happening.

Then Carmen was before him. She took his hand and stroked it down across her back, then below.

The Prince found himself lying on the floor. He had freaked out. The presence of an audience had not stifled so powerful an effect.

"I have won you," Carmen said. "I will take you away to my water domain where we will share endless love."

"But I was going to take him!" Metria said, outraged. She was so angry that sparks were flying from her hair.

"Tough luck, sister," Carmen said. "I won him fair and square. Or rather, fair and rounded. He's mine."

"We'll see about that," Metria said. "If I can't have him, nobody can!" She extended both hands, and magic sparked between them. "To the Void with you, Voila!" Scintillating power shot out, surrounding him. Then he faded out. Only Hapless was left, a used-up actor.

"And that is the end of the play," Zed said, returning to the stage. "But not the end of the story. Prince Voila was banished to the Void, where he became the Horn, required to float around unclogging snags in the progression of others to the Singularity in the center of the Void. The Prince no longer exists, only his memory, and not much of that. Now there is only you, Horn."

The Void Horn hung there, assimilating this news. He had been given a past, and a lost identity. Would he accept it?

"He has to commit now, or the moment is lost," Zed murmured.

The gorgon took the stage again. "Princess Carmen was so grieved by the loss of her beloved that she retreated to her kingdom and wept such a storm of tears that it flooded the area and became the Region of Water. Only the return of Prince Voila can console her. Not the actor in the play, but the real Prince, now cruelly masked as a horn of emptiness. You!" She gestured appealingly to the Horn. "Come to me, my love!"

Was she serious? Would she sacrifice herself for the good of the Quest? Would it work?

The Horn bobbed in air. Was that acquiescence? The gorgon was about as attractive a creature as any man could hope to see, let alone win. She was offering a lot. Assuming the Horn identified with the story Prince and felt like a man.

"But to do that, you must first escape the Void. That can only be done by becoming the Totem, which in the company of a living person has power to travel anywhere. If you do that, and help us complete our Quest, I will take you to my water realm when it is done and we will be as happy together as anyone can imagine. Because I am the Totem of Water, in the adjacent Region. We're neighbors, with similar interests in maintaining our domains. We can do it together, if you join us."

The Horn, swayed by her appeal, and surely by her nude loveliness, nodded. Hapless suspected that no male could have turned her down, including himself. In fact he felt a pang of loss. She was not to be his bad girl. Not his girl at all.

"Now, Faro," Zed murmured.

Hapless conjured the drum set. Faro put it on and started beating the drums in the pattern of the Void. It was compelling.

The Horn floated toward her, and finally touched without sucking her in. He became the Totem, in the shape of the Horn. But on its side was a picture of Prince Voila, looking rather like Hapless. It was the only model available. Prince Voila would surely become more individual, when.

Faro ceased playing and picked it up. "Oh, I feel the power of Nothing," she said.

Then she held it out to the gorgon. Carmen took it and kissed it. "Together," she repeated. It was a promise.

"Now let's get out of here," Zed said.

Faro led the way up the slope, away from the deadly gulf. They followed in her wake, the only place where this direction was possible.

They walked up to the shimmering curtain, and through it. They were back in the Region of Water.

"Bye, Quest," Metria said, leaving skid marks in the air as she took off. "It has been an education." She was gone.

Or almost. "I could have won you," her voice came back to Hapless. "If those hussies hadn't been so strict with the rules."

"Begone, spook!" Feline snapped.

Carmen touched the Totem again. "This is my kingdom," she said. Then she reverted to her own Totem state, and Feline put her away.

"I think we can be friends," Feline said. "She did come through for us."

Hapless and the others were glad to agree. The sustained tension of the Void drained from them. They sank blissfully to the damp ground.

Chapter 14

WEST TERN

They walked on out of the Region of Water and emerged to Xanth Proper. It was a huge relief. Not that Hapless disliked the Region of Water, but he preferred to be clear of all the Regions now that their business there was done.

"Let's camp right here for a day," Zed said. "We've all been under considerable stress."

"Amen," Feline agreed. "And Ah-women and Ah-children too." Then she turned to Hapless. "Which reminds me: we need to look up Merge and Myst."

"You—want them with us?"

"Considering the alternatives we just play-acted, yes."

He didn't argue; he wanted them too. "But we're not where we left them. How can we—"

"I thought you'd never ask," Faro said. "I'll fly. You look."

Feline changed to cat form and jumped on ahead of him. Faro spread her wings and took off, her eyes closed.

"Turn to the left," Hapless said. "That's south, where they were."

She turned, and they flew south at gradually increasing height.

In a scant five moments, maybe four and a half moments, he spied them. He waved, and they waved back. Faro waggled her wings, though she could not see them herself. "Glide down, straight ahead," he told Faro.

She did, and landed neatly near the two as he announced the ground. "I could do this with my eyes closed," she said.

Hapless jumped off, and so did the cat, changing in midair. He ran to Merge and swept her into his embrace. Then he kissed her. She was an absolute delight, both ways.

"Why Hapless, you're so bold," she said breathlessly.

He was taken aback. "I'm sorry. I was just so glad to see you I lost my—"

"I'm teasing," she said, and kissed him back. "I was afraid we'd never see you again, knowing you were going to brave the Void."

"We have a story to tell about that."

"In due course," Feline said behind him. "Now let's switch partners." She was with little Myst.

Hapless sat down to join the child, while Feline hugged Merge. "Did you miss us?" Myst asked.

"I, uh—"

"I knew you'd say that. But we missed you." She flung her arms about him and kissed his nose. He knew right then that he did want her for a daughter.

They walked north to rejoin the Quest, catching up on bits and pieces of their adventure. "You mean you have the Void Totem with you now?" Merge asked Faro.

"Yes." She held up the little Horn. "The prince says you're pretty, but not as pretty as Carmen."

"Carmen?"

"The Water Totem. She's a gorgon."

"A gorgon!"

"Tame, for now. She won't hurt you."

By the time they rejoined the camp, Merge had the essence of their excursions into the Regions of Water and Void.

"We've been thinking," Zed said. "We have the five Totems, but if they are all needed to handle the Orb, we had better get in some practice. We need to be thoroughly conversant with them before we tackle the big stuff."

"How much of a challenge are you looking for?" Merge asked.

"One big enough to allow us to stretch our new muscles, as it were. These Totems are almost hideously powerful, but we're only just beginning to appreciate their qualities."

"We met a dog," Merge said. "Her name is Rachel; she's a Service Dog from Mundania who visited Xanth a few years ago and liked it, so now she's here permanently." She smiled. "It seems she couldn't talk in Mundania, but can talk here. She has been exploring Xanth, now that her pups are grown, and says there's a village near a comic strip that is going to need a lot of assistance. She's trying to find someone who can help. It's her nature to help."

"A comic strip?" Zed asked. "They are normally limited to the worlds of Ida."

"It seems that one got loose somehow and landed in Xanth near the Village of West Tern. The villagers have been mining it for puns, which are more valuable since the virus wiped out so many. But now a mob of monsters is moving in, wanting to take over the business for themselves. They're laying siege to the village. If it doesn't get help, it will soon be rubbed out."

Zed looked around at the others who had gathered to hear about this. They nodded. "This may be what we are looking for. I believe we are equipped to handle monsters."

They all looked at Hapless, expecting him to make the decision. What could he do? "Uh—"

"Then it's decided," Zed said. "We'll camp here tonight, and tomorrow go to help the village. Where is it?"

"I don't know," Merge confessed. "But Rachel does. She can lead us to it. I understand it's not far from here."

"And where is Rachel?"

"She's in the vicinity where we were, south of here, sniffing out prospects with her boyfriend Woofer. Had I known we might be able to help her—"

"I can find her," Myst said.

"Could you show Hapless?" Faro asked.

"Sure."

"Go with him," Merge said. "While Feline and I catch up on things."

Thus suddenly Hapless was back in the air, this time with the child riding before him. "Oooo!" she exclaimed, loving it.

They flew south again, Hapless directing. When they reached the place where Merge and Myst had been before, the child was ready. "Hold me in while I fog," she said as they landed. "There's a wind."

He put his arms about her, and she fuzzed into fog. His body shielded it from the wind just enough. Soon she solidified again. "That way," she said, pointing.

They followed her directions, and before long caught up with a pair of dogs snoozing under a tree: Woofer and Rachel. Woofer was nondescript, but Rachel was a German shorthaired pointer. Myst jumped down and conferred briefly with them.

She returned. "They'll be at the camp tomorrow morning, and will lead you to West Tern," she reported. "Rachel says thank you; she had about given up finding anyone with a chance to save the village."

They returned to the camp, where the others had made things comfortable. That night Hapless shared a blanket with Feline and Merge again, one holding each of his hands. It occurred to him that this might be their way of keeping his hands out of mischief, but he loved it anyway.

In the morning the two dogs were there to lead the way. The party followed. They passed East Tern, which was occupied by birds, then took the Tern Pike to West Tern. They saw the comic strip, winding sinuously across the landscape, and the monsters, poised to charge the village at high noon.

"This looks bad," Zed said.

"The puns won't bother you if you stay clear of the strip," Merge said.

"I mean the siege of monsters. They are surrounding the village."

Merge smiled. "Those, too. We will have to pass through their line. They will allow it, because to them it means all the more meat for their feast. It's departure from the village that they won't allow. Except for me— they know I'll douse them with anti-pun virus elixir that will incidentally make them sweet for an hour. They can't stand that."

"You must have encountered them before," Zed said.

"Yes. I am not entirely defenseless."

"First we need to explain to the villagers that we're allies, not more monsters," Feline said, glancing at Hapless.

His job, of course. "Lead me in," he told Rachel.

The dogs did. Feline came along, and Merge, with Myst. They passed the goblin checkpoint, and the ugly male goblins leered openly at the women. "We'll have something to do with you before we eat you," one told Feline.

"Yes, you'll get your eyes scratched out," Feline said. She did not mention her Totem, which gave her far more power than that.

"Me first!" another goblin called.

"Wait your turn," a third one said.

The goblin sergeant was a bit more sensible. "Why are you taking your friends into this trap, multi-girl?" he asked Merge. "You know they don't share your immunity."

"It's not a trap for them," Merge replied evenly. "It's a trap for you. If you're smart you will give up this siege and go far, far away."

All the goblins burst into crude laughter. "We love it when you make jokes, pretty thing," the sergeant said. "Are you sure you won't join me for a really hot plumbing? Maybe all five of you with five or ten of us?"

"Quite sure," Merge said. "Please don't be crude in the presence of my daughter."

They laughed again. "We'd plumb her too, if we found some glue to hold her in place."

Merge marched grimly on without responding further.

"I could let Carmen wash him out," Feline murmured. "One look will do it."

"No. It's his male-goblin nature. Only if he physically attacks you."

Hapless was impressed by the way Merge handled the goblins, and by her restraint.

"She's a nice person," Myst confided. "It's a problem."

They walked on into the village. A few barricades were up, but it was plain that they were inadequate. The villagers were in a somber depression. They knew they were doomed.

"This is Hapless," Rachel said to the Village Elder. "He can help."

"I am not sure anyone can help at this point," the Elder said. "They will converge within the hour. We are doomed. Our men will be slaughtered, our women raped and slaughtered, our children made into slaves."

"We can help," Hapless repeated. "We are on a Quest, and have captured the five Totems of the Regions. They have power."

The man looked at him. "You are either more powerful than you look, or a madman."

"We don't have time to argue," Feline said. "I have the Totem of Water."

"Can you demonstrate?"

Feline held up her Totem. Water poured from it in a torrent, splashing on the ground and quickly flooding it. "More?" she inquired.

The Elder picked up his dropped jaw. "That suffices."

The flow stopped. "Thank you," Feline said, smiling.

"The other members of our party are two crossbreed centaurs and two crossbreed dragons," Hapless said. "I will bring them in now so you know that they are friends, not enemies."

"Monsters!" the Elder said fearfully.

"No. They are Companions of the Quest."

"Monsters!" the other villagers echoed. They were so stressed that they were unable to accept the distinction. Was their irrationality going to destroy the effort, and with it their village?

Hapless got a notion. "Companions," he repeated. "I'll prove it. Have you ever heard of monsters playing lovely music in harmony?" Actually there were some musical monsters, but maybe the ignorant villagers did not know of them.

"Monsters aren't musical," the elder said. "But—"

"I'll show you." He conjured Feline's kit. "Play," he said.

She didn't argue. She put the small violin to her chin and played a truly lovely theme. The villagers paused in their developing panic, surprised and soothed.

Hapless turned to Merge. "Please, will you go back and tell the others to come here one by one? Starting I think with Zed; he looks almost ordinary."

"Yes, dear," she said, and hurried off with Myst.

Dear? Why not? They were in love.

"She's no monster," the elder said, appreciating Feline's music. "She's a cute young woman."

Hapless held up his hand in a stop signal, and Feline stopped playing. "Show them your nature, briefly," he told her.

Feline handed him the violin, then changed to cat form. She arched her back, spat, then changed back. "I'm a crossbreed," she explained. "But thank you for calling me cute." Then she took back her kit and resumed playing.

The villagers, silenced, listened.

Zed trotted in, with Myst riding his back. "They called him striped meat," she reported. "He ignored them."

Zed could make the earth shake, literally. As the goblins might soon discover.

Hapless conjured the saxophone. Zed played it, joining Feline in a mellow harmony. The villagers listened, charmed.

"Centaurs aren't monsters either," the Elder said, though without his former conviction.

"None of them are monsters," Hapless said.

Faro arrived. "Those goblins need a whole-body caustic enema," she muttered.

Hapless conjured her drum set, and she commenced a rhythmic beat. The Elder didn't try to protest that winged centaurs weren't really monsters.

Next came Nya, as a naga. The villagers eyed her bare upper torso, as they had Faro's, and did not protest. Hapless conjured her harmonica, and she joined the others in perfect harmony.

"Neither are naga," the elder said.

Hapless stopped Nya and took her instrument. "Show them your nature, briefly."

She changed to dragon form, then back to naga. He returned her harmonica and she resumed playing. She was definitely a monster, but the villagers were catching on.

Finally Quin arrived, in harpy/serpent form, and Hapless conjured his accordion, then had him change briefly to his steam dragon form. He was definitely a monster, but the villagers no longer were concerned. The lovely music had made its point.

They brought the piece to a neat conclusion, though they had never played this one before. Somehow the music was always right. They set down their instruments.

"They aren't monsters," Hapless said. "At least, not enemy monsters. They're on your side."

"Not monsters," the elder agreed.

"But the real monsters are coming," Myst said, returning from a fuzzing out. "They're all around."

"Get under cover, villagers," Hapless said. "Stay close to me in the center. This may get wild."

There was a small dais in the center circle of the village. The villagers crouched down around it. Hapless mounted it and looked around. Sure enough, he saw a contingent of flying dragons coming in from the north. "Quin, you handle those," he said. "Blow them away."

Quin assumed full dragon form and faced the other dragons. He opened his mouth and blew. A gale of air blasted out. It struck the dragons and knocked them literally out of the sky. They landed in a tangle on the ground.

The villagers cheered.

But the dragons weren't done. They righted themselves and slithered along the ground toward the village, breathing fire.

Quin exhaled again, harder. The wind coursed along the ground, blowing up sand, wrenching bushes out, and sending bits of debris flying into the dragons' snouts. Yet still they came, forging through the flak.

"I can take care of that," Nya said.

"No, wait," Hapless said. "This could be a diversion. We need to be ready for the others. He's holding them back for now."

Indeed, the very ground before the dragons was getting scooped out by the gale. They were not making any progress.

"Nickelpedes at ten o'clock," Myst announced.

"Those are yours, Feline," Hapless said. "Don't let them reach the dais."

Feline stood facing the northeast. Soon the ground before her was alive with the dread armored insects, each one capable of gouging out nickel-sized chunks of flesh. Anyone stepping into that living carpet would not be worth a plugged nickel. It was flowing toward the dais.

"Any time now," Hapless murmured, hoping that nothing had gone wrong with her Totem.

"I want to get them all committed, so they can't retreat."

"Uh—"

"Don't worry," Myst said. "Aunt Feline knows what she's doing."

Feline patted her on the head. "Right, dear."

The nickelpedes swarmed right up to within a few paces of the dais. The villagers shrank back in horror.

Now at last Feline acted. A virtual wall of water washed out from her, splashing down onto the insects. They were borne away, helpless in its fierce current. It kept coming, spreading out across the area, forming a rising puddle, then a pond, then a lake. The nickelpedes didn't have a chance; they were drowning.

"Big snake at seven o'clock," Myst announced. She was pretty good as a spotter, thanks to her sensitivity in mist form.

Hapless looked. It was a giant land serpent, its body as thick as the height of a man. It would neither be drowned nor blown away; it was simply too big. "Nya," Hapless said.

The naga assumed dragon form and oriented to the southwest. She looked like a toy compared to the approaching monster, but she slithered out to meet it. When they came snoot to snoot, Nya lifted up her forepart and breathed a warning wisp of fire.

The gargantuan creature looked at that and shook with laughter. Obviously a little jet of fire couldn't hurt it.

Nya breathed out a rocket-blast of fire. That toasted the serpent's snoot and made it draw back in surprise. But now it was annoyed. It gaped its ponderous and mottled jaws and lunged forward to take in the whole of Nya.

Nya exploded into a stellar fireball. The closing mouth was illuminated by brilliant light before it dropped to the ground as ashes. The serpent had literally lost its head.

The villagers applauded. They knew now that the rescue party was deadly serious about saving the village.

But the siege was hardly over. "Bogies at three and five o'clock," Myst announced. "Goblins and wolves." She paused. "The Garbage Goblin tribe, I think; they're bad. Rabid wolves, by the smell of it. Can't let any spit touch you."

"Zed, the goblins," Hapless said. "Faro, the wolves."

The centaur faced east, where the goblins were charging in, preceded by their smell. "I have heard of the Garbage Goblins," Merge said. "They simply swarm over their opposition, reducing it to garbage. Then they fish out what they like."

"They'll have a problem this time," Zed said grimly. Then the ground under the horde shook just enough to make its power felt. When they ignored that, it shook harder, and a crack opened up in their midst, swallowing more. When they still came on, a volcano formed, erupting and pouring out molten lava. The goblins were quickly buried, becoming crisps.

"You tried to warn them," Merge said.

"I did. But it can be hard to reason with marauding goblins."

Meanwhile the wolves were loping in, their eyes red with madness, their saliva dripping. There would be no reasoning with them either.

"I hate this," Faro said. "Hang on, folk." Then she lifted her Totem. It expanded into the full-sized Horn and started sucking. The suction intensified, trying to draw in the whole world, but the villagers behind it stayed low and were not moved. The wolves, however, bounded straight into it. And disappeared. They were in the Void.

It was done. The Companions eased off their totems and the tumult faded. All around the village was devastation, from flooding, lava, wind, fire, and suction. But the land would recover in time. There would be no more monsters attacking.

"Our job is done," Hapless said, satisfied. "We shall be on our way."

"Oh, no!" the Elder said. "You must accept our grateful hospitality tonight. You saved us from a five-fold horrible fate."

Hapless glanced around. The others nodded. "We accept," he said.

The villagers provided them with a surprisingly capacious house. Then the villagers came one by one to thank them for saving the village and the lives of all within it. "We thought we were doomed," one woman said. "I was ready to slit my child's throat so she couldn't fall into the hands of the monsters."

Hapless knew she wasn't exaggerating. They had been desperate, for good reason.

"We were glad to help," Merge said. "We were lucky the dogs knew where you were."

The Elder came. "It is time for the celebratory feast, where you will be duly feted."

"Oh we don't need—"

Merge put a hand on his arm. "Thank you," she said. Then, to the others: "You just saved their lives from a terrible end. They have to honor you. Just nod and smile and it will soon be over."

It occurred to Hapless that she was socially practiced where he was inadequate. She would make a good companion.

They followed her advice, and it worked. It wasn't at all bad.

Then alone together in the evening, Feline told Hapless. "Call a meeting."

"Uh?"

"Zed has thoughts."

"Oh."

"I have some thoughts," Zed said. How had she known? "The Totems are amazingly potent. We had no trouble vanquishing the monsters. In fact, I believe any one of us could have done it alone. We could have flooded, burned, blown, buried, or sucked them all to oblivion."

The others nodded agreement.

"That is what bothers me," Zed said. "We have amassed a phenomenal amount of power. Enough, perhaps, to destroy Xanth if we put it to that fell purpose. We don't yet know the limits of it. We might generate the storm of the century to blow away all structures, or a fire that laid all forests bare, or make an earthquake that leveled everything, or simply siphon everyone into the Void. Power tends to corrupt. We shall need to be careful that we are not corrupted by it."

"Good point," Faro said. "We will need to return the Totems once we have accomplished our Quest. To give up that power before it corrupts us."

They looked at Hapless. "Well sure," he said. "Wasn't that always the plan?"

They nodded as if appreciating something he did not. What was he missing this time?

"But I am thinking that we may need more practice," Faro said. "We will be going up against the Goddess Isis, and by stray accounts she's an imperious b—bad girl." Had she started to say something else? "We don't know what she will be up to. We had better be prepared for anything."

"What are you thinking?" Zed asked her.

"That the Totems provide us with terrific physical power that I think no one could stand against, not even a goddess. So I think she would not meet us on that front. But there are other kinds of power."

"Such as?" he prompted her, evidently having a notion. Centaurs did tend to see eye to eye on things, perhaps because their eyes were at the same level.

"Such as illusion. She might clothe herself in completely unexpected appearances, such as a sea serpent or the king of Xanth. How would we know?"

"How indeed," Zed agreed rhetorically.

"Or she could be in a castle that turned out to be a gulf for us to fall into. With illusion you can't be sure of anything, not even the level ground ahead of you. We might flounder around, blowing things away, burning things, flooding things that looked like enemies but were actually innocent folk. She could make utter fools of us, and our powers would be use-less or counterproductive."

Zed nodded. "And how do you propose we prepare for such a chal-lenge?"

"We shall need to be ready for virtually anything." Faro quirked a smile as she glanced at Hapless. "To think outside the box, perhaps."

"In what manner?"

"There is a comic strip nearby. We might assist the villagers with their mining of puns."

"Oh, bleep!" Nya said. "I was hoping you wouldn't think of that."

The others pondered the suggestion. "Those comic strips have a hor-rendous reputation," Feline said.

"Folk can get sick in them, from their inversions and nonsense," Quin said.

"In sum, a perfect challenge for our equilibrium," Faro concluded.

Feline glanced at Hapless. "Time for you to make the decision."

What could he do? "We'll try it tomorrow."

"We knew you'd come through."

They had known he could be browbeaten into doing what they wanted. Yet it did seem to make sense. It should prepare them for their encounter with the goddess. Assuming they could be prepared.

They settled down to sleep. The two centaurs stood a bit apart, dis-cussing Mundane Quantum Theory. Hapless couldn't help overhearing part of it.

"It never made sense to me," Faro said. "The idea that reality is not fixed until someone observes it. Where was the universe before anyone observed it?"

"No one ever accused the Mundanes of being unduly rational," Zed said. "It is more devious that that. As I understand it, the universe exists in an infinite number of alternate possibilities. When we observe one, the alternates collapse into a single reality. Or it may be that at that point we recognize a single reality, abating our uncertainty. We make a snapshot, as it were, fixing it in place."

"These are the same Mundanes who don't believe in magic?" she asked cuttingly.

"I'm glad we live in Xanth."

Their dialogue continued, but Hapless tuned it out. He did not have a centaur mind. He just wanted to rest.

Feline, Merge, and Myst boxed him in as usual, and he loved it as usual.

"You did well," Feline whispered in his right ear, kissing it.

"Very well," Merge whispered in his left ear, kissing it.

"Hey, you're floating too high," Myst protested. "Get back on the floor."

They all laughed. They loved teasing him, and he loved being teased.

In the morning they went with the villagers to the nearby comic strip. It writhed and scintillated like a living thing, which maybe it was in its fashion. As they stood beside it, almost touchingly close, color washed across the boundary wall. Letters appeared: MAKE MY DAY.

"We normally don't enter it," the Elder said. "We spot a likely pun, reach in, and pull it out. It's like fishing in a violent stream."

"We will be entering it," Zed said. "We want to figure out how to maintain our bearings even in the midst of chaos."

"Do not use your Totem powers," Faro said. "That could be dangerous, as things may not be what they appear to be."

"Myst and I will wait by the side where you enter," Merge said. "That way you will know you have succeeded if you come out where we are."

"We'll know," Hapless agreed, dry mouthed.

"We should stay together, at least the first time," Zed said. "We can hold hands and step in, then step out again, testing the water, as it were."

"If anyone gets separated," Faro said. "Step out immediately."

They linked hands in a circle of six and stepped in.

It was instant chaos. Hapless knew the others were still with him, because Feline held his right hand and Faro held his left hand. But he couldn't see them. What he saw was a tree with extremely odd fruit: dolls with singe eyes in their foreheads. They were little cyclopses. But where was the pun? He knew that he'd be locked into place contemplating the sight until he got the pun.

"Focus," Feline said, squeezing his hand. "You're the last one. We can't move until you do."

Then he had it. "Eye Doll a Tree! Idolatry."

"Good enough. Now we'll step back together to get out of the strip."

"Just let me grab a doll for the villagers," he said.

"No!" she cried. But she was too late; he had let go of her hand and

Faro's hand and grabbed a doll. He got it, and turned around to rejoin them.

They were gone. Too late he remembered the warning: stay linked. Now he was alone in the comic strip.

But they had to be close. He stepped toward the boundary, only there was no boundary any more. What he saw instead was a set of young dragons lining up at a line. Suddenly they were off in a cloud of alcohol fumes, racing along the track. What were they doing? He had to figure it out before he could move on. Sure he knew that young dragons, like other teens, like to race. But where was the pun? For a moment his noggin blocked up. Then it cleared: they were drag(on) racing!

He went on, seeking the boundary wall and thus the way out. There was a man with a book, *Principia Mathematica*. Hapless recognized it as a math book. This must be a mathematician.

"Pardon me, sir. Do you know the way out?"

The man ignored him.

Hapless tried again, this time getting in his face. "Please, sir—"

The man tapped his ear and shook his head. Oh, he was deaf!

So Hapless made an elaborate gesture of trying to walk away. Would that get through?

The man looked at him somewhat blankly, then made a sweeping gesture that Hapless somehow recognized as a mathematical construct: a sine wave.

The deaf mathematician communicated in sine language. That made a certain sense, but since Hapless didn't speak it, it was no help. He had to give it up.

"Thank you, sir," he said, keeping it polite. "My best to you, and to your wife, who I presume speaks cosine language."

He tried to turn around to go back, but remained in a skelter of obscurities. Where was the boundary? He had no idea. What use was it to solve a pun, if he just came up against another pun?

Then he remembered: Think outside the box. The comic strip was like a box, hemming him in. He'd never get free of it if he followed its rules.

But what was there to think of? His problem was immediate. He needed to get out of here, instead of being constantly flummoxed by drifting puns. Actually, it wasn't the puns that were messing him up—it was the environment. Things kept changing, so that he couldn't get a fix on reality.

Then he remembered the bit of dialogue the centaurs had had about reality. That the Mundanes believed that it wasn't fixed until someone observed it. Crazy—yet wasn't that the case here? Could he fix it by observing it? By making a snapshot? That was certainly outside the box.

He concentrated. SNAPSHOT.

Something changed. He looked around. The environment was locked in place. The deaf mathematician was fixed in his sine. The two dragons were frozen in mid race. Beyond them the Eye Doll a Tree was still.

He had made an observation and collapsed the alternates into a single static reality. Only he remained free to move around.

Good enough. Now he was able to make out the boundary wall. He strode to it and through it, emerging into Xanth proper.

Except that there was no one there. Where were Merge and Myst? The villagers? It wasn't frozen; he could see tree leaves fluttering in a breeze. What had happened?

"I went out the other side!" he exclaimed. He would have to go back.

So be it. What good was gumption if he didn't use it? He stepped back through the wall and was back in chaos. Everything had changed.

This time he faced what he recognized as an emulation of the Void. It was spitting out birds. Hawks, in fact. As they emerged it slowly got smaller.

What could he make of a black hole that let hawks escape?

Then he got it. "Hawking radiation."

But this time he knew how to handle it. He concentrated. SNAPSHOT.

It froze. He walked on through the tableau, past myriad stilled puns.

And there were the mathematician, racing dragons (now a bit farther into their race), and the Eye Doll a Tree. And beyond that were the five Companions. They were caught in an attitude of concerned looking. They were trying to find out where he had gone.

He tucked the cyclops doll into his belt, then resumed his place and took Feline and Faro's hands. He focused. RELEASE SNAPSHOT.

The chaos resumed. "Let's get out of here," he said loudly.

They backed out as a group and were in Xanth proper again.

"What happened?" Feline and Faro asked almost together.

"I let go to grab a cyclops doll," he said, showing it. "A pun for the villagers."

"You vanished," Feline said severely. "We couldn't find you anywhere. Then you were back."

"It's a middling size story."

"We had better have it," Faro said.

Hapless narrated it. "So you see, I drew on your dialogue," he concluded, addressing Faro. "To think outside the box. And it worked. I made a snapshot that enabled me to get around in the comic strip without being swamped by its environment. I think that's the breakthrough we need to handle the Goddess Isis."

"Perhaps it is," Zed agreed thoughtfully. "We had better all learn the technique."

They practiced it, one by one. First Feline entered the strip alone. She seemed to flounder for a generous moment, but then the strip seemed to crystallize around her.

She stepped out leading a witch by the hand. "She's so sentimental," Feline said. "I had to get her out of there."

"But she's a witch!" Zed protested. "Witches aren't sentimental."

"That's sedimental, catsup," the witch snapped, not at all sentimental. "I'm a sand witch."

"Oh. I guess I missed the pun."

"I'll show you. Hit me."

"But I was trying to rescue you, not abuse you."

"Do it anyway."

Feline shrugged and slapped the witch across the face. The blow landed, but had a peculiar effect. The witch's face dissolved into sand, followed by the rest of her body. In two thirds of a moment she was a pile of sand on the ground. Feline, caught by surprise, was half standing on it.

"Oh!" Feline said. "I didn't mean to do that."

The sand mounded, humped, and rose into a human figure. "I can't be abused," the witch said. "I just dissolve into sand. I lie there, picking up everything in sight from the ground." She smirked. "You have nice panties, dear."

"Sedimental," Zed agreed with three-fifths of a smile.

"Anyway," Feline concluded. "I made the snapshot technique work, and the witch is the proof."

"My turn," Faro said. She stepped into the comic strip.

As before, there was a scant moment, then the strip coagulated around her. She had snapped it. She emerged hauling a man by the arm. "This is Phil," she said.

"You bet I'm Phil," he said. "Phil A Buster. I never stop talking. You'll never get anything done, ha ha."

"I've heard of him," Zed said. "I thought he lived in Mundania."

"I live everywhere that anything needs to be accomplished," Phil said proudly. "I keep talking until there's no point any more."

"Well, move it, Buster!" Zed snapped.

"Oh, bleep," Phil said. "There's a motion on the floor." He walked away.

"Sorry I didn't get a better example," Faro said. "I didn't realize how bad he was."

Next was Zed. "I'll try not to get a person," he promised. In due course he emerged with a colorful egg.

"Uh-oh," Faro murmured. "That looks like a darning egg."

"What's the problem with a darning egg?" Zed asked, setting it down.

The egg proceeded to wobble along. "Oh! Darn, Darn, Darn!" it exclaimed.

"Oh." But Zed, too, had mastered the snapshot technique.

Nya went next. "No darning eggs," she said as she stepped through. She emerged with a delicious-looking piece of pie. "Don't eat it," she warned. "It's humble pie. Its best use is for arrogant folk who seek to enter the Good Magician's castle without undertaking the challenges."

Myst took the pie, promising to deliver it to the villagers without nibbling it herself.

Then came Quin. He emerged hauling a statue. "Statue of Limitations," he explained. "It tells folk what is impossible."

"Can we capture the Goddess Isis?" Hapless asked.

The statue looked at him. "You can, but you may wish you hadn't."

That was not encouraging. But what could they do but go on?

Chapter 15

ISIS

Next day, rested, they bid parting to the villagers. Hapless opened the box.

There was a lovely woman in shorts and a halter, wearing hair curlers and sandals, sitting on a crude wooden throne. The words were ISIS ORB.

"Can that really be her?" Hapless asked, surprised. "I thought she'd be in a shining royal gown."

"It must show her when she's not making a formal presentation," Feline said. "I suppose even goddesses don't wear their finery all the time; it would get soiled."

"That must be it," he agreed. But he still wondered.

The path, to their amazement, led straight to the comic strip. Could she be in there? Or did they merely have to pass through it to reach her?

"I am glad we practiced how to handle the comic strip," Zed said. "We did not know we'd be using that knowledge so soon."

"But we shouldn't need it while we're on the path," Faro pointed out. "It protects us from bad things."

"And what happens once we reach her, and the path ends?" Feline asked.

"We'd better have our mission in hand," Zed said.

Hapless studied the picture. Isis' legs were crossed, and she was showing a fair degree of thigh. He did not want to admit how much that turned him on, or the way her halter showed extra flesh around the edges. She was one superlatively sexy creature, regardless of her clothing.

Feline snapped the box shut. "We're going to complete our Quest, not see the sights."

"I suppose this is farewell, again," Merge said sadly. Myst stood with her, misting.

"No," Feline said firmly "Come along, both of you."

"You want us along?" Merge asked, surprised.

"Moral support. We fear the goddess may be the bad girl, since Carmen wasn't. It may take both of us to shield him from that. Men can be wickedly tempted by bad girls."

"Even by their pictures," Merge agreed. "Even in dishabille." She had evidently noticed Hapless' attention. What could he say? He *was* attracted.

"That's right. We need to be sure Hapless does the right thing."

"Then we'll come," Merge agreed gratefully, and Myst was sunshine again.

Was this smart? There could be serious danger. Yet he was glad to have them along.

"We should not have to link hands this time," Zed said. "But we should remain alert."

"Oh, yes," Faro agreed.

They formed a single file line and followed the path through the wall and into the comic strip. There was chaos, but now it was safely off the path. The details were blurry, as they were through the comic strip wall. They had, in effect, walled off a path-shaped section.

"I'm almost disappointed," Feline said.

"I see a pun!" Myst exclaimed happily, pointing to a foggy outline.

"What is it, dear?" Merge asked, squinting.

Hapless squinted too. The thing looked like a wooden box overflowing with dolls. Except that the dolls were moving. They were small people. Some of them clutched pencils, which they used to sketch pictures on any available surface.

"A chest of drawers," the child said.

A subdued groan went through the party. "Let's move on," Zed said. Centaurs generally were not partial to puns.

They ignored other puns along the way, though Myst tittered several times as she observed them.

The path did not pass through the comic strip and emerge on the other side. Instead it turned to follow the strip lengthwise. Where was it going?

"Surely the goddess could not live in the strip," Feline said, voicing Hapless's thought. "The puns would drive her crazy."

"Unless she is already crazy," Merge said. "Some say the gods are mad."

"Would that make her easier or harder to deal with?" Faro asked.

"Excellent question," Zed said. "It may be a presumption to assume that she will be rational."

"She looked rational in the picture," Hapless said.

"She looked sexy," Feline said. "That's not the same."

"You, of course, being in a position to know," Zed said with a smile.

"Females know it; males don't. That's why they are so foolish about women."

"And it is a woman we are up against." Zed pondered briefly. "It occurs to me that we have gathered power and practiced countering illusion. But what about dealing with a sexy woman? Some call Isis the goddess of sex."

"Fertility," Faro said. "That, too, is not the same."

"But close enough. Maybe we should consult with Carmen, now that she's on our side."

"If you wish."

They paused to gather around, the path coincidentally becoming wide enough at this point. Coincidentally? There was more to these paths than showed.

Feline touched her Totem and the gorgon appeared, garbed in an exceedingly tight halter and extremely short skirt. Skirt? But she wore her tail. The skirt actually made it look like legs, at least where it stretched across the hips. Hapless assumed she also wore the kerchief and dark glasses; his eyes were too firmly locked on her torso to make sure. "I thought you'd never ask." She flounced the skirt, though there was hardly enough to flounce. The eyeballs of the males flexed in perfect harmony.

"So will the goddess try to freak out the males?" Feline asked.

"No. She'll be more subtle. She'll flash them just enough to make them docile, then deal with the females."

"Deal with us for what?"

"She'll want to know exactly why we're here. She'll know we're on a Quest, because she'll see the path, but she won't know our specific object. Then she'll decide whether she wants to cooperate."

"And if she decides not to cooperate?"

"Then we'll use the Totems, of which I am one, to force her to. Then we'll be dealing with an angry goddess."

"But if we win our case and get our wishes granted, will it matter?"

"Yes, because we will not be able to safely release her. It will be like letting a bomb detonate. Hell has no fury, etc."

"Thank you," Feline said. The gorgon made a final flirt of her skirt that came yea close to freaking out the males, then faded.

"Now we know," Zed said as he cracked his eyeballs loose first left, then right. The other males were no better off.

"I believe her," Quin said. "We're in for mischief."

"I'll try to talk her into cooperating," Hapless said. "Maybe she'll listen to reason."

The others burst out laughing. "She's a *goddess*," Feline said. "Why would she bother with reason?"

It seemed he had, as usual, said something foolish. Which made him wonder, for the Nth time, why he had been selected for this Quest. He was probably the least capable, physically and mentally, of them all.

Merge picked up on his mood. "There's just something about you," she murmured.

"Yes," Myst agreed.

And what could that possibly be?

They resumed their trek. Now the path slanted upward. It did not emerge from the roof of the comic strip, if there was a roof; the height seemed not to matter. They rose above the rest of the strip like a coaster-roller ride, heading into the sky.

"Look!" Myst cried. "A castle!"

They looked, and it was true: in the sky ahead was a magnificent castle with turrets and pennants galore, a lovely sight. Its foundation was lost in dark mist, but its pinnacles were bathed in golden sunshine.

"There was no castle here when we entered the comic strip," Zed said. "It has to be illusion."

"It's Isis's castle," Myst said. "I love it!"

Hapless remembered something. "Caution," he murmured. "Remember our practice with illusion. Look, but do not indicate that anything is amiss."

Then he and the others made mental snapshots of the castle. The result was amazing. It was a crude wooden structure with a tin roof, sitting on the ground. Nothing at all fancy.

But the illusion made it a glorious multi-tiered edifice floating in the sky.

"Your faces," Merge said. "You are seeing something I am not."

"We'd better pause here," Hapless told the others. Then he brought Merge and Myst into a close huddle. "You did not get practice nullifying illusion. I think you need to learn it now. Simply concentrate on making a snapshot of what you are looking at, freezing it in place. That will make a still picture without the illusion. Only what's physically there."

They tried, and tried again. Then the child got it. "It's wood!"

"Yes. Wood enhanced by illusion. That must be so that we won't try to enter the castle and fall right through it; there needs to be something to touch."

Merge tried again, and again. Then at last she got it. "Oh, my!"

"We will pretend we see only the castle," Hapless said. "Since it is obviously fashioned for our benefit. But we will also know the reality. That may make a difference, if things get difficult."

"Such as if we see a smoky dragon charging us," Zed said. "And it's really just a broomstick."

"So we don't jump out of the path and lose our protection," Feline said.

Merge nodded. "Thank you for the warning. I would have jumped."

"Yes," Hapless said. "She will maintain the illusion as long as it seems to be fooling us, and we'll maintain the semblance of being fooled as long as we can."

"And you thought there wasn't a reason for you to lead the Quest?" Feline asked. "You're the one who figured out the snapshot technique."

Hapless shrugged. "Lucky guess."

"Maybe."

They went on, openly admiring the castle. "The goddess must be really good with magic, to make such a castle," Myst said brightly.

The castle loomed close, just as impressive as it was from a distance. The front entrance was (seemingly) solid stone, with a massive glass door in which they could see their reflections. As illusions went, it was impressive, because it meant it was interacting with them instead of being fixed in place.

Hapless stepped up and tapped on the door. The glass rang, making a kind of chime. Then the door slowly opened. They were being admitted.

An ornate hallway led to a grandiose chamber whose walls were sparkling glass through which sunlight filtered, forming prismatic bands of color. There was a fountain, and there the beams curled into rainbows. It was artistic and delightful. But the snapshot showed light leaking in through cracks in the walls and ceiling, and the fountain was a bucket of water.

In the center was a mighty throne of pure diamond. On it sat the Goddess Isis, wearing an ankle-length white linen dress expertly pleated with alternating horizontal and vertical patterns, as if patched together in sections, but each "patch" was of exquisitely artistic design. Her head and neck were covered by a finely wrought leopardskin mantle, and she wore a crown consisting of a pair of cow horns, between which was a bright circular plate as big as her head: the solar disk. But her feet were bare.

The snapshot showed her on her wooden throne, in halter and shorts, as in the box. The only thing that didn't change was her beauty of face and figure. It seemed that she didn't need illusion there.

"And who may you be?" the Goddess inquired. Her voice was mellow yet authoritative.

Hapless stepped forward. "I am Hapless, leader of this Quest. These are my Companions and companions."

"And I am the Goddess Isis, mistress of my domain. What is your Quest?"

"We have wishes to be granted. We need the Orb to grant them."

"And what are these wishes?"

Hapless reeled them off. "Feline wishes to be loved for something other than her curves. Zed wants to find true love. Nya wants to find her purpose. Quin wants to find out how to become human. Faro wants to get over her fear of heights. And I want to find a musical instrument I can play."

"These are garden variety wishes. You hardly needed to undertake a Quest to achieve them."

That was the uncomfortable truth they couldn't admit without putting their whole Quest into doubt. "We understand the Orb can grant them."

"The Orb is potentially the most powerful force in your realm. To invoke it for such minor favors is like conjuring a fire-breathing dragon to light your candle. You can't be serious."

Hapless was getting nettled despite her beauty. "We are serious. Lend us the Orb, grant our wishes, and we'll depart."

"And if I don't?"

Hapless nerved himself to say it. "Then we shall have to take it from you."

The Goddess pursed her lovely lips. "That you can't do."

"I think we can. But we'd rather settle with you peacefully than have to fight you."

"It seems you do not appreciate the complexity of the challenge. Perhaps your Good Magician is making sport with you by sending you on an impossible mission."

"I don't believe that," Hapless said stoutly, though he was beginning to wonder.

"Perhaps this will dampen your unbelief. Do any among you recognize untruth when you encounter it?"

"You mean when someone's lying?" Myst asked. "I can tell."

Merge nodded. "She can. She senses the atmosphere."

"I smell the air," Myst agreed.

Isis did not laugh. "Truth can come out of the months of babes. Very well, attend to me child, and tell your associates whether I am speaking the truth." She paused, took a breath, and said: "The reason you can't take the Orb is because at present it does not exist. I alone can make it exist, and I am not inclined to do that."

Myst turned to the others. "She's telling the truth."

The others looked at her, surprised and dismayed.

Myst fidgeted. "But it's not the whole truth."

"Clever girl," the Goddess said. "Tell me, child, can you tell the truth about things as well as people?"

"Sure. Like this fancy castle is just a wooden shack with a tin roof, and you're in shorts instead of a royal gown."

An expression crossed Isis's face that was somewhere between surprise, admiration, and pure fury. But the Goddess quickly erased it. "So it seems we have no secrets here. All of you knew?"

"We knew," Hapless said.

"And what else don't I know about you that relates?"

She would know soon enough anyway. "We have the five Totems."

Isis glanced at Myst. "True," the child said. "They went into the Regions and got them, 'cause they knew they'd need them to make the Orb work."

Isis contemplated Hapless with a new appreciation. Her gaze was disquieting. "It seems you came prepared."

"Uh, yes."

"But can you actually use them?"

Hapless looked at the others. "Maybe a very brief demonstration?"

Feline smiled, but not in a very nice way. "Merge, Myst, go join Hapless. This will be rough around the edges."

Mother and daughter came to hold Hapless's hands.

"Maybe three seconds, on my mark?" Feline asked. The others nodded. "Three, two, one, mark."

At that point Feline spurted a blast of water toward the Goddess, Nya sent a jet of fire, Quin emitted an explosive blast of air, Zed made the ground shake with a small earthquake, and Faro's Horn sucked in the Goddess's wooden throne as she hastily leaped clear. It was all over in three seconds.

The chamber was in a shambles, in illusion and reality. Isis herself was both wet and scorched; her halter was askew, and her hair was a mess.

"You did ask," Hapless said, his eyes starting to crystallize.

"I did," the Goddess agreed, as she righted her halter, surely to Feline's relief. Hapless's eyes resumed motion. She was clearly impressed but not affrighted.

"So what's the whole truth?" Hapless asked.

"To understand that, you would have to know more about me."

Hapless glanced at Myst, who nodded. More truth.

"Then tell us more about you," Hapless said.

"You might find it dull."

Hapless looked at the others. Then he spoke again. "Tell us anyway."

"As you wish. Make yourselves comfortable in a convenient crater."

They found places to settle down, Myst went to sleep on Merge's lap, and Isis began to speak. Maybe she used an illusion assist, because Hapless found himself almost in the scene, sharing her perspective.

"I was born (confusion, in a moment sorting itself into a scene of the internal Stork Works) about eight thousand years ago, along with my brother Osiris. We loved each other from the start." Indeed, the baby girl was kissing the baby boy. In fact it soon went farther than that; they seemed not to be bound by the Adult Conspiracy. Of course this was a long time ago, and not in Xanth.

"We grew up together, and in due course I married my brother, and was true to him. We were satisfied. But we had not reckoned with the jealousy of other siblings. Our sister Nephthys loved Osiris too, and one night made herself look like me so he thought he was with me, and they made love. I was furious when I learned of it, but what could I do without alerting my husband to the deception? So I was silent, but saw to it that my sister never had access to him again."

Hapless wasn't sure what else she could have done. Osiris had been a faithful husband, as far as he knew.

"Worse was our brother Typho, Nephthys's husband, who was jealous of Osiris's power and possibly of his wife's infidelity with Osiris, and wanted to kill him. But how could he? Osiris was stronger than he, and I was constantly alert against further mischief. But Typho was cunning. He managed to get Osiris's measurements, then made a chest of that exact size and brought it to the banqueting room to show it off. It was richly ornamented and beautiful; he promised to give it to anyone who fit it. All the others tried lying down in it, but none fit perfectly. The last to try it was Osiris himself, and he lay down in it. Whereupon the conspirators rushed in and clapped the cover on, and nailed it down and poured melted lead over to seal it. Then they carried it away to the Nile River and on to the sea, where it floated away and was lost amidst the waves." There was that coffin, disappearing into the sea.

When Isis heard the news, she cut off one of the locks of her hair, and put on a mourning gown, and searched the whole country for the chest. Because it was her power to restore life to the dead, and she wanted to revive Osiris if only she could find him. But for years she was unsuccessful, catching only fleeting rumors that turned out to be false. Until at last she received news from demons that the chest had floated to the coast of the city of Byblos and gently lodged in the branches of a bush by the shore. In a short time, buoyed by the ambiance of the chest and the body within it, the bush had grown up into a large and beautiful tree, which grew around the chest on every side and hid it from outside view.

Furthermore, the King of Byblos saw the tree and was amazed by its unusual size. So he had the tree cut down, and made that part of the trunk into a pillar to support the roof of his house. Isis traveled to Byblos and settled herself down by the side of a fountain, refusing to speak to anyone except the queen's maids. The townsfolk marveled at the sight of this lovely woman, whom they did not know to be a goddess. When the queen's maids came, she saluted and caressed them in the kindest manner, and plaited their hair, and imbued them with a wonderful perfume that issued from her own body.

When they returned to their mistress the Queen Astarte, she marveled at the loveliness of their hair and fragrance of their bodies, and wanted to meet this remarkable stranger. Thus the anonymous Isis was brought into the presence of the Queen, who conversed with her briefly, was charmed, and made her a nurse to one of her sons.

Isis fed the child by giving him her finger to suck instead of the breast, and such was her power that this fed him well. She also every night put him into the fire, in order to consume his mortal part, replacing it with immortal flesh. She kept watch over him by transforming herself into a swallow and hovering around the pillar and bemoaning her sad fate. But one night the queen stood watching her, saw the child all in flame, cried out in protest, and that deprived him of the immortality he would otherwise have had. But he was otherwise uninjured, and the queen realized that it was no ordinary nurse who took care of him. She was sorry she had interfered.

Then Isis identified herself, and asked that the pillar that supported the roof be given to her. This was done, and they replaced it with another. Isis cut it open, took out the chest, then wrapped the remainder of the trunk in fine linen, poured perfumed oil on it, and returned it to the king and queen. Then she threw herself upon the chest, making such a loud and terrible lamentation that the younger of the king's sons was frightened out of his life. But the elder son, whom she had cared for, survived, and she took him with her when she set sail for Egypt. When the river sent forth a rough breeze she was angry, and dried up its current. Even natural things learned not to mess with the Goddess.

She conveyed the chest to a desert place, and thinking herself to be alone, she opened the chest and laid her face upon her dead husband's face. She embraced the corpse, weeping bitterly. But the little boy had sneaked up behind her and saw what happened. In her sudden anger she gave him so stern a look that he died of the affright. Then she hid the chest in a secret place, for it would take time and preparation for her to develop the magic to bring her beloved back to life. But Typho discovered it, and tore the body into fourteen pieces. That forced Isis to make another search for the pieces, using a boat made of papyrus to maneuver through the fen. When a crocodile threatened her she gave it such a look that ever since no crocodile has ever attacked a papyrus boat. In time she found all the pieces of the body but one: the privy member. She needed that to generate a son who would avenge the murder of his father. So she made an imitation member, and reanimated her beloved for a while, all she could do in the circumstance, and used that to (signal the stork) and beget her son, Orus. She raised him, and his father visited him from the other realm and instructed him in arms and gave him the incentive for vengeance.

In due course Orus, grown, challenged Typho, and they fought for many days until Orus got the better of him and made him prisoner. He turned Typho over to Isis for safekeeping while he rested. And Isis, the giver of life, discovered she could not deliberately kill her brother, despite what he had done. She loosed his hands and set him free.

When Orus learned of this, he was so angry that he laid hands on his mother, pulled off her royal headdress, and cut off her head. He transformed the head into that of a cow, and put it back on her body. So she lived, but not in a nice manner. She had become a cowgirl.

"But the greatest indignity was when the Christians came," Isis concluded. "They were a recent sect that borrowed my history, but put the name of the Virgin Mary on me, and the name Jesus on my son Orus. Thereafter few knew who I was; my identity had been stolen by the newcomers. They even took over our sacred holidays, renaming them to be Christian. That religion spread rapidly throughout the Roman Empire and continued after its demise; it was very popular, of course, but I myself had become anonymous."

She shrugged. "And that is my ancient history. I was betrayed by my sister, and my brother, and then by my son, and finally by my worshipers, after five thousand years of doing my utmost for them. It leaves a sour taste, and has rankled for a thousand years."

Hapless, expecting to oppose the Goddess, found himself in deep sympathy with her plight. To suffer identity theft, and see the credit that should have gone to her taken by another—that was maddening and humiliating. She was older than she looked, by about six or eight thousand years, but she had a case.

"Now we know your background," Zed said. "But that is only the preparation for us to understand your whole truth. How does this relate to our use of the Orb?"

Isis nodded. "Now you understand why I am disenchanted with what you call Mundania. I tried my best to help my worshipers and the men in my life, but in the end I was betrayed, by all except my beloved Osiris, who was similarly betrayed, and died. That realm has nothing left for me. So I looked for a new realm, and a new start."

She took a breath. "This time I would leave the faithful suffering wife and mother bit behind, so as not to get bleeped again. This time I would focus on just one thing: my own selfish desires. I would stop being the good girl, who is a patsy, and start being the bad girl, who knows what's what and how to get what she wants."

Hapless could not refute her logic. She had certainly given the positive role its chance. But he was sorry it hadn't worked out for her.

"I searched for centuries," Isis continued. "I checked all the alternate mythologies. But they tended to be misogynistic, reducing women to serfs or worse, and with limited roles for aspiring queens. Until recent times, when new kinds of fantasy developed. And I rather liked the look of Xanth. It had plenty of magic, and a population in need of religion. So I applied to the relevant Demons, Earth and Xanth: where I came from, where I wanted to go. They allowed me to move to Xanth only if I performed a significant service for them, so I was constrained to agree."

"Service?" Zed asked.

"To guard the magic Earth had won from Xanth, and see that no one stole it. Because it remained in the Land of Xanth, where Demon Earth himself could not guard it. He wanted one of his own for the role, and the Demon Xanth had to agree."

"The Orb!" Hapless exclaimed.

"Not exactly."

"Now you're getting evasive again!"

Myst was awake now, having slept through anything that might have strained the Adult Conspiracy. "No, she's near the Whole Truth now. It's complicated."

Isis smiled stunningly. "Thank you, child."

"So what is it, exactly?" Zed asked, no more patient with this circularity than Hapless was.

"The magic could not be handled by a regular mortal," Isis said. "It required someone with formidable magic of her own. That meant a sorceress, demoness, or a goddess. Sorceresses are mortal, and demons can't be trusted. That left me. But neither Earth nor Xanth completely trusted me. They feared I had ambition for power."

"And don't you?" Zed asked.

"Of course I do! What's the point of coming to a new realm, if not to rule it? But they begrudged me that favor. In fact they set it up so that there were formidable constraints that effectively prevented me from achieving it. Not completely, because then I would have spurned the deal; there had to be a chance. It was a compromise. There is a route, but it is devious in the extreme. I had no choice but to accept the deal; otherwise I would not have gotten into Xanth at all. I am not pleased." She frowned, and the nearest potted plant wilted.

"Constraints?" Zed asked.

"First, I was confined to the idiotic comic strip. That is normally limited to the first World of Ida, Ptero, but I managed to disrupt the flow slightly so that a section got loose and landed on Xanth proper. Second, I was allowed to employ only illusion for my personal use. Hence this castle, which is more apparent than real, as you have discovered. Back home in Egypt I could have made it real. Third I could not touch the cache of magic directly; it could be drawn on only through the control mechanism of the Orb. The Orb bears about the same relation to the magic as your Totems do to their Regions: they can draw on their power, but don't change the nature of the Regions. Fourth, I could not use the Orb myself; only some third party can do that. Fifth, even that third party can control the Orb only via the combined powers of the Totems."

Now Hapless was getting a glimmering. "We have the Totems. That's why we had to get them."

"Smart boy," Isis said, her tone implying nothing of the kind. "Without the Totems you would be completely unable to address the Orb, and thus be unable to make it perform. You did come prepared."

"But you said there is no Orb," Zed reminded her.

"There is no Orb now," Isis agreed. "It has to be brought into existence. Just as you brought the Totems into existence."

"By taming their guardians!" Feline exclaimed. "Does that mean what I think it means?"

"Surely it does, catgirl."

"But where is its guardian?" Hapless asked, perplexed.

The five Companions merely looked at him. So did Merge and Myst. And so did the Goddess. He was being stupid again.

Oh, no! "*You're* the guardian!" Hapless said.

"In that sense, yes," Isis agreed.

"So we have to—to tame you."

"In a manner. But you will not accomplish that feat by force. This is my temporary domain; I will counter any attempt. I am not an animal like the Region guardians. You must deal with me on my terms."

"You'll do it voluntarily?" Hapless asked, not trusting this.

"Of course not. Once I become the Orb, I will lose personal volition. You will be my master. That does not appeal."

"Then why are you talking with us?" Hapless asked. "Why did you let us in?"

"Could I have barred you?"

"Well, no. But you are treating us like guests."

"That is part of the illusion. You are not guests; you are an invading army."

"We just want to get our wishes granted!"

"I don't suppose I could persuade you simply to give it up and depart?"

"No," Hapless said.

"Then we shall have to engage in serious negotiation. You want to invoke the Orb in order to get your innocent little wishes granted. I want to use it to achieve ultimate power in Xanth. I could grant your wishes on my own, without invoking the Orb. Would that be satisfactory to you?"

Hapless was surprised. "Uh—"

"What's your price?" Zed asked.

"That Hapless invoke the Orb and use it only to grant *my* wishes."

Zed nodded. "Because you can't use the Orb yourself, even when you *are* the Orb. You need him to draw on its immense power to further your own wish."

"You would have to trust him to do it," Feline said.

"Why me?" Hapless asked. "I'm nobody."

The Goddess turned to address him. "Several reasons. Your party consists of five crossbreeds and yourself. A crossbreed won't do for my purpose."

"Why not?"

"Because I will need to marry you, and for that I need a full human male."

"Marry me!" Hapless exclaimed. Feline and Merge looked as appalled as he was. The bad girl was making her move boldly and publicly.

"I take that as an exclamation rather than as an offer."

"It's astonishment," Hapless said. "You're a goddess! I'm nothing."

"You are far from nothing, Hapless. You are what is available. Not many suitable prospects blunder into the comic strip. Apart from that there are three reasons for me to choose you. You are a virgin; that is precious to a woman who has had seven thousand years' experience with supremely potent males. That fleeting initial naiveté is charming. Second, your formidable talent, which you understand only in part, that is responsible for your success so far in the Quest. Third, a quality of your character. That is most important."

"But—"

"Shall we discuss the terms of engagement?"

Hapless was completely flustered. "I—"

"In both the military and romantic aspects," Zed said.

Isis faced the others. "You want your wishes granted. I want my wish granted. I am offering to grant yours if you will grant mine."

"That is for Hapless to decide," Feline said, and Merge agreed.

They all looked at him again. "No!" he said.

"You do not want your friends to achieve their wishes?"

"I—I—not that way."

"So it will not be voluntary on his part," Isis said to the others. "Then it is to be a contest, if not war. One of the three of us must prevail. Give us an hour alone together. If he wins, you will have your wishes granted and I shall not have mine. If I win, all of us will have our wishes granted, my way. Except that he will marry me, not either of you two maidens. Is this fair?"

The Companions, together with Merge and Myst, exchanged a look that might sour butter. What were they thinking of? The whole thing was preposterous.

"Yes, it is fair," Zed said.

They were agreeing? "But—"

"Our dialogue has just begun," Isis said.

Then the castle and the Companions vanished. They were alone together.

Chapter 16

ORB

"What—" Hapless asked, as eloquent as ever. They stood in a wide pleasant meadow with flowers all around. A sparkling blue river flowed through it.

The Goddess took him by the hand. She now wore a lovely gown, and her hair framed her head like a holiday bonnet. She was so beautiful that merely looking at her made him light-headed. "I am courting you," she explained. "This is a magnetic moment, capable of attracting folk into love."

"But I love Feline and Merge!"

"They are counting on that. But they know that it is better to limit my effort to an hour rather than allow me to besiege you for an indefinite period. It's a compromise."

"You—you're going to seduce me?"

"That would be an understatement. It is your love I want, not just your body."

"Because you want me to control the Orb to—to—"

"To grant me my freedom from the restriction of the comic strip, and to restore my full powers of magic, which are by no means limited to illusion."

"I don't want to do that. I don't think you would be good for Xanth. And I don't want to leave Feline and Merge in the lurch."

"Of course you don't, Hapless. You're a nice, dull, decent guy."

She had his number. "They're nice girls."

"And you surely feel guilty for experiencing even a passing reaction to a naughty girl."

"Yes."

"This about that, Hapless. Bad girls don't have the limitations of good girls. We can address men in ways impossible for nice folk."

"Uh, so—"

"Would a good girl ever do this?" She reached through his clothing as if it didn't exist and touched him in a manner he had never before imagined. "Or let him do this?" She took his hand, passed it similarly through her dress and put his finger in a spot he had hardly known existed.

"No!"

"But you liked it, didn't you?"

He had to admit it. "Yes."

"Bad girls can make better lovers than good girls. After we're married, I will take you into realms of rapture beyond your wildest imagination."

"I don't want to marry you!"

"That is what this hour will decide. You need to give it a fair chance."

"No!"

"If you close your mind, I will have to take stronger measures."

"What are you talking about?"

"Like this." She faced him, put her hands on his shoulders, and drew him in. Suddenly the whole of her was in contact with the whole of him, and her hands were on his rear, kneading it.

Belatedly he caught on. "We're not wearing anything. Our clothing is illusion."

"Exactly. We can banish that illusion if you prefer."

"No!" He yanked away from her. Illusion had become his own protection from thorough embarrassment.

"You have elected to give the tour a fair chance."

"Uh, yes." Because she would forcefully seduce him in seconds otherwise, and he would be lost. She had made that clear. Worse, part of him wanted it to happen.

"Let's start with a canoe ride."

"Canoe?"

"Here." There was a small low narrow green boat in the water before them. "Step in, Hapless."

"I've never been in one of these before. I don't know how to—"

She handed him a double-bladed paddle that appeared in her hands. "It will come to you." Then she sat opposite him, her knees almost touching his. They were parted, and he had to look away before he freaked out. Her legs were the finest he had seen.

"You may look," she said. "You won't freak. I'm not wearing panties."

He was not at all sure of that. Just the thought of panties, or their absence, made his eyeballs quiver dangerously in their sockets. He tried dipping the paddle in the water, and abruptly the canoe was moving smoothly forward. He couldn't be that competent; he had little idea what he was doing.

Oh—more illusion. They were probably sitting in a still canoe, or even just a box, and the scenery was going past them. He could verify that with a snapshot, but that would also show her complete nakedness, so he didn't. It wasn't that she might object; it was that he was trying not to get halfway freaked out. He needed to keep what few remaining wits he had about him.

They were coursing along the river, the flowery banks passing in a colorful display. Then the river angled upward, and they floated into the sky. The meadow disappeared; they were now on a placid lake, with flowering water lilies and friendly fish coming to the surface to observe them. It was a celestial lake extending to the stars, which reflected in its surface.

"Oh, it's so sweet of you to bring me here," Isis said, leaning forward. Naturally her décolletage dropped, displaying her perfect breasts.

"Uh—"

Then she was kissing him. Surprised, he lost his balance. The canoe overturned and they both splashed into the warm water. Their clothing dissolved away. So did the paddle; they were swimming nude.

"What a wonderful surprise!" Isis exclaimed, kissing him with more passion. He tried to resist, but couldn't; his arms went around her almost involuntarily, and he kissed her back. He had had heavenly kisses before; this was heaven squared.

Then she drew back. "But we have other sights to see. Keep our place."

Keep their place? As if this could be resumed at another time? "Uh—"

"Ah, here is the canoe." They scrambled back into it, her body flashing in numerous ways, surely none of them accidental, and were immediately dry. The water was probably illusion too.

"But I lost the paddle."

"And you are up the creek without the paddle," she agreed. "Fortunately we don't need it anymore."

And it seemed they didn't, because they were no longer in a boat, but in a car, one of a chain of them on a track. It was a coaster roller! By the coast, of course.

They angled steeply upward into the starry sky, then crested the highest mound and started down. "Eeee!" she screamed and flung her arms about him as if terrified. Actually he found this descent nervous too, and didn't mind. But this frequent personal contact was having its effect. He increasingly liked being close to her. She smelled faintly of new mown hay, and her skin was like linen.

They zoomed to the base, then coasted up to the next peak, where she kissed his ear. "Thank you for saving me," she whispered.

"You're welcome." They both knew he had done no such thing, but this was a kind of game wherein she found new ways to flirt.

The coaster passed stars and galaxies, then dropped into a tunnel and raced underground, marking lights flashing rapidly past. A dinosaur loomed, jaws spreading wide, and Isis screamed again and wrapped her arms about Hapless's head, burying his face in her bosom. He didn't mind that either.

The coaster slowed to a stop. Was the ride over? "Oops," Isis said. "There's a breakdown. We'll have to wait for the repair crew."

An illusion ride needed repair? She just wanted more time to seduce him. She was making progress; his body made that clear.

"No. Let's walk," he said.

Her irritation hardly showed. "I love your leadership."

Yeah, sure.

They climbed out of the car to stand on the track. That gave way, and they plunged down through darkness to land in a pile of soft sugary jell. Lemon meringue!

"It's a giant pie!" he said as his eyes acclimatized to the dim light.

"It's too much to eat." She pulled him down, smearing yellow kisses on his face. "Lick me off."

Lick her off? Why not? He put his face to her bare bosom and started licking off lemon fluff. She writhed beneath him, giving him more than pie to eat.

It was too much. He drew her in close and pressed her to him so that meringue squeezed out from between them. The confection wasn't half as sweet as her body. He kissed her madly, and she kissed him back, meeting him exactly halfway. She was simply too delectable and too willing; he had to finish it.

Yet somehow he did not. He paused.

"There is a problem?" she inquired.

He realized that there was. "I can't do it."

"Of course you can. This is one thing I must not do for you; it has to be your initiative. But the way is open, the channel clear." She spread her arms and legs.

"I want to. But I can't."

Now she was genuinely concerned. "Why not?"

"I can't betray my good girlfriends or the Quest. It just wouldn't be right."

"How can there be anything wrong about this transcendent mutually fulfilling passion?"

"If I do it, I lose the contest, and must marry you and help free you from your comic strip prison. I wish I could help you, and I know I'd really enjoy your continued company, including the naughtiness, but I just can't."

She was amazed. "You're passing me up for a Quest you no longer need to achieve all of your wishes? Knowing how much I want you to complete it? Are you an utter fool?"

"Yes," he said, ashamed. "I guess I am."

"It isn't as if I am a stranger. You know my entire life history. You don't know theirs."

"I guess it's that I have interacted with them more."

"It is true that we met more recently, but you can interact more with me, and more significantly." She spread her legs wider. "Right now. Deeply."

He wanted to. He knew he would never get another chance with a creature like this. But he couldn't. "It's—it's not the same."

She visibly reassessed. "Then let's discuss this. Is it that they are mortal?"

"Maybe. I'm mortal."

"And I'm immortal, or as close to it as makes no significant difference. Actually gods can be killed, but only by other gods, and there aren't any others in this vicinity. Like attracts to like; I understand that. But there are other aspects. Have you considered that one of them is a crossbreed?"

Hapless was baffled. "What is your point?"

Her lips pursed in another kind of assessment, but she dropped that one and went on to the next. "The other is saddled with a child."

"I love that child!"

Another swift shift. "Then what is it you see in them?"

"Feline has curves."

"My curves are curvier than hers." She took his hand and ran it over those curves, proving her point.

"Uh, yes. I guess I really love her for more than her curves."

"She teases you mercilessly."

"I like it when she does that. It's her way of paying attention to me."

"And the other? You loved her without knowing her at all."

"Yes. There must have been an enchantment. But Merge is surely one of Xanth's finest women, regardless, and the work she does eliminating the anti-pun virus is worthy."

"At present I am limited to illusion, but if I recover my power, I will be happy to enchant you similarly."

He nodded. "I guess you could. But I don't think it was a love spell, exactly. It was more as if we were destined for each other, and we knew it the moment we met."

"Except that you already loved the cat woman."

"It's a picklement," he agreed ruefully.

"You're not being very haved."

"Uh, what?"

"Not behaving well."

Oh. "I guess I'm a klutz from any angle."

"Where is your common sense?" she asked impatiently.

"I guess I don't have much of that."

"You're hopeless!"

She had set him up for his favorite line. "No, I'm Hapless."

The Goddess looked as if she were about to explode, but not in laughter. "You're something else."

"Yes. I really don't know what they see in me. They're not captives and they don't care about power, so they don't need me."

"Of course you don't know. You're a man." Her tone suggested that this was not exactly a compliment.

He was vaguely nettled. "And you do know?"

"I do. It's the same thing I see. You're committed, innocent, and manageable. You'd make a perfect husband."

"They'd make perfect wives. Either of them."

"So would I. The difference is that I would make you King of Xanth, feted by all, with virtually unlimited power. There might be some in Mundania too; the Mailer Daemon is a friend of mine, with connections to a lot of folk. I came from Mundania; he came from Xanth."

"And you would be the power behind the throne."

"Yes, of course. I can't exercise power here in my own name; it has to be through you. But that's all right. I could accomplish a lot with this kingdom."

He shook his head. "I'd rather be with my two good girlfriends."

"You can be, Hapless! You can have them both as concubines, and as many others as you want. It's the royal way."

"They wouldn't be happy that way."

She eyed him with a certain impatience. "You care about that?"

"Yes. I love them and I want them to be happy."

"Our definitions differ."

"Yes. I guess that's why I can't make it with you. You are not my type."

"Indeed I am not." She sighed. "And my time is up. Your intractable naiveté proved to be beyond my wiles. I have never encountered that before in a man. You have won."

The illusion dissipated. They were on the floor before the wooden throne, with the others sitting in a circle around them.

Hapless was amazed and embarrassed. "You saw it all?"

"We did," Feline said.

"There was too much hugging and smooching," Myst complained. "Not enough coaster-roller riding."

"Some of the details were fogged out, fortunately," Merge said.

And he had been talking about Feline and Merge. He tried to remember what he had said, hoping he hadn't mortally offended them. "Uh—"

The two got up and came to him. Feline kissed him on his right ear. Merge kissed him on his left ear. Apparently they did not feel offended. He was relieved. They were evidently in a forgiving mood.

"Now it is time to conclude our mission," Zed said. "We have wishes to be fulfilled, and by the terms of our agreement, you must grant them, Isis."

"True," the Goddess agreed. She was now fully robed, with no sign of lemon meringue.

There was a pause. "Well?" Zed asked.

"Not yet."

"Are you reneging?"

"No. Merely invoking the small print. No time limit was set for the completion. I will get around to it when I am ready."

"And when will you be ready?" Faro asked.

"Maybe in a century. Maybe two."

"But we'll be faded out by then!" Feline protested.

Isis shrugged. "Perhaps you'd like to consider rephrasing the deal to include immediate settlement."

"At what price?"

"Give me Hapless, and control of the Orb."

"But you *are* the Orb!"

"That's why I need Hapless, and the members of the Quest, with the five Totems. To invoke and control its power. I can't do it myself."

"That's the deal you lost!"

The Goddess shrugged again. "I will honor the deal we made. In due course."

Zed looked at Hapless. "Is this something you're ready to consider?"

That answer was easy. "No."

"But we seem to be at an impasse. Isis won't cooperate without getting you."

"Then we'll do what we came to do," Hapless said.

The others nodded. It was the answer they had been waiting for.

"You have decided to wait?" Isis asked brightly.

"No," Hapless said. Then he started conjuring musical instruments and passing them out. In two and a half moments all five Companions had theirs. They spread out in a circle around Isis.

"You're going to play music?" the Goddess asked dismissively.

"Maybe you overlooked another detail of the fine print," Hapless said grimly. He gestured, and the others started playing their instruments.

"What detail?" Isis asked, alarmed by the sound.

"Enforcement," Hapless said.

"I'm getting out of here!"

"I believe we can reach you anywhere in the comic strip," Hapless said, advancing on her. "And you can't leave the comic strip."

She backed away from him. "This is preposterous!"

"Unless you'd like to reconsider the timing? We'll still settle for the deal we made, if our wishes are granted now."

"And mine is not? Forget it!"

"I'm sorry you feel that way. Now you will lose more than time."

She tried to escape him, but he had her pinned against the wall of music. He reached out and took her hand.

And she was the Orb: a great glowing sphere sitting in his hand, whose translucent interior showed the Goddess struggling to get out. She was indeed a prisoner.

The music stopped. The Orb remained. It was Hapless's Totem, the center of power. Now all he needed to do was figure out how to make it perform.

Well, he could ask Isis. She could no longer try to balk his will; he was her master now. He held up the sphere. *Isis*, he thought.

She stood in place, inside. "Yes, I am your slave," she agreed. "I must answer immediately to your bidding." Her thought was mental, but he heard it as her voice. "I am also obliged to warn you before you go wrong, so you will not come to harm via your ignorance. There are cautions."

"Cautions? We just want to have our wishes granted. How do we do that?"

"Let me put it on speakerphone, so all of you hear."

"Okay."

"The power the Orb controls is immense," she said, and the sound was amplified so that it filled the house. "It could tear Xanth in half. Any carelessly phrased wish could be taken literally and become disastrous."

"What's so careless about just wishing for, say, love?"

"I am getting to that. For example, you might want a drink of tea. If you said 'Make me a glass of tea,' you could become that glass of tea. That would be an error from which you could not recover. Because of your careless phrasing."

Hapless shuddered. He could readily make such a mistake. The others reacted similarly. This device was more than they had bargained on.

"Or if you asked to visit the moon, you could land amidst a lake of spoiled green cheese and drown."

"We do want to be careful," Hapless said. "How do we safely make it grant our wishes?"

"You tell me informally, and I will rephrase it to make the wording safe. Then you can get your answer."

"Very well. We have six wishes."

"Its aura of power also tends to corrupt the user, at best making him overconfident. At worst, making him insatiably power hungry."

Hapless felt that aura. It made him feel slightly giddy. "Okay. I'll try not to be too confident. Now about the wishes—"

"Wait. There is more. The Orb is what can be called an attractive nuisance. Creatures are attracted to it, so it is best to keep it hidden at all times when not in use. Otherwise—"

"Are you trying to stall?"

"No, Hapless. I am trying to enable you to use the Orb safely."

"Oh, come on! It can't be that complicated." Hapless flipped the sphere up into the air, and caught it like a ball.

"Don't do that!" Isis screamed in near panic.

"Don't do what? This?" He tossed it up again.

An ugly bird swooped down from seemingly nowhere and caught the Orb in its beak. It flew on, swallowing it, disappearing through a hole in the wall.

Hapless and the others stared after the bird. "Oops," Hapless said, chagrined.

"She did try to warn us," Zed said.

"I'll catch that bird," Faro said, and launched into the air. She crashed into the wall, taking a section of it out, and flew on.

"I just keep messing up," Hapless said. "I thought she was only trying to scare us."

"She was trying to warn us, as it seems she is obliged to do," Zed said. "But the aura was already making you careless."

"Yes." Because now Hapless had no confidence at all.

"Maybe we no longer need the Orb," Feline said thoughtfully.

"We don't?" Hapless asked.

"I already got my wish."

"You did?"

"When you were being courted by the Goddess. She said her curves were better than mine, and she was right. And you said you loved me for more than my curves."

"I do," Hapless agreed.

"That's my wish. To be loved for more than my curves. You said it in a moment of candor, not realizing I was listening."

"You're not mad?"

"Of course I'm not mad, Hapless! You granted my wish before we invoked the Orb." She walked to him and kissed him ardently. "Now I know it has happened. I don't need to be concerned any more. I don't need the Orb."

"Uh, okay," he agreed.

"And Faro," she continued. "Did you see what she just did?"

"She took off after the bird with the Orb."

"Yes. And she did it alone. Her eyes were wide open. How could she have done it if she still feared the heights?"

The others stared at her. "How, indeed," Zed said.

"Maybe it happened when she got her Totem, the Void Horn, and didn't realize, because she's so used to walking on the ground when unridden. Maybe her fear will return when she gives up the Horn. But right now she doesn't need the Orb either. Two down."

Zed nodded. "Two down."

"And Hapless. I think I made the connection when he conjured our instruments so we could play the Goddess into the Orb. He has his instrument."

"I do?" Hapless asked.

"Your instrument is yourself. You make the rest of us play. Without you we can't do it. You're a musical conductor."

Hapless stood open-mouthed. She was right! He had unconsciously conducted them as they circled Isis and played. He was his own musical instrument.

"And it's not just music," Merge said. "He organized the Quest. He's a conductor of people."

"But I'm such a klutz!"

"You are," Feline said fondly. "So no one suspects you of being the leader you are."

"And I think it is coming clear why you were selected for this Quest," Zed said. "You are steadfast. You would not betray the Quest or your friends no matter how much the Goddess tempted you."

"And she tempted you pretty hard," Quin said.

There was the heavy sound of wings. Faro glided back in through the smashed wall. "I caught it," she said, and produced the Orb. "It was quite a chase high in the sky, but I would not let the bird get away. I made it cough it up."

Feline looked at her. "Are you aware of what you just did?"

"I saved the Quest, I think."

"You flew alone," Hapless said. "High in the sky, you said."

Faro looked at herself. "I lost my fear of heights!"

"We conjecture that your Totem is responsible," Zed said. "Possibly the effect is temporary."

"Oh, I don't think so. Not only did I fly high, I reveled in it. I was focusing on the bird, yes, but I felt the power of the air as I forged through. It's my realm!"

"Surely it is," Zed said gravely.

Faro caught the tone. "Don't even think what I think you're thinking! You sought to find true love. You found it! I am your love, and I will not desert you just because I can fly. I will trot along happily by your side most of the time."

Zed looked relieved. "Then I think it is four down."

"Four down?"

"Feline is loved for other than her curves. You can fly. I have love. Hapless has found his musical instrument. Only Nya and Quin remain."

"And we are a couple," Nya said. "We relate well as dragons. But I'm still looking for my purpose, and Quin still wants to become human."

"About that," Zed said. "I believe you were thinking of forming a physically human compromise. But humanity is more than the physical. It is the mental, which you have, and the social, which you also have. Doesn't that suffice?"

"I suppose it does," Quin agreed, surprised.

"And Nya," Zed continued. "You seek to find your purpose. There's an obvious one: with your combination of traits, you could be an envoy, a connection between the dragon folk and the naga folk. Does that appeal?"

"Actually it does," Nya said. "And I must say, I have found a temporary purpose supporting the Quest. So it is true: I don't need the Orb."

"Did we do all this for nothing, then?" Hapless asked, dismayed.

"By no means," Zed said. "We required the experience of interaction with each other, rising to challenges, gaining a better understanding of ourselves and our world, to achieve these breakthroughs. The Quest for the Orb enabled us to focus; without it we would not have met each other and would not have found our answers."

"Which maybe was what the Good Magician had in mind," Feline said. "Now we can dump the Orb."

But Hapless wasn't so sure. "I'd like to be certain our wishes are complete. Maybe Faro's fear of heights will return when she gives up the Horn. Maybe Quin does really want a fully human form. I don't want to give up the Orb until I'm positive we're done with it."

"Ask Isis," Nya suggested.

Hapless lifted the Orb. "Uh—"

"I heard," the Goddess said on the speakerphone. "You are right to be uncertain. Faro's fear will return when she no longer has the magic of the Void at her beck. Quin does want a physically human form. The Orb can grant both."

"But there's a caution?"

"Always. It is this: your first use of the power of the Orb will expose you to the Temptation of Power."

"Temptation?"

"There are three Temptations. The first is that of Passion. I have already exposed you to that, and you resisted, thanks perhaps to your love of the two good girls. The second is Power. The third is Knowledge. This will affect you primarily, Hapless, and the others to a lesser extent. Your second use of the Orb will strengthen that desire. You will want more, and more, until you are thoroughly corrupted."

"But I wouldn't use it for myself."

Isis smiled. "Temptation always wears a beneficial mask at first. It is easy to justify. But in time the justifications become shallow, and finally are dispensed with entirely. Power becomes its own object."

"Not for me."

Her smile was sad. "Trust me in this, Hapless. I have been the route.

At first I sought only to be the best wife and mother I could be, wanting nothing for myself. But in time I kicked over the traces and became the grasping, deceitful creature I am today. The progression is insidious, with never a clear stopping point. It's like putting on weight. Have you seen how fat Mundanes are getting? They don't want to be fat, they hate it, but they keep putting on the pounds. Because they lack the discipline to pass up the tasty cakes and drinks they so like. It's obvious, they know better, but they continue. Power is like that, only worse. Once a person tastes it, he wants more of it, and more; what he has is never enough. He thinks he can stop it at any time, but he deludes himself. He reasons that he deserves it. There's always a rationale, but the reality is that it is a craving that can never be completely satisfied and will in time inevitably destroy the seeker. The love of Power is the most addictive thing there is."

"She is making sense," Zed said, and the others nodded. Even little Myst, who was evidently not too small to want more power for herself.

"Well, I wouldn't be corrupted," Hapless said.

"So thinks every inexperienced person," Isis said. "Tell, me, Hapless, if you discovered you could transform yourself into any other kind of creature, whether a mouse or a dragon, would you do it?"

"I guess, if I needed to. But—"

"And you could similarly transform any other person, merely by invoking the Orb, becoming the greatest transformer ever seen in the Land of Xanth, would you?"

"Well, I—"

"And others flocked to you, begging you to transform them into better forms, or to give them riches, or beautiful slave women, and you could do it almost without effort, would you?"

"I guess."

"And if the line of supplicants got to be endless, everyone wanting something, without limit, and be mad at you if you didn't do it?"

Hapless became annoyed. "I'd tell them to go away. What right have they to beg favors from a stranger?"

"That is the beginning of arrogance. You will become imperious, like a king. That is corruption."

She did seem to have a point. So he changed the subject. "Why are you telling us this?" Hapless asked.

"Not because I want to," the Goddess said. "Because I am required to. When you made me become the Orb, you also invoked its constraints, which I am obliged to interpret for you. I have to warn you about the cliff you are about to step over, even though I know you will ignore the caution. It's a thankless chore."

"What do you advise? To throw away the Orb?"

She winced. "No, don't do that. Someone will find it, because it seeks to be found, and that person will become corrupted by it and probably do incalculable harm. No, instead you must decommission it. Release me, then release the Totems, so that no one will be able to draw on this power without going through what you did, braving the five Regions and then tackling me. Chances are that won't happen in a century, or in a millennium, or ever. Your lives will return to their utter dullness, but Xanth will be safe, at least from this particular threat."

"But if I release you, you'll try to seduce me again, and make me do your will."

"Indeed. This is another thing about Power, whatever form it takes: it can be as difficult and dangerous to release as to acquire. You can't just let it go and forget it."

"Bleep," Hapless muttered.

"Uneasy is the head that wears the crown. Believe me, I understand."

Hapless put away the Orb. "I guess we have some thinking to do."

"But it's your decision, Hapless," Feline said.

Hapless sat down beside Myst, who was playing with illusion balls borrowed from a fragment of the wall that Faro had broken. "What do you advise?"

"Fix Faro. Quiet Quin. Orbit Orb. Marry Mom."

Hapless kept a straight face. "What do the rest of you think about this advice?"

"I'm not completely sure about that last," Feline said, with only the suggestion of a trace of a smile.

"If I may translate," Merge said, "my daughter thinks you should grant the wishes of Faro and Quin, then shut down the Orb. Then, if Feline is amenable, marry me and adopt Myst."

The child clapped her little hands. "Yes! Aunt Feline can help with the wedding."

They looked at Feline.

"Are you a virgin?" Feline asked Merge.

How did that relate? Hapless was confused yet again.

"What's a virgin?" Myst asked.

"Someone who's never done more than kissing and hugging a friend," Feline said.

"Oh," the child said. She took her illusion balls and went to play by herself, not caring to be bored by any such dull adult discussion.

Now Merge answered Feline's question. "Yes. I am a virgin."

"Do you want to marry a virgin?"

Merge was startled. "Why no, actually. I always expected to marry a man of experience. Then there would be no, well, fumbling." She blushed delicately.

"I love Hapless, but I don't think I have to marry him," Feline said. "There are fields yet to play, tomcats to tease, now that I know that my curves aren't everything. I'll always be his friend, and yours. Suppose I de-virginate him and turn him over to you to marry?"

"Oh, would you? I would be so grateful."

"After we conclude the Quest," Feline said with the trace of a bit of an obscure smile.

"Yes, of course."

So they had agreed, without consulting Hapless. They had made the decision for him. But he liked the result. He could marry Merge without alienating Feline.

Chapter 17

SHADOWS

They went outside to a pleasant illusion meadow. The snapshot showed it to be a weedy barren, but that was fine; they needed flying space.

"First, let's verify that you aren't cured of your fear, Faro," Hapless said. "Give me the Horn, and fly without it."

The winged centaur gave him the Void Totem. It did not throb with power; it was inert in his hand. He could not command it, only she.

Faro trotted forward, then spread her wings and leaped into the air. And immediately stalled and landed again. "The fear is back," she said tightly.

Hapless returned the Horn to her. "Try it again."

She did. This time she sailed up to treetop height, then spiraled higher with no problem. It was definitely the Totem.

When she landed, Hapless raised the Orb. "What is the exact protocol?" he asked Isis.

"First you must orient the five Totems to focus on the Orb. Each must activate briefly. That in turn activates the Orb so that it is ready to function. It's a safety feature. You never want to activate it carelessly."

"Totems," Hapless said.

The five gathered around. He could tell by the power throbbing in the air that the Totems were now activated.

"Next step?"

"Faro must touch the Orb and make her wish, which I will intercept and rephrase. That should do it. But remember, your invocation of the Orb's power will affect you also."

"I know." He glanced at the Orb in his hand. "I just want to be sure there's no shadow of a doubt."

"Oops!"

"What?"

"It pulsed. You made a wish."

"What wish?" he asked, nettled and nervous.

"That there be no shadow of a doubt. I didn't think of it as a formal wish, so did not intercept it. It slipped through, and I fear the Orb acted. It had been activated, and you were touching it when you spoke."

They all stood in place, as if afraid to move. How right she had been about never activating it carelessly!

"What did it do?" Zed asked.

"Something relating to shadows. I can't quite nail it."

Hapless looked around. Everything seemed normal. "I guess nothing's wrong," Hapless said.

"I don't like this," Isis said. "Please don't speak of any desire or preference in the presence of the Orb. It's not safe."

"I won't," Hapless agreed. "Faro, your turn."

Faro stepped up and touched the Orb with one finger. "I wish to have no fear of heights."

There was a pause. "I have processed it," Isis said. "It should have taken effect."

Faro handed the Horn back to Hapless. Then she launched into the air. She flew high. "I'm cured!" she called down from well above their heads. "Oh, I'm so pleased!"

The others applauded. "So are we all," Zed said.

She glided down, landed, and recovered the Horn. Then she took off again. It made no difference. That was evidently what she was verifying. She could now fly with or without the Totem. That simply, it had worked.

But Hapless felt a stronger affiliation with the Orb. He knew this was because of the exercise of its power, but that did not change the feeling. He did want more of it. But there remained one more wish to make.

"Now Quin," Hapless said. "Phrase your wish carefully before you speak it."

The dragon with the harpy front end slithered forward to touch the sphere. "I wish I could make a completely human form that I could assume at will, without sacrificing my present forms."

There was another pause. "I have processed it," Isis said.

"Change," Feline suggested.

Quin disappeared. In his place stood a handsome naked man.

"Well, now," Feline said approvingly.

"Did it work?" the man asked. It was Quin.

"Look in the unbroken wall," Feline said. "At your reflection."

Quin walked to the illusion glass wall of the house beside the meadow and stared at himself in its mirror. "It worked," he repeated. "Glorious! I am all man in this form."

"You sure are," Feline said, contemplating his midriff. "And well endowed."

But Hapless had received another jolt of affinity with the Orb. Already he did not want to give it up. Which meant it was time to do so.

"Perhaps a smudge of illusion would be in order," Merge suggested, if not blushing red, at least managing pastel pink.

Quin fetched some fogginess from the wall, and applied it to his groin. Now only obscurity was visible there.

"Where is your shadow?" Feline asked. For the sun was out and shining warmly.

They all looked. Quin had no shadow.

"What's this?" Nya asked, pointing to the ground where Quin had stood before. There was his shadow. By itself.

"And this?" Faro asked. For she had no shadow either. At least not where she stood. Her shadow was where she had been standing before.

None of them had shadows. All their shadows had stayed in place when they moved.

"This is distinctly odd," Quin said. "Something changed recently."

"When I spoke of the shadow of a doubt," Hapless said. "And the Orb reacted."

"Now we know what happened," Zed said. "It separated our shadows from our bodies. The shadow of a doubt. That did not show up until we moved, and then it took us a while to notice. The local trees and bushes still have their shadows, because they haven't moved."

"Subtle," Faro said. "But we had better comprehend it, lest there be aspects we don't like."

"Have you grown, Hapless?" Faro asked. "You seem taller."

"I, uh—"

"We are all taller," Merge said.

"I don't feel different," Hapless said.

"The shadows haven't changed," Zed said, looking down at his. "Neither position nor their size or shape. But we are changing. I fear this is mischief."

"We're changing the way shadows change!" Feline said. "Getting longer as the day progresses."

"That's a reversal," Faro said. "Normally we hold our form, while the shadows change."

"Now that we are separated from our shadows," Nya said, "It seems that the truth about the connection is being revealed. Normally the shadows absorb the change. Deprived of them, we are suffering it ourselves. We do need our shadows."

"But what happens at night?" Zed asked. "When shadows normally disappear? Will we fade out entirely?"

"Or become infinitely large?" Faro asked.

"I think we'd better get reattached to our shadows," Feline said. "If the Orb can do this, it can undo it."

"Uh—" Hapless began.

"Spit it out, man," Feline said. "There's a reason why not?"

"Maybe," he said. "Each time I use the Orb, its power over me increases. Originally it hardly appealed to me. Now I want to use it again. I'm being corrupted by the desire for its power."

"We were going to win the Orb, get our wishes granted, and quit with the Orb, weren't we?" Feline asked. "You're changing your mind?

"Not yet. But each use of it affects me. I can't be sure which one will tip the balance."

"This is relevant," Zed said. "Power is known to corrupt. We have felt empowered by our Totems. Now Hapless is being affected by the Orb. It should be decommissioned as soon as possible."

"After we fix the shadows," Feline said.

The others considered for much of a moment, and agreed. "Our wishes have been granted," Quin said. "It may be that the granting of all six wishes via the use of the Orb would have completed the corruption. As it is, only two, perhaps three wishes have been granted, the third inadvertently. If reversing it counts as another wish, then the corruption would be two thirds complete. This is only conjecture."

"But persuasive," Zed agreed. "We had better fix the shadows, then immediately decommission the Orb. That should be our safest course."

They were agreed. Hapless lifted the Orb. "Isis—"

"I heard," she replied on speakerphone. "The parameters are not as simple as a straight six-count, but as an approximation it will do."

"Parameters?" Merge asked.

"Variable boundaries," Zed said.

"The shadows are probably the less risky course," Isis said. "Constantly changing your sizes may be awkward, but not as final as getting corrupted."

"My curves are already getting seriously distorted," Feline complained. Indeed, she looked stretched out, too tall and thin for her figure.

"I did not achieve a full human form only to have it constantly distorted by the time of day," Quin said. "I want it to be handsome."

"Let's gamble," Nya said. Her human portion was getting awkwardly elongated, while her serpent portion was compacted. It was not an esthetic effect.

They took a quick vote, and agreed to gamble.

"You may be sorry," Isis said. "Undoing a prior wish isn't as easy as making a new one. The phrasing is critical. I hope I get this right." A keyboard appeared before her, in the sphere, and she typed busily. "There. I think I have it properly couched. Ready?"

"Ready," Hapless agreed, dry-mouthed. "I hereby make that wish."

There was a jolt. The shadows zipped to rejoin their owners. But the folk had not thought to go stand by their own shadows. Quin, in manform, suddenly had the shadow of a centaur. Feline had the shadow of a harpy/dragon crossbreed. The others seemed to have their own shadows, at least.

Well, Hapless and Merge had exchanged shadows. Hers was big and clumsy, while his was small and refined.

"They will correct themselves," Isis said. "Just give them time to acclimatize. Shadows are not the brightest things." She smiled, indicating a pun, but no one was much amused.

But now Hapless was assaulted by the worst siege yet. He felt the power of the Orb infusing him, taking possession of his spirit. It was trying to make him its own. He fought it, but its power was greater than his.

"Don't fight it, Hapless," Isis said. "Flow with it. You are not yet lost."

"What do you care?" he demanded, nervousness giving him an unkind edge.

"I do care, Hapless. You own the Orb, and I am your servant. I am trying to guide you to your best outcome. Do you know what a riptide is?"

"No."

"It's a shallow water current that occurs when the tide is going out. If you get caught in one, there are two ways to handle it. One is to swim as strongly as you can toward the shore, hoping to overcome it and not get washed out to sea. The other is to flow with it, letting it carry you, saving your energy. Then you can ease out of it, into regular water, and swim shoreward from there. That's the smarter course."

It sounded like good advice, but he didn't trust it, or her. "Are you trying to get your way, and become queen of the Orb?"

"That, too. But the Orb is yours; I can bask in its power only by influencing you. If you stay with it, you will be king. I will be your queen. I am part of the package, Hapless; you will need me to exercise its power smoothly. You are simply not competent."

He knew that was true. "What of Merge!"

"Do you suppose she would ever agree to your complete corruption by the Orb? Unless you exercise your magic power to change her mind and corrupt her too. You can do that. You can do almost anything."

"No!"

"You still have those endearing civilian attitudes. But face it, Hapless: You are caught in the riptide. Are you going to handle it smartly or stupidly?"

What choice did he have? "Show me how to handle it smartly. But if you betray me, when I have power I will make you regret it."

"And you could do that. I would much rather work with you than oppose you. Here is your course of the moment: study the shadows."

"We just fixed the shadows!"

"You fixed the literal shadows. Now it is time to address the figurative ones. Look at your associates standing around you. Do you see their historical shadows?"

"Their whats?"

"Let me come out and help you, Hapless; it will make it easier."

"Come out," he agreed.

She formed before him, her royal robe just loose enough in front to provide a tantalizing glimpse of the rounded contours within. "Thank you." She kissed him on the cheek. He liked it far more than he cared to admit. "Consider Nya, the naga/dragon crossbreed with the bosom that is returning to its natural attractive shape."

He considered Nya, as she was standing directly before them. She seemed frozen in place. They all were. "Yes."

"Her physical shadow is adjusting its contours. But focus on her historical shadow."

"I don't see it."

"Use your snapshot technique, and modify it when you get a glimmer."

He tried, and did begin to get a glimmer. There were shadows extending both before and after the Naga. "What are they?"

"The one behind is her past. Follow it closely and you can see her associates before she joined you, right back to her original family."

He saw them, all standing still along the extended shadow. Right back to the meeting of her parents at a love spring. "Wow!"

"Love spring encounters do tend to be graphic," Isis agreed. "A love spring doesn't care about social events; it simply forces instant breeding. There's not much real love in it, truth be told, just overwhelming passion."

"So I see," he said, impressed. He was a virgin, and had not seen action like this before. It was mesmerizing. He had had no idea that this was the way it was done. He really did need Feline's advice. Or Isis's.

"I will tryst with you in a love spring, if you wish."

Temptation flared, but he fought it down. "What about the other shadow? The one going forward?"

"Follow it."

He traced it carefully forward. Nya in due course married Quin, and they had a fine time as a dragon pair. Then one day they blundered into a dragon net set up by goblins, and both were suddenly captive, then killed, cooked, and eaten. "No!" he cried in anguish.

"It does not need to be," Isis said. "You can warn them, so that they can avoid the dragon net."

"I'll do that!"

"But that will count as a wish, a foretelling of the future, and will commit you more firmly to the Orb."

"Oh. Still, to help a friend—"

"Understand this, Hapless. Every creature comes to an end eventually. You can't prevent all passages, or even any one, given enough time. You can expend yourself, corrupt yourself, and in the end it will make very little difference. Every case will be severely tempting, but you will be better off ignoring them all."

"Bleep you!"

She smiled. "I merely advise you of reality. You may do what you choose to do. Try watching your own future shadow."

"I can do that?"

"Not far, because your looking will cause your future to change, and the original future will dissipate, to be replaced by a new one, which will in turn also dissipate. But you can see ahead a day or so at a time, and this can enable you to follow the course to become King of Xanth. There is no power like the ability to see the future and to change it at will. You will be king."

"But I don't want to be king."

"Think of all the good you could do as king. You could seriously benefit all your friends. And consider this: I will be your queen. Look at a typical night."

He looked, and his shadow, guided by her, showed the two of them in the throes of such passion that the air was shimmering and nearby candles were melting into puddles. "Hoo!"

"Every night, Hapless," she said. "All night, if you wish. Daytime too, if you wish. I have had thousands of years experience being a good wife; I do know how to do it. I also know of herbs and spells to make a man endlessly potent. There is no effective limit to your potential pleasure."

He was tempted again. To help his friends, and to be with her . . .

She was of course aware of his desire. She pursued her advantage. "But if the pleasures of Power are not enough, consider those of Knowledge."

"Knowledge?"

"You can know all things. Never again will you be considered ignorant. The mysteries of existence can be yours to fathom."

"Mysteries?"

"Did you ever wonder why the universe, including Xanth, Mundania, Fornax, and all else, even exists? Why there is something rather than nothing? For it must have started with nothing."

"Uh, no." But now he was intensely curious. Why *was* there anything?

"That question has perplexed philosophers for millennia, and they have never had a satisfactory answer. But you can have the answer, via the Orb. All you have to do is ask it."

"I—"

"Then there is the riddle of life. How did it come to be, when originally there was only inert matter? How was the original transition made from non-living goo to living goo? This too has perplexed alchemists and scientists. But you will be able to visit the scene and actually see it occur."

He was awed. He did want to do that. "Uh—"

"And the mystery of consciousness. That has balked philosophers from the outset. How did it first arise, and why? Because without it we are all mere blobs of protein."

He did want to know, now that she had tweaked his mind. "Um."

"These and endless other mysteries will be yours to fathom. You will know everything you care to know, from the nature of the universe down to the color of a lady's panty." She flounced her skirt, almost showing the fringe of a panty. "Nothing will be too large or too small for your attention."

That was phenomenally tempting. Then he thought of something. "Merge. What of her?"

"Follow her future shadow."

He did. There was Merge, with Myst, both disconsolately going about their business of searching out remnants of anti-pun virus to neutralize. He zoomed in close to look at their faces and their eyes. Both sets of eyes were bright with tears.

He knew why: they had loved him and lost him to the bad girlfriend. To the Orb. To Passion. To Power. To Knowledge. They were protected by his beneficence so that no personal harm came to them, but they were not happy. They had wanted to be with him, as wife and child.

That wiped out all else. "I'm going back to them," he said.

"You will have to give up all of what I have shown you."

"Yes."

She shook her head. "Amazing."

Then the scene reanimated. He was no longer looking at shadows. "We are decommissioning the Orb," he announced.

"Oh, Hapless!" Merge exclaimed, and Myst clapped her little hands.

"How do I do it?" he asked Isis.

She frowned but answered. "Simply hold up the Orb and say the words 'Orb be Free.' Then have the others do the same with each of the Totems."

Hapless hesitated. The lure of the Orb tore at him, incalculably precious. It could all so readily be his! Could he really give it up?

Then he looked at Merge and Myst, and his reluctance dissipated like an ice cube in a furnace. "Orb be Free."

The Orb dissolved into smoke. That reformed into the Goddess Isis. "Now at last it is clear why a klutz like you was selected for this mission," she said. "You are virtually incorruptible. You value the feelings of a woman and child more than you do absolute power. Only one man in a million would do what you have just done, and there aren't that many men in Xanth."

"Sorry about that," he said, and he was. She might be the Bad Girlfriend, but she was not a bad goddess. He could have been happy with her. But there was no point in dwelling on that. The decommissioning was not yet complete. "Companions, it is your turn. Hold up your Totems and say the same words I did, to them."

The others did. One by one their Totems reverted to their guardians, who hastily fled the scene. They were left with almost nothing.

Only the gorgon Carmen lingered for a moment, as beautiful as ever despite her kerchief and glasses. Beside her was Prince Voila, who would join her in her Region, at least for an extended visit. "I think you must be lonely, Isis," she said. "So am I, though the prince may help. Visit us in the water realm if you like. I'm willing to share." She glanced at Voila, who seemed nothing loath.

"I can't leave the comic strip," the goddess said. "But if you care to visit me here, you will be welcome."

"It's a date." Carmen hugged her and vanished with Voila.

It occurred to Hapless that if any two supernatural women understood each other, these were the ones.

But he had other business. "We'll be moving on now," Hapless said. "Fare well, Isis."

"Fare well, Hapless," she replied, and now the tears were in her eyes. "For what it's worth, you have won my respect." Then she faded out of the scene.

"Let's get out of here," Hapless said.

They went into snapshot mode, and soon picked their way out of the frozen comic strip. They emerged roughly where they had entered it.

There were two dogs. "Rachel! Woofer!" Myst cried, running to hug them both.

"To what do we owe the honor of this visit?" Feline inquired.

"The princesses are organizing an informal musical ensemble, but they are missing a few things," Rachel said. "I told them I know of someone who could help."

"Princesses?"

"Melody, Harmony, Rhythm. The triplets."

Feline visibly digested this. "What are they missing?"

"Instruments, ability, a conductor."

Feline laughed. "They're joking!"

"No, they really want to do it. They want to travel around Xanth and give concerts for grateful audiences."

"This seems like a big ambition, considering what they lack," Zed said.

"They hope to recruit some competent musicians, and learn the ropes."

"But if they lack talent, this is nonsensical," Faro said.

"They're *princesses*," Rachel reminded them.

She had a point. The terms princess and common sense hardly fit in the same sentence, but what royal folk wanted generally came to pass.

All eyes came to focus on Hapless. What could he do? "I guess we can give it a try."

"This way," Rachel said.

They followed her to a copse where stood a young man. "Back so soon, Rachel?" he asked.

"They'll help," the dog reported.

"Yes they will, Bryce," Merge said. Evidently they were acquainted.

Hapless stepped forward. "I'm, uh, Hapless. I'm a, uh, conductor." They shook hands.

"I'm Bryce Mundane. Rachel and I came to Xanth together four years ago. I'm older than I look; I was youthened. It's a long, dull story. We do need a conductor. We have Xanth's two finest musicians, but they aren't used to playing in concert. And the princesses have never joined a group. Now suddenly they have this idea, and sort of have to be humored."

"Uh—" All he could think of was how he could have abolished "uh" forever if he had accepted the Orb. He just wasn't a very sharp conversationalist.

"I see you carry the box," Bryce said.

"The box?"

"That's the one that enabled our passage to Xanth. It has what you need, whatever it may be, even if you don't know it. All you need to do is open it."

Hapless considered the box. It should be useless, now that the Quest was done. He shrugged, and opened it.

There was a small cylinder. No picture. He took it out. It lengthened into a wand. A conductor's wand. His musical instrument. Apparently this was meant to be.

Then the box disappeared. It seemed that he was truly through with it. He hoped that he would continue to be able to think outside it, even if he didn't have it there to remind him.

"This way," Bryce said. "The princesses are waiting."

And there before them was a beautiful castle that Hapless somehow hadn't noticed before.

"Caprice Castle," Rachel said. "It travels."

"It wasn't there before," Bryce said. "You'll get used to it."

Hapless wasn't sure he would ever do that.

Hapless found himself walking beside Nya and Quin. "Uh, you guys— be hyper alert for dragon nets. You never can tell when you might run afoul of one."

"We will," Nya agreed, humoring him. But maybe the warning would be enough.

Now the princesses came out to meet them. There were three of them, similar but not quite identical, with cute little crowns. They looked to be about twenty years old. They stood together so that Bryce could introduce them. "Princess Melody." The one in a green dress, with greenish hair and blue eyes, nodded, smiling.

"I'm the prettiest," Melody said, though in truth there was little to choose between them.

"Princess Rhythm." The one with red hair in a red dress smiled. Only her eyes did not match, being green.

"I'm the naughtiest," Rhythm said proudly.

"Princess Harmony." She had brown hair and eyes, and was in a brown dress.

"I'm the smartest," Harmony said. "Soon I'll marry Bryce."

"You will not!" Bryce sputtered as all three princesses laughed. Was it a joke? Then he returned to the introductions. "The Princesses are general-purpose Sorceresses. Any one is the match of any other Sorceress. Any two of them working together square the effect, and the three together cube it. So it is best to humor and perhaps to be a bit wary of them."

"Uh," Hapless said, daunted.

"We'll gather here outside, on the patio," Melody said. "Princess Dawn, the proprietress of Caprice, will be along soon." She glanced at Hapless. "I understand you can conjure instruments."

"Uh, yes."

"Excellent. Picka and Piper have their own, and the three of us too, but anyone else who wants to play will need them."

"And here come Picka and Piper now," Princess Rhythm said.

Hapless tried not to stare. Piper was a normal young man, but Picka was a walking skeleton. All bones, no flesh.

"They are Xanth's finest musicians," Princess Rhythm continued. They were? Hapless kept his mouth shut. "Picka Bone, Princess Dawn's husband. Piper, who in his other form is a musical monster. Now let's organize the ensemble."

Princess Dawn's husband? Musical monster? Hapless had to clamp down on his incredulity lest it explode and blow him to pieces.

The two males sat beside each other, and the three princesses nearby.

Feline poked Hapless in a rib. "Your cue," she said.

Oh. Hapless went to stand before them, feeling hopelessly awkward. But what could he do? He lifted his wand and waved it.

The music was instant. Piper had a small flute he played with such expertise that it was like music from heaven. Picka detached his clavicles, the shoulder bones, and used them to play his ribs. Weird as it looked, the sound was perfect.

The three princesses had their own instruments. Harmony had a harmonica, Rhythm had a drum, and Melody sang, an almost bell-like soprano. Individually and together they were divine. As an ensemble, it was wonderful. He was conducting, but he felt as if he were doing so from a divine cloud.

The piece ended of its own accord, and Hapless collapsed the wand.

Then the players put aside their instruments and clapped their hands, applauding. "Rachel was right," Piper said. "You are the conductor we need."

"But I, uh, just waved my wand. You could have done just as well on your own."

They shook their heads. "We have tried it," Princess Melody said. "We are all good individually, but we lacked coordination. We overrode each other's themes, we got the timing wrong. Only just now, with you conducting, did we get it right. Thanks to your magic."

"You are the third greatest musician of Xanth, perhaps even the second or the first," Piper said, and Picka nodded his empty head. "But your talent is expressed through others, empowering them."

"Well, uh—"

"Now let's add your Companions of the Quest," Melody said.

"Um—"

The five Companions came up and took seats on the patio. Hapless conjured their instruments, and they made ready to play them. Now it was an ensemble of ten.

Feline made as if to poke another rib from a distance. "Conduct, dummy."

Hapless conducted, and all ten participated. It was a new piece, wonderfully coordinated, phenomenally lovely. This time he felt as if he were perched atop the moon. It was absolutely glorious.

When it finished, they applauded again. "Oh, that was so great!" Zed said, setting down his saxophone.

"Oh, Princess Harmony, I was inspired to use the harmonica by your example," Nya said. "It was amazing, playing here with you."

"And my drum was inspired by you, Princess Rhythm," Faro said. "I will remember this experience forever, even if we never do it again."

"Oh, we'll do it again," Rhythm said. "Now that we've got our group."

"I am minded to try one more round," Piper said. "Some of our associates are not musical. Hapless, does your talent include them?"

"Uh, I suppose so. Anyone seems to be able to play in my presence."

"Dear?" Picka said.

Princess Dawn stepped forward. "I am not at all sure about this." She was a lovely figure of a woman, several years more mature than the triplet princesses. "Perhaps I should check Hapless first."

"Check?" Hapless asked.

Princess Dawn approached him confidently. She reached out to touch his hand. "Oh, my!" she said. "Your talent and character are both special."

"They are?"

"I should explain: I am a Sorceress, as are all the descendants of Great Grandpa Bink. My talent is to know all about any living thing I touch. So I have just been apprized of your encounter with the Goddess Isis, and the full nature of your formidable magic talent. We owe you a lot, Hapless."

"I, uh—"

"Your modesty becomes you. Now I am curious to see whether your talent works on me. Please conjure me a musical instrument."

"Uh, what one?"

"Any one. The least likely one."

"A bassoon," Picka called mischievously. "The most difficult instrument in an orchestra."

A bassoon appeared in Hapless's hands. He gave it to the princess.

"Oh, my," she said. "I have never even touched one of these before. I have no idea how to play it."

"Try," Hapless suggested.

She tried, holding it before her and putting her mouth to the thin mouthpiece extending from its middle. And suddenly she was playing a compelling theme.

The members of the ensemble applauded.

"So it is true," Dawn said, surprised despite her understanding of Hapless's talent. She took her place beside Picka.

Several other non-musicians accepted instruments and joined the group, including Merge and Myst with their big and little xylophones. Then Hapless raised his wand and conducted them, and they all played marvelously together. It always happened when he conducted: each player, and the larger group, were perfect, needing no written music or rehearsal.

"That does it," Dawn said, flushed. "You and your group will stay here at Caprice and join the ensemble. You were able to enable me to play an instrument I'd never touched before, and play it well. Your talent is simply too valuable to allow to go to waste." She glanced at the assembled

Companions with their instruments. "Between concerts, we can use the other talents of the members of your Quest. Nya, we will be visiting some obscure sections of Xanth, where your ability to relate to dragons, naga, and other crossbreeds will be valuable." Nya nodded, satisfied. "Quin, there are some sections where the human form is preferred, but a dragon form may become necessary to keep the peace." Quin nodded. "Zed and Faro, our children are away today, visiting Castle Roogna with the other dogs, but they will return tomorrow and will absolutely love to ride you, on the ground and in the air, if you can tolerate it." Zed and Faro nodded; they would be happy to entertain children, in a context like this. "Feline, we have dogs galore here, but no cats at present. We need one. No castle is complete without a cat." Feline nodded; this was something other than her curves.

Hapless was impressed. Princess Dawn clearly knew how to manage things. She must have touched the Companions and ascertained their natures.

Dawn took a breath. "Now Woofer and Rachel will show you to your rooms."

"I'll share his room," Feline said. "We have business to attend to."

"Not Merge?" Rachel asked.

"Not until they are married."

Dawn looked at Merge, who nodded, faintly blushing. "Of course," Dawn said smoothly.

Princess Harmony approached. "I will show them to their room," she told the dog. Rachel nodded and went on to the next.

"I am so pleased to make your acquaintance, Hapless," Harmony said as she gently guided them through the labyrinth that was the interior castle. "In fact, it's an honor."

"But I'm nobody," he protested.

"A nobody with character."

"I didn't do anything."

"It's what you didn't do," Harmony said seriously. She looked into his face, and he was abruptly aware that this was far, far more than a triplet princess. Not only was she remarkably pretty, she was indeed a Sorceress, with powers he hardly guessed, and she was smart, informed, and dedicated.

But still her remark confused him.

"Didn't do?"

"I am slated to be the next King of Xanth, in due course. I have been preparing for the role for years. First I have to persuade Bryce to marry me; he remains uncommitted, but I don't think he can hold out much longer. He does love me, as I love him."

King of Xanth! The position he would have usurped, had he gone with the Goddess Isis. She knew!

She kissed him on the cheek. "We are going to get along." She paused at a door, one among many. "This is your room. I'm sure you will find it an education."

"Oh, yes," Feline agreed, taking his hand possessively.

And Hapless realized that what he had here as an ordinary person was more valuable to him than what the Goddess had offered. A useful place in society, facilitating music. Friendship. Love. Not to mention what Feline had in mind for him.

For one thing, there were no suggestive shadows.

AUTHOR'S NOTE

On Apull 8, 2013 (in Xanth we use the Ogre Months, which are more dynamic than the dull ones of drear Mundania) I received an email letter from Heather Pryzstas: "One of the best things about being a mom has been watching my daughter grow to love reading as much as her father and I do. Now I get to share my love of Mr. Anthony's work with her as well, and she's devouring them just as I did (and still do!). She asked that I find a way to deliver the attached letter. I promised I would try my best."

This, of course, is music to an author's ears, hearing from dedicated fans who perpetuate the love of his writing so that future generations are similarly enthralled. The secret is the magic dust that wafts out from between the pages of the book and addicts the unwary reader to fantasy. But in these days of electronic publication (no physical pages) that is less reliable, so we still depend on long-time fans.

Here is her daughter's letter:

Hello. I am Laurana Pryzstas age 10. I am a great fan of all your books Mr. Piers. I know I am probably just another piece of fan mail in a huge pile but all I ever wanted was a letter from you. I have an idea for a book called Isis Orb. It's about a group of strangers [who] want to get their wishes. They are Quin the polite harpy dragon crossbreed who wants to find out how to become human. Then there's Nya the dragon naga with wings who wants to find her purpose. Also there's Zed the centaur whose father was a Mundane zebra so he has stripes he wants to find true love. The other two are the human cat crossbreed who wants someone who will love her even without curves. Last but not least is Fear O Heights, the winged centaur who wants to know how to get over her fear of heights. The story is that many years ago the Demon Xanth and Demon Earth made a wager and Xanth didn't win. So Earth took a chunk of his magic in the form of the Isis Orb and hid it in the deepest core of Xanth. Now the Good Magician tells the group to find and control the Orb they must get the four totems of Fire, Air, Earth, and Water. The fire totem is the fire faun of blazing flame which is protected by an actual fire faun. Then there's the six headed griffin of air protected by a six headed griffin. Next is the great six winged steam dragon of Earth protected by a six legged steam dragon. Lastly is the gorgon sea monster protected by itself again. I would love to see my ideas published one day but all I really want is a letter from you.

Sincerely

Sorceress Laurana

PS: my talent is to change anything!

PSS: That's just the beginning of the story. I figured you could fill in most of it.

I considered the idea. I was then writing Xanth #39 *Five Portraits*, but a year later, in 2014, I tackled *Isis Orb*. Well, I did fill in a few details. There are five Regions of Xanth; Laurana had not mentioned the Void, though obviously she knew of it because she had five characters to fetch the totems. There was a roughly similar story in *Swell Foop*, so I had to avoid being too close to that. When a series gets to be 40 novels long, it's tricky to avoid stepping on its own toes. The name Fear O Heights was too obvious, so I made it a cruel nickname, digesting it down to Faro (Fear O). I researched the ancient Egyptian goddess Isis, who turned out to have an interesting history, and figured out how she could get involved in Xanth, which is not her mythology. Mainly I reshaped the story to avoid introducing five major characters together; the reader needs to get to know and appreciate them one by one. So they became Companions on the Quest.

I introduced a new character to lead the Quest, Hapless, who then inter-acted with each of the others, spaced out. (Oh, come on, you know what I mean; it's not a pun.) This is a standard device in novels: a way to see the main characters from another viewpoint. It went on from there, as you should have just read. (If you're one of those characters who reads the Author's Note first, stop it this instant.) It's an adult novel, as all the Xanths are, which means that Laurana's mother may have to check it first. As I told a critic, I refuse to censor my series for the sake of an audience for which it was not intended. Children read Xanth at their own risk from parents who think a child should not know what a panty is until age 21, if then. Fortunately few parents remember its naughtiness, and most chil-dren are too smart to tell. And it answers the question writers often get: where do you get your ideas? From my readers, obviously, and this is a prime example. Now you know.

My main research reference on Isis was *The Gods of the Egyptians* by E A Wallis Budge. It was there that I saw the theory that Christianity spread rapidly in the Roman Empire because it was merely a paste-over of familiar Egyptian mythology, easy to accept because the essence was unchanged. I'm not sure I believe that, but certainly Isis does, and she resents being displaced by the new fad after being dominant for thou-sands of years. Who knows; maybe her turn will come again. In fact, as I wrote this novel there was a new source of violence in the Near East as the Islamic State of Iraq and Syria, known as ISIS, started conquering cit-ies. Can that be coincidence? Isis was Egyptian, but surely her influence extended to nearby regions.

Meanwhile, Mundane life continued. My wife and I had our 58th anni-versary during the writing of this novel. What's the secret of a long mar-riage? Marry young, stay with it, and live a long time. I'm pushing 80 at this writing. We bought a chocolate covered cheesecake to celebrate. That's the septuagenarian idea of celebration. I had a scare, though; just as I completed the first draft of the novel, my backup flash drive flashed an error message and shut down its menu. It was permanently gone. I could no longer export my material. I got in touch with my geek—that's a com-puter nerd, not an insult—Brian Smith, and he came over and struggled, but could not find that menu. I have remarked that I have no belief in the supernatural, outside of Xanth, so the supernatural does its best to mess me up. That menu was gone to fantasyland. But he did show me another way to address the drive, so that I could use it again. So the novel was not permanently locked in the system, and you did get to read it. Yes, I know my literary cri-tics wish it had been lost; too bad for them.

I also had a personal malaise: the left side of my crotch became uncomfortable, verging on painful. What was the cause? We finally figured it out, we think. I normally use a scooter, the kind you push with your foot, to go out along our three-quarter-mile drive through our tree farm to fetch in our morning newspapers and our daily mail. It's a supplementary exercise, and I do take my exercise seriously. But it got a flat tire. I patched it, but it went flat again. So I bought a new inner tube, and that fixed it. But when I remounted it, it scraped. I went halfway crazy trying to get it right, but it just didn't work. So I renovated my wife's bicycles to use instead, and that worked, but then the main one of those got a flat that refused to be fixed—yes, I tried, but it was opening up along the central seam—so we took it in to the shop, where they pointed out that the old tires were coming apart. So we replaced both tires and got it tuned up, and then it was fine. But it cost more for that repair than the bike had cost new. That made me pause. Then when I got the groin discomfort, we figured it was the bike seat; this is a known problem for some riders, as the seat jams a nerve in the groin. So I tried riding by standing on the pedals, but that turned out to be awkward and uncomfortable. I needed to get back to my scooter. Which didn't work.

Sigh. Have I mentioned that life in Mundania can be dreary? But sometimes there may be a bit of magic. My printer ran out of toner, so we bought a new toner kit, which was eye-poppingly expensive, more than the bicycle, actually, and the store had a sale on paper, buy two get one free. So we bought two boxes of reams, and got the third; we can always use paper. Then I packed the three new boxes into the closet where we store paper, and that was a chore because those boxes weighed fifty pounds apiece and the available space was jammed. I had to clear out junk from the back to make room. And part of that junk was the old front fender on the scooter, which I had to remove years ago when the replacement tire didn't fit right. You could almost see the light bulb flash over my head. So I removed the rear fender, and the scooter worked again. Now you could call that a chain of unlikely coincidences leading from toner to scooter. Or you could call it a magic reminder right when I needed it. Do you really believe in coincidence?

I use a number of reader suggestions in each Xanth novel. I had trouble with my first Xanth publisher about this, and finally had to leave that publisher in order to have the freedom to write Xanth my way, humor, readers, and all. Fitting in reader notions can get tricky; I try to use ones by "new" contributors before using repeats by "old" contributors, but sometimes the best notions are by repeaters. So it's always a compromise, and there's always a backlog of as-yet unused ideas. Sometimes they sneak into the Author's Notes instead. Consider this letter by Daniel Christopher June. Adult Conspiracy warning: parts of this letter are unsuitable for children of any age, from 5–50. If you are one or more of those, do not read.

Greetings, Piers. I've read you since I was in third grade. My dad read *Crewel Lye* and stopped reading it during the stork signaling scenes. Naturally his imposition of the Adult Conspiracy made me read them and I read the whole set, though not the last ones. In the third grade I declared I would be a writer like you, and that is what I finally became.

Xanth is a real place; you can go there. I went there and said "My name is Daniel," and they said "You are in denial of what?" I said "My name is Dan June," and they said "Yes, the dungeon for you." So they stuck me in the dungeon. I had to use a latrine, and it was kept by a woman named Latrina. She fell in love with me, but she always got p*ssed off. Finally she pushed me in the Latrine and a monster dolphin was inside. I was swallowed up, but broke through her stomach and into her womb. There was baby Dolph in a former life as a Dolphin. There was a twin with him. I said hey, Dolph, don't hit her, she was changed shape in a purpose so he would have better purpose. When he was born, the father demanded where this purpose came from, and the mother explained she was true to him. Just in time, Dolph turned back into a Dolphin; that's when he first used his special talent. I swam with the Dolphins. My talent is the learning of all other talents. So I learned all their talents. I changed shape too. I changed shape into a flying fish and flew out of the water into land. I saw a statue to Piers Anthony. Somebody left their sandwich there, a peanut butter honey sandwich. I wonder who made the honey? Not bees, but ants. It appears ant honey had gotten all over the statue to Xanth's overgod. I felt bad about this so I ate the honey. It made me crazy and I fell into a bush of tics. I went crazy when they bit me. I started doing antics. I was frantic. I had tickles. I went psychotic. I was a goner, traveling the land as a madman.

Finally a kind woman said to get rid of ticks you need tickles. She tickled me. Slowly the ticks came off. All of them, except the romantic. The woman was kind to me. She said her name was Sherry. She poured me a glass of wine, sherry, and shared it with me.

You've been my inspiration all my life. I hope you were well.

No, I obviously had a sick mind, abetted by readers like him. Good thing he didn't write in the month of JeJune. Are you through not reading? Good. It's time for the remaining credits. I had, as usual, more reader notions than I could cram into this novel without risking its structural integrity, not to mention sanity; some will have to wait for next time. Some were worthy of more than a passing mention, so I saved them rather than waste them here. It's a constant compromise.

Title and idea for the novel, plus Companions Quin, Nya, Zed, Feline, Fear O' Heights—Laurana Przystas, as described above. Conjuring any musical instrument, West Tern, East Tern, Tern Pike—Tim Bruening. Cylla Cybin (psilocybin)—Priscilla Uhrin. Carve air into a solid mass, Water Lily—Rohan Willoughby. Wanna Bee, Null and Void—Tina Kelley. Eli, of the 7 days—Eli Borchgrevink. Mundane man immune to panties—Douglas Harter. Alley Cats with a bowling alley, ear wigs, Rachel Dog, darning egg, humble pie, separating shadows, clothes horse—Mary Rashford. Bowling with bowls of berries—Darrell Jones. Smart Alec—Ann Dragera Dragonclawz. Nose the scenter of the face—Dean Howell. Deciphering Gibberish, Kumquats and Goquats—John Estren. Izadora Dahlia Crow—Jeff Oscar. Eggsplore, Eggscited—Jennifer Nichols. Fast Food, Swiss Army Cheese—Josh Davenport. Box containing what folk don't know they need—A J Billingsly. Punch Bowl—David Wells. Demon Destroy-Her—Shirley Francis. A bit of background here: she is the sister of the late Barry David Khelder, who suggested the Demon Contest that became the basis for *Luck of the Draw*. Her notion is just mentioned here, but it intrigues me, and might become the basis for further exploration in a future novel. More Demons messing with Xanth? That could be serious mischief. Bees allergic to honey—James Patterson. Eye Candy—Brittani Dunsmore. Hush Puppy Dog—Roger Vazquez. The Chaos Butterfly, Tern of Events, Flying Buttresses, Centaur Stage Coach, Statue of Limitations, Outhouse—Richard Van Fossan. AutoCrat—Michael Mitchell. Exsangui Nation—Dexter Smith. Villains—why heroes exist—Clayton Overstreet. Peter Reddick—Tim Reddick. The cemoness C Duce—Tom Marrin.

Ari twins—Ari Tsivkin. Spelfie—Amber. Opti-Mist—Joshua Davenport-Herbst. Rain Bow, Hardly Harpy—Miriam Kleit. Julius Saucier—Michael Trimble. Corncob Unicorn—SheRissa Schultz. Monti—Monti Fleck. Pomegranite—Pastor Ben Cleveland. Palm of Granite—Diana Litsch. Foot Stool—Emma Archambault. Passing Thoughts, Mushroom—Wiley Kohler. The Thought that Counts—Paul White. Person who changes color with temperature—Brittany Westly. It seems I credited her in *Luck of the Draw* but didn't actually include the character, so here she is again. (These things happen as I near my dotage.) Eye Doll (A) Tree—Jessica Edwards. Drag Racing, sine language—Naomi Blose. Hawking radiation—James Blakeney. Sand Witch—Laura Kwon. Phil A Buster—Misty Zaebst. Chest of Drawers—David Seltzer. Magnetic Moment—David D Stanton. Not being haved—David Leo Novacek. Mailer Daemon is from Xanth—Randy Gordon. Punnish letter in Author's Note—Daniel Christopher June. And my credit to my proofreaders, Scott M Ryan and Anne White.

If these novels have not given you more of a bellyful than you can stomach, you can check my website at www.HiPiers.com, where I do a monthly blog-type column and maintain an ongoing survey of electronic publishers for the benefit of aspiring writers. Sometimes it seems that half my readers are aspiring writers. I wish they all could be successful authors.

ABOUT THE AUTHOR

Piers Anthony has written dozens of bestselling science fiction and fantasy novels. Perhaps best known for his long-running Magic of Xanth series, many of which are *New York Times* bestsellers, he has also had great success with the Incarnations of Immortality series and the Cluster series, as well as *Bio of a Space Tyrant* and others. Much more information about Piers Anthony can be found at www.HiPiers.com.

TALES FROM
THE LAND OF XANTH

FROM OPEN ROAD MEDIA

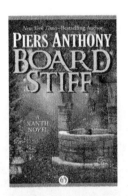
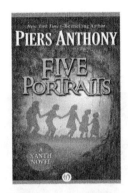

OPEN ROAD

INTEGRATED MEDIA